February's Son

Alan Parks

W F HOWES LTD

This large print edition published in 2019 by
W F Howes Ltd
Unit 5, St George's House, Rearsby Business Park,
Gaddesby Lane, Rearsby, Leicester LE7 4YH

1 3 5 7 9 10 8 6 4 2

First published in the United Kingdom in 2019
by Canongate Books Ltd

Excerpt from 'My Coo Ca Choo', Words and Music
by Peter Shelley, Magnet Music Ltd (PRS)

A CIP catalogue record for this book is available
from the British Library

ISBN 978 1 52886 342 1

Typeset by Palimpsest Book Production Limited,
Falkirk, Stirlingshire

Printed and bound by
T J International in the UK

MIX
Paper from
responsible sources
FSC FSC® C013056
www.fsc.org

For Mary Mackay Robertson

'Death is not the worst thing that can happen to men.'

– Plato

'Night time's a lonely time . . .'

– Alvin Stardust

He sits down, looks at what he's done. Down to his trousers and vest now, hard work this thing he's doing. Still an occasional moan from it, gurgle and cough as the blood runs back down its throat. He's tired but he's close to the end now. He stands back up, calls it a fucker again, spits at it. Tells it why he's here even though it must know. Tells it again and again. No response. He takes a swinging kick at the side of its head. The moon emerges from the clouds, illuminates the scene in cold, heartless light.

He takes the Polaroid camera he's bought himself out the holdall. Sticks a flashcube on the top and aims the camera at it. Familiar click as he squeezes the button, bulb fizzes, camera makes a grinding noise then the cardboard-backed photo slides out the back. He sticks it under his arm. Moves in, takes another one, closer this time, shoves that under his other arm and waits the two minutes just like it says on the packet. He peels the backs off, ghostly reverse image on the paper. He lets the wind take the paper out his hands, watches it fly up into the air then slowly descend over the side of the building. Nice little present for someone to find. The pictures are still sticky. He holds them by the corners, lays them on the ground, tries not to look at them too much, keep that for later.

Gurgling has stopped now, no more misty breath leaking out its mouth. Dead. He takes the ivory-handled razor out his pocket and moves in. He's being a Good Boy not doing it while it's alive. He smiles, not like he hasn't done it before, maybe he's getting soft in his old age. He says her name, tells her it's all for her own good. Wishes she was here watching, knowing what he'd done. He lifts his arm and the razor comes down. An arc of dark red blood flies past his shoulder and splatters into the puddles on the ground.

10TH FEBRUARY 1973

CHAPTER 1

McCoy stopped for a minute, had to. He put his hands on his knees, bent over, tried to catch his breath. Could feel the sweat running down his back, shirt sticking to him under his jumper and coat. He looked up at the uniform. Another one of Murray's rugby boys. Size of a house and no doubt thick as shit. Same as all the rest.

'What floor is this now?' he asked.

The big bastard wasn't even breathing heavily, just standing there looking at him, raindrops shining on his woollen uniform.

'Tenth, sir. Four more to go.'

'Christ. You're joking, aren't you? I'm half dead already.'

They were making their way up a temporary stairway. Just rope handrails strung between scaffolding poles, stairway itself a series of rough concrete slabs leading up and up to the top of the half-built office block.

'Ready, sir?'

McCoy nodded reluctantly and they started off again. Maybe he'd be doing better if he hadn't just finished two cans of Pale Ale and half a joint when the big bastard had come to get him. Him and Susan were laughing, dancing about like loonies, Rolling Stones on the radio, when the knock on the door came. Big shadow of the uniform behind the frosted glass. Panic stations. Susan trying to open the windows and fan the dope smell away with a dishtowel while he kept the uniform talking at the door for as long as he could. Just as well they'd decided against splitting the tab he'd found in his wallet.

They climbed a few more storeys, turned a corner, and at last McCoy could see the night sky above them. It was grey and heavy, moon appearing every so often through the clouds and the falling rain. He stood for a minute, taking in the view, getting his breath back. Glasgow was laid out beneath him, dirty black buildings, wet streets. He walked to the side and looked out, didn't want to get too close, no walls up here, just more rope handrails. Worked out he must be facing west, the dome of the Mitchell Library was right in front of him, university tower behind it in the distance. Below them the new motorway they were building cut through what was left of Charing Cross, a wide river of brown mud and concrete pilings. He heard footsteps behind him and turned.

Chief Inspector Murray held out his hand. 'Sorry it's a day early but Thomson's away until Monday. Need someone working this soon as.'

For some reason Murray was wearing a dinner

suit under his usual sheepskin car coat. Full shebang: dickie bow, cummerbund, silk stripe on the trousers. Only thing spoiling the dapper effect was the pair of black wellies he'd tucked the trousers into.

'Lord Provost's Dinner,' Murray said, noticing him looking. 'North British Hotel. Food was bloody swill. Never been happier to be called away to a murder in my life.'

'Still trying to get you to take that Central job?' asked McCoy.

'Still trying, still not getting anywhere. No matter how many fancy dinners they invite me to.' He took the unlit pipe out his mouth, pointed into the darkness. 'Follow me, good pilgrim, for I am not lost.'

A path of damp stamped-down cardboard boxes led towards the far corner of the roof. There must have been ten or so people up here already, uniforms milling about, two technicians carrying the tent, even Wee Andy the photographer, almost lost in his duffle coat and a big woolly scarf. He could hear distant sirens; saw two ambulances crossing the river over to their side, blue lights spinning. Meant it wouldn't be long until the press boys were here. Was hard enough to keep a murder quiet, never mind this one. A body found at the top of an unfinished office tower only a couple of minutes' walk from the *Record* office? No chance.

'Quite a view from up here,' said Murray pointing. 'Can see the cathedral. If it wasn't pissing with rain you'd even be able to see the People's Palace.'

'Great,' said McCoy. 'Well worth climbing up fourteen bloody storeys for.'

Murray shook his head. 'And here was me thinking leave might have changed you, but no, still the usual moaning-faced bastard that you are. How'd it go anyway? You go and see him?'

He had. Three two-hour sessions in a draughty back room in Pitt Street. Question after question.

How did you feel when you pushed him off the roof?

How did you feel when you saw the dead body?

How did you feel, really feel, inside at that point? Did you feel guilty?

What he'd really felt was an overwhelming desire to lean over the desk and punch the bastard in the face but he knew if he did he'd never get signed off so he sat there saying as little as possible, watching the clock. It was only when he got home he'd started thinking about the last thing the bloke had said to him.

Do you still feel happy being a policeman? Is it what you really want?

McCoy nodded. 'Statutory three appointments all attended. Signed off. Psychologically fit for duty.'

Murray grunted. 'How much did you have to bribe him?'

'So what have I missed?' McCoy asked. 'What's the big news from—'

'There's the boy!'

They turned and Wattie was walking towards

them, anorak, bobble hat and a pair of Arran wool mittens. He looked more like an enthusiastic toddler than a trainee detective.

He took a mitten off and pumped McCoy's hand up and down. 'Thought you weren't due back until tomorrow?'

'I'm not. Couldn't keep away. Well, not when there's some big bastard at your door telling you Murray needs you now.'

Wattie grinned. 'Did you miss me? Because fuck me, I didn't miss—'

'Watson!' Murray had had enough. 'Get this crime scene secured now! Stop acting like a bloody schoolboy!'

Wattie saluted and walked back through the rain towards the lights being set up on the far corner of the roof.

'How's he getting on?' asked McCoy, trying to fasten the top button of his coat, not easy with numb fingers.

Murray shook his head. 'Bright enough, but he treats everything like a bloody game. Need you to knock some sense into him.'

'What's the story then?' McCoy asked, looking round. 'How come we're freezing our balls off on the top of this building?'

'You'll see soon enough. C'mon,' said Murray.

McCoy followed him along the cardboard path leading towards the other side of the roof. Three steps behind Murray again, just like always. Was like he'd never been away. Cardboard beneath his feet already starting to dissolve with the rain and the amount of people walking on it. Two uniforms were huddled over in the corner, big umbrellas being held over them not doing much to keep the water off. Both of them were fiddling with the battery packs, trying to connect them.

'Fucking bastarding thing,' said one, then noticed Murray. 'Sorry, sir, just give us a minute.' He grunted and finally managed to push a plug into the socket in the side. 'Should be all right now,' he said, putting his fingers into his mouth, trying to suck some feeling back into them.

'Well then,' said Murray. 'What are you waiting for?'

The uniform nodded and clicked the switches down. Bright white light bounced back up off the wet roof. McCoy held his arm over his face, peered out through half-closed eyes. He'd never been good with the sight of blood, any blood, never mind this much. He took an involuntary step back. Edge of his vision was starting to blur, he felt dizzy. He shut his eyes, took deep breaths, tried to count to ten. He opened them again, saw the red everywhere, and turned his head away as fast as he could.

'Christ! You could have warned me, Murray.'

'Could have but I didn't,' said Murray. 'Need to get over it. Told you a million bloody times.' He looked over at the illuminated corner of the roof and grimaced. 'Mind you, this is bloody hellish.'

It was. The blood was everywhere. Splattered up

the half-finished walls, dripping from a flapping tarpaulin. Some of it had started to freeze already, red ice crystals glinting in the light from the big lamps. But most of it was still sticky and wet, giving off the familiar smell of copper pennies and butcher shops.

McCoy pulled his scarf across his mouth, told himself he was going to be okay and tried to concentrate. There wasn't any way round it. To get any closer to the body he was going to have to step into the big puddle of blood. There was more cardboard laid down in it but it had half soaked up the blood, wasn't going to make much of a difference. He put his foot down gingerly, felt the congealing blood tacky against the sole of his shoe. A tarpaulin snapped in the wind and he jumped, heartbeat going back to normal as he watched it break free and float off over the side of the building into the darkness.

He took a few deep breaths and stepped in, folded the edges of his coat over his knees and squatted. Tried to block out the cold and the rain, the sheer amount of blood, and tried to think about what he was looking at. It was a young man, late teens, early twenties. He'd been sat up against a pile of metal scaffolding poles, legs pointing out in front of him, arms hanging down by his sides. His left leg ending in a mess of tangled blood and bone, foot just attached.

Whatever he had been wearing had gone. All he was left with was a pair of underpants, pale skin of his legs and torso bluish in the bright lights. The words 'BYE BYE' had been cut into his chest, blood running down his torso.

McCoy counted down another ten like the doctor had told him and looked up into the man's face. Despite everything, his hair was still combed into a neat side shed, raindrops on it glistening in the big lights. Below it, one of his eyes was completely gone, socket empty, some sort of vein emerging out of it, dried blood sticking it onto his cheek. His jaw was hanging slack, broken it looked like. There was something stuffed into his mouth. McCoy knew what it was going to be before he looked. He looked. Wasn't wrong.

He stood up, ran for the side, feet sliding as he went, just made it to the edge before he was sick. When he'd finished he spat a few times, trying to clear his mouth of the taste of stomach acid and flat lager, watched it spiral down.

A tap on his shoulder and Murray handed him a hip flask. He took a deep pull, swirled the burning whisky round his mouth and swallowed it. Murray was shaking his head at him, looking at him like he was a uniform on his first day. He handed the flask back and Murray looked at him disapprovingly.

'Give us a break, Murray. That your idea of fun, eh? Switch the big fucking lights on when I turn up? Christ, they've even stuck his cock in his mouth.'

'Aye, that's right, McCoy. This whole murder scene's been arranged just to give you a fright.'

McCoy nodded over at the body. 'How did we know he was here?'

'Anonymous phone call into Central,' said Murray.

'From whoever did it?'

Murray nodded. 'Who else? No other bugger would know he was up here.'

'Sir?'

They turned. Wattie was standing there with a clear evidence bag. 'One of the uniform boys found these.' He handed the bag to Murray.

Murray took out his torch, switched it on and pointed it into the bag. Three used flashcubes, bulbs fizzled and spent, and two Polaroid backs, the cardboard left when you peel the picture off. He turned the bag and they could see the ghost photo on them. Reverse images of the man's destroyed face.

'Christ,' said McCoy. 'Pictures for later. Lovely. Might be fingerprints on them?'

Murray nodded.

'What do you mean for later?' asked Wattie.

McCoy made a wanking gesture. Wattie groaned.

'Mr McCoy, nice to see you back.'

He turned and Phyllis Gilroy the police pathologist was standing there. Seemed to have some sort of tiara thing on under her Rainmate, pearls round her neck, bottom of a pink chiffon dress poking out beneath her black rain slicker.

'North British?' asked McCoy.

She nodded. 'Mrs Murray was indisposed so

Hector kindly invited me along as his partner. Unfortunately we didn't get to stay very long. Had to leave before the turn. Moira Anderson. Pity, she has an excellent voice, I think.'

'You look very . . .' McCoy searched for the word. 'Dressed up.'

'I'll take that as a compliment,' she said, 'of sorts.'

'Did you have a look?' asked Murray.

'Indeed I did.'

'And?'

'Provisionally?' she asked. As always.

Murray sighed. As always. 'Provisionally.'

'Gunshot to the front of the head, specifically the left eye. As you will have noticed, that had the effect of pretty much removing the back of the head. There is another gunshot wound to the left ankle which seems to be post-mortem. Other than that he's been knocked around a bit, scratches and scrapes and cuts. And of course, the amputation of the . . .'

She hesitated for a second.

'The penis.' Carried on. 'The words on his chest look post-mortem too but I'll have to double-check . . .'

'Why no clothes?' asked McCoy.

'That, Mr McCoy, is a question for you rather than me, I fear. However, were I to conjecture I'd say he wanted the BYE BYE on the chest to be on display, first thing one would see, but as I said it's only conjecture. Now, if Hector will give us

14

the go ahead I'll get the ambulance boys to start packing him up?'

Murray nodded, and she walked off across the roof, gesturing to the ambulance men that they were good to go.

McCoy watched her go, looked at Murray and grinned. 'Hector is it now? Didn't know you and the esteemed Madame Gilroy were so pally.'

'Secret weapon. She's perfect for fending off the top brass. She's cleverer, richer and posher than the lot of them put together. I just hide behind her and smile. Stops them pressuring me about Central.'

McCoy blew into his hands. He was freezing, driving rain had pretty much soaked him through. Icy wind blowing round the top of the building wasn't helping much either. 'Do we know who he is? Nightwatchman, something like that, maybe?'

Murray held up a clear plastic bag with a bloody wallet in it. 'Don't know, but this was sitting next to the body. Whoever did it wanted him identified quickly.'

McCoy took the bag off him, fished out the wallet, trying not to get too much blood on his fingers. He flipped it open, managed to read the name on the driving licence.

'No,' he said. 'No way.'

He dug further in the wallet, found a folded-up bit of newspaper. He unfolded it. Read it. Couldn't believe it.

'Christ, it is. It's him.'

15

He held up the newspaper. Murray peered at it, too dark for him to read. Got his torch out, pointed it at the clipping. Illuminated the headline.

DREAM DEBUT FOR NEW CELTIC SIGNING

CHAPTER 2

'Seriously? You don't know who he is?' asked McCoy.

'Why would I? Never been to a football match in my life,' said Murray.

'Not even seen him in the paper? On the TV? Charlie Jackson?'

'Two teas. One wi' sugar?'

The woman was leaning out the caravan hatch, two chipped mugs held out in front of her. McCoy took the one with sugar, handed the other one to Murray. The tea van was parked outside Tiffany's in Sauchiehall Street, prime position to catch people coming out the dancing. Van had been there for years, selling teas, coffees, rolls and sausage. McCoy remembered stopping at it on his first night on the beat. He took a sip of the tea. As rotten as it was then. Still, at least the mug was warm.

'So who does he play for then, this boy?' asked Murray.

McCoy shook his head, didn't believe what he was hearing. Half suspected Murray was just doing it to annoy him. 'Celtic. He probably played today. Draw with Partick Thistle.'

17

'Today?' asked Murray.

'Aye, at Parkhead. He made the first team a year or so ago, never been out it since. Very talented boy. When he's on he's fucking magic, reads the ball better than anyone I've seen. Probably be off soon, or he would have been I should say. Liverpool would have got him, Clough, someone like that.' He looked at Murray again, still not quite believing him. 'C'mon, you must have heard of him.'

Murray shook his head, patted his jacket looking for his tobacco. 'No. Bloody game should be banned. Just another excuse we don't need for the idiots in this town to knock lumps out each other.' He looked at his watch. 'It's quarter past nine now. Was called in at seven. So when did this game finish?'

'Usual. Quarter to five,' said McCoy.

'Not much time to do that,' said Murray, nodding up at the office building. 'Must have got hold of him just after the match.'

'Poor bugger,' said McCoy. He thought for a minute. 'You know something? I just don't get it. Why would anyone want to shoot Charlie Jackson, carve some shite into his chest? What's he ever done to anyone? He's what, twenty-two? All he's ever done is kick a ball.'

They moved into the side of the caravan to let a group of girls clattering through the puddles in platform boots pass by. They had skimpy wee dresses on, halter tops, coats held over their heads to keep the rain off their hair. Even if it was pissing down and freezing it was still Saturday night. Bit of weather wasn't going to stop a Glasgow Saturday night.

'That photographer boy Andy seemed to know a bit about him,' said Murray, watching the girls joining the end of the queue already forming outside Tiffany's.

McCoy looked surprised. 'Andy? What'd that wee prick have to say about it?'

'Said he'd taken pictures of Jackson for the sports pages, chatty young lad apparently. Told him all about his fiancée, plans for the big day.'

McCoy dimly remembered a picture of Charlie Jackson and a girl in the paper, some big charity do. 'A dark-haired lassie? Good-looking? That her?'

Murray put his mug up on the counter. 'That's her, and, according to young Andy, she's Jake Scobie's daughter.'

McCoy had brought his cigarette up to his mouth, was about to take a drag. Stopped. 'You're having me on.'

Murray shook his head. 'Need to get it checked out but he seems certain.'

'Charlie Jackson is Jake Scobie's future son-in-law?' McCoy shook his head. 'How the fuck did I not know that?'

Murray shrugged. 'What? Harry McCoy's not as clever as he likes to think? Wonders will never cease.'

'Very funny,' said McCoy.

'Maybe the boy didn't know what he was letting himself in for.'

19

'How could he not? Can't be anyone in Glasgow who doesn't know who Jake Scobie is.' Something dawned. 'That's got to be why he's been killed. Maybe Charlie Jackson was playing away, if you'll pardon the expression, and Scobie found out. Maybe he—'

'Maybe's the bloody word! I don't know what happened and you certainly don't know what happened. That's what we need to find out. It's called being a polis.'

McCoy was on a roll.

'Makes you wonder what Jackson did to his daughter. Must have been something bad. Maybe he got another lassie pregnant, that might explain the cock-in-mouth scenario.'

Murray looked exasperated. 'I'm talking to my fucking self here. We don't know who did it. Got that?'

McCoy nodded. 'Yes, sir.'

'First principles, not bloody fantasies. Okay?'

McCoy nodded again.

Murray seemed temporarily satisfied. Had managed to locate his pipe, now came the process of getting it lit. He knocked the barrel on the heel of his shoe. 'How d'you think he got him up there?'

'Arrange to meet him nearby? Put a gun in his back and march him up the stairs? But why go all the way up there? Doesn't make any sense, too much chance of him getting away, even with a gun. Why go to all that trouble? Why not just kill him in his flat?'

They looked up at the half-built building. 'No one to see you up there,' said Murray. 'Or hear the gun. All the time you want to do what you want. That's why.'

The crime scene lights at the top of the building were still on, shining out in the rain like some kind of lighthouse. McCoy didn't want to think about what had gone on up there, how many of Jackson's screams went unheard, how much pleading there had been, how much pain. Still, didn't see how the office building made sense. Why not some waste ground or an empty house? Plenty of those around here. Be a lot easier.

'Maybe the office block is one of Scobie's jobs? He runs a security firm, doesn't he?'

Murray nodded. 'Amongst other things.'

'He could have cancelled the guards, made sure there was no one around to see what was going on.'

'Get Wattie to check, give him something to bloody do,' said Murray.

'Will do. Shooting someone in the head, that's like an execution.'

'Something a hit man would do,' said Murray.

'Okay, and don't go nuts again but Scobie's got one of those,' said McCoy.

Murray unclipped his bow tie, opened the top button of his dress shirt. 'That's better. I can bloody breathe now.'

He looked at McCoy. 'Kevin Connolly.'

McCoy nodded. 'Don't know that much about him apart from he does Scobie's dirty work.'

'Well, I do,' said Murray, finally getting his pipe lit. 'He's a right nasty piece of work is our Connolly.'

'Nasty enough to do that to Charlie Jackson?'

'Oh aye. Something like that's not a problem for Connolly. Was at one of his trials, prosecution lawyer described him as "a truly evil man". Way he grinned when he said it, Connolly seemed to take it as some sort of compliment.'

'Did he get done?' asked McCoy.

Murray shook his head. 'Too many witnesses who suddenly forgot their testimonies and Archie Lomax in his corner. Archie Lomax is many things, but he's also a bloody good lawyer. Don't think Connolly's done jail time for anything serious for years. Scobie needs him around, happy to pay Lomax to make sure he is.'

He looked back up at the building. 'What we really need to find out is how he got to the top of that bloody building.'

'Hang on,' said McCoy.

He left Murray standing there and hurried across the road. The paper seller outside the Variety Bar was packing up for the night, pulling the headline paper from under the crossed wires on the wooden board in front of him – *TRAGEDY IN CHURCH* – and crunching it into a ball. Luckily he had one *Sports Times* left. McCoy gave him the four pence, flicked through it on the way back. Found what he was looking for by the time he got back to Murray.

'Jackson was on the bench. Didn't play. Need to find out what happened between the end of the match and . . . you know. You going into the shop now?'

Murray shook his head. 'Pitt Street. Need to do a report for the Super getting in.'

McCoy nodded. 'Okay. I'll go back to the shop, see if I can get hold of Scobie or his daughter. Quite looking forward to disturbing Archie Lomax's peaceful Saturday night. You know Jackson was a left-footer?'

'A Catholic?' asked Murray.

'Jesus! No, well, I don't know, maybe he was, probably was if he played for Celtic, but he was actually left-footed is what I mean. Always scored with his left.'

'Ah. That why he shot his left ankle, you think?' asked Murray.

McCoy shrugged. 'Could be. Mind you, not easy to play football with the back of your head blown off. Not sure a broken ankle's gonnae make much of a difference.'

Murray sighed. 'Someone'll have to tell the boy's family and quick. Every one of those uniforms up there'll be racing to a phone box as soon as they get down, straight on to the *Record* for their tenner. If word of that thing on his chest gets out I'll bloody hang for someone. Need that kept back to weed out the fucking nutters. He a local boy, this Jackson?'

McCoy nodded. 'Maryhill, I think.'

Murray took off his hat, scratched at what was left of his ginger hair. 'So that'll be me then. What a fucking mess.'

McCoy watched Murray get into the waiting squad car, drained the rest of his rotten tea, put the mug back on the counter. The queue outside Tiffany's was starting to shuffle in. Groups of giggling women passing half-bottles of vodka. Boys in their leather and denim jackets getting soaking but trying to show they were too hard to worry about something like rain.

Jackson must have been about the same age as them. Nice-looking fiancée, great football player, good-looking boy. Had it all in front of him. McCoy lit up, took a deep drag, started walking into town. Not any more he didn't.

Turned out Lomax beat him to it. By the time McCoy got back to the shop there was a note on his desk telling him to phone Mr Lomax at home as soon as he could. He cursed, crumpled it and threw it in the bin. Then he phoned the number. Posh Edinburgh voice answered, wasted no time.

'Ten o'clock tomorrow morning at my office. Mr Scobie wants to have a chat.'

McCoy put the receiver down, sat back in his chair and had a look around. Didn't seem like much had changed in the three weeks he'd been off. Desks covered in papers, full ashtrays, files and dirty mugs. Wee plug-in radiator in the corner doing its best and failing to heat up the room.

Apart from the desk sergeant he was the only one in. Saturday night was always their busiest night. Everyone out dealing with the usual shite. Fights and drunks, knives and crashed cars. Battered wives and slashed boys.

He took the two bacon rolls he'd bought on the way out their damp paper bag and started eating, realised he was starving.

He was so engrossed in the rolls and the copy of *Titbits* he'd found on Wattie's desk he jumped when the phone on his desk rang. He picked it up.

'Central. McCoy speaking.'

'Harry, my wee darling! The very man. What you got to tell me about a certain young football—'

He hung up before she could get any further. Mary at the *Record* hot on the trail. Hadn't taken her long. The phone rang again so he leant over and unplugged it at the wall, sat back up and that's when he noticed it. Thomson's corkboard. Been up there so long he'd stopped seeing it. Pictures of big-titted girls he'd cut out from the *Sun* or *Men Only*, a poster telling you to look out for Colorado Beetle in your potato plants, and a front page from a few weeks ago.

HERO COP FOILS KILLER ON ROOFTOP

He walked over and pulled it free of the drawing pins, took a closer look. God knows where the paper'd got the picture of him. He looked about ten years younger. Wouldn't have looked bad at all if someone hadn't drawn a moustache and a pair of wee glasses on his face and a speech bubble coming out his mouth – *I'm shiteing it up here!*

He shook his head, pinned it back up, and that's when he noticed it, pinned in between a picture of George Best and a picture of Jinky Johnson. Charlie Jackson was running away from the goalmouth, green-and-white strip, hands held up, expression of utter joy on his face, teammates trying to catch up with him to celebrate. He looked ecstatic, not a care in the world. He unpinned the picture, put it in his wallet, walked back to his chair, plugged in the phone, called Susan, told her he'd be late.

11TH FEBRUARY 1973

CHAPTER 3

Most of the lawyers McCoy dealt with had offices down on the Saltmarket right beside the courts, all the better for picking up stray clients. Not Lomax, though, he was up in Blythswood Square, smack in the middle of the most expensive area of town, in amongst all the bankers and the corporate offices. Wasn't that far from the shop and the rain had gone off so they decided to walk.

Sunday morning in this part of town was dead. All the offices and shops shut up. Just the distant clang of St Aloysius' bells as they walked up West George Street, past the RAC Club with its Union Jack flying, and into the square. Nothing grand, just a rectangle of grass with benches round it surrounded by wrought iron fencing.

Was a funny place, Blythswood Square. Schizophrenic. During the day it was full of men in pinstripes and secretaries in wee business suits going in and out the offices, making deals, looking important. Soon as the offices shut and night fell everything changed. Became a different kind of square entirely. The girls started appearing. Old, young, didn't matter, all of them dressed in mini skirts, high heels and jackets that were too flimsy for the weather. They stood on the corners, chatting, smoking, keeping one eye on the cars circling round and round. If one stopped it didn't take long, they leant in the window, decided a price, then got in. Two different worlds separated by a couple of hours.

Number 42 Blythswood Square was a three-storey building of grey stone, marble steps leading up to a smart black door. Murray rang the brass doorbell above the nameplate LOMAX & LOMAX and they waited. No reply. Murray pressed it again, muttering under his breath. Still nothing. He turned to McCoy.

'Where is the prick? Sure it was ten he said?'

McCoy looked at his watch, tried to stifle a yawn. 'Only ten past, maybe he's a wee bit late.'

It was almost half past when he turned up. Murray'd just declared that he'd had enough and was going back to the shop when McCoy saw the car.

'Sir,' he said, nodding over.

A gold Jag was turning into the square, exhaust billowing out behind it in the damp air. It circled round, then pulled in to the pavement in front of them. Door opened and out stepped Archie Lomax, looking immaculate as always. Chalk-stripe suit, polished black brogues, navy Crombie. No tie the only concession to the weekend. You didn't get to be the highest paid criminal lawyer in Glasgow by turning up looking a mess.

Murray got in first. 'About bloody time, we've been standing here for half an hour.'

Lomax held his hands up in apology. 'Sorry, gents, roads blocked outside Bearsden. Some burn has burst its banks, had to go round the long way, couldn't be avoided.'

'Half a bloody hour,' said Murray again.

Hadn't got his money's worth from Lomax, he wasn't contrite enough for his liking. Wasn't going to get it, though. Lomax just ignored him, unlocked the big black door, pushed it open, held it wide for them. They followed him up the stairs, furnishings and fittings getting steadily more luxurious as they climbed. On the third floor Lomax unlocked a heavy glass door and they went in.

'Welcome to the inner sanctum. Don't usually have men of the constabulary in here but the boardroom is being redecorated so needs must.'

Lomax's office covered most of the top floor of the building. Carpets were dark green, dotted with faded oriental rugs, pale blue walls hung with gold-framed paintings of old sailing ships. His desk sat in front of the double windows looking out over the square, not so much a desk as a long slab of glass held up by spindly steel legs, leather swivel chair behind it. Only things sitting on it were a metal frame with a row of silver balls hanging from it by black threads, a notepad and a thick file. If the office was meant to be impressive, it was. He clicked a switch and warm air started blowing.

'Drink?' he asked, walking over to a large antique globe with legs. He flipped up the top half to reveal gleaming crystal glasses and expensive bottles. McCoy spied a bottle of Chivas, was about to say yes, but Murray got in before him.

'As I'm sure you are aware, Mr Lomax, we're on duty. Where's Scobie?'

'Please yourself,' said Lomax, pouring a good measure of Johnnie Walker Black Label into a tumbler. He settled himself down behind the desk, pointed at two leather armchairs in front of it. 'Make yourselves comfortable.'

They struggled out of their coats and scarves – room was heating up already – and sat down. Lomax took a heavy fountain pen from his inside pocket and unscrewed the top, wrote the date on the notepad in front of him.

'Couple of things before we start, gents. My client has volunteered to come in here and speak to you. He only heard about the dreadful incident a few hours ago. Obviously he's extremely upset so I'm sure you'll appreciate how helpful he's being coming here today. Secondly,' he looked at each of them in turn, 'this conversation is very much off the record, in the spirit of cooperation and the hope of bringing a swift conclusion to things. Understood?'

Murray took his time, brushed a bit of lint off his trousers, moulded the crease on his trilby sitting on his lap before he spoke. 'Your client is a piece of scum, Mr Lomax.' He looked round at the paintings on the wall, the deep pile carpet, the Bang & Olufsen stereo system in the corner. 'All these trappings that he's no doubt paying through the nose for don't change a thing. Jake Scobie is still scum. Always has been, always will be. The fact that he pays you means you may have to act like he's a respectable businessman, but thankfully I don't. Now where is he?'

McCoy had to hand it to him; Murray was not one to be intimidated by anyone. Not even a big lawyer like Lomax.

Lomax looked indignant, had just opened his mouth to reply, when the buzzer went. 'Looks like my client is here,' he said, getting up. He leant into Murray as he passed him on the way to open the door. 'Keep your grandstanding under your hat if you please, Mr Murray. It's not only tiresome, it's pointless and, believe me, I've heard it all before.'

'What's he doing this for?' asked McCoy after he'd gone. 'Normally Scobie wouldn't talk to us for love nor money, and now he's volunteering for a little chat? After he's got his pet hatchet man to kill his future son-in-law? I don't get it.'

'Me neither,' said Murray. 'Normally takes a week of going back and forward with Lomax until he'll even admit Scobie is his client, never mind set up a meeting.'

'Must be your way with words,' said McCoy.

33

Murray was about to answer when Scobie and Lomax appeared. Lomax pulled another chair round behind his side of the desk and they sat down.

Scobie was dressed just like Lomax. Suit and a Crombie, shiny shoes, white shirt. On Lomax they looked like the clothes he was born to wear, on Scobie they looked more like a costume, dressing-up clothes. There was one other big difference between the two of them. Lomax, unlike Scobie, didn't have a dirty big scar running from his ear down across his left cheek and into the side of his mouth. Looked like someone had tried to hack half his face off, which, knowing the people Scobie ran with, they probably had. He was a small man, Scobie, and like all the best hard men, slight too, built like a welterweight.

'Morning, Jake,' said Murray.

'That's Mr Scobie to you,' he said, leaning forward.

Lomax held his hand across him, a restraint. 'As I said, gents, Mr Scobie has volunteered to come here. Some respect is in order.'

Murray grunted.

McCoy knew Scobie and Murray had too much water under the bridge for a civilised chat, so he thought he'd better step in. 'What was it you wanted to see us about, Mr Scobie?'

Murray didn't look happy at him saying 'Mr' Grunted again.

'It's a delicate matter,' said Lomax, shifting

round in his seat towards McCoy, grateful for a more receptive audience. 'Might be easier if I speak on Jake's behalf.'

Jake was looking at them with contempt, barely nodded. 'Fire away,' said McCoy. 'We're all ears.'

Lomax looked relieved, sat back in his chair, settled down to tell the tale. 'Mr Scobie has some information that may be pertinent to the unfortunate fate of Charlie Jackson. As you may know, Jackson was only months away from becoming Mr Scobie's son-in-law. Consequently he's very upset about what's happened, as, naturally, is his daughter.' Murray made a noise somewhere between a snort and a laugh. Lomax ignored him, kept going. 'Mr Scobie has an occasional employee, a Mr Connolly—'

'Occasional employee?' said Murray. 'Now you really are taking the piss.'

Lomax, not looking happy at the interruption, sat forward, laced his fingers together. 'As Mr Scobie's accountancy records will show, Connolly is indeed an occasional employee.'

'Employed as what exactly?' asked McCoy as innocently as he could manage.

'Ah . . .' Lomax looked at the notepad in front of him, couldn't find any inspiration, turned to Scobie. 'What was his official title again?'

'Gardener,' said Scobie, deadpan.

This time Murray laughed out loud; even Lomax had half a smile on his face. 'We are off the record, gentlemen?' McCoy nodded, Murray almost did.

35

'In a situation this grave I feel the best option is to be as open as possible. I think we all know who Mr Connolly is and what kind of work he does for Mr Scobie, no need to elaborate. Unfortunately Connolly has become a problem. Connolly has always been – how shall we say? – somewhat unstable. Regretfully that instability has become more pronounced of late. It seems he has formed an unnatural interest in Mr Scobie's daughter, Elaine.'

McCoy raised his eyebrows; things were getting interesting.

Lomax went on. 'About a year ago he started sending her letters, following her, turning up wherever she was. She became an obsession, an unreciprocated obsession to say the least. Miss Scobie tried to laugh it off at first, but then she became alarmed and then she became seriously frightened. This courtship, for want of a better word, culminated in her coming home one night to find him sitting in the living room of her flat holding a bunch of flowers.'

Lomax glanced at Scobie. Another nod. Carry on.

'At that point she felt she had to tell her father. After she and her father made it perfectly plain there were no reciprocal feelings, Connolly became convinced that this was simply due to her fiancé, Mr Jackson. That he had somehow turned her against him. In his twisted mind he started to believe that without Charlie Jackson in the picture

Miss Scobie would come to her senses and fall for him.'

'Hence the BYE BYE on his chest,' said McCoy. Lomax nodded.

'Nasty,' said McCoy. 'Imagine that. A nutter like Connolly taking a fancy to your daughter.'

Lomax carried on. 'You may have read recently that Charlie was injured – hamstring trouble. Couldn't play for a couple of weeks. In reality he'd been attacked by an associate of Connolly. He tried to break his shin with a hammer. Luckily his aim wasn't too good and he only inflicted a rather nasty flesh wound. The club and ourselves thought it better it didn't become common knowledge. Shortly after that incident Connolly disappeared, cut off all communication with the Scobie family.'

'Did you look for him?' asked McCoy.

Scobie answered before Lomax could stop him. 'Oh, I looked for the cunt all right, looked every-where. Nobody hurts my family and gets away with it. When I find him I'm going to splatter the cunt from here to—'

Lomax's hand went up again. 'Jake,' he hissed. 'Please.'

Scobie didn't look happy but he sat back, hands gripping the arms of the chair. He reached into his pocket, took out a packet of Regal and lit up.

'Okay?' asked Lomax.

Scobie nodded.

Order restored, he went on. 'It seems that Mr Connolly is a very hard man to find. He has a habit of staying in short-rent flats, hotels, boarding houses, moving around a lot.' He smiled. 'Perhaps a wise move for a man like that. The Scobies eventually gave up, hoped he had moved on, gone to London, somewhere like that.'

'Until this morning,' said McCoy.

'Until this morning,' said Lomax.

McCoy sat back on his chair. Time to throw the grenade. 'That's a lovely wee story, Mr Lomax. But I'll tell you what I'm thinking, eh? Maybe Mr Scobie there just wasn't too keen on his future son-in-law and got Connolly to take care of it. That's what he usually does for you, isn't it, Mr Scobie? Takes care of nasty wee problems, makes them go away, weeds in your roses, that sort of thing.'

Lomax's hand came up again, but Scobie was having none of it this time and pushed it away, stood up before Lomax could stop him.

'Who the fuck are you, you prick? You calling me a fucking liar?'

McCoy was the picture of innocence. 'I didn't say that.' He turned to Murray. 'Did I say that?'

Scobie was red-faced, spat through clenched teeth, 'That boy was like a son to me. Understand that? That going in your fucking head, is it? If I get—'

'Jake! Please!'

Scobie looked at Lomax, took a second, then nodded and sat down. Suddenly he seemed deflated, confused, almost as if he was going to cry. All of this seemed like it was new to him. Not used to not being the one calling the shots, running the show. Was new for McCoy too. The only emotion he'd ever seen on Scobie's face before was anger. Never seen him look like he did now, like a man who was hurting.

'Well, Mr Scobie, I'm sorry to hear of your loss,' said Murray, standing up. 'From the look of it, Connolly may well be responsible. However, what the motive was and who was involved remains to be seen.'

Lomax screwed the lid of his pen back on. 'Be assured, Mr Murray, my client is telling the truth.'

Murray smiled, put his hat back on. 'Who knows, Mr Lomax? Maybe he is. Always a first time for everything. Isn't that what they say? We'll be in touch.'

'You buy all that?' McCoy asked. They were back on the pavement in Blythswood Square, stamping their feet, waiting for a squad car to turn up.

Murray shrugged, turned his collar up against the wind. 'Don't see why not. If Scobie had just wanted rid of that boy he'd have been a lot less obvious about it.'

'Unless he did something to his daughter, something he wasn't happy about.'

'Could be. We'll get her in, see what she's got to say for herself.'

'Can't see Lomax letting that happen without a fight. Or him being there,' said McCoy. 'But I'll give it a try.'

A patrol car turned into the square, started the one-way circuit.

'How were the parents?' asked McCoy.

'Them? They were great. Only son shot in the fucking face then chopped to fuck? They opened a bloody bottle of champagne. How do you think they were?'

'Sorry,' said McCoy, feeling like an idiot.

The car pulled up, uniform got out and came round to open the passenger door. 'At long bloody last,' Murray growled at him, turned to McCoy. 'You call Lomax when we get back, tell him we want Elaine Scobie in the station tomorrow morning. Rattle his cage.' He went to get in the car, realised McCoy wasn't following.

'You not coming back?'

'I'll walk. It's only ten minutes.'

'In this weather?'

'Clears the head,' said McCoy.

Murray shook his and got in the car.

No offence to Murray but McCoy needed a break. Couldn't face being stuck in the back of a stuffy squad car while Murray ranted and raved about what scum Scobie was and how Lomax should be struck off for defending scum like him. Besides, McCoy liked walking, gave him the chance to think without the noise and distractions of the shop. So he buttoned up his raincoat, started walking down the hill back towards town.

When Scobie had come into the office McCoy had thought he'd be intimidated, impressed maybe.

The great Jake Scobie close up. But he wasn't, far from it. All the things that made up Scobie – the clothes, the scar, the temper – were beginning to feel wrong, dated. Was like Scobie was stranded back in the days when he'd come up through the ranks, still living in the time of the razor kings and honour amongst thieves. Would have been as well wearing spats and talking like George Raft. Scobie in the North, Ronnie Naismith in the Southside, McCready in Govan. Suddenly they seemed old, like kings who could be toppled.

McCoy handed the money over, pocketed the wee red notebook, stepped out of R. S. McColl's and back onto Sauchiehall Street. New case, new jotter. Force of habit. He peeled the price ticket off the front and put it in his pocket. Realised he didn't have a pencil, should have bought a new one of those as well. Was a mystery to him where everything he had disappeared to. They all went. Pens, fags, gloves, house keys more than a few times.

He was nearly at Treron's when he noticed him. Charlie the Pram. McCoy didn't know his real name but he'd seen him around town for years, wandering around, talking to himself. Just another lost soul amongst the many. Charlie'd found an old Silver Cross pram somewhere – hence the name – and, as always, it was full of wire, ginger bottles, anything he could try and make some money from. Charlie had good days and bad days. Never knew if he'd talk to you or just stare through you.

'You all right, Charlie?' asked McCoy.

Charlie turned, nodded. A good day then. He tapped the window of Dunn & Co. 'I'd a coat like that once. Good tweed coat.'

'That right? What happened to it?'

'It's hanging on the back of the kitchen door,' he said, as if it was obvious.

McCoy dug in his coat pocket, found a pound note and handed it to him, told him to get a hot breakfast. Charlie took it and slipped it between the folds of the filthy tartan rug he had wrapped around him.

'Can I tell you something?' he said.

McCoy nodded, tried to look at his watch without Charlie seeing. Was already slightly regretting stopping.

'Sure. Fire away.'

'I had a house once, an old manse, lovely it was. Three boys at school, pretty wife.' He pinched the skin on his forehead, a habit; it was covered in small cuts and scabs. 'Was all mine. Until they found out.' He looked at McCoy, eyes panicked. 'They found out and they tried to drown me but I got away. That's what they do if they catch you. They boil you in tanks of dirty water and bleach until the skin peels off you.' And then he started to cry.

McCoy patted his shoulder. 'C'mon, Charlie. Not going to happen anytime soon. Get yourself a hot breakfast, eh? Make you feel better.'

Charlie nodded, wiped his nose with his sleeve,

went back to staring at the tweed coat, pinching his forehead, blood starting to run into his eyes.

McCoy left him there, kept walking down the hill towards Stewart Street. He did what he could. Gave them some money, listened to their stories, tried to treat them like human beings. Maybe it was a kind of bribe. Guys like Charlie wandered all over the city without anyone noticing them, they saw things. Guys like Charlie had given him information more than once. Information worth a lot more than a couple of bob for a cup of tea. At least that's what he told people he did it for anyway.

He stopped at the zebra crossing, waited. If Scobie was telling the truth, if he was out to get Connolly, which seemed more likely than not, Connolly was fucked. Either Scobie found him and killed him or the polis found him, put him in jail and Scobie got someone to do the same thing in there. If he was Connolly he'd be gone already, further than London – as far as he could go.

The rain was back on, turning into sleet, grey clouds scudding across the sky. McCoy stood in the doorway of Grandfare for a minute, lit up. The news about Charlie Jackson should be in the paper and on the radio this morning. Mary from the *Record* wasn't going to give up easy, not on a story like this. The shot in the eye, shot to the ankle, carving in the chest. Did that mean something, the places he'd aimed for? Or was it just Connolly getting his kicks? And the bloody pictures he'd taken for later? Proof of the job done, maybe, to send to Scobie. He finished his fag, flicked it out into the road, turned his coat collar up and ran through the sleet towards the doors of Central.

CHAPTER 4

McCoy tried to walk in without Billy the desk sergeant clocking him. Thought he'd managed it. Billy's head was down, *News of the World* spread out in front of him. No chance. Billy had a sixth sense. Looked up, fat face already clouding over.

'At long bloody last! C'mere, you!' he said.

McCoy sighed, walked over to the desk. 'How's things Billy? No seen you for a—'

'Fuck up,' said Billy. 'Here.'

Handed McCoy a pile of notes all with the same message on them. *Call Mary at the* Record *ASAP*.

'Daft cow's been phoning all bloody morning, right cheeky article she is too. "Why don't I know where he is?" Do me a favour, McCoy, and call the daft bint, because if you don't, next time she calls I'm going to come and get you and drag you here to this bloody phone. Got it?'

McCoy nodded, lied. Said he'd call her soon as he could and walked through to the office. Murray was already standing in front of the big blackboard so he slipped in behind his desk like some schoolboy late for class, tried to shrug his wet coat off. Wattie

45

winked at him as he sat down, tapped at his watch. Mouthed 'you're late'.

He was. Most of the squad were already there, sitting on the edge of desks, notepads out, serious faces. Murray must have put the fear of God into them already. Room smelt of fags and wet wool coats drying in the heat of the radiators. He sat at his desk, slid the copy of *Titbits* into the bin, got his wee red jotter out, found a ballpoint pen in one of his drawers. Tried to look like he was all ears.

There was a picture up on the board, blown-up mug shot of Connolly. He looked late thirties, balding, pleasant face. Kind of guy you wouldn't remember passing in the street, somebody's neighbour, somebody's brother-in-law. There was something familiar about it though. McCoy felt like he'd seen him somewhere, couldn't think where.

Murray took the empty pipe out of his mouth, pointed at the picture. 'Kevin Connolly. Date of birth eleventh February 1943. Multiple—'

'Birthday boy,' said Wattie.

'What?' asked Murray, looking exasperated.

'His date of birth. He's thirty today.'

'Finished?' asked Murray. Few sniggers from round the room. 'Can I get on with my bloody job now?'

Wattie nodded, looked down at his notepad, back of his neck going red.

Murray carried on. 'Multiple arrests for assault, one attempted murder charge, one charge of kidnapping, one charge of serious sexual assault.

46

A very dangerous and a very violent man. Hard to estimate how much damage he's inflicted over the years.' He shook his head. 'But, thanks to Jake Scobie and his money, Archie Lomax has managed to get him off with almost all of it.'

'What's the connection exactly?' asked Wattie, attempting to redeem himself.

McCoy smiled to himself. Wasn't so long ago Wattie had stayed at the back of the room during briefings, too scared to speak. Now he was leaning on Thomson's desk, chewing a pencil, making notes and asking questions. Supposed it was progress. Even if he still looked too young to even be in the force, never mind in a briefing like this.

'Connolly and Scobie have been joined at the hip since Connolly started working for him,' said Murray. 'They come from the same street in the Calton. Means a lot to someone like Scobie. Their maws knew each other. People say Scobie's the brains and Connolly's the brawn but it's not as simple as that. Scobie's more than able to take care of himself so Connolly gets reserved for the really nasty jobs. Nastier the better as far as he's concerned. Enjoys hurting people. Was convicted of aggravated assault in' – he checked the file he was holding – 'October '71, spent five months in Barlinnie. Other than that, our Mr Connolly has mostly led a charmed life, sorting out Jake Scobie's problems, making them go away and getting away with it.'

McCoy looked up at the picture again. Must have seen him in the shop or at the courts, something

47

like that. In the picture he looked like butter wouldn't melt in his mouth. Nice open features, half a smile on his face. You can't really be charging me with anything, can you?

Murray continued. 'For those of you who have been living under a rock and our more junior colleagues' – Wattie stood up and bowed to general catcalls – 'Jake Scobie started out as a tally man, collecting debts. Worked his way up – mainly by taking out his employer Robbie Craig with a machete – to be the boss in around '62. Past few years he's been trying to clean up his act, investing in property, keeping a good distance from the illegal stuff, just another Glasgow businessman.' He paused. 'Except he's not. He can hide behind Lomax and his charity dinners and his suits from Forsyth's but be assured he's still running his rackets. Now, since Mr McCoy has finally managed to come back from his holidays' – more catcalls – 'I'll let him run through the situation with Scobie and Connolly. McCoy?'

McCoy stood up, made his way to the blackboard. Ran them through this morning's meeting. Told them about Connolly, his falling out with Scobie, his previous attack on Charlie Jackson and his obsession with Elaine Scobie. Sat back down.

Murray took over. 'Charlie Jackson. Twenty-two years old. Good son, good friend, shining career, about to get married.' He pointed to the picture of the footballer. 'Kevin Connolly is our primary suspect. There is only one thing we have to do.'

He paused, looked out at the assembled team. 'Find him before Scobie does. I am not giving that cunt the satisfaction of getting to Connolly before we do.' He clapped his hands. 'So! Previous addresses checked, known associates interviewed, get round the touts, someone must know where he is. I want him found and quick. Understood?'

A few mumbles.

'I said understood?'

Chorus of 'yes, sir'.

Murray nodded, satisfied, walked back towards his office shouting 'McCoy! Watson!' over his shoulder.

They followed him into the office, sat down. McCoy looked around. Murray's office hadn't changed in years, no reason why it would have changed in the past three weeks. Same old pictures of him looking young in a rugby strip, signed rugby ball on his desk. Stink of pipe tobacco and Ralgex. Piles of folders and files covering most of the available space. Murray rifled through the big pile in front of him, found what he was looking for and pushed a bit of paper across the desk.

'Lomax called. Connolly's last known address, he got it from Scobie,' he said.

'Lomax called?' asked McCoy. 'He's getting very helpful all of a sudden.'

Wattie picked it up, read it. 'Stronsay Street? Where's that?'

'Just off the Royston Road, I think,' said McCoy.

'Where's the Royston Road?' asked Wattie.

McCoy rolled his eyes. 'I keep forgetting you're

from Greenock. They got actual streets there or is it just one big shithole?'

Murray banged his fist on the desk. The two of them shut up, looked at him guiltily.

'McCoy! You're supposed to be helping Wattie here do his papers, teaching him how to be a detective, not scoring bloody points. Holiday's over, McCoy. Start concentrating!'

McCoy muttered, 'Sorry, sir.'

'Right. You two away and have a look at the flat, see what you can see. Hopefully you can pick up an idea of where he's gone.'

'Any luck with getting the daughter in for an interview?' asked McCoy. 'Lomax stonewalled me.'

Murray's face darkened.

'Apparently she is "too distressed to speak to us". Lomax buying time until he gets her story straight, more like. We'll try again tomorrow. If it's the same again I'm going to make him get an official medical certificate for her or I'll arrest her for perverting the course of justice.'

'What did he say about bringing her into protective custody?' asked McCoy.

'That got nixed too. Apparently the bold Elaine told Lomax that Connolly would never harm her and she was fine where she was,' said Murray.

'More fool her,' said Wattie. 'Does she know what he did to her boyfriend?'

Murray rummaged through the papers on his desk again, came up with a copy of the *Sunday Mail*. Picture of Charlie Jackson on the front.

'Well, if she didn't, she bloody does now. Her and every other bugger in the city.'

'Some uniform called in and got their tenner then,' said McCoy.

'Aye, and if I find out who it is, his feet won't touch the fucking ground. At least the carving on his chest still seems secret. Better bloody stay that way. Let me know how you get on at Connolly's. Oh and . . .' He looked through the papers on his desk. Again. Found the one he was looking for and handed it over. 'Charlie Jackson's flatmate, another football player apparently, plays for Celtic as well—'

'Nae luck,' muttered Wattie.

'You say something, Watson?' barked Murray.

'No, sir!' said Wattie smartly.

'Go and see this flatmate. See what he knows about Jackson and Connolly, if Jackson ever talked about him. And find out if he saw him after the match. Club are saying Jackson left the ground at half five as per usual. Nothing out the ordinary. Need to track his movements.'

They stood up to go. 'McCoy, you stay here a minute,' said Murray.

He sat back down. Murray waited until Wattie shut the door behind him, leant back in his seat.

'You okay?' he asked. 'I can leave you here on a desk for a while.'

'I'm fine. I've had three weeks pottering around

the house, going to the appointments. Any more time off and I'll be climbing the walls. Need to get working again.'

'You sure? No shame in—'

'I'm fine, Murray! Honest.'

Murray held his hands up. 'Fine! Christ . . . Don't know what I'm asking this for but how's your pal, Cooper?'

'Okay, I think. I heard he got out the hospital,' said McCoy.

'You keep away from that thug,' said Murray. 'He may have helped you out—'

'He did more than help out. He was in the bloody hospital for three weeks because he tried to help me out.'

'Aye well, that was his choice. You keep clear of him. You hear me? I've told you once and I'm no telling you again.'

McCoy nodded. Didn't have the energy to argue. 'I will.' He stood up. 'By the way. Connolly? I'm sure I recognise him from somewhere, sure I've seen him before.'

'He's been in and out of here and Pitt Street for years. Must have seen him then,' said Murray.

'Must have.'

He shut Murray's office door behind him. Shouted on Wattie to go and get the car. He didn't know where he'd seen Connolly but one thing he did know. Wasn't in the shop or Pitt Street.

CHAPTER 5

'The manager of Jackson's club Glasgow Celtic, Jock Stein, has issued a statement. "On behalf of myself and everyone associated with the club, we wish to express our shock and dismay at the untimely death of Charles Jackson. Not only was he an excellent football player, he was a fine young man and our thoughts are with his family at this time." Two men were injured in Belfast today as a bomb they were—'

McCoy leant forward and switched off the radio, sat back in his seat, started digging in his pockets for his fags. He pushed the cigarette lighter in. Waited.

'You ever see him play? Jackson?' he asked as they slowed down to let a funeral procession pass.

Wattie nodded. 'Not bad.'

McCoy snorted. 'Not bad? You're joking, aren't you?' Lighter popped out, McCoy held the hot element up to his cigarette. 'Best left foot for years and you know it. You Rangers boys just can't see past the strip, can you?'

Car was getting stuffy with the smoke and the

heater blasting out hot stale air. McCoy rolled the window down, felt the rain on his face.

'Murray wasn't even sure if you were coming back,' said Wattie. 'Said you were rattled by what happened with the Dunlop boy, the whole thing. He was worried, you know.'

'That right?' said McCoy flatly.

Last thing he wanted to hear about was Wattie and Murray having cosy wee chats about his state of mind. That's what happened if you got signed off. Suddenly everyone thinks you're fair game. Everyone passing judgement on your mental state. And every bugger thinks the same thing. 'He's no the same any more.' Far as he was concerned they could all fuck off, Murray and Wattie included.

Wattie pulled up at the lights. 'He was just worried. Didn't want to lose you, that's all. You're still the golden boy no matter what happens.'

McCoy pointed to Stronsay Street. 'Aye well, I'm back, so he can rest easy. Left here.'

End of conversation.

Stronsay Street was in a scheme sitting on a hill at the back of Royston. Rows of identical council houses with neat wee gardens in front. Huge towers of the Red Road flats in the background. Wattie was peering through the windscreen counting.

'Twenty-two, twenty-four, twenty-six.'

'Twenty-eight,' said McCoy, pointing up ahead.

Connolly's flat was the top left of a four-in-a-block.

They parked behind a Beetle up on four bricks and got out. The garden in front of the flat below seemed to be some sort of gathering ground for gnomes and little statues of fish and birds. There was a wishing well in the middle of the lawn, plaster Scottie dog and plastic cat beside it. Path was lined with plastic flowers and foil windmills. Even had a sign planted in the lawn.

ENJOY THE GARDEN BUT LOOK DON'T TOUCH!

'That sign's enough to make you want to kick one of those gnomes to fuck,' said McCoy.

Wattie looked up at the windows. White net curtains just like the rest of the flats. 'What if he's in there?'

'He's not. Half of bloody Glasgow's looking for him. Last place he's gonnae be is at home.'

They headed up the path. Eyes of the gnomes upon them.

McCoy was right. Connolly wasn't there but Scobie's boys definitely had been. If the broken lock didn't give you a clue then the floor covered in upturned furniture, ripped clothes and smashed crockery would. They stepped between the debris, made their way down the hall and into the living room.

McCoy righted a slashed armchair and sat down while Wattie wandered around, picking things up at random.

'I'll check the bedroom,' he said.

McCoy nodded, let him go. He sniffed. Was a smell of bleach, looked like a couple of bottles had been emptied over the carpet, stamped through. Pale patches in the brown swirls. Connolly's scattered belongings seemed mostly to consist of war novels and porn mags. Floor was strewn with them. Nazis and naked women on fur rugs. A message had been left just in case Connolly was stupid enough ever to come back. Red spray paint across the living-room wall.

YOU ARE DED YOU CUNT

'Don't suppose being able to spell is a qualification for being one of Scobie's goons,' said McCoy.

'Probably not,' said Wattie, walking back into the room. He picked up a painting of Ben Nevis and put it back on its nail.

McCoy looked round the living room. 'Any point in us being here?'

'Nope,' said Wattie, stepping back to see if the picture was straight. 'Apart from shutting Murray up. Don't think there was ever much here in the first place. Not sure he even stayed here. No food in the fridge, no TV, no post. There's a few clothes in the drawers in the bedroom but that's about it. They've slashed up the mattress and his bedclothes. Doesn't look like they found anything either.'

He sat down on a wobbly coffee table, picked

up a copy of a book called *Assignment Gestapo*, started flicking through it.

'Could interview the neighbours, I suppose. See if they saw anything?' he said.

'Do you really want to talk to the bastard with the gnomes?' asked McCoy.

'Not if I can help it.'

McCoy stood up. 'Me neither. Right, we've seen his flat. Duty done. Let's go.'

He walked back towards the door and stood on something that made a sharp crack under his shoe. He lifted a torn copy of *Men Only* up and there was a splintered cassette box under it, yellow BASF cassette in it. He picked it up, looked around. 'See anything to play this on?'

'Hang on,' said Wattie. He pulled the sofa right side up. 'Bingo'. A wee cassette player was lying there, cover smashed. 'Let's see if it works.'

It did.

They watched as the spindles turned and a voice came out the speaker. As if watching it was going to help them understand.

'August thirteenth, sixteen stone fourteen pounds. August fourteenth, sixteen stone fourteen pounds. August fifteenth, sixteen stone fourteen pounds. August sixteenth, sixteen stone thirteen pounds. August seventeenth, sixteen stone fourteen pounds. August eighteenth, sixteen stone fourteen pou—'

McCoy leant over and pressed the fast forward button, held it down for a minute or so, let it go.

'September twelfth, sixteen stone fourteen pounds. September thirteenth, sixteen stone fourteen pounds. September fourteenth, sixteen stone fifteen pounds . . .'

Didn't take long to go through the whole tape. The same thing over and over again, two sides of a C30 cassette. Ended on January 11th.

McCoy leant forward and switched it off.

'What the fuck is that about?' asked Wattie.

'Fuck knows,' said McCoy, reaching for his cigarettes. 'Maybe he's in Weight Watchers.'

He looked around for something to use as an ashtray. Suddenly wondered why he was bothering; the place was trashed anyway, wee bit of ash wasn't going to make any difference. Tapped his ash onto the carpet. 'All this is just ticking boxes. What we really need to do is just find the bugger before he decides someone else is in the way of his great love affair.'

'And how are we going to do that?' asked Wattie.

'Not by interviewing the bloody flatmate, I'll tell you that, but if we don't we'll never hear the end of it. You ready to enter Paradise?'

Wattie didn't look happy. 'Do I have to?'

McCoy ground his cigarette into the carpet, pocketed the cassette.

'Yep. Do you good to see how the other half lives.'

CHAPTER 6

'What's the flatmate's story then?' asked Wattie as they drove up and over Todd Street from Shettleston.

McCoy dug in his pocket, got the note from Murray out. 'Peter Charles Simpson.'

'Never heard of him,' said Wattie.

'Me neither,' said McCoy. 'In the squad apparently.'

'Must be shite then.'

They parked beside the school in London Road and walked up towards the red-brick stadium.

'If my dad could see me now,' muttered Wattie glumly as he walked through the double doors of the offices at the front of the stadium.

'He'd turn in his grave,' said McCoy.

'Naw,' said Wattie. 'He's still alive, he'd give me a punch in the chops.' A woman behind the reception desk told them Peter would be down in the changing rooms, pointed them to a stairway.

The changing rooms were deserted, their feet loud on the tiled floor as they walked in. A young man was sitting on a bench by an open locker folding up a tracksuit. He looked up.

'Mr Simpson?' asked McCoy. 'Said you'd be down here.'

He nodded, stood up. They introduced themselves, he shook their hands. Simpson was tall, blond, zipped-up tracksuit, sandshoes. 'Peter,' he said. 'Just call me Peter. Mr Simpson's my da's name.'

McCoy took out his wee red jotter. 'Fair enough. Maybe we can just start with yesterday. Could you tell us what happened after the game?'

He nodded to a bench and they all sat down. 'We finished up here about the back of five. Charlie was on the bench and I was just here watching so didn't take long to get ready. Didn't have to have showers or a debrief, anything like that.

'We got home about half five or so. Watched the end of *World of Sport*. Charlie made some toasted cheese. We ate it, he ironed a shirt, said he had to get ready.'

'Ready for what?' asked McCoy.

'He didn't say exactly. I just thought he must be meeting Elaine. Usually did on a Saturday night. He got changed, a taxi peeped his horn outside, he shouted cheerio from the hall and that was it.'

'And that was it?'

Simpson nodded, still looked a bit shell-shocked. 'That was it until I heard it on the news this morning. Still cannae believe it.'

He shook his head, eyes started to tear up. He rubbed at them.

'So what's she like then, this Elaine?' asked Wattie.

'Wears the pants, but I think he quite liked that. Told him where to be and when. Even bought his clothes for him. Got him all the trendy gear. Didn't see so much of him once they started going out.'

Simpson stood up, opened the locker door. There wasn't much inside: a couple of pairs of football boots, a tin of Brut talc, balled-up socks. The remnants of someone's life.

'Just packing his stuff up for his maw,' he said.

Somehow it was always that kind of stuff that stuck in McCoy's mind. The blood spatter on the 'Souvenir of Blackpool' plate hanging on the kitchen wall. The scrapes round the lock on the inside of the cellar door. The discarded socks at the bottom of the locker. Was the kind of stuff he thought about when he woke up in the middle of the night and couldn't get back to sleep. The damage done.

'McCoy?'

He turned and Wattie was looking at him.

'Sorry, he ever mention a man called Connolly?' asked McCoy.

Simpson sniffed, tried to settle himself. He shook his head. 'Don't think so. Who's he?'

'He works for Elaine's dad,' said McCoy.

'The famous Jake Scobie,' said Simpson. 'Thought the sun shone out of Charlie's arse, he did. Wanted to be his big pal.'

'And what did Charlie think about that?' asked McCoy.

Simpson hesitated. 'He didn't really like him.

61

But he was a bit scared of him, didn't want to offend him.'

'Why didn't he like him?' asked McCoy.

'Jake used to take him out for a drink. Supposed to be just Jake and him, but when they got to the pub all Jake's mates would mysteriously turn up. Jake would kind of parade him about – look at me with my Celtic player son-in-law, that sort of thing. Charlie is a shy guy really, he didn't like it.'

'How did a shy guy end up going out with someone like Elaine?' asked Wattie.

'Easy. He was in the first team. Good-looking. Going places. Women were always coming on to him. Elaine set her cap at him and that was that. It happens.'

'Happen to you?' asked Wattie, grinning.

Simpson smiled. 'Not yet. Hopefully one day.'

McCoy and Wattie stood up to go. 'Anything else occurs to you, let us know, eh?'

They were halfway across the changing room when Simpson spoke.

'There was one thing,' he said. 'He was a bit drunk couple of weeks ago. We'd been to some club dinner thing, were coming back in the taxi. He said he thought maybe Elaine was seeing someone else.'

'Did he say who?' asked McCoy.

Simpson shook his head. 'He didn't know who it was, just had the feeling she was getting a bit tired of him. As if she was busy with someone else. Someone new.'

He's ordered a tea and a scone. Smiled at the waitress, made some small talk about the bad weather.
He can do these things. Shift. Shift what he is, what
people think he is. He fingers the pictures in his
pocket. Remembered the first time he'd heard about
a Polaroid camera. Couldn't believe it. Meant that
finally he could take the kind of pictures he wanted.

He looks round. Treron's tearoom. Third floor of
the department store on Sauchiehall Street. Him
and a sea of ladies in hats and gloves. He looks
like a dutiful son awaiting his elderly mother, like
a loving husband meeting his wife after a day of
shopping.

Sometimes he can see it, he thinks, in the half-light,
in the gloom of a darkened bedroom, the beam of a
torchlight shining in someone's terrified eyes. What
he is. The dried and flaking blood on his hands and
clothes. The skull shining through the skin. But when
he blinks it goes. What he is.

He can see himself sitting here with her. Her
showing him something she's bought downstairs, him
smiling and saying it looks nice. He forces his finger
down onto the hard plastic corner of the Polaroid in

his pocket, pushes harder until he feels it burst through the skin. Blood on blood.

He stood up, needed to get to Jessops before it closed. Wanted to buy three more packets of film. After all, he was going to need it . . .

CHAPTER 7

Mc Coy trudged up the steps to Susan's flat. Could feel his socks squelching inside his shoes. Wondered why everyone he knew lived on the bloody top floor. The wee boy who lived downstairs was sitting on a step wrapped up in an Arran jumper and a balaclava, surrounded by Matchbox cars, McCoy stepped over him, patted his head.

'You all right, Bobby?' he asked.

Bobby nodded. Wasn't one to talk much.

He reached the top landing, pressed the bell. Even though he was spending most nights there now, they were still at the stage where he didn't have a key. Heard footsteps then the door was pulled back quickly and Susan stepped out the flat, closing the door behind her. Didn't look happy.

'What's up?' he asked.

She'd a pair of faded jeans on, T-shirt with a picture of Che Guevara on it, long cardigan, hair tied up in a scarf. Even when she wasn't trying she still looked great. She pushed some strands of hair behind her ear.

'Who exactly is Stevie bloody Cooper?' she said.

He wasn't expecting that. 'What?'

'Him, whoever he is, and some giant thug have been in the bloody flat for half an hour. Sarah was round for a cup of tea, was so awkward she left. The two of them rang the doorbell looking for you. When I said you weren't here they said they'd wait. Bloody barged in before I could stop them! Who the fuck is he, Harry?'

'Stevie? He's the guy that was with me in the house. With Teddy Dunlop. I told you!'

She looked amazed. 'Him? That's the guy who got cut with the sword?'

McCoy nodded. 'Stevie. He's a friend of mine—'

'A friend? Are you joking? He looks like he's going to stab someone any minute. I was scared, Harry! I didn't know who he was—'

'Stevie's fine. You don't need to worry about him.' McCoy tried to calm her down, gave her a hug. Could feel she was shaking. Not good. 'I'll take care of it. Okay? He's a pal. Wouldn't hurt a fly.' He let her go, looked into her eyes. 'Okay?'

Susan couldn't have looked less happy if she tried. 'Just get him out of here. Please?'

Harry nodded.

'And you're remembering what tonight is? Need to get ready.'

McCoy nodded. Hadn't. Did now.

'Course I do. I'll sort it.'

McCoy walked into the living room of the flat, Susan following behind. Stevie Cooper was sitting in the armchair by the bay window, mug of tea in his hand, flicking through a copy of *Spare Rib,* of all things. Cooper wasn't even the most surprising sight. That was Jumbo. All six foot three of him sitting on the settee munching his way through a plate of biscuits.

Cooper sat back in his chair, put the magazine down. 'No at your flat, no at the station, not even at the fucking pub.' He put his mug down next to the coaster on the coffee table. 'If I didn't know better I'd say you've been avoiding me, Harry.'

McCoy shook his head. 'Come on, Stevie, I wouldn't do that.'

'I should fucking hope not,' Cooper said. 'Not after what I've been through. But you know what, Harry? You're making me wonder. Two fucking visits. Three weeks I was in that hospital, on my back, forty-two stitches, all because of you, and two fucking times you came to see me. Two times. Not good.' He shook his head. 'Not good at all, eh, Jumbo?'

Jumbo shook his big stupid head, replied through a mouthful of shortbread crumbs. 'Not good, Mr Cooper.'

'C'mon, Cooper,' said McCoy. 'I wasn't avoiding you. I had things on, had to go and see the psychologist, all sorts of shite.'

Cooper sat back and lit up a cigarette. He was dressed as he always was: blue jeans, short-sleeved shirt, red Harrington jacket. His blond hair was neatly parted and swept over in a Jimmy Dean quiff, smell of Bay Rum coming off him. Jumbo didn't quite match his boss's sartorial elegance. A brick shithouse squashed into old jeans, plimsolls and a red woolly jumper.

Cooper looked McCoy up and down, at the worn suit and the soaking shoes and the tweed coat with a cigarette burn in the arm. 'So how's your wee world been getting on, Harry?'

'Good. Back at work. I think that—'

'That right? Well, I think too. And what I think is you and I need to have a wee chat.'

'All right,' said McCoy. 'How's about tomorrow? I can—'

Cooper looked at him, smiled and shook his head. 'Not tomorrow,' he said, standing up. 'Now.'

'Hotspur Street' was all Cooper said when McCoy asked him where they were going. No more information forthcoming so McCoy gave up trying.

The three of them walked up Byres Road. It was busy, as a road full of pubs would be. Crossed Great Western Road and kept going up Queen Margaret Drive. McCoy tried to see if Cooper was walking funny, if the sword damage had affected his legs, but he seemed fine, usual rolling stride like a sailor on deck. They crossed the bridge over the Kelvin and Jumbo stopped to throw a penny into the running water below.

'If you cross a river you should throw a penny into it,' he said. 'Protects you from bad luck.'

'That right?' said McCoy.

Besides granting luck to the penny throwers, the river also acted as the great divide in this part of Glasgow. The area they'd come from, the leafy West End, was full of students, smartly dressed women, academic-looking blokes. Lecturers at the university, workers at the BBC Studios.

Once they'd crossed the river it was a different story. Now they were in Woodside, Maryhill. Dark streets full of flats where the people who worked in the wee factories and workshops around the canal lived. More Cooper's scene.

Hotspur Street was up on the left, a road of tenements overlooking a swing park. Cooper stopped outside the second close. 'Up here,' he said.

They climbed the stairs to the top floor and Cooper knocked the door. A few steps then the door was pulled back, revealing the last person McCoy had expected or wanted to see. Iris. She looked equally pleased to see him.

'Fuck sake!' she said. 'I hoped you'd fallen off that bloody roof too.'

'Nae such luck. Thought you were running a sauna now,' said McCoy as they walked in.

'I was. Then Mr Cooper came to his senses, realised what an asset I was.'

'Got sick of your moaning more like,' grunted Cooper. 'This way.'

He pushed the door open and they went through into the main room. It was dark and hot, smelt of stale beer and stale sex. There was a bloke asleep on the couch, snoring away. He'd no shoes or shirt on, just braces hanging down by his sides.

A young girl, eighteen or so, falling out her lacy dressing gown, was carefully pouring a bottle of Tennent's into two mugs. Mission accomplished, she handed one to the other occupant of the room. He was a big fella, no shirt either, just fleshy shoulders and a beer belly covered in black hair and a pair of long boxer shorts. He took the mug from the girl and drew her close. They swayed back and forward, moving to the music coming from the record player in the corner. 'Three Coins In The Fountain'.

Neither of the dancers took much notice as they made their way through to the kitchen beyond, just kept swaying to the music.

'Thought you were closing down the shebeens,' said McCoy. 'Not opening up another one.'

'Comes in handy,' said Cooper. 'I sleep in the back bedroom sometimes, get Iris to make me breakfast. She likes doing it. That right, Iris?'

Iris plonked a couple of bottles of beer down on the table. 'Do I fuck. C'mon, Jumbo, you can help me get rid of that fat lump on the couch.' They left, and McCoy looked round. Kitchen was big, pulley on the ceiling full of drying bedclothes, crates of drink and towels everywhere, just like every other shebeen he'd ever been in. A bright blue budgie in a cage on a stand in the corner. Whistled at him when he tapped the wire bars.

'Didn't know you were such a soft touch when it comes to Iris,' said McCoy, sitting down.

Cooper shrugged, opened the bottles and handed one over. 'Needed somewhere to go when I came out the hospital, Memel Street's a fucking zoo these days. Iris had been moaning away so I set her back up. Suits us both. Besides, she was shite in the sauna, put the punters right off.'

Cooper took a gold lighter from his trouser pocket, lit up, handed the packet over. McCoy took one. Jumbo reappeared, sat down in the corner, started cooing at the budgie. Last time McCoy'd seen him he'd just managed to stop Cooper killing the poor bastard. Now they seemed glued at the hip. Wasn't like Cooper to need muscle, he could take care of himself, no trouble. Injury that had put him in hospital must have taken its toll after all.

Cooper took a long slug of the beer. 'Tasty wee bird that. How long's that been going on?'

'Few weeks,' said McCoy.

'And you're shacked up there already? Must be love.'

McCoy shrugged. Wasn't sure how happy he was about Cooper knowing who Susan was or where she lived. 'How's the back?' he asked.

'Fine,' said Cooper too quickly.

McCoy knew Cooper too well to think he would tell him the truth. Men like Cooper prided themselves in dealing with anything, be it a pub landlord not paying his dues or a life-threatening wound in your back. He was up and about but the amount of stitches he'd had and the presence of Jumbo told the real story. He was sitting funny too, straight; looked like he might have a brace on under his shirt.

'Jumbo?' said Cooper.

Jumbo was up and standing by him in a second. 'Mr Cooper?'

Cooper held out a quid. 'Away and get me some fags.'

Jumbo looked down at the open packet on the table, fifteen or so left in it. Was about to say something then didn't. Took the money and headed for the door. McCoy watched him go, waited until he'd left before he spoke again.

'You sure you're okay, Stevie?' asked McCoy.

A flash of anger. 'How many fucking times do I have to tell you? I'm fine. Stitches are out. All fixed, raring to go.'

He leant forward, put on a posh woman's voice. 'And how about you, Mr McCoy? Has this event affected you psychologically?'

McCoy shook his head. 'Shows how much you know. Psychologist was a man. And from Shettleston of all places, had more of a Glasgow accent than I do.'

Cooper laughed, leant behind him to get another couple of beers from the crate. 'You doing that Celtic lad by the way?' he asked.

McCoy nodded. 'You hear anything?'

'What's to hear? Scobie lost control of that nutter Connolly a long time ago. The guy's a fucking psycho. He cannae find him now either, got all his boys running about town like blue-arsed flies.'

'How come Connolly's gone off the rails all of a sudden?' asked McCoy. He wanted to know what Cooper knew; easiest way was to act daft.

Cooper looked dismissive. 'Everyone knows that. Elaine Scobie. Cannae leave the lassie alone. Cunt's obsessed.'

'You know her?' McCoy asked.

Cooper shook his head. 'No really. Used to see her around couple of years ago, out and about in the town. Used to like the nights out. Liked the bad boys too.'

McCoy looked puzzled. 'Charlie Jackson wasn't a bad boy.'

'Nope, pure as the driven snow him, fucking good player as well. Every father-in-law's dream.' Cooper shifted himself in his seat, winced. 'That Elaine wised up right enough.'

'What? She had enough of the single life?'

Cooper snorted. 'Aye right. All she's doing is making sure Daddy leaves her the money. Settled down with a Celtic player, started staying in nights watching the telly. What more could Scobie want? Got cancer, I hear. Year at the most. Gonnae be a fucking war in the Northside when he goes. Place'll be up for grabs.'

'Thought Bertie Waller was all set to take over,' said McCoy.

'Aye well, that's what Bertie Waller thinks, but

73

Bertie Waller's just another stupid old cunt.' He shook his head, looked at him.

'What the fuck am I telling you this for? Doing your job for you. You fucking polis know bugger all about bugger all.'

'So this a social visit, is it?' asked McCoy. 'Concerned for my mental state, were you?'

Cooper shook his head. 'No, it's not, and am I fuck so don't come the cheeky cunt.' He sat back in his chair, winced again. 'You know something? There's fuck all to do when you're lying in your hospital bed for three weeks. Boring as fuck. Especially when your pals don't even come and visit you—'

'Stevie, I—'

'Can it. You're forgiven. I don't blame you. I wouldnae go near a hospital unless I had to.'

'You sure you're okay, though?' asked McCoy.

'Christ! How many times? Fit as a fiddle. Never better. Dirty big scar on my back but the lassies seem quite taken with it. Wounded bloody soldier.'

Cooper never was a very good liar; that's why he hardly ever did it. Hadn't got any better.

'So what's with Jumbo then? How come he's a fixture?'

Flash of anger across Cooper's face. 'Jumbo carries things. That's what. That okay with you?'

McCoy held up his hands. 'Just asking.'

'Asking too bloody much. You ask Murray to get rid of Naismith like I asked you?'

74

'I've been off work, Stevie. I haven't seen him. I can—'

'Don't worry. It's done. No thanks to you. The stupid cunt got himself caught with half of bloody Watches of Switzerland in his office. He'll get a couple of years at least.' He nodded over at the empty chair by the budgie. 'Hence Jumbo. Nothing like that is gonnae happen to me. From now on I'm holding nothing, carrying nothing.'

'Good idea,' said McCoy.

'Aye well, I'm full of them the day.' He reached into the pocket of his Harrington, took out a folded bit of newspaper and held it out to McCoy. 'As I said, not much to do in the hospital. So you end up reading the paper.'

McCoy took the paper, unfolded it. Was half a page of the *Herald*. Cooper must have been really bloody bored if he was reading the *Herald*. A picture taken at some function in the Central Hotel. Four middle-aged men. Three in dinner suits, one in a dress police uniform.

POLICE CHIEF RETIREMENT DINNER

McCoy didn't know what he was supposed to be looking at. Looked over at Cooper.

'The polis,' he said. 'Look at him properly.'

McCoy took another look. Just made it to the kitchen sink before he was sick.

CHAPTER 8

By the time he left Cooper and got back to the flat McCoy was running late, very late. He held up his hands in acknowledgement, said sorry as he came into the flat, already taking his jacket off. Susan looked like thunder. He got his orders. Had to be washed, shaved and into the new suit and tie in ten minutes.

He hurried into the bathroom, took his shirt off and ran the hot tap, got his shaving foam out the wee mirrored cupboard. He pressed the can, squirted the foam onto his hand and spread it round his chin.

Cooper had been quiet, persuasive. None of his usual bluster and threats. He said it was simple. What had been done was done. Nothing could change it. All that was left was revenge. And they were the ones to do it.

He pulled the razor down his face, scraping noise against the bristle, waved the razor in the water in the sink.

He had listened to Cooper, agreed with what he was saying, and then he had said no. He was as surprised as Cooper was. For the first time in his life he had said no to Stevie Cooper. He couldn't do it. The past was the past. Gone. And he wasn't going back there, not for anyone. No matter what had happened. No matter how angry Cooper got. No matter how many threats he made.

He rubbed the remains of the shaving foam off his face with a towel. Looked at himself. A thirty-year-old man, a detective, shaving himself at his girlfriend's flat. Whatever had happened, he had moved on. He had managed to leave it behind and that's where he needed it to stay.

He dragged a comb through his wet hair, brushed his teeth.

Funny thing was he felt calm, not what he had expected at all. Decision had been made. Case closed.

He walked through to the kitchen and presented himself for inspection. Only one nick on his neck, suited and booted and ready to go. Susan had a dress on, wee flowers all over it, deep neckline, had her hair up, looked a million dollars. She looked McCoy up and down, moved in and straightened his tie. Kissed him.

'I've seen worse,' she said.

The Malmaison restaurant was hushed, a comfort zone of linen and waiters, silver service and good wine. Room was softly lit with candles on the tables, chandeliers above. Susan took McCoy's hand and led him towards a table under the minstrels' gallery. Other diners a mixture of well-dressed couples and groups of rich-looking businessmen. McCoy put a smile on his face as he passed them all, tried to look like he belonged here, like he belonged with Susan.

They sat down. Waiter arrived with menus and a wine list which he opened with a flourish and gave to McCoy. He promptly handed it to Susan. No use pretending, he knew as much about wine as she did about being a polis. They were here for an early Valentine's dinner. Susan was working Wednesday night so she'd arranged this.

'Who is that guy anyway?' asked Susan, reading the menu.

No need to ask who she was talking about.

'Told you. He was there in the house when Dunlop—'

'I know that, but why was he there? What's he to you?'

The waiter appeared and they ordered. Steak for him, venison for her. Bottle of Malbec, whatever that was. Waited until he'd left until he replied.

'Stevie? He's an old pal. He's a good guy underneath it all.'

She looked at him. 'Didn't look like it. Looked like a right nasty piece of work. And who was Lurch?'

'Jumbo. His pal.'

'What happened to his finger?' asked Susan, holding up her left hand.

'Eh?' asked McCoy.

'Jumbo. He only had half of one finger.'

'That right?' said McCoy. 'I never noticed.'

78

The wine arrived. Susan tasted it and deemed it fine. Waiter poured them two glasses and McCoy made a start on it and the wee basket of bread rolls.

'So how does he make his money, this Stevie?' asked Susan, watching McCoy shoving most of a roll in his mouth.

McCoy tried to chew it down, replied. 'Does a bit of this and that. Why? Why are you so interested in Stevie Cooper all of a sudden? Thought we were supposed to be whispering sweet nothings into each other's ears, not talking about my pal.'

Susan wasn't going to be derailed easily. 'Does he deal with prostitutes, run them?'

'What?' he asked, looking over at her. He wasn't the only one; a middle-aged lady in pearls had heard her too. Looked somewhat surprised at the subject of the conversation.

'Does he?'

'Well, I suppose so—'

'Good!' Susan looked delighted. 'Exactly the kind of person I need to talk to for my thesis.' she said. 'You could arrange it.'

The thought of Susan and Stevie Cooper having a cosy chit-chat about the economics of sexual exploitation was more than he could cope with.

'Don't know if Cooper'd want to talk to you about something like that, to be honest,' he said. 'He's not exactly what you'd call chatty.'

'You can ask him, though?' she asked.

McCoy nodded. He'd worry about that later.

There was something much more important on his mind right now. His steak had just arrived.

He hadn't been looking forward to the evening much – posh restaurants weren't his natural habitat – but he enjoyed himself. Ate his steak, drank more than his fair share of red wine and played footsie with Susan under the table. They left about eleven, both pleasantly woozy, got back to the flat and McCoy opened the cigar box, sat on the end of the bed and started to roll a joint.

'I could get used to places like that,' he said, pushing his shoes off.

'That right?' said Susan.

'Yep. Need to win the pools, mind you, but that could happen,' he said. 'I'm a lucky man.'

'You've won the pools already, you've got me,' she said, getting under the covers.

He was down to his skivvies now. He handed her the joint and she lit it up.

'Christ, is there any tobacco in this?' asked Susan as she blew out a cloud of strong-smelling smoke.

'Not much.' He grinned, trying to find an ashtray amongst the wee plants and ornaments on Susan's dressing table.

'Are you getting in or are you just going to parade around the bedroom in your pants?'

He turned round, waggled his bum at her. 'I might just do that,' said McCoy. 'Why? Is it turning you on?'

Susan looked at him. 'Exactly how much brandy did you have?'

'Same as you, three.'

Susan shook her head. 'I had one.'

'Ah,' said McCoy, stepping out his skivvies and getting into bed. 'That might explain it.' He snuggled in beside her. 'Put that joint down.'

'Or what?'

'Or I'll bloody burn myself when I jump on you. Give.'

Susan smiled, handed the joint over and McCoy stubbed it out in the ashtray, put it on the bedside table.

'Now, c'mere.'

They rolled together, embraced. He moved down her body, kissing her, grinned up at her as he gently pushed her thighs apart. Did what she liked as she held onto him, fingers tightening as she got nearer. She was halfway there already when he moved up and in between her legs. They moved together, breathing getting heavier, faster. She had her hands round his waist, whispering in his ear, pulling him closer. 'Come on, McCoy, come on . . .'

She fell asleep quickly afterwards, like she always did. He lay there smoking a last cigarette, ashtray sitting on his chest, and did what he always did – let the events of the day run through his mind. Wondered how rich you'd have to be to eat at Malmaison every night. Wondered if Susan would forget about having a chat with Stevie Cooper. Wondered why Elaine Scobie was so sure Connolly wouldn't hurt her.

He was kidding himself, though; there was only one thing he was really thinking of, only one thing he couldn't get out his mind. The folded newspaper cutting Stevie Cooper had shown him. The policeman smiling out in his dress uniform.

He shut his eyes.

Tried to let the wine and the brandy and the Red Leb do their work.

Tried to sleep.

Didn't.

12TH FEBRUARY 1973

CHAPTER 9

McCoy put his mug of tea on the pile of *Phone Mary at the* Record notes on his desk and sat down, yawned. He'd finally got to sleep about the back of three. Felt like an unmade bed. There was a dun-coloured folder sitting in the middle of the desk. McCoy recognised the neat fountain pen capitals. Gilroy the medical examiner had attached a note to the corner: *Wasn't quite sure who to give this to then remembered your sympathy for those fallen on hard times.*

McCoy shook his head. Care about one jakie and that's you, tarred for life. He opened the autopsy report, started reading. So now he knew what the *TRAGEDY IN CHURCH* on the paper seller's board was. One Paul Joseph Brady had hung himself in the Hopehill Road Chapel, St Columba's. As far as McCoy could remember, killing yourself was a mortal sin. Doing it in a chapel just seemed to be taking the piss.

He skimmed through the rest of it. Age approx 30–35. Death by broken neck caused by body weight. Body was undernourished, showed evidence of long-term alcohol abuse. Cirrhotic liver damage, scarring on lungs caused by smoking. Previous evidence of broken arm in childhood. Nothing unexpected, except that by looking at his picture McCoy would have said the man looked nearer fifty. Life on the street takes its toll, right enough.

He closed it over. Hanging yourself wasn't a crime. Wasn't quite sure what he was supposed to do with the report. Shove it in his drawer in case anyone ever came looking for it, he supposed. He checked it again, no mention of any next of kin.

He got out his fags, lit one up, inhaled, coughed, inhaled again. Why would you kill yourself in a chapel? For someone like Brady the way out was standard. Fill yourself with paracetamol and cheap vodka and jump off a bridge over the Clyde. He looked at the picture again. Paul Joseph Brady. Had to be a Catholic. Maybe he just wanted to be nearer his God to thee when he checked out.

McCoy sat back in his chair, looked round the office. Usual noise of chatter, people on the phone, a uniform waiting to see somebody, hat on his lap. Thomson wandering round with the *Racing Post* collecting lines to go to the bookies. Robertson collecting mugs off everyone's desk, his day to make the teas. Wattie was the exception, working hard, receiver jammed into his neck, list of hotels and B&Bs in front of him. Looking for Connolly.

Wasn't quite sure why, but one of the questions the psychologist had asked him kept going round and round in his mind. *Do you still feel you want to be a detective?*

Did he? Truth was he'd never really thought about it, not for years anyway. Joined up straight after he'd left school and just kept his head down and kept working. What else would he be if he wasn't a polis? That's what he was, as much part of him now as the colour of his hair or the scar on his eyebrow he'd got from Jamie Gibbs.

He yawned again, took a sip of his tea, gave himself a shake. He opened the red jotter. Wrote

Charlie Jackson

Connolly

'That it?'

He looked up and Murray was standing over him.

'We can call off the troops now, McCoy's on the case.'

'Very funny,' said McCoy.

'Get Watson. We've had a tip-off,' said Murray. 'Sounds kosher.'

The St Enoch's Hotel was right in the centre of town, a huge Victorian building above St Enoch Station. Up until a few years ago, the station had been the main route south but it was closed now, all the lines moved to Central. They'd cemented over the long platforms and tracks and turned them into a huge car park. The glass-and-iron roof of the station was still there, full of broken panes and nesting pigeons. No more steam trains and *Flying Scotsman* to shelter, just the parked cars of Glasgow's shoppers.

The hotel itself was still open. Just. What had once been an ornate red sandstone frontage was now black with soot and neglect, chicken wire wrapped round the more fragile carvings in case they fell off and hit someone. A couple of the upper floors were permanently closed, curtains in all the rooms shut, windows stained with pigeon droppings and grime. The whole building looked like it was hanging on for dear life. Incessant rain wasn't helping the picture look any prettier. Low grey clouds looked like they were only yards above the building's spires and towers.

McCoy and Wattie drove the unmarked Cortina up the ramp past the pen sign and parked outside the front entrance. McCoy got out, yawned and stretched, still knackered, and walked over to where Murray was standing under the awning. He was looking up at the hotel, empty pipe clamped in his teeth. Took it out, used it to point at the windows on the top floors.

'Spent the first night of my honeymoon in there. Look at it now, fucking shithole.'

'Where'd you spend the rest?' asked McCoy, lighting up.

'Eh? Oh, Whitley Bay.'

'That any better?' asked McCoy.

'Not much,' said Murray, looking round. 'Where's Watson?'

'Here, sir,' said Wattie, locking the car. He wandered over, joined them, looked up. 'What a dump. Cannae believe it's still actually open.'

'Used to be something in its day. I can remember it,' said McCoy.

'Certainly was,' said Murray. 'Honeymoon suite cost me a bloody fortune.'

'Connolly's flat was a waste of time,' said McCoy. 'Nothing there. But the flatmate told us Charlie Jackson thought Elaine was seeing someone else.'

'Did he now,' said Murray. 'Connolly, you think?'

McCoy shrugged. 'He didn't know. Could be.' He looked up at the hotel. 'So what's the story here?'

'We got a tip from a bloke that works at the front desk,' said Murray. 'One of Billy's touts. Says he's sure Connolly's here. Not using his own name, calling himself Mr McLean, but he fits the description. Been here for a couple of days, he says.'

McCoy was still looking up at the building; clouds of sparrows were whirling round the roof, looking for somewhere to land.

'He in there just now, is he?' he asked, turning to Murray.

He nodded. 'Bloke thinks so. He tends to come and go via different doors, must be about twenty of them in this dump. They should have knocked it down when they closed the bloody station.'

'Scobie and his cronies can't have been looking that bloody hard,' said Wattie. 'Great big hotel right in the city centre. He's no exactly keeping a low profile, is he?'

'Would you stay in here?' asked McCoy.

'Nobody would,' said Murray. 'Probably why he's here.'

A single-decker coach drew up at the entrance, Caledonian Tours and a big Lion Rampant painted on the side of it. The driver honked the horn and they moved to the side to let it park.

Murray pointed one way then the next. 'There's pairs of uniforms at every exit door and these two clowns' – he nodded at a pair of big constables – 'are covering the front. We go up and chap Connolly's door, see if he's home.'

McCoy waited for the rest of the plan. Didn't come. 'Is that it?'

'Is that what?' said Murray.

'That's the plan? The bloke's a bloody nutter! And we're going to chap his door and see if he wants to come for a wee hurl in a polis car?'

Murray looked unimpressed. 'He's a villain like every other, no bloody Superman. Get a grip on yourself, McCoy. Now, c'mon.'

The hotel lobby was vast, an ugly and worn-out combination of pea-green carpet and beige walls. A group of pensioners with wee suitcases were milling around, making their way out towards the coach and the next stop on their tour of Scotland's most miserable hotels. The restaurant was through glass doors, white cloth-covered tables stretched for miles, waiting for diners who were never going to appear.

The bar was next door. Tartan carpet and a few Highland landscapes on the walls. Barman wearing tartan waistcoat and an expression that would turn milk. Looked like the kind of place you would go to have a last drink before topping yourself. A fat man with a gold piped uniform sitting at the reception desk looked up and gave them a nod.

'It's the second floor,' said Murray. 'Two one four.'

They started up the big marble stairway. Wattie looked as nervous as McCoy felt.

'You sure that's it, sir? We just chap the door?' McCoy asked.

'What else do you suggest?' said Murray. 'Machine-gunning the cunt through it?'

'Fair enough.' He decided to shut up. Couldn't help but remember what Charlie Jackson had looked like, eye and the back of his head gone, blood seeping into the puddles around him.

On the second-floor landing, two corridors of yellowing doors stretched off either way. Half the bulbs were missing in the overhead globes, stained carpets, occasional tray of congealing food outside a door. Looked more like a marginally more upmarket Barlinnie than anything else.

'Wattie, you wait here by the stairs. If he gets past us you stop him,' said Murray.

Wattie looked more surprised than scared. 'Me?'

'Aye, you,' said Murray. 'You're a big bugger. Flatten him.'

Wattie nodded at them, tried to look alert and ready for any eventuality. Some hope.

Room 214 was halfway down the corridor. It was only when they stopped outside the door that McCoy realised he'd been walking on his tiptoes.

He looked at Murray, who looked at him and pointed at the door. He sighed, knocked it hard. Here we go.

'Mr Connolly! Police! Need you to open the door.'

Nothing.

He looked back at Murray, who nodded at the door impatiently. He knocked it again.

'Mr Connolly. Glasgow Police. Need you to open up now!'

Nothing again.

'Maybe he's gone out one of the other doors. Uniforms might have got him already?' said McCoy hopefully.

'Pan it in,' said Murray.

'What? You sure that's a good idea?'

'You heard,' said Murray. 'Knock the door in.'

McCoy looked around, walked back up the corridor and pulled a large red fire extinguisher off the wall. Weighed a ton. He stood at the door with it. 'You sure?'

Murray nodded so he stepped back, took it in both hands and launched it at the lock. The door cracked and splintered but held. He swore under his breath and swung it again. This time the door gave way, swung into the room, leaving a handle surrounded by splintered wood still attached to the lock.

'Mr Connolly? You there?' he shouted.

The room was gloomy, just a sliver of weak morning light seeping in through the net curtains.

McCoy stepped in, immediately recoiled at the smell. Was like rotten food and something like blocked drains. He turned round to look for the light switch and that's when the chair hit him.

It just missed his head and caught him on the shoulder but he went down all the same. Had a brief glimpse of Connolly's bald head above him before he brought it down again. One of the chair legs went right into his chest, hurt like fuck. He cried out, tried to roll away. Looked up just as Connolly jumped over him and rammed the chair legs into Murray's chest, pushing him back, pinning him against the corridor wall. One of the legs digging into his chest, the other digging into his windpipe. Connolly rammed the chair forward and Murray let out a horrible gurgling as the leg burst through the skin and dug further into his neck.

McCoy got himself up onto his knees but that was as far as he got before Connolly turned and whacked him across the side of the head. He didn't know what it was he'd hit him with but it was hard and heavy, got him right on the temple, knocking him back against the bedroom wall and that was that.

He could only have been out for a minute or so. He came to, head spinning, seeing tiny flashes of light. He looked up. Connolly was gone and Wattie was crouched down over Murray.

'He okay?' McCoy managed to get out.

Murray struggled up, pushed Wattie off to the side. 'Of course I'm bloody okay! Get after him!' he bellowed at Wattie. 'Move!'

Wattie scrabbled up and started running down the corridor towards the stairs.

McCoy sat up and rubbed at his head, could feel a lump there already. Looked down, two squares of blood were coming through his shirt. 'What the fuck happened?'

Murray was pressing buttons on his radio, shouting into it. All he was getting was static; he chucked it at the wall, shouted, 'Fucking thing!' Then rounded on McCoy.

'I'll tell you what bloody happened. He got past me and you, brushed Wattie aside like a bloody fly and he was off like the clappers.'

'Uniforms'll get him then,' said McCoy, holding out his shirt and looking down into it. Blood was running down his chest.

'Some bloody chance of that. Fucking useless, the lot of them!'

An unlucky uniform appeared at the top of the stairs and got both barrels. Murray shouting orders at him about covering exits, watching the car park. Seemed like a waste of time to McCoy but it was probably making Murray feel better.

He crawled towards the bed and pulled himself up on it. Eased his jacket and shirt off, looked at himself in the dresser mirror and winced. The square dent from the chair leg on his chest was bleeding badly, raised red welt. Had a horrible feeling he'd a couple of broken ribs.

He leant in for a closer look and that was when he noticed them. Behind him, reflected in the mirror. Twenty or so old milk bottles lined up against the wall, each of them full of different levels of dark yellow piss. He looked away and groaned, the smell thick in the back of his throat.

He pushed the bathroom door open, looking for a drink from the tap, and suddenly the smell got even worse. He pulled a worn towel off the rail over his mouth and tried to breathe through that. Couldn't believe what he was looking at. The bath was full of paper bags stuffed full of shit, flies buzzing and crawling over them. Each of them complete with a weight written on them in ball-point pen: 4oz, 5oz. Realised they were grouped together by similar weight. He groaned, spat the taste out his mouth into the sink, wiped his mouth with a wad of toilet paper. There was an open paperback on top of the cistern.

Sven Hassel. *Assignment Gestapo.*

Big burning tank on the front. Shaving kit was on the shelf, navy blue wash bag with a drawstring. He pulled it open. A bottle of Brut aftershave, facecloth, nailbrush and a bottle of pills. He took the bottle out, gagging again at the stink. No chemist label on it. Two different kinds of pills, black bombers and Mandies by the look of it. He slipped the bottle into his trouser pocket, put the wash bag back.

Back in the bedroom he pulled the curtains wide and opened the window as far as it would go, tried to avoid the stink of the piss, breathe in the fresh air. Realised the bottles were marked too; amount in each one written in chinagraph pencil on the side.

He opened the dresser drawers. Nothing much, a couple of shirts. Nothing much in the wardrobe either. Just some dirty Y-fronts and a pair of trousers on a hanger. Connolly certainly did travel light. He started feeling a bit dizzy again so he sat back down on the bed, started breathing deeply. It hurt each time he breathed in, ribs must be fucked right enough.

Realised there was a picture pinned to the wall right in front of him. It was the picture that he'd seen in the paper. Charlie Jackson and his fiancée Elaine Scobie at the Provost's Ball. Charlie looking young in a dinner suit, Elaine in a long dress, hair pinned up with a flower in it. Charlie's head had gone in an angry scribble of blue ballpoint pen. Beneath it there was something written on the flowery wallpaper in pencil, hard to make out. McCoy leant to the side, let what light there was from the window hit the wall.

BYE BYE CHARLIE
Everything tastes the same.
My soul sometimes leaves my body.

He sat back, uttered a quiet 'fuck me' under his breath.

'You all right?' asked Murray, stepping into the room.

'I'll live,' he said. 'You?'

Murray nodded, rubbing at the welt on his neck with a bloodstained hanky. 'What's the bloody smell?'

McCoy gestured at the bottles. 'Don't go in the bathroom, it's even worse. The sick bastard's been keeping all his piss and shit and measuring it.'

'He's been what?' Murray was staring at the bottles in disbelief. 'Jesus Christ.'

McCoy pointed at the writing on the wall.

Murray read it, shook his head. 'Fuck's that supposed to mean?'

'No idea. Think Lomax was right after all. He has gone fucking nuts. Did we lose him?'

'Looks like it. Did you no see him when you came in?' asked Murray.

'You're joking, aren't you? Aye, I saw him. That's why I let him clobber me with a fucking chair. What about you?'

Murray sat down on the other bed and shook his head. 'Maybe I'm not as young as I used to be. Didn't know what was happening until you were down and he was stabbing me with those bloody chair legs.' He looked up. 'What you grinning at?'

McCoy shook his head. 'Two of us. Glasgow's finest. Brought to our knees by some loony armed with a bedroom chair. Maybe put in for a medal, eh?'

Murray shook his head. 'C'mon. After this shitshow I need a bloody drink.'

'Nowhere, sir. Uniforms didn't move from the exits, didn't see anything. Nobody came past them. We could search the building but it's almost four hundred rooms . . .'

'So where the fuck is he?' asked Murray.

Wattie shrugged. 'He's either hiding somewhere in the hotel or he managed to get out some other way.'

Murray put his glass back on the table. They were sitting in the empty lounge bar, tartan everywhere. Smell of damp in the walls. Miserable bartender polishing a glass and looking at them suspiciously. Only other patrons were two old ladies sipping sherry.

'He'll be gone. No way he's going to stick around here.' McCoy took a sip of his pint, waved his arm around. 'This hotel is fucking huge. Even if we'd covered the exits there's windows, service entrances, delivery chutes, loads of ways he could have got out.'

Murray knew he was right, just didn't want to admit it. 'So what do we do now?'

'Nothing we can do. He'll turn up. Don't think Connolly's ever been out of Glasgow in his puff. He'll no be going anywhere. Not while Elaine Scobie's here. We're looking for him, we've got our touts looking for him, even Scobie's cronies are supposedly looking for him. He'll turn up. Just need to go in mob-handed next time, make sure he doesn't get away.'

He held up the paperback he had found in Connolly's hotel room. 'He's underlined something in here.'

'Oh aye,' said Murray, looking sour. 'What?'

McCoy read it out. '"The colonel had died badly.

98

He had begged and pleaded and babbled hysterically, with tears down his cheeks, of the favours he could arrange for them if only they would spare his life. His last despairing words had been to offer them free use of his wife and daughters . . ."'

'That supposed to be about Jake Scobie?' asked Wattie.

'Might be,' said McCoy. 'Really need to get Elaine Scobie to come in. Picture of the hotel-room wall's proof if we even needed any. He's obviously obsessed; she's not safe.'

Murray nodded. 'I'll have another go at Lomax.'

McCoy finished his pint, stood up, winced.

'Where you off to?' asked Murray.

'Boots the chemist and Marks. Aspirin, some plaster for these bloody cuts and a new shirt. You?'

'Into the shop for a couple of hours then back home to change. Got dinner at the City Chambers. Some charity thing. All I do these days is go to bloody dinners.'

'Perils of being a big boss.' McCoy pointed at his neck. 'Make sure the dress uniform doesn't cover your war wound, give all the lady councillors a thrill. I'll catch up with you later, see where we are.'

'We need to be bloody somewhere,' said Murray gloomily. 'Between the press and the Super this Charlie Jackson thing needs to get sorted. Press went national today.' He looked up at them and for the first time McCoy noticed he was starting to look old. More grey in his beard than ginger. 'He'll no be happy we lost Connolly today.'

'We'll get him, sir. Not be long.'

McCoy headed for the door, hoped it was true.

He was crossing the shabby foyer, almost at the hotel's front doors, when they burst open in front of him. Jake Scobie and two of his boys were standing there trying to look like the bloody cavalry.

'You get him?' Scobie asked, looking round.

'Not this time,' said McCoy. 'Got away.'

'For fuck sake!' Jake's shout echoed round the empty foyer. Fat guy behind the desk looked up in fright.

Murray appeared beside him. 'Scobie? What are you doing here?' he asked angrily.

Jake's colour was up, fists bunched. 'You lost him, you stupid cunt, didn't you!'

Murray stepped forward; McCoy put his arm out to stop him going any further. Way Scobie was shouting the odds, he was definitely looking for a fight, and way Murray was feeling, Murray would be more than happy to give it to him.

'Mr Scobie, can I ask you how you knew we were here?' asked McCoy.

'What?'

'Can't be a coincidence you turning up here, can it? How did you know we were here?'

Jake looked exasperated. 'What's that got to do with anything? You had Connolly and you let him go! Fucking useless shower. Usual polis shite.' He shook his head. 'Can see I'm going to have to do this myself.'

Murray was still pressing against McCoy's arm, trying to get to Scobie; could feel the weight of him. McCoy held firm. Last thing this investigation needed was Murray and Scobie going at each other in the foyer of the bloody St Enoch Hotel.

'I'll ask you again, Mr Scobie. How did you know we were here?'

No response, just a glare. One of his boys cleared his throat, spat on the carpet.

'Okay, Mr Scobie, let me explain things to you in simple terms. You are refusing to tell me how you knew the police or Kevin Connolly were here. If it turns out you are bribing or pressuring any officers on this case for confidential information that led you here, I'll arrest you and make sure you spend the next couple of months in Barlinnie, Archie Lomax or no fucking Archie Lomax.'

McCoy wasn't quite sure where all this bravado was coming from, but it seemed to be working. Scobie had been expecting a screaming match about how shite the polis were and that was the last thing McCoy was going to give him. He was talking quietly, calmly, even though his heart was racing.

'Any answers, Mr Scobie?'

Scobie looked at him. Whether he was or not, he obviously thought McCoy was serious. He pointed at him, started talking, saliva flecking the corners of his mouth.

'Listen to me, you jumped-up fucking cunt.

I know your name, where you live. You and the fat cunt behind you. When this is over I'm gonnae pay you both a wee visit. You remember that.'

He turned, nodded to his boys, walked out the double doors.

I liked the St Enoch Hotel. The room, the bed, the empty floors upstairs. I slept up there sometimes. Woke up in the middle of the night, in the dark, walked the corridors. Listened to the mice in the walls, the pigeons in the roof, and the whispers of the dead. I found a pile of scud mags in one of the rooms, cotton hanky on top stiff with dried spunk. Maybe someone had been there before me but I thought I recognised the girls in the magazines, thought I knew them. Maybe I'd bought the magazines myself? Couldn't be sure.

The older one, the one with the hat, had come to talk to Scobie once. Acting the big man, talking shite, just another puffed-up polis without a clue. I should have got the chair higher, pushed the leg hard into his face. His eye.

The big clock hanging from the roof of Central Station says half past four. I am a free man. Stay wherever I want. Start my collection over again. Was vital I kept a record. Really should be weighing everything. See what's leaving my body.

I bought a Mars Bar from the newsagents. One and three quarter ounces. Unwrapped it and took a little bite. Grimaced. Everything tasted the same.

CHAPTER 10

McCoy walked back into the office, swallowing two aspirin with a gulp from a bottle of Irn-Bru. He stopped a second, put it and the Marks bag down on his desk, and burped loudly. Felt better. Rolled the six notes from the desk sergeant telling him to call Mary at the *Record* into a ball and threw it twenty feet towards the bin beside Wattie's desk, raised his hands in triumph as it went straight in.

'No bother!' he said. 'You see that?'

Wattie looked up from his paperwork. 'Marvellous.'

McCoy took off his jacket, started to pull his tie loose. 'Christ, what's up with you?' he asked and immediately wished he hadn't as Wattie started his rant.

'I'll tell you what's up with me. Every fucking thing that nobody wants gets dumped on my desk. Look!'

He stood up, spread his arms wide. McCoy had to admit he had a point. His desk was covered in all sorts of shite.

He went on. 'Files that nobody's put back, phone messages for every cunt in here, the tea kitty tin, Thomson's fucking requisition forms! I'm supposed to be a junior detective, supposed to be learning things, not the bloody office junior!'

McCoy pulled his shirt from his trousers, started unbuttoning it. 'Finished?'

Wattie sat back down, looking glum. 'And while you've been out bloody shopping I've spent the last two hours phoning every bloody B&B and boarding house in Glasgow.'

McCoy pretended to step on something, bent down to pick it up, held out his hand to Wattie. 'Your dummy. Think you must have spat it out.'

Despite himself, Wattie laughed. 'Arse.'

'Detective Arse to you, Watson.' He got his shirt off, started to unwrap the new one. Wolf-whistle from across the room. Thomson grinning at him.

'Thomson! You've finally realised you're working with a sex bomb?'

'Seen more muscles on a bloody worm,' said Thomson.

McCoy was trying to get the tin of Elastoplast open. Eventually managed to prise a nail under the lid and pop it up. He got a couple out, started the equally difficult process of getting them out their wee wrappers. Noticed a large brown paper bag on Wattie's desk. 'What's that?'

'More shite. Why are you in such a good mood anyway?'

'Don't know,' he said, sticking a big plaster on one of the cuts on his chest. 'But it doesn't happen often so you better make the most of it.'

He really wasn't sure why he was in such a good mood. Adrenaline from the confrontation with Scobie probably. Plus Murray had taken him aside after, told him he had done a good job diffusing the situation, the right thing. Golden boy, right enough.

'Okay, gonnae take this then?' Wattie held out the brown paper bag. 'Remember that guy that hanged himself in the church—'

'Chapel,' said McCoy. 'What about him?'

'This is his personal effects. What am I supposed to do with the bloody things?'

'Here,' said McCoy, sticking the other plaster over the cut above his left nipple. 'Give us them.' He lowered his voice. 'I've got the autopsy report. I'll put it with them and dump it all on Thomson's desk when he goes out.'

Wattie handed the bag over, went back to trying to clear his desk. 'Thomson!' he shouted. 'How about moving your shite off my desk?'

Thomson held his hands up. 'I didn't bloody put anything on your desk.'

McCoy left them arguing, sat back down, looked at his old shirt, decided it was beyond saving and put it in the bin, buttoned up his new one. The bag Wattie had given him was pretty light for a man's final possessions. He opened it. Folded suit and shirt smelling of sweat and fags. Least his underwear and socks weren't in there. His wallet was sitting on the top. McCoy got it out. Opened it.

A pawn ticket for a watch, a wee prayer card. St Jude, patron saint of lost causes. Hadn't done much for this poor bugger. He turned it over. The back of it was covered in Bible verse references written in neat ballpoint pen. Usual ones: Corinthians 13.4, John 3.16, Matthew 11.28. He'd had the Bible rammed down his throat for so many years at the schools and the homes that he knew most of them by heart.

Pulled out a cracked photograph of a woman standing in front of a garden fence, baby in her arms. Him and his mum by the look of the clothes, looked like it was taken in the '40s. A wee card with times and places of AA meetings on it. Least the poor bugger had tried, he supposed. Bit of folded newspaper. McCoy unfolded it, wondered why he'd kept an article about planting bulbs early for spring, realised he was looking at the wrong side and turned it over. A function room in a hotel. Three businessmen and a policeman in a dress uniform.

POLICE CHIEF RETIREMENT DINNER

Immediately felt dizzy, sick. Looked up. Thomson reluctantly picking up folders from Wattie's desk. Murray talking to some big guy in uniform about the Melrose score. He tried to breathe, to take slow breaths, stop the spinning in his head.

He looked back down at it, the picture. Looked closer. The policeman in the dress uniform had something written above his head, blue ballpoint pen capitals.

PSALMS 56.4

One he didn't know. He shouted over to Thomson, 'We still got those Bibles?'

Thomson dropped the files on his desk, nodded. 'Pile of them still in the storeroom.'

McCoy hurried off, got one, came back and sat at his desk. They'd been bought for the Bible John case. Put away when the trail went cold. He flicked through, found Psalms, nineteenth book of the Bible between Job and Proverbs. Could still recite them after all these years. Found chapter 56. Found verse 4. Read it.

'In God I have put my trust; I will not fear what flesh can do unto me.'

Sat back in his chair. Could hear Thomson yelling at Wattie, telling him it wasn't his bloody stuff on his desk anyway, the radio in the background going through tomorrow's weather. Himself breathing.

He read it again.

Told Wattie his chest was sore and he was taking an early one. Made sure no one was looking and put the wallet into his pocket, the autopsy report under his coat and walked out the door.

McCoy stood outside the chapel door for a while, smoking, trying not to turn around, go back to the shop and bury himself in Kevin Connolly and Elaine Scobie and Wattie and Thomson grumbling at each other. Didn't really like being in the office but somehow the thought of it felt comforting now, somewhere safe. But eventually he did what he always knew he was going to do. Dropped his cigarette onto the red gravel, ground it out. Pulled the heavy chapel door open.

Been a long time since McCoy'd been in a chapel but the smell was still the same. Hit him as soon as he walked in. Floor polish, candles and a faint trace of incense. The chapels he remembered going to when he was a wee boy were dark and cold, designed to instil fear and obedience. At least this one looked a bit friendlier than that.

Interior wasn't the usual dark stone; was white plaster and wood, roof shaped like an upturned ship, high windows letting in the last of the afternoon light. There were two big vases of flowers on either side of the altar, some sort of tapestry embroidery thing up on the wall, all bright colours and rainbows, 'HEAR THE WORD OF THE LORD' in big multicoloured letters.

Some things hadn't changed. There was still a dirty big crucifix on the back wall. Jesus looking down on them all, plaster face wrought with agony and disappointment. He could remember being battered in front of a crucifix just like this one. Sister Helen was her name. Hitting him and hitting him with a leather belt, grabbing him by the hair, making him look up into the eternally disappointed face of Our Lord Jesus Christ.

Telling him he was worthless, that his mother

and father had abandoned him because he was wicked. Telling him he better change his attitude or this would happen every day. Telling him that he was less than a dog in the street. Funny thing, realised now that she couldn't have been more than nineteen, twenty. Wondered how she'd manage to get so much hate into herself in such a short life.

He sat down on a pew, tried not to cross himself automatically. The priest was up at the altar arranging the chalice and all the rest of the stuff whose names he couldn't remember. He was a young guy, tall, late twenties, black suit, ginger hair. He looked up, saw McCoy and smiled, went to walk back through to the chapel house.

'Need a word,' said McCoy, voice sounding very loud in the empty chapel.

The priest stopped, turned and walked back towards him. 'How can I help you?' he asked, holding out his hand to shake. 'Father Monaghan.'

McCoy held out his police identity card. 'Need a word about Paul Brady,' he said.

The priest dropped his hand, sat down in the pew in front of him. Looked like he knew this was coming.

'Did you know him?' asked McCoy.

'Not as well as I should have.' He smiled weakly. 'Not enough to really help him.'

McCoy looked round. 'This where he did it then?'

The priest nodded, pointed over McCoy's head.

'Attached a rope to a pew in the balcony and lowered himself over the edge. I found him when I opened up for six o'clock mass.' He crossed himself. 'Was too late to do anything, he was dead already.'

'What was he like?'

'Quiet. I tried to talk to him but he seemed very shy. I got the impression he was living rough; looked better on some days than others. I gave him our leaflet about soup kitchens and hostels and told him to come and have a chat any time he wanted.' He smiled again. 'Wasn't enough really, was it?'

'How often did he come in?'

'Couple of times a week maybe, always early mass, sat near the back. Last time was a couple of weeks ago, when we had that really cold spell. He seemed in a bit of a state, half frozen, came in the chapel just to warm up, I think. It was quiet so I made him a cup of tea, sat with him for a while.'

'What did you talk about?'

'I tried to get him to go to the Simon Community down at Clydeside. I knew they had a few spaces, told them I would call them, make sure they were expecting him. He said he would go, but to be honest he wasn't making an awful lot of sense. Not sure it really went in.'

He thought for a minute.

'I don't think he was drunk, maybe just confused, a bit mixed up about times, where he was. He said something about not being allowed to go to his mother's funeral, how someone at the Great Eastern had stolen some money from him and did I know where it was. I let him talk on, seemed like he just wanted someone to listen to him. He said he'd seen one of his uncles—'

McCoy sat forward. 'What?'

'Said he'd seen an uncle. He was so mixed up I wasn't sure if it was recently or a long time ago. I can't remember what he said his name was—'

'Kenny?' said McCoy.

The priest looked surprised. 'How do you know that? Yes, it was. Did you know him?'

McCoy shook his head. 'What did he say about Uncle Kenny?'

'As I said, he wasn't making an awful lot of sense. He just said he'd seen him. I said to him that maybe his uncle could help him out, take him in for a bit, maybe?'

'And what did he say to that?'

'He laughed. And then he started crying.'

The big front doors behind them opened; a blast of cold air and two boys came rolling in. They were laughing, pushing and shoving each other. Immediately stopped when they saw the priest. Knelt and crossed themselves.

'Go and get ready, boys. I'll be through in a minute,' said the priest.

They nodded and hurried off behind the altar.

'Wasn't so long ago I was an altar boy myself.' He smiled. 'Some of the older members of our congregation still treat me like I am.'

'Did he ever come into confession?' asked McCoy.

'Once. He only came in once.'

'When?'

The priest didn't reply.

'When?' repeated McCoy.

The priest looked up, eyes red. 'The night before. The night before he did it.'

'And what did he talk about?'

The priest shook his head. 'You know I can't say anything about that.' He looked behind him at the altar. 'I'm sorry, I should get ready.'

He went to stand up and McCoy grabbed his arm.

'He hung himself in your fucking chapel. Tell me!'

The priest tried to pull his arm away but McCoy held tighter. He needed to know. 'Doesn't make any difference now. The poor bastard's dead. So you tell me what he said to you.'

The priest squirmed, tried to get away.

'Fucking tell me!'

McCoy didn't realise he was shouting until he heard his voice echoing around the chapel.

The priest looked at him, open-mouthed. 'You know what Brady said, don't you? I can tell by your face.'

McCoy dropped his arm and started to back away.

'Hold on!' said the priest. 'Please! We should talk. Maybe I can help—'

McCoy got up, started walking towards the door, walking quickly, needing to get out as soon as he could. He could hear the priest calling to him, asking him to come back, voice echoing in the empty chapel. He ignored it, kept walking. Priest called him again, was saying something about the need to unburden, about the strength of prayer.

McCoy pushed the heavy doors open and stepped out into the cold clean air. The door banged shut behind him. No more priest, just the noise of the evening traffic on the Garscube Road. Sounded good. He leant against the wall of the chapel. Realised he was crying.

McCoy walked down Renfield Street trying to work out what he was doing. Who was he kidding? He knew fine well what he was doing. He was lighting the fire. He'd been doing that since he walked into the chapel and now he was about to pour petrol on it. No going back after this. The streets were empty, a cold Monday night in February. He passed Forsyth's windows, full of suits he couldn't afford to buy, and stopped outside the entrance to the restaurant.

This was it, last chance to stop the train. Knew if he went in, there was no going back. He thought of Brady hanging in the chapel, of all the other boys who might have done the same thing, and the ones like him and Stevie who had managed to keep going. He owed them. He dropped his cigarette on the pavement, stood on it and opened the door of the Jade Sea.

He walked up the stairs, wondering why Chinese restaurants were always on the first floor, pushed the door open and went in. The restaurant was decorated like some kind of oriental garden: wee pagoda roofs over the booths, plants and fish tanks, a brightly painted wooden dragon hanging from the ceiling. Effect somewhat lessened by the brown swirly-pattered carpet on the floor.

A smiling waiter in a dickie bow approached, menu in hand. McCoy pointed over at a booth in the corner. Cooper and his second-in-command Billy Kerr deep in conversation with some guy with black slicked-back hair and a long leather coat on. He went to walk over and Jumbo appeared out of nowhere, stood in front of him.

'Sorry, Mr McCoy. Private conversation.'

He looked over and Cooper held up five fingers. Mouthed 'five minutes'.

McCoy sat down at a table, Jumbo sat down beside him, tried to slide a copy of a wee *Battle* comic under the table before McCoy could see it. Too late.

'*Gott im Himmel!*' said McCoy nodding at it. '*Name of a dog!*'

Jumbo looked a bit puzzled. 'I've got this because Mr Cooper says I have to practise my reading.'

'Fair enough. Not a bad idea.'

McCoy lit up, dropped his match in the ashtray. Jumbo watched him, face blank as usual, huge

115

hand holding the comic. Couldn't have been older than seventeen, eighteen. More like a giant kid than anything else. But the muscles under his jumper and the sheer fucking size of him meant he was sitting here keeping guard over Cooper.

'So what's it like then, working for Stevie?' asked McCoy.

Jumbo smiled, face lit up. 'I like it. Mr Cooper's a good man to work for.'

'That right?' asked McCoy. 'How's the hand?'

Jumbo looked flustered. Held it out. One finger half gone, one mangled.

'I had to do it, you know,' said McCoy. 'If I didn't things would be worse. I didn't want to.'

Jumbo nodded. 'I know. If you hadn't come he would have killed me.'

It wasn't a phrase or an exaggeration, just a simple truth. Cooper would have killed him just like he'd killed his mate. And all for stealing a tally book.

McCoy shook his head. 'You sure you're okay with all this, Jumbo?'

He nodded. 'I've got a job, somewhere to stay. I'm lucky.'

McCoy nodded. Maybe he was. What else was a guy like Jumbo going to do with his life? He'd never get a proper job, maybe day labourer if he was lucky. He nodded at the comic.

'Okay, let's hear you,' he said.

Jumbo opened it up. Started. '"Darn signal came through stren, stren-G?"'

He looked up.

'Strength,' said McCoy. 'You say strength. The G is silent.'

Jumbo looked at him in puzzlement.

'I know,' said McCoy. 'Don't ask me, just the way it is.'

Jumbo carried on. '"Strength three, but I got the gist—"'

'Not gist, jist. You pronounce the—'

'FUCK!'

They both turned, looked over to the other side of the restaurant. Cooper had a knife in his hand, well, the handle, to be precise. The blade was deep in the guy with the leather coat's hand, pinning it to the table. He was sobbing, nodding, agreeing with whatever Cooper was hissing into his ear, face twisted in pain.

From what he could see through the foliage Billy was trying to reason with Cooper, get him to calm down. He didn't seem to be having much luck. Opposite effect in fact. Cooper told him to fuck off and drove the knife further into the guy's hand. Another scream.

'Christ,' said McCoy wincing. 'What's going on over there?'

Jumbo looked over, shrugged. Kept going with his reading.

'"It's urgent. You better get over to the old man."'

McCoy sat back in his chair. Wondered why he was still friends with Cooper. Wondered why he didn't just do what Murray kept telling him.

Keep away. Jumbo was still reading. Paying no attention to what was happening across the other side of the room. Must be inured by now.

Cooper pulled the knife out and the man slumped against Billy. Billy wrapped his hand in a linen napkin, pulled him out the booth and dragged him towards the door.

'Okay, Harry? Give us a minute,' he said cheerily as he huckled the terrified man past them.

Jumbo kept droning on. '"Okay, mate. I will send a message to the front—"'

'How's it going?' Billy Weir was back, standing there with his hand out. They shook. McCoy liked Billy. Far as he was concerned he was the only one of Cooper's boys who had any sense. Billy grinned. He was young too, early twenties if that, black hair cut short, little splatter of blood on the cuff of his shirt.

'Had to get rid of that tosser before he started annoying the boss any more. Stupid arse wouldnae be telt. More fool him.'

He bowed theatrically. 'His Majesty will see you now.' Tapped Jumbo on the shoulder. 'C'mon, pal, let's go for a walk, buy some fags. Mr Cooper wants some peace.'

They left and McCoy wandered over to the booth, waited as the waiter wrapped up the bloody tablecloth, dropped it in a bucket and laid out a fresh one.

'You again?' said Cooper mildly. 'Want some dinner?'

McCoy nodded. Cooper told the waiter to start

the food coming. He never ordered anything, just left them to decide what was good that day.

'What was all that about?' asked McCoy.

'My business,' said Cooper, wiping the bloody blade of the knife on another napkin and putting it in his jeans pocket.

McCoy put the autopsy file down on the table, wallet on top of it.

Cooper pulled them over to his side, opened the file, skimmed it. 'Some bloke's hung himself.' He grinned. 'Well, at least they cannae pin that one on me.'

McCoy tapped the name. Cooper read it again.

'Paul Joseph Brady. So? Who's he when he's at home?'

'Joey. He's Joey,' said McCoy.

Cooper looked up at him. 'What? Wee Joey? Naw.' He looked at the photo stapled to the front again. 'You sure?'

McCoy nodded.

'Poor bugger,' said Cooper. 'Never did have much going for him.'

McCoy opened the wallet, took out the clipping from the paper, flattened it out. Cooper looked at it, raised his eyebrows.

'He had this on him when he hung himself. He must have recognised him too.'

'What's that?' asked Cooper, pointing at the writing above the policeman's head.

'Biblical quote. *"In God I have put my trust; I will not fear what flesh can do unto me."*'

A waiter appeared, started laying plates on the table. Cooper sat back, let him fuss, arranging the food, side plates and bowls, cutlery. Kept his eyes on McCoy. Eventually the table was to the waiter's satisfaction. He bowed and walked off.

'Uncle Kenny,' said Cooper.

'Uncle Kenny,' said McCoy. 'Give me a day or so, I'll have a look in the files. Find out where he lives.'

'And then we beat the living fuck out him,' said Cooper.

McCoy nodded. 'And then we beat the living fuck out of him.'

Cooper grinned. 'Why don't you just do what I say when I say it, McCoy? Save time.'

'Because I'm an arsehole. That right?'

'Indeed it is.' Cooper picked up a spare rib, started gnawing at it. 'Got some good news today. Billy phoned from Hong Kong. Supply line back up and running.'

'So the great plan's taking shape?'

Cooper nodded. 'Things are going to change, Harry, change big-time. What you doing the night?'

'Nothing planned,' said McCoy.

'Good,' said Cooper, dropping the rib bone back onto his plate. 'We've no been out for ages. You can come fishing with me.'

To be honest, he didn't have much else to do, couldn't think of a real reason to say no, so here he was, sitting beside Jumbo in the back of a

Zephyr listening to Cooper and Billy Weir discuss how many more boys they were going to need. Verdict seemed to be five or six. That decided, Billy turned the radio up, started to sing along to 'My Sweet Lord'. Badly.

Luckily he didn't have to endure it for too long; they weren't going far, just along Argyle Street to the Gallowgate. The Land Bar to be exact, although being that exact about the Land Bar wasn't easy; it seemed to change its name every five minutes. Last time McCoy had been in it, it was called the Civic. Something else before that. Reid's maybe?

Cooper leaned over the back of the seat, handed McCoy a half-bottle of vodka. McCoy took it, took a swig. Held it out to Jumbo who shook his head.

'What exactly is it we're doing again?' McCoy asked.

'Finding new blood,' said Cooper. 'Way things are going we're going to need it. Some guy that leads off one of the shitey wee gangs over this way's supposed to be no bad. He's got a couple of mates too. Comes recommended.'

McCoy took another drink of the vodka, grimaced, wondered what kind of person found up-and-coming gang members to recommend. They pulled up at the lights at the High Street. Watched a woman pushing a pram and dragging two weans struggle across the road. Rain was still pouring down, wet streets reflecting the car head-lights. Jumbo humming to himself, drawing smiley faces on the condensation on his window.

'These guys know we're coming?' asked McCoy as they set off again.

Billy looked at him in the mirror, grinned. 'Not exactly.'

The Land was just like every other shitey pub in Glasgow. Worn-out lino, few tables and chairs, two dirty wee windows and a couple of striplights in the ceiling illuminating the faded wallpaper and the line of no-hopers lined up at the bar. They shuffled in, found a table while Jumbo went up to the bar.

The back area was filled with young guys, obviously their patch. Long hair, denims, the occasional leather coat. All of them smoking, all of them staring at Billy and Cooper. All trying to work out what the fuck Stevie Cooper was doing in their bar, all of them desperately trying to look like they didn't care.

'So that'll be the gang then?' said McCoy as Jumbo put the drinks down on the table.

'Look like a bunch of cunts,' said Cooper mildly.

'Am I going to get my head kicked in here?' asked McCoy. 'Because if I am, can we get it over with and go somewhere else for a drink? This place is bloody miserable.'

'No, you're no, so shut it,' said Cooper. 'You can just sit there and watch.'

'Great,' said McCoy. 'What a night out. Glad there was nothing on the telly.'

Billy stood up, drained his pint. 'May as well get this show on the road.'

Cooper nodded.

Billy walked over to the bunch of lads. There was a shuffling, a changing of positions, couple of hands went into pockets, gripped chibs. Defiant stares from the braver ones.

'Which one of youse is Tony Reid?' he asked.

A tall red-haired guy stepped out the pack. Denims, white granddad shirt, Fair Isle tank top. 'Who wants to know?' he asked.

'Me, ya prick. C'mon,' said Billy. 'Someone wants a word.'

He turned to walk back towards Cooper but Reid didn't move, just stood there.

'Christ,' said Billy. 'Gonnae be like that, is it?'

'Looks like it,' said Reid.

Billy muttered something under his breath about not having enough time for this, stepped forward and headbutted Reid in the face. He dropped, Billy grabbed his hair before he hit the ground and started dragging him along the floor towards Cooper.

The group of lads stepped back, started looking anywhere but at Billy dragging Reid across the filthy floor.

Billy hauled him up, sat him on a chair opposite Cooper. Reid looked dazed, blood streaming from his nose. All bravado gone.

'You know who I am?' asked Cooper.

Reid nodded.

'Someone recommended you. Said you could handle yourself. That right?'

Reid nodded again.

'Well, in that case this is your lucky day. Need you and two others. You work for me, deal with Billy.'

Reid looked at Billy doubtfully. Billy smiled at him, winked.

'All good?' said Cooper.

'Yes, Mr Cooper.'

'That's the boy. Billy'll fill you in, me and my business associate are going along the road for a drink.'

Cooper stood up, looked at McCoy.

'Oh me?' said McCoy, surprised. 'Sorry, didn't know who you meant. Great.'

Cooper shook his head.

They walked back along Gallowgate into town, Jumbo following a few steps behind. Rain was getting worse so McCoy pointed up ahead to the Tolbooth. Couldn't face walking any further, he was soaked already. Besides he liked it, the Tolbooth, well-run pub, good beer. Cooper didn't seem quite so sure. Grumbled about there never being any women in it, just bloody old men. But it was warm and it was near. McCoy won out.

They settled down near the fire, started to dry out. Jumbo happy with his Coca-Cola and some coppers for the one-armed bandit. They were a good few pints in, been through where Cooper was going to find another couple of lads, why Billy was a good number two, how shite the Scotland team were, before Cooper started talking about what they were really there for.

'Wasn't only that cunt Uncle Kenny I was thinking about when I was in that bloody hospital,' he said. 'Started thinking about the future.'

'Sounds serious,' said McCoy.

'It is. What am I? Thirty-two? Getting too old for the shite I've been doing. No more street fights, no more fucking tally books.'

'You like fighting, though,' said McCoy.

Cooper nodded. 'Doesn't like me so much any more.' He glanced at McCoy. 'Tell anyone this and I'll fucking bust you, okay?'

McCoy saluted.

'Seems my back's a bit fucked. Major muscle damage. That cunt with the sword really did a fucking number on me.'

The news wasn't a surprise to McCoy, he'd seen the way Cooper moved now. The surprise was he was admitting it.

'It's no that bad, is it?'

Cooper shrugged. 'Might be. I've to go back in a couple of months, see some specialist. Anyway, whatever the fuck happens with it, it's time for me to move up, been fucking about for too long. Things are changing, starting to fall into place: me, you, Billy Weir, Billy Chan's on board.'

'Me?' asked McCoy.

'Aye, you.'

'What am I supposed to do?'

'Keep your head down, get promoted.' Cooper grinned. 'I might need a friend in high places one day.'

McCoy ignored that one; no matter how friendly him and Cooper were there was no way he was becoming his pet bloody policeman.

'So, the new boys? The plans for world domination? When's it all kick off then?'

'Soon enough,' said Cooper. 'Just need another couple of pieces to fall into place and we're off to the races.' He stood up. 'Meanwhile, let's get pissed.'

A couple of drinks later they were getting there. Billy Weir had come and gone, came to tell Cooper he had picked up another few decent lads at the Land to join the cause. He'd also dropped off a couple of grams of speed – passed them under the table.

McCoy came out the toilets wiping his nose. Knew starting doing speed at eight o'clock on a Monday night was a bad idea but couldn't stop himself, especially after a few pints. He sat down by Cooper, felt the familiar chemical taste dripping down the back of his throat and took a big slug from his pint.

Cooper was surveying the bar, eyes wide. Didn't look happy. 'Told you this place was full of old bloody men.'

He had a point. The two of them and Jumbo seemed to be the only punters under sixty.

'Where'd you fancy going?' asked McCoy.

Cooper turned to him, grinned. 'Funny you should ask.'

★　★　★

Half an hour later they were sitting in the Gay Gordon's in Royal Exchange Square, drinks in front of them. They had a bit of trouble getting in. Doorman took one look at Jumbo and told them it was regulars only. Cooper had smiled, told him to go and get Chan before he punched his fucking face in.

Seemed to work. Chan the manager appeared at the door all smiles and handshakes and drinks tickets and guided them in. Was like walking into some giant shortbread tin. The carpet was tartan, the walls were tartan, pictures of stags and Highland warriors on the walls. He walked them through the back to a booth in the cocktail bar, sent a waitress wearing a mini kilt over to take their order.

Wasn't the first place McCoy would have wanted to go but Cooper seemed happy, smiling at the waitresses, making wisecracks, knocking back the drinks.

'Any particular reason we're here?' asked McCoy.

'You'll see,' said Cooper. 'Just hold your fucking horses.'

Speed was making McCoy want to talk, that and the drink giving him enough confidence to ask the question.

'Remember in Memel Street?'

'What?' Cooper turned distractedly, had been eyeing up two girls sitting at another booth.

'You said Murray was dirty, on the take.'

127

Cooper was looking at him, listening properly now.

'Is he?' McCoy asked.

The waitress appeared with another tray of pints and whiskies. Coke for Jumbo. Placed them down on the table carefully. Winked at Cooper and wandered back to the bar.

'No. I made it up because you were annoying me. Happy now?'

'Did you really?'

'Fuck sake, McCoy, I just told you, didn't I!'

He was about to ask him again when the lights dimmed and the James Bond theme started thundering over the speakers.

Cooper leant over, shouted in his ear. 'This is why we're here.'

A voice boomed over the music. 'Ladies and gentlemen, the Bryan Marley Dancers!'

Six girls emerged from the dry ice flooding the stage, stepped into the spotlight. All wearing bikinis, all carrying revolvers. Music switched to Shirley Bassey belting out 'Goldfinger' and they starting dancing, pointing the guns at the audience as they moved round the stage.

McCoy sat back in the booth, sipped his whisky, watched as the girls started winding themselves round the columns holding the ceiling up, legs up, stilettos pointing. Wasn't sure if Cooper was lying now or then.

Had the feeling that was exactly what he wanted.

My head hurts. Been hurting all day. Hit it off a wall a couple of times, sometimes it works. Not this time, though. I go for a walk in the rain, thinking the cold will calm it down. Stop on a bridge over the Clyde. Watch the water.

I can't be sure but I think I see a body floating in it, arms outstretched, spinning as it disappears under the bridge. A body floating in the water, just like they did in the Rhine in 1944.

I can see lights in the sky, see colours round the streetlights. Crunch six aspirin.

Take a half-bottle of vodka from my new coat pocket. Drink it as I walk up the town, swallow over three black bombers. Start to feel better. Decide I need to fuck someone, pretend it's her. Feel her hair in my hand, the curve of her arse, her tit in my mouth. That will make my head better.

I walk up Sauchiehall Street, hand rubbing my cock through my pocket. Am already hard by the time I get to Blythswood Square. I imagine I am crossing the Rhine, Mauser over my back, Porta and the Legionnaire beside me, German girls for the taking.

I watch for a while then pick a girl with black hair just like hers.

Oh my love, I say as I bend her over and come in her, not long now, not long now . . .

13TH FEBRUARY 1973

CHAPTER 11

The picture of the grieving widow in the paper hadn't done her justice. She really was a stunner. Her dark hair was cut short now, flicked off her face, big blue eyes and a figure that would stop a clock. Elaine Scobie was leaning back against an old draughtsman's cabinet wearing a blue silky jumpsuit thing, green platforms and an expression of contempt. Couldn't have looked less happy to see them if she tried.

The draughtsman's cabinet wasn't the only thing McCoy wasn't expecting to see in the boutique. The shop was full of stuff that had been salvaged from God knows where. Old tram signs, Victorian busts of dead generals, wooden plant stands with ferns growing in chamber pots on them. Place was so full you could hardly see the clothes. They seemed to be dotted about at random, like an afterthought. McCoy looked at the price tag on a wee blouse hanging from a stag's antlers. Was more than he'd spent on his suit.

'Somewhat mob-handed, aren't you?' asked Lomax, looking rather amused by the whole thing. He was suited and booted as usual. All chalk stripe and flowery tie. 'Didn't realise we would be entertaining the full set.'

'More the merrier,' said Murray. 'Mountains coming to Muhammad.'

Elaine Scobie smiled unconvincingly and screwed the last of her black Sobranie cigarette into a big marble ashtray. 'This going to take long, Archie?' she asked. 'I do have an appointment later.'

Lomax gestured towards two battered and cracked leather Chesterfields at the back of the shop. 'Gents, take a seat.'

They sat down and immediately sank too far down into the depths of the sofa. Struggled to sit back up to a normal level. Murray, McCoy and Watson were on one, Lomax and Elaine on the other. Old Louis Vuitton travelling trunk between them with another marble ashtray sitting on the old Union Jack draped over it.

They'd got the word that morning. A call into the shop from Lomax's office. The interview had finally been agreed to. Nowhere as normal as the shop or his office. The boutique it was. It seemed Miss Scobie's distress was finally under control. Looked more than under control to McCoy, looked positively submerged.

A young girl dressed like she was on *Top of the Pops* was hovering about, huge purple baggy trousers and a striped polo neck. She squatted down beside her boss.

'Anything I can get you, Elaine? You going to be okay?' she asked.

Elaine shook her head, the suffering martyr. She took the girl's hand, squeezed it. 'No thanks, Margo, I'm fine. Just turn the sign to closed as you go, eh? Thanks, doll.'

Margo smiled at her then gave the three men on the couch a look that would curdle milk. 'Will do,' she said.

They waited a minute until she'd gone, then sat in silence. Tick of a big old train station clock on the wall seeming ominously loud. Wattie was looking round, eyes wide.

'Have you had the Golden Dawn long, Miss Scobie?' he asked. 'It's quite some place.'

'Two years,' she said. 'I don't really have time for this small talk, Mr . . .'

'Watson,' he said, starting to blush.

'Watson,' she said. 'Could we just get on with it?'

McCoy stepped in. 'Fair enough. So could you tell us when was the last time you saw Mr Jackson?'

She looked at Lomax, who nodded, leather attaché case across his knees serving as a desk for his notepad.

Elaine sat forward, picked some lint off her trouser leg. 'The day before . . . the day before he died . . .' She looked up at the ceiling, lip trembled for a second, then she carried on. 'Friday. He came into the shop before he went for training. We went for a coffee.'

'And this would be what time?' asked McCoy.

'We weren't open long. About half ten? He has to get to training by twelve.'

135

'Where did you go?' he asked.

'Epicures in West Nile Street, it's where we always go. Why does this matter?' she asked, looking exasperated.

'Just trying to build up a picture,' said McCoy. 'That was the last time you saw him?'

She nodded.

'And how did he seem to you? What did you talk about?'

'He was fine, Charlie was always fine, he wasn't a worrier. We talked about the game coming up, what to get his father for his birthday, the usual.' She shook her head. 'I don't know.'

Lomax leant over, held her hand. 'Don't worry, Elaine, you're doing fine.' He looked over. 'Mr McCoy?'

McCoy nodded. 'And the night Charlie . . . Where were you?'

'I went to a party in Doddy Laing's house in Milngavie. Archie was there.'

They all turned to Lomax.

He smiled. 'Indeed I was. Excellent do. Doddy's not shy about sharing his largesse, I'll say that for him.'

'I stayed the night,' she continued. 'Fiona, Doddy's daughter, is a friend of mine. They woke me up at seven, my dad was on the phone with . . .' She looked down at her lap, seemed to steel herself. When she looked back up her eyes were glassy with tears. 'With the news about Charlie.'

To complete the dramatic moment Lomax

reached into his suit pocket, brought out a spotted silk hanky and handed it over. He glanced over at the three of them as Elaine dabbed at her eyes, trying to preserve her make-up.

'Gents, as you can see Miss Scobie is very upset, unless this questioning is vital I'd like to draw it to a close now.' He made to stand up when Murray spoke.

'Sit back down, Mr Lomax,' he said. 'I'll let you know when the interview is over.'

Lomax was caught. He hovered, bent over, deciding which way to go, then sat back on the couch. 'Well, let's get it over with as soon as possible then.'

'And when did you last see Kevin Connolly?' asked McCoy.

Another glance at Lomax, another nod. To McCoy it was obvious. She'd been coached through all this already, probably had a couple of practice runs. Question was: why?

'It was the end of November last year. I came home from work and he was sitting in my flat, bunch of flowers and a box of chocolates. He didn't have a key, must have broken in. I was scared, really scared, so I called my father and he came straight over. I left them to it and I haven't seen him since.'

'Was that the first indication that his attitude to you had changed? The first time you were worried?' asked McCoy.

She shook her head. 'For years Kevin Connolly

was a family friend; I've known him since I was a wee girl. He's always been like an uncle, my dad's best friend. But in the past year or so things changed.'

'How?' asked McCoy.

'He'd started looking at me differently, accidentally touching me, turning up here at the shop, at restaurants, everywhere I went. Think he was following me. It was creepy. Finding him in my flat was the final straw.'

McCoy and the others listened patiently as she ran through more of the script. How Connolly had started harassing her, how Connolly had always disliked Charlie. How upset she was to think of Charlie alone on top of that building. How she would never get over his death.

McCoy nodded sympathetically for a while. Wasn't long until he was sick of listening her run through the points Lomax had obviously coached her on. He wanted a cigarette, he wanted something that was actually going to help him with the case, but most of all he wanted off the uncomfortable bloody sofa. Time to get things going.

He smiled at her, tried to look puzzled. 'Maybe you can clarify something for me, Miss Scobie,' he said. 'Help me understand what was going on?'

She smiled back. 'What's that?'

'Connolly was your boyfriend, wasn't he? Until you chucked him for some glamour-boy football player? That the story?'

Lomax looked shocked, drew in his breath,

138

started scribbling on his pad. Not Elaine. She sat forward, face only inches from McCoy's. He could smell her perfume, see the blue of her eyes. See the fury in them.

'If you think a remark like that is funny then I feel sorry for you. If you were being serious then I feel even sorrier for you. Kevin Connolly never was, is, or will be my boyfriend. If the extent of your investigative powers is asking ridiculous and insulting questions like that, then I'll be asking Archie here to put in a complaint, and I'll be asking for someone else to be assigned to this case. My fiancé has been murdered and all you can do is try and score cheap points. You know what, Mr McCoy? You should be ashamed of yourself.'

She stood up, walked into the back office and slammed the door shut behind her.

McCoy sank back into the Chesterfield. 'I hate to spoil a dramatic exit,' he said, 'but I haven't finished.'

Lomax stood up. 'Oh, I rather think you have, Mr McCoy, I rather think you have.' He opened his briefcase and dropped his notepad into it. 'Let me see you gents out.'

They found themselves back out on Union Street waiting for a squad car. Traffic was back to back, hardly moving. Pouring rain had brought everything to a halt. They stood under the awning of the Golden Dawn trying to stay half dry.

'Sorry about that,' said McCoy.

'Fuck them,' said Murray, 'and the horse they rode in on.'

He got his pipe out, tried to light it with a Zippo stinking of petrol. 'It was a legitimate question to ask; only problem was the answer wasn't in Elaine's script.'

'Wasn't just me then?' asked McCoy.

Murray shook his head. 'Been coached through the whole thing. Two reasons Lomax would have done that. Either she was so nervous he was worried she'd get flustered—'

'Think we can forget that one,' said Wattie. 'No way she suffers from nerves.'

Murray nodded, blew out a cloud of blue smoke. 'Or she'd been told exactly what to say and what to leave out.'

'You don't really think she was Connolly's girlfriend, do you?' asked Wattie. 'She's about twenty years younger than him for a start. And she's too good-looking.'

McCoy and Murray looked at each other.

'Sheltered life these Ayrshire boys live right enough,' said Murray. He looked up the road at the stalled traffic, still no sign of the squad car. 'One bit of bloody rain and this whole bloody city grinds to a halt.'

'So why were we interviewing her then?' asked Wattie.

'It's called poking the midden, son, poking the midden,' said Murray. 'See what crawls out. Oldest trick in the—'

'McCoy, you bastard!'

They all turned. Shout had come from across

the road. A small woman bundled up in a fur coat was waving frantically at them from the kerb opposite.

'You, ya bastard! Wait there! Do not fucking move!' she shouted.

Murray raised his eyebrows. 'A friend of yours, McCoy?'

McCoy shook his head, looked resigned to his fate. 'I wouldn't go that far. Mary Webster. *Daily Record.*'

They watched as she weaved her way between the cars, gingerly stepping through the puddles in huge platform boots. Finally made it to their side of the road. Up close she looked about fifteen: wee button nose, eyes outlined in lime green and a woolly hat with a bunch of plastic cherries dangling from it.

'Off out, Mary?' McCoy asked.

'Uh-uh.' She shook her head. 'Don't you sweet-talk me, you cheeky bastard. You hung up on me!'

Murray and Wattie had taken the opportunity to move off and were pretending to look at the cakes in the window of the Lite Bite, keeping their heads down.

'When?' he said, trying to look puzzled. 'Wasn't me, Mary. Must have been someone in the office.'

'I left you about twenty bloody messages!' she squawked.

'Did you?' Looked like he was trying to think. 'Ah, I know what's happened. You didn't leave them with Billy the desk sergeant, did you? He's

141

terrible at delivering them. I'll have to have a word with him.'

She looked dubious. 'Thousands wouldn't, McCoy, thousands wouldn't.' She took a packet of cigarettes out her bag. Lit up, waved her fingers at him, green nail varnish, and blew smoke in his face.

'Divinely decadent, don't you know,' she said in a husky voice.

McCoy looked at her blankly.

She tutted. 'What are you doing here anyway?' she asked.

He nodded back over his shoulder. 'The grieving widow.'

'What? The delectable Elaine? Good-looking girl, but Christ does she know it. And let's be honest, she wouldn't know grief if it crawled under her dress and shouted in her fanny. Readers love her, though. Can't get enough.'

'You know what?' said McCoy. 'You always did have a lovely turn of phrase, Mary. Maybe you should think about becoming a writer, something like that.'

She stuck her tongue out at him.

'That what you're doing here, is it?' he asked.

She nodded. 'And I'm late as well. Madam won't be happy. Pages four and five tomorrow. How we met, how he popped the question, how much I miss him. Usual shite. I've got to get it in by ten. To be honest I'd be as well sitting at home and making it up myself.'

'True love no run deep then?'

She stopped, looked at him. 'Hang on a bloody minute. Why should I be giving you the benefit of my wisdom? What did you ever give me, you hangy-up bastard?'

He grinned at her.

'Fuck off! Believe me, one drunken shag counts for sweet FA. Especially when it was from you. I've had more thrills taking my knickers off and riding my bike over the cobbles. Give.'

He held his arms out. 'I've got nothing to give, Mary. First time I get something I'll be straight on the phone. Promise.'

Nothing. She smoked her fag, examined her nail polish.

'Come on, Mary, be a pal. For old times' sake.'

She snorted. 'Don't make me boak. I'm still trying to forget that night of horrible sexual degradation.' She looked up and down the street like a spy. 'I don't know why I'm telling you this, but she's no exactly grieving alone.'

'What?' he said.

'Way she's acting? Give me a fucking break. He's been dead, what, two nights? And she's all wee chats on the phone, giggles. Call it feminine intuition but who gets all dressed up like Bianca bloody Jagger just to spend a night in? I don't think so, no, siree. There's someone else if you ask me. Doesn't seem that broke up about poor Charlie and what that bastard wrote on him—'

'Who told you about that?'

She looked triumphant. 'I knew it! You could have fucking well told me that, McCoy. Anyway, that's as good as a confirmation so fuck you.'

He shook his head, knew he'd been done good and proper. 'You sure about this other bloke?'

She nodded. 'Oh, I'm sure. A woman knows these things.'

'Know who he is?'

She shook her head. 'I answered the phone once for her. Whoever he is, he didn't go to school with Archie Lomax. Sounded dog rough.'

'Older?' he asked.

She nodded. 'Could be.'

McCoy thought. 'So what's the plan after your wee tête-à-tête?'

'She was talking about going for a drink.' She rolled her eyes. 'Doesn't like being in the flat by herself, the wee lamb.'

'You let me know if you do? asked McCoy.

She folded her arms, looked like she meant business. 'And you'll give me something real?'

They heard the bell and the door of the Golden Dawn opened behind them. Archie Lomax poked his head out, looked at the two of them, didn't look too happy.

McCoy nodded at Elaine. A deal. She smiled.

'I didn't realise you two knew each other,' said Lomax. 'Mary, she's ready for you now.'

'Just coming, Archie,' said Mary, voice shifting from deepest Bridgeton to posh West End. She dropped her cigarette into a puddle, stood on it.

144

'Bye, Mr McCoy.' She leant over, kissed him on the cheek. 'And thanks.'

The door shut behind her and McCoy realised there was some sort of poem painted over the window of the boutique. He stepped back.

YOU ARE A CHILD OF THE UNIVERSE
NO LESS THAN THE TREES AND
THE STARS

He stopped reading there, already felt queasy. Murray and Wattie wandered back over, both looking very pleased with themselves.

'She seemed very friendly,' said Wattie, trying to keep a straight face.

'Fuck off, Wattie. It's about time—'

Horn sounded and they turned. Thomson drew up in an unmarked Rover. Murray opened the door. 'Saved by the bell, McCoy. Saved by the bell,' he said and got in.

CHAPTER 12

The afternoon lull. A low hum of people talking on the phone, the occasional yawn, tap of the new electric typewriters, a curse as it goes wrong. McCoy is working, not working at what he should be, but working nevertheless. He'd got the staff book off Diane in Records. List of everyone in the Scottish Police Force. Rank, home address, next of kin.

Chief Constable Kenneth Ralph Burgess, Glen View, Strathblane Road, Strathblane.

Uncle Kenny's face peers up from the page. Head of Dunbartonshire Constabulary. Dunbartonshire's big, covers a lot of places – Clydebank, Cumbernauld, Lenzie – places where they have children's homes, Borstals, reform schools, scout troops, army cadets. The kind of places Uncle Kenny likes. The kind of places people like Uncle Kenny go.

He can remember Joey now. Quiet wee boy, scared of his shadow, wasn't much different from him but Joey didn't have Stevie Cooper looking out for him. So he got bullied, wet his bed, cried all the time, a natural victim. Stevie even battered him a few times, down in the basement, while

146

Uncle Kenny and whatever other men were there that evening looked on.

Gathered in a circle. Flipping the lids off bottles of beer, nervous laughter, sweaty rings under their armpits, beady wee eyes taking it all in, putting their hands down their trousers, rearranging their underwear to accommodate their growing hard-ons.

Stevie battered Joey because that's what happened down there sometimes. A wee wrestling match to get the juices flowing. Two boys down to their pants and vests trying to batter fuck out each other, trying to batter fuck out each other because it was simple, because sometimes if you won you got to go back upstairs before the fun started.

'I said McCoy!'

McCoy turned and Murray was standing at his desk. 'Jesus, what's up with you?'

McCoy sat up, tried to shake himself back to the here and now. 'Sorry, sir. Miles away.'

Murray shook his head. 'Fat lot of good that does me.' He handed him a sheet of paper. 'Connolly was in Barlinnie for five months starting in October '71. We should look at his cellmates. One of them might be a pal we don't know about.'

'Good idea,' said McCoy, taking it.

'Aye, it is, and you should have bloody thought of it.'

'I'll get onto it,' said McCoy.

Murray went to go.

McCoy called after him. 'Sir, you know Chief Constable Burgess?'

Murray nodded. 'Aye. Ken. Dunbartonshire. Met him a few times at various dinners. Why?'

'What's he like?' asked McCoy.

Murray looked suspicious. 'Why d'you want to know?'

McCoy looked innocent. 'No reason. Just saw a picture him in the paper the other day. That who they want you to replace, is it?'

Murray nodded. 'Head of Central goes to Dunbartonshire, I go to Central. Trouble is I'm no bloody going. Keep asking, no matter how many times I tell them no. Mind you, no like Ken to be in the paper, tends to keep his head down. Bit of a Holy Roller, I think. Church of Scotland, an elder, all that stuff. Lives over Strathblane way, I think. Bit of a dry stick for my tastes but he's well thought of. That okay for you, is it?'

'Aye, was only asking.'

'Well, now you're told.' He started walking back towards his office. 'Get on those bloody cellmates. Now!'

McCoy picked up the phone and called Barlinnie.

Murray, Wattie and McCoy were sitting at a Formica table in the Pitt Street canteen, teas in front of them. Murray had yet another meeting about Central so they came to him. McCoy liked the canteen, was on the top floor, good view. Had a comforting smell of food and cigarette smoke, stewed tea and burnt toast. Radio on in the background. The New Seekers still trying to teach the world to sing.

Apart from the women behind the counter scrubbing at the macaroni on the big metal dishes left from lunchtime, they were the only ones in there. McCoy had his wee red jotter open in front of him. Blue ballpoint writing over two pages.

He sipped his tea, started. 'So, three cellmates in the time Connolly was in. Clifford Reid, in for aggravated assault—'

'I know that name,' said Murray.

McCoy nodded. 'Wouldn't surprise me. List of shitey arrests as long as your arm. Housebreaking. Breach of the peace. Reset. Goes on and on. Anyway, doesn't matter. He's in Cardonald Cemetery now, died last year.'

'Good riddance to bad rubbish,' said Murray. He looked over at the women behind the counter. 'Watson, away up and see if they've got any cakes or biscuits left.'

Wattie rolled his eyes and stood up. 'You want anything?' he asked McCoy.

'See if they'll make me a cheese sandwich,' he said. Hadn't eaten anything the night before because of the speed, stomach was empty.

'They're shut, they'll no make it,' said Wattie. 'You've no chance.'

'Use your charm, they all like you. So you keep telling me.'

Wattie grinned. 'I'm a good-looking guy,' he said. 'Why wouldn't they?'

'What have I told you two about bloody carrying on?' said Murray, sounding exasperated.

Wattie muttered, 'Sorry, sir.' Headed off to the counter with a cheery smile on his face. 'All right, Lena? How's things?'

'Next one,' said Murray.

'Next one was Stuart McPhee, currently in Strangeways after battering his wife to death with a hammer.'

'Jesus,' said Murray shaking his head. 'What's up with these bloody people?'

Wattie appeared with a plate of biscuits, sat down. 'That's your whack. Lena said you can shove your cheese sandwich up your arse. Or words to that effect.'

'Great. Thanks for nothing, Lena. Number three is a weird one. Dr George Abrahams.'

Murray took two biscuits, stuffed them in his mouth, chewed down.

'A doctor in the jail?' asked Wattie, supping his tea. 'That's weird.'

'Gets weirder. Abrahams was a big cheese at Ninewells Hospital in Dundee. Consultant psychiatrist or something like that. I don't remember it, but was all over the paper apparently.'

'What did he do?' asked Murray, dunking another two biscuits in his tea.

'Was charged with assaulting a patient,' said McCoy, picking one up from the plate before Murray managed to eat them all.

'He battered one of his patients?' asked Wattie.

McCoy tapped the jotter. 'That, Mr Watson, is

where you are wrong. He's a doctor after all. He didn't do something as run-of-the-mill as battering them. Oh no, the bastard lobotomised them.'

Murray and Wattie looked at him. 'He did what?' asked Murray.

McCoy was enjoying the telling of the tale. 'Spoke to a guy called Mason up at the Dundee shop. He worked on the case, told me all about it. Ninewells has a big psychiatric wing. Specialises in lobotomies—'

'Christ, I didn't think they still did those,' said Murray. 'Thought they'd stopped them years ago.'

McCoy shook his head. 'Everyone else has. Still quite keen on them up there, apparently.' He shrugged. 'That's Dundee for you.' Carried on. 'Anyhows, there's a patient, a young woman, forget her name. Parents are rich. Father owns half of Tayside. Girl's a bit of a wild one, few arrests for breach, public nuisance. Lawyer pleads, tries to get her off a custodial sentence by saying she'll go into Ninewells for psychiatric assessment. Abrahams examines her, does an interview, recommends a lobotomy.'

'Fuck sake!' said Wattie.

'Exactly. Parents say absolutely not. All she's done is drink too much, throw a hairy fit at some woman in a shop and threaten her with a steel comb. No exactly crime of the century. The bold Abrahams? He does it anyway. Daughter comes home a vegetable. Father predictably goes nuts, employs some big advocate from Edinburgh, gets

151

Abrahams done and struck off from the medical register.'

'And where is he now?' asked Murray.

'Flat in Whitevale Street in Dennistoun,' said McCoy.

'Bit of a comedown for a doctor, isn't it?' said Murray, picking up the last biscuit. 'Go and pay this nutter a visit, see if he's heard from Connolly.'

'Will do,' said McCoy. He stood up. 'Come on, Casanova. You can drive.'

Three o'clock and it was already getting dark. The joys of Glasgow in the winter. McCoy yawned, watched an ambulance speed into the Royal, lights and siren going. He found his cigarettes in his pocket, pushed in the lighter on the dashboard. Waited for it to pop out.

'What is a lobotomy?' asked Wattie.

'Eh?' said McCoy.

Wattie looked sheepish. 'I'm no sure what it is, exactly.'

McCoy lit his cigarette off the glowing element, put it back in the hole. 'They cut the front part of your brain out.'

Wattie winced. 'What does that do?'

'Makes you calm. So calm you don't know who you are or what the fuck is going on. Makes you a bit of a vegetable. Eh, right here.'

Wattie indicated, waited for a gap in the traffic on Duke Street, turned in. Eighteen Whitevale

Street was opposite St Anne's Church. Had to park further down the road, funeral cars just about filling the whole street. Wattie took the keys out the ignition, nodded at the crowd of people coming out the front door.

'Must have been popular, whoever he was.'

'Everybody's popular when they're dead,' said McCoy. 'Not around to annoy you any more.'

'Fuck sake,' said Wattie. 'I'd forgotten what a cheery bastard you were.'

They made their way through the crowd of mourners and climbed up the stairs. Top bloody floor as usual. Was a neat close, tiles on the walls, smell of bleach coming off the wet steps. Wattie knocked on the door. No response, he knocked again.

'He's no in. And don't mess up my bloody stairs. I've just done them.'

They turned. Door across the landing had opened and a middle-aged woman wearing a flowery pinny was standing there.

'It's Tuesday. Be on Saracen Street,' she said.

'He'll be on Saracen Street?' asked McCoy. 'What? Does he work there?'

She shook her head, looked at them like they were daft. Started recounting by rote. 'Monday Argyle Street, Tuesday Saracen Street, Wednesday Victoria Road, Thursday Sauchiehall Street, Friday Byres Road. Never changes.'

'And what does he do on these streets?' asked Wattie.

'Walks up and down. You cannae miss him,' she said and shut the door.

They looked at each other. Wattie shrugged. 'Search me.'

Amazing how trusting people are. A simple knock on the door was all it took. And now I'm here. The thing in the bath is making a noise so I stamp on its face a few times. Blood bursts out from under the duct tape and pools round its head.

Last night I thought I saw the light go back into the bulb when I switched the light off. My abilities are increasing. I am maintaining equilibrium. Same amount out as went in. Nothing left behind. No dead food or dead water or dead air polluting my body. Headache gone. Knew it would when I came in that girl. Gave her two quid extra.

In my pockets I have two Mars Bars, two grams of speed, sixteen Mandies and a bottle of Irn-Bru. Enough to last a couple of days.

I flick through his wardrobe, same size as me. A couple of nice suits, shirts. I try on a pair of shoes. Brogues. Lobb's. They fit me perfectly. Things are aligning. I smile.

In the kitchen I look at the half-eaten bowl of cornflakes, the folded paper, the cold coffee. Having his breakfast, looking forward to another day. Another day of clocking in and doing what you are told. Maybe he will thank me.

CHAPTER 13

Turned out the woman with the pinny was right. Abrahams wasn't difficult to spot. Not difficult at all. They'd parked by the library, just started walking up Saracen Street when Wattie stopped, pointed up ahead.

'That'll be him then,' he said.

McCoy took a look, heart sank.

Dr Abrahams was a small neat man, car coat, flat cap, wee round specs, the kind of man you wouldn't notice unless, like Abrahams, he was carrying a dirty big sign on the end of a stick. Hand-painted, very neat, looked like he'd used those wee enamel paints you get to paint Airfix models. Waterproof. Just as well, the rain had started up again.

McCoy read the sign out: 'Depression! Nymphomania! Drunkenness! Anxiety! Hysteria! Melancholia! Mania! All can be cured by LOBOTOMY. Ask me why the GOVERNMENT won't allow it.'

'Christ,' he said, shaking his head. 'Why us?'

They stood and waited as he walked down the street towards them. People mostly ignored him, seen him before, too busy going in and out the shops or trying to pick out their own bus in the steady stream of them heading up to Lambhill and Springburn. Some school kids, brown paper bags of steaming chips in hands, laughed as they walked past. Boldest one shouted, 'Loony!' before they ran.

A woman in a man's duffel coat with a hairnet and no teeth took one of his wee pamphlets, promised to read it. McCoy stepped out from the butcher shop awning they were sheltering under as Abrahams approached.

'Dr Abrahams, can we buy you a cup of tea, have a chat?'

The wee man looked doubtful. 'Are you followers of my crusade?' he asked. 'I haven't seen you before.'

'Not exactly,' said McCoy. 'But you can tell us all about it. C'mon, it's pissing down.'

They walked back up Saracen Street towards Joe's. Streetlights had come on, shop windows lit up in the gloom of a rainy winter afternoon. The bell above the door rang as they stepped into the cafe. It was a wee place, typical tally cafe. Window steamed up in the cold, smell of coffee, hot milk and salt and vinegar. List of ice cream prices on the wall amongst the cigarette adverts and the pictures of celebrities who had been in. A middling crop. Lulu, Bill Tennent, Mary Marquis, Moira Anderson and, for some reason, Alvin Stardust. Some kids hyped-up on Coca-Cola, ice cream and sweeties stood up to go and Wattie commandeered their table.

'You order at the counter,' said Abrahams, still looking suspicious.

McCoy walked up, man behind it had his wee notebook out already writing. 'One hot orange and one hot peas for the Prof.' He looked up. 'What he always has. What you two boys want?'

'Couple of teas,' said McCoy.

The man nodded, pulled the page out of the wee notebook, handed it to a tired-looking woman with a failing beehive hairdo. Smiled. 'Sit down, be right over.'

Abrahams carefully leant his sign against the plastic-covered bench seats, dug in his wee bag of pamphlets and handed them one each. Red capital letters on the front. As big as they could get and still fit on the page.

THE CONSPIRACY TO STOP THE PRACTICE OF LOBOTOMY AND ITS DETRIMENTAL EFFECT ON THE MENTAL HEALTH OF THIS COUNTRY BY DR GEORGE ABRAHAMS MRCPsych

McCoy looked at it, flicked through a few pages. More red capitals, diagrams of brains. More exclamation marks.

'Print this up yourself, did ye?' he asked.

Abrahams nodded. 'I had to.'

'That's a shame,' said McCoy. 'There's a mistake on it.'

Abrahams looked doubtful. 'I don't think so. I proofread it myself. If there was a mistake I'm sure I would have noticed it. Maybe there's just some terms you are unfamiliar with?' He picked up the pamphlet, started flicking through. Looked up at them. 'Where is the mistake?'

McCoy took the pamphlet, closed it, tapped the front. 'Right there on the front cover.'

Abrahams stared at the front cover. 'I don't see any mistake.'

'No? It says you're a doctor. Not any more you're not.'

'Peas, hot orange for the Prof. Teas for you, lads. Sugar and milk's there on the table. You need anything else give me a shout.' They sat in silence as the man put the stuff down on the table, faffed about with the teaspoons and the serviettes. Waited for him to leave.

'What do you want?' asked Abrahams flatly.

McCoy took out his police warrant card. Put it on the table. 'No need for alarm, Mr Abrahams. Just a chat about your old pal, Kevin Connolly.'

'Kevin Connolly?' Abrahams looked blank. Or more accurately tried to look blank.

'Can't remember him? Funny that.' McCoy pulled the plate of hot peas towards himself. 'Sooner you remember who he is, sooner you can eat your peas and we'll be on our way.'

Abrahams looked defeated. 'He was my cellmate. After my trouble. In Barlinnie.'

'Your *trouble*?' said McCoy, smiling. 'That's a nice way of putting it. Not sure that's how the lassie's parents saw it but hey ho.'

Abrahams looked exasperated. 'If they only had the wisdom to see what benefits a lobotomy—'

McCoy held up his hand. 'Can it. You can keep that shite for your pamphlets. So, Connolly and your good self. How did that go? Two of you stuck in that wee cell twenty-three hours a day?'

Abrahams took off his glasses, started polishing one of the lenses on his serviette. 'It was difficult for me. Very difficult. Kevin Connolly was a psychopath.' He put his glasses back on, blinked a few times. 'I was a psychiatrist for almost twenty years, worked in institutions up and down the country, dealt with many men who had committed terrible, violent acts, and in those twenty years I can safely say he was the only real psychopath I ever met.'

He looked up at them, smiled weakly. 'A perfect specimen in some ways.'

'And you were locked in a cell with him,' said McCoy.

Abrahams nodded, tried to swallow. Took a drink of his hot orange. 'I wasn't sure I was going to get out of there alive. Not sure I slept properly for the three months he was in there with me.'

'Did he threaten you?' asked Wattie.

Abrahams shook his head. 'Quite the opposite. Was studiously polite. Read his books most of the day. Very fond of Sven Hassel. Gory books about

160

the war, concentration camps, that sort of thing. *True Detective* magazines.'

'How did you know he was a psychopath?' asked McCoy.

Abrahams took a packet of ten Regal out his pocket, took a nipped one out and lit it up, hand shaking as he held the match to it. 'I had never been to prison, I wasn't sure of the etiquette. One night we were in our bunks, after lights out. Was a scorching night, nobody could sleep. We were talking about all sorts, seemed to be in a good mood. I asked him what he had done to be in there.'

Abrahams looked at them again. He looked scared somehow, like he was frightened to even talk about Connolly. 'So he told me. In great and explicit detail. Then he told me all the other things he'd done that he hadn't been caught for.' He took another deep draw on the hot orange. 'The worst thing was that I could hear him masturbating as he told me.'

'Fuck,' said Wattie.

Abrahams smiled. 'Not quite what I was used to. After that I started to ask him questions from the Standard Test.'

'Standard Test?' asked McCoy.

He nodded. 'There are various ones, all fairly similar. It's just a standard set of wide-ranging statements, the patient answers yes or no to each question. It helps determine a diagnosis.'

'What kind of statements?' asked McCoy.

'Let me think, I'm a little rusty these days.' He paused for a minute, remembered. '*Evil spirits possess me at times. I have nightmares every few nights. My sleep is fitful and disturbed.*' He smiled. 'One you'll like: *I enjoy detective or mystery stories.*'

'How did he react to the test?' asked McCoy.

'I didn't ask him the questions directly, was too frightened he would know what I was up to and react badly. A couple of questions a day, maybe, in passing conversation. Disguised.'

'How? asked McCoy.

'Well, I wouldn't ask, "Are you easily awakened by noise?" I'd say, "Did you hear the noise last night? Think someone was banging the doors?" That sort of thing. Didn't take too many questions to prove what I already knew.' He shrugged. 'That he was a psychopath.'

'You ever seen him since?' asked McCoy.

Abrahams shook his head. 'Thankfully not.'

'Any idea where he would be?'

He shook his head again. 'No idea. If I were to guess I'd say back in prison. Or dead by his own hand.'

McCoy pushed the dish of peas back towards Abrahams and they stood up to go.

'Any chance he contacts you, let us know.'

Abrahams nodded. Picked the two pamphlets up off the table, held them out. 'You've forgotten your pamphlets. If you wish some more for your colleagues there's an address on the back.'

162

CHAPTER 14

The rain was still on when McCoy left the shop. To his amazement, Mary had actually called him. Maybe their night together hadn't been that bad after all, or more likely he was kidding himself and she just wanted to trade. After all, it was one drunken night a few years ago, hardly the romance of the century. To be honest, it was hard to remember how their night had gone, the two of them were so drunk and stoned. Still. He checked his watch. Was running early so he stepped into the Red Lion in West Nile Street for one. Hair of yesterday's dog.

The smoky wee pub was mobbed, mostly men propping up the bar and a group of women from the wet fish shop across the road in one corner. Were always in here after work, all perms and clouds of Capstan. He stood at the bar and ordered a Tennent's, took his damp coat off, shook it and put it up on the bar. Went to pay the barman and found the pamphlet in his pocket. Funny wee guy, that Abrahams. Had to have been something at one time, psychiatrist at Ninewells in Dundee; now he was reduced to wandering the streets with a

163

sign telling the world lobotomies were a good thing.

His auntie had had one. Auntie Mary, his dad's oldest sister. Been in and out of mental hospitals for years then she came home for the weekend with a big smile on her face. Didn't have a fucking clue where she was or what was going on but didn't seem to mind. Maybe Abrahams was right. Maybe someone like her was happier with the operation after all.

Maybe Joe Brady would have been better with one. Maybe then he wouldn't have hung himself. Maybe he'd have been better off not able to remember anything. The priest at Hopehill Road was right, he knew exactly what Joe had told him in the confession box. He knew because he could still remember them all, each and every one. Uncle Kenny, Father Trent, Mr Just-Call-Me-Daddy, all those fuckers who used to turn up at the home. Smiling, giving you sweeties, asking if you wanted a ride in their big posh car. Made you wonder how many other kids had turned out like Joe, too damaged by what happened to go on any longer.

Boys like him and Stevie. Taken from 'unsafe families' they used to say. Placed into care for their own protection. Wasn't even ironic, it was just horrible. And he couldn't deny it, knew it wasn't really going to change anything, but he was really going to enjoy kicking fuck out of dear old Uncle Kenny. Kicking the fat fucker until he was bleeding and crying and pleading for mercy. Just like he had been.

Smell of wet fish and cigarette smoke alerted him that one of the fish-shop women had nudged in beside him at the bar.

'What's up with you, son?' She was peering at him through blue cat's eye glasses. 'Look like you've seen a ghost.'

He smiled at her. Told her he was fine, just thinking. She nodded, held up her glass. 'Have a whisky. It'll help. Good for the brain.'

He bought her one, bought himself one too. They clinked glasses and chucked them back. She said thanks, made her way back through the crowd towards their corner. Sweetheart Stout tin tray covered in port and sherry glasses held out in front of her, Capstan hanging out her mouth.

In a way she was right. He had seen a ghost. Just wasn't quite sure who it was. He looked at himself in the mirror above the gantry. Him or Joe Brady or Uncle Kenny? Knew thinking about this stuff wasn't going to do him any good so he finished his pint, put his coat on. Time to do his real job, try and find out what the fuck was going on with Elaine Scobie and Kevin Connolly.

McCoy nodded at the doorman in his peaked cap and uniform as he held the door of Rogano's open for him. Tried not to feel the man was looking down on him. After all, he had a suit, a tie and an overcoat on, problem was they weren't the right ones. Not expensive enough. Rogano's was the kind of place Archie Lomax and his chums frequented. Lawyers and businessmen who had gone to the same schools and same universities, were members of the same golf clubs and lodges. Not people like him who had grown up in care and still bought their clothes in the Burton's sale.

He left his coat in the cloakroom at the door, smoothed himself down and wandered into the front bar. Rogano's had been built in the '30s and hadn't changed since. It was like stepping aboard an art deco ocean liner, all bird's eye maple and flowing lines. He squeezed into the bar beside an advocate he recognised from the High Court and ordered a whisky and water. He really wanted a beer but he wasn't sure if they sold it and he wasn't going to ask. He'd just recovered from what the drink cost and put the glass to his lips, when he heard her.

'Harry McCoy? What are you doing here?'

He turned to see Mary and Elaine sitting in a dimly lit booth, bottle of red wine on the table in front of them. Elaine was dressed to kill, black dress with low neckline, hair slicked back. Mary seemed to be wearing some sort of American baseball jacket and a cloth cap. He walked over.

'Mary, Miss Scobie. Small world.'

'Sure is,' said Mary. 'I didn't know you two knew each other?'

'We don't,' said Elaine. 'He interviewed me this morning.'

McCoy waited for the invitation to sit down that didn't come. 'Okay then,' he said. 'I'll be off, I just dropped in for a nightcap.'

'That a habit of yours, Mr McCoy?' said Elaine, taking a cigarette from Mary's packet on the table and lighting up. 'A nightcap at Rogano's?'

'Now and then,' he said.

Elaine inhaled, then blew out a long stream of smoke. 'Really? You do surprise me.'

McCoy went to walk away and she sighed theatrically. 'Sit down, Mr McCoy,' she said. 'If you've gone to all the trouble arranging this farce you may as well stay for a drink.'

They shuffled along and McCoy eased himself into the booth. Elaine poured him a glass from the bottle. He could smell her perfume, no idea what it was but it smelt expensive.

She looked at them both. 'You in on this, were you, Mary?'

Mary snorted. 'You're joking, aren't you? I've had enough of this one to last me a lifetime.'

Elaine took a sip of her drink, sat back against the banquette, totally in control of the situation. Pretended to think, drummed her fingers on her chin.

'Okay, let me see if I've got this right. You, Mr McCoy, turn up out the blue and I fall for your, frankly, non-existent charms, ignore the fact that I have no lawyer present and start talking to you about Charlie, Connolly and my father until I'm blue in the face. That about it?'

'Well . . .' said McCoy.

'Exactly how stupid do you think I am?'

'Not stupid enough to fall for it, apparently.'

Elaine smiled and raised her glass. 'Touché.'

They clinked glasses then Elaine leant in towards him, blue eyes staring into his. 'Now, no offence, Mr McCoy, but why don't you just fuck off and think yourself lucky I'm not on the phone to Lomax and your superiors already.'

McCoy sat back, swallowed the rest of his wine. She'd had her fun but now he was starting to get tired of Elaine Scobie and her superior attitude, really fucking tired. He smiled at her.

'I tell you what, Miss Scobie, before I go, why don't you ask yourself this question? Why am I bothering hanging round this jumped-up shithole trying to talk to you while you act like I'm the fucking shite beneath your shoe? One reason. One reason I'm here and one reason I'm bothering. Kevin Connolly is a psychopath. He shot your boyfriend, but not before he'd beaten him all over the roof of a fucking skyscraper, took pictures while he was doing it so he could have a good wank over them afterwards—'

'McCoy!' said Mary. 'Fuck sake!'

'What? Oh, sorry. Am I putting you off your drinks? Nice expensive red wine and all. Well, I'm sorry about that, but Connolly's out of control and the chances are the next person he'll come after is you. That's the only reason I'm here. Let us get you into protective custody for a few days until we catch the bastard. Is that really such a stupid idea?'

Elaine looked at him. The smirk was gone, face

was white, bottom lip trembling. 'If you're still here in two minutes, I'm calling Lomax.'

McCoy stood up, shrugged. 'Fair enough. I tried. It's your funeral.'

He stood in Rogano's doorway and lit up. Felt a bit of an arse, his great plan come to nothing. Rain was off but the wind was up. His dad always said he could smell snow coming, something to do with his sinuses. Maybe McCoy had inherited it, was pretty sure there would be snow in the morning. Air had that icy feel in the back of his throat.

The door behind him opened and Elaine appeared. Black fur coat draped over her shoulders.

'Looking to call Lomax?' McCoy asked. 'There's a phone box corner of Buchanan Street and Gordon Street. Knock yourself out.'

'I'm not looking for a phone box,' she said. 'I want to talk to you without Mary listening in. Is there somewhere we can go?'

They walked round to the Horseshoe. Wasn't a bar McCoy liked, too big, too full of arseholes and loudmouths, but it was the nearest one he could think of. He held the door open for Elaine and they went in. As usual it was mobbed. He pushed through the crowd and found them a wee table at the side of the long bar. Elaine looked round at the sea of ruddy-faced drinkers bundled in their coats, at the old men huddled over their pints and roll-ups and sat down. By the look on her face it didn't seem to be the kind of place she liked either. She took her coat off, laid it across her knees.

'Be back in a minute,' said McCoy. He nodded down at her coat. 'I'd keep a tight hold on that if I was you.'

He pushed into the bar, ignoring the tuts and curses, and ordered two whiskies and a pint. Brought them over. 'Didn't think you'd want to risk the red wine in here,' he said, putting the whisky down in front of her.

Elaine picked it up and took a sip. Grimaced. Looked at him. 'You're wrong.'

McCoy pulled out the stool and sat down, took a pull on his pint.

'About the red wine? Everything in general?'

'About Connolly,' she said.

'Don't think so,' he said. 'Fucker clattered me with a chair this morning. Left a hotel room full of bottles of his own piss and shite. He's not a well man.'

'He would never hurt me,' she said.

McCoy shook his head. 'There's no way you can know that. He's not the man you knew. Way he's acting seems like the wheels have come off. Right bloody off.'

'I do know,' she said.

Sounded like she was trying to keep herself in check, not get angry. Not used to being disagreed with.

'He blamed Charlie for it all, only Charlie, for turning my head, for taking me away from him.

As far as Connolly's concerned I'm the innocent one. I've done nothing he's angry about.' She took another sip of her drink. 'Anyway, that's not really why I'm here. I need to talk to you about my dad.'

'Oh aye,' said McCoy, raising his eyebrows. 'Fire away.'

Bell rang, shout for last orders. Most of the customers got up and made for the bar. McCoy looked at Elaine expectantly but she shook her head.

'Connolly hates the fact my dad likes . . .' she stumbled. 'That he liked Charlie, worshipped him, in fact.' She smiled. 'Sometimes I think he liked Charlie more than he liked me. The son and heir he never had.'

She pushed a strand of hair back over her ear. 'My mum couldn't have any more kids after me. My dad tried to be good about it, but you could tell he missed having a son. If I'd been a boy I would have . . .' She thought, searched for the right phrase. 'Would have carried on his business, if you understand what I mean. But instead I got a shop full of pretty wee things and an expense account at Fraser's. I was just a lassie.'

McCoy shook his head. 'Even you don't believe that. Don't think anyone would ever call you "just a lassie".'

She looked at him. Smiled. 'Are you trying to flirt with me, Mr McCoy?'

'Are you fishing for compliments, Miss Scobie?'

She grinned. 'Maybe Lomax was right about you

after all. He thinks you're bright, the coming man, as they say.'

'Great. Been waiting my whole life for a recommendation from Archie bloody Lomax. Your dad?'

'Sorry. When Charlie came on the scene, Connolly got pushed to the side, became an employee again, instead of one of the family.' She took out a packet of cigarettes, the box opened like a tray, revealing black cigarettes. She lit one up. 'I think that's what sent him over the edge. He lost his place in the family, in the hierarchy. When he got someone to go for Charlie's leg, that was the final straw. After that Dad fired him.'

'Fired him?' asked McCoy.

Elaine nodded. 'Connolly's worked for my father since he was a teenager. He's never done anything else in his life. Then suddenly he's out in the cold. No job, no family, no nothing. If there's anyone Connolly's angry at, it's my dad. That's who you need to be looking out for.'

McCoy laughed. 'Come on. If there's anyone who can look after himself, it's your dad. Believe me, he was happily effing and blinding at me this morning for a start.'

'I don't think he can. Not any more.' She hesitated, trying to decide whether to say it or not. 'He's been diagnosed with lung cancer.'

McCoy made himself look surprised. 'What?'

'Lung cancer. They want to operate in a couple of weeks. He's in his late sixties, scared. Not what he was.'

'Maybe so, but he's still Jake Scobie,' said McCoy.

She shook her head. 'No, he's not . . . not the way you mean.'

Bell rang again. Fat bloke in a white short-sleeved shirt behind the bar started shouting, 'On your way!' Crowd started grumbling, finishing off their pints, heading for the doors.

McCoy tried to be reasonable. 'Look, even if he's not what he was, he's got protection, heavies, his boys with him all the time.'

'That's the trouble. That's all they are, boys and thugs. That's all he's got now Connolly's gone.' She drained the last of her whisky. 'People think Connolly's a thug, that he just did my dad's dirty work, but he's more than that. Connolly's clever, cleverer than anyone thinks. If he wants to get to my dad, he will. Can you just get some police to watch him? Follow him? Make sure he's okay?'

'Put a protective tail on Jake Scobie? Are you joking? After his performance this afternoon? You really think my boss is going to approve that?' said McCoy.

Eyes flashed, voice got steelier. 'Fine. So you just wait, let Connolly get to him? Saves you police the trouble? That it? I might've bloody known.'

'That's not what I meant,' he said.

'Really? You sure? Jake Scobie out the picture, that not what the Glasgow Police have been wanting for years?'

'Look, if you're really worried about your father

173

then maybe we could have a word with the local boys, get them to—'

Elaine stood up. 'If you're not going to do anything, fine, but don't patronise me. For Christ's sake save me from that.'

'I wasn't trying to—'

'Thanks for the drink,' said Elaine, pulling her coat over her shoulders. 'And thanks for nothing.'

He watched her walk out the bar. She really did have a gift for the big dramatic exit. Sat there nursing his whisky. He'd fucked up tonight good and proper. No way Elaine was going to talk to them again now. Maybe he was off his game, out of practice after three weeks off. Not concentrating. Mind elsewhere. Too much Uncle Kenny and Joe Brady.

The pub door opened and a couple came in, snow on their coats. Barman told them no chance. Well, at least he was right about one thing. He had smelt the snow.

McCoy looked at the clock beside the bed. Half four. He sighed, got up reluctantly. Flat was freezing but he needed a pee. Badly. He'd found a couple of cans when he got in from the Horseshoe. Drunk them and tried to work out how they were going to get to Uncle Kenny without being caught. Was paying the price now.

He padded through to the bathroom. Soon realised why he was so cold. The back courts out the bathroom window were already thick with snow, big clumps of it coming down. He peed, flushed the toilet and walked back through to the bedroom. Put his socks and yesterday's shirt on before he got back into bed. Didn't help. Was still freezing.

At last I can see what I need to see. You. You turning the bath taps on. Pouring some coloured liquid in, frothing the water. I am already hard, straining at my trousers. I undo the belt buckle and they fall to the ground.

Now the skirt, now the blouse, and you stand in front of the mirror in bra and knickers. You look at yourself as you tie up your hair. I push my underwear down. I spit in my palm. I move closer to the windowpane as you take the bra off and I see your breasts and my hand is starting to move and I hear another groan from the thing in the bath, a groan of pain, makes it better.

My hand moves faster, urgent now. Another cry from the bath and I come in the sink, judder and groan. I lick the spunk from my fingers, wash the rest down the drain. You are in the bath now, hidden from my sight.

I have come once but I need to come again. I need to judder and spurt and think of you, Elaine, and the puff of black hair between your legs. I turn to the thing in the bath. I grab its hair, pull the duct tape off its mouth, tell it if it makes a noise or screams or doesn't do exactly as I say I will kill it. It nods. I stick it in its mouth.

14TH FEBRUARY 1973

CHAPTER 15

Thomson was waiting for him on the Prince of Wales Bridge, silhouetted against the early morning sun, suit collar up, hands deep in pockets. He was pacing to and fro, trying to keep warm. McCoy trudged down the hill towards him, glad he'd thought to wear his wellies. He'd even found the horrible scarf his neighbour had got him for Christmas and wrapped it tight round his neck before he left his house. His flat was freezing, ice on the inside of the windows, as bad as being outside. He could only find one glove in the drawers, didn't seem worth the bother. He approached the cordon of uniforms, nodded at Big Gordy, who stepped aside to let him through.

'Welcome to the Winter Wonderland,' said Thomson.

The River Kelvin was the only streak of colour in all the white. The grey water was choppy, running fast about thirty feet below them. McCoy could hear a dog barking in the distance and the crackle of a police radio; other than that, nothing. The snow had silenced the city. Kelvingrove Park may as well have been in the bloody Highlands instead of the West End of Glasgow. The six acres of park in the West End were normally full of dog walkers, kids, people using it as a shortcut to get to work. Not today. Just the uniforms, the snow and Thomson standing watch on the bridge.

'Wattie come for you?' he asked as McCoy approached.

McCoy nodded. 'We had to leave the patrol car on Gibson Street and walk, couldn't get any closer. Cars abandoned everywhere. There's even a bus stuck at the bottom of the hill, can't get up, keeps slipping down. Chaos.' McCoy looked at him again. 'You not got a coat?'

Thomson looked miffed. 'I left the bloody thing up in Dundee when I was visiting the weans.'

'Arse. How's that going anyway?'

'Great,' said Thomson glumly. 'Don't know what's worse, the fact they're getting on with Bob or the fact I can't help myself being angry about it. Still, as long as they don't start supporting Dundee United I can live with it.' He put his fingers in his mouth, tried to suck some feeling into them, nodded upriver. 'If you peer over you can see him.'

McCoy brushed the snow off the stone balustrade and leant over. Looked down. Couldn't see anything, just the grey water. 'Where?'

Thomson leant in beside him and pointed. 'There, about twenty yards up the river.'

He was pointing at a little island of rocks and branches in the centre of the current. The man's body must have drifted downriver and got caught up in it. His top half was out the water, propped up on the island, bottom half still in the river, water eddying and swirling around him. The body was naked, pure white in the cold. His right arm was bent behind him at an impossible angle, an angle that could only mean the bone was broken.

'The parkie saw him this morning, called it in about six,' said Thomson.

McCoy looked around. 'Is Murray no here?' he asked.

Thomson shook his head. 'On his way from Jordanhill. It's taken him an hour to get as far as the Crow Road. I wouldn't hold your breath.'

Wattie appeared through the row of uniforms, woolly bunnet, big anorak, carefully carrying three paper cups of Bovril, trying not to slip in the snow. He put them down on the bridge wall, cursing as one overflowed and burned his hand. McCoy took one. He never drank Bovril but it was hot. How bad could it be? He sipped it and found out. Grimaced.

'They no have any tea?' he asked.

'Fuck off,' said Wattie, sucking his fingers. 'Was hard enough getting that.'

'Fair enough,' said McCoy.

Thomson kept pacing back and forward, trying to stay warm. 'The problem we've got is we can't get him out the bloody river. The divers can't get here for another few hours, called out to some capsized boat in Leith last night. They're still on their way back.'

'What about the River Police?' McCoy asked.

'They only cover the bloody Clyde, so the cunt of a sergeant took great delight in telling me this morning.' He rubbed his hands together and stuffed them in his pockets. 'I've closed the park but I don't know what else we can do but wait.'

McCoy squinted in the sun and sipped the horrible Bovril. 'Anyone reported missing this morning?'

Wattie shook his head. 'I checked, but it's chaos. Traffic accidents, people stuck in their cars, phone lines down. There's a good chance nobody's even noticed he's missing yet.'

'Who is he?' McCoy asked. 'Any ideas?'

Thomson shrugged. 'Fuck knows. Can't really see his face from up here.'

They all peered over the bridge to look. Wattie seemed to have the best eyesight. 'Dark hair, looks old, about sixty-odd. He's got a scar, I think, a scar across his cheek. Looks like someone's taken a razor to him.'

'Great,' said Thomson. 'All this for some fucking hard man—'

'What side's it on?' asked McCoy.

Wattie squinted again. 'Left.'

McCoy peered harder. Sinking feeling in his stomach. He couldn't be sure, eyesight wasn't what it was, but somehow he knew.

'I think it might be Jake Scobie,' he said.

'Eh?' said Thomson. He looked closer. 'You know what? You might be right. It does look a bit like him.'

McCoy kicked at the pile of snow by the wall. 'Fuck!'

'What's up wi you?' asked Wattie.

'She told me last night, said she was worried about him. I thought she was talking shite.'

'Who did?' asked Wattie, sounding exasperated.

'Elaine Scobie,' said McCoy. 'Fuck!' He kicked the snow again.

'Fuck sake! Calm it! Are you sure it's definitely him?' asked Wattie.

They all leant over the bridge as far as they could.

'Look at his face,' said McCoy. 'I'd recognise that scar anywhere.' He pointed. 'It's him all right, look at his—'

And then Scobie opened his eyes.

McCoy dropped his cup of Bovril into the river. Thomson started swearing and Wattie started running.

Thomson found his radio, started barking into it, calling for an ambulance. Wattie ran along the bridge, vaulted the fence by the walkway and started climbing down to the riverbank, pushing his way through the rhododendron bushes and long grass, snow flying everywhere.

'Where the fuck's he going?' asked Thomson as his radio started squawking.

McCoy shook his head. 'Christ only knows, maybe just trying to get a closer look.' Then it hit him. 'Oh fuck. He's not going in, is he?'

Wattie had reached the river's edge now and was bent over, unlacing his shoes.

Thomson looked horrified. 'For fuck sake, the stupid arse's gonnae drown himself.'

They started running along the bridge, desperately trying not to slip, and down onto the bank. Thomson was ahead, pushing his way through the bushes. Snow going all over them. By the time they got down to the bank Wattie had stripped down to his trousers, vest and socks. Now he was this close, McCoy could see how fast the river was going, swollen with snowmelt, how dangerous it looked.

Thomson grabbed Wattie's arm. 'No way! And that's a bloody order. You'll drown or you'll freeze. We have to wait. It's not safe.'

McCoy was bent over, hands on knees, trying to catch his breath. 'C'mon, Wattie, don't be stupid. It's too bloody dangerous.'

Wattie pulled the vest over his head and started undoing his belt. 'He's still alive. It's worth trying. Can either of you two swim?'

Thomson looked sheepish and shook his head.

'I can,' said McCoy. 'But that's not the point, the water's too fast—'

'I swam for the county. I've got a lifesaver's badge. I did five miles in the fucking sea off Arran!' He looked at Thomson and McCoy. 'You can't swim and you're just back after being battered to fuck. It's me or it's nobody. What's it going to be?'

Thomson looked at McCoy. McCoy looked at Thomson. Neither of them knew what to say.

Wattie looked back and forward at them. 'For fuck sake! Come on! Make a bloody decision!'

'You sure you can do it?' asked Thomson.

'I'm sure!' said Wattie. And standing there he looked like he could. Big shoulder and arm muscles, broad chest.

Thomson nodded his head. 'Okay. Go.'

Wattie pushed his trousers down, peeled his socks off and started wading into the icy water in his skivvies.

'Don't do anything fucking stupid,' McCoy shouted.

'Don't worry about me, just get the ambulance,' Wattie shouted back.

McCoy took out his cigarettes, couldn't find his matches. Thomson got out his lighter and held it to McCoy's cigarette then his own. 'I can't fucking believe this.' Thomson turned to McCoy. 'What should I have told him?'

'He wanted to go. He's got the best chance of any of us. You did the right thing,' McCoy said, not sure he believed it.

Wattie was chest-deep now. On the opposite bank a fox was watching them, sniffing the air. Wattie took a deep breath and dived under the water, re-emerged a few yards upstream and started to do the crawl towards the island of rock and branches where Scobie was caught up.

He was battling hard but he didn't seem to be making much progress; every time he made some headway towards the island the current pushed him back. He stopped for a minute, treading water, looking round to get his bearings. Before he could start swimming forward again the current seemed to overcome him and his head went under, the water carrying him away from the island and down under the bridge they'd been standing on.

'Fuck sake!' Thomson was running back and forward on the bank, trying to spot him in the fast-moving water. 'Can you see him? Christ! All this for Jake fucking Scobie!'

McCoy scanned the water. No luck. All he could see was browny-grey water and the occasional branch caught in the current. The uniforms on the bridge started shouting. He looked up. They were hanging over the bridge, pointing down beneath them.

Wattie was hanging on to the edge of the bridge. He looked frozen, his face and shoulders pale against the stone, lips blue.

Thomson splashed into the river, shouting at the top of his voice, trying to make himself heard above the rushing river. 'Stay there, Wattie! Don't fucking move! We'll come to you!'

He turned back to McCoy, his voice full of panic. 'Can he hear me?'

'I think so.'

McCoy didn't know whether he heard him or not, but the next thing he knew Wattie'd taken a deep breath and pushed himself off from the bridge, swimming back upriver towards Scobie. McCoy groaned and Thomson started swearing.

Wattie stopped, treading water again, head swivelling from side to side, trying to gauge how far he was from Scobie. The current started pulling him back but he was swimming hard against it, slowly getting nearer and nearer to the island.

McCoy was muttering under his breath, 'Come on, Wattie, come on.' Felt sick in his stomach, wished he hadn't let him go in.

A last push and Wattie managed to get level, grabbed onto one of the branches and pulled himself up next to Scobie's broken body.

The uniforms on the bridge started clapping and hollering. Thomson grabbed McCoy, hugged him and they started jumping up and down.

'He did it! He fucking did it!'

Wattie lay on the little island panting, exhausted. He leant over, stuck his hand into Scobie's mouth and scooped out some dirt and leaves. Scobie started coughing, spluttered, vomited up a gush of river water.

'He's alive!' Wattie shouted.

'Stay there!' shouted McCoy. 'Stay there, Wattie! Don't move! We'll get a rope! We'll get you out!'

Wattie raised a tired hand in acknowledgement and then he did the one thing McCoy hoped he wouldn't. He cupped Scobie under his chin, let go of the branch, and they both slipped back into the river.

'No!' shouted Thomson, voice echoing round the silent park. 'I'm going to kill him. I'm going to fucking kill him! Can he no fucking listen?' He was stabbing at the buttons on his radio, trying to get reception. 'I swear the minute he gets out the fucking water he's dead.'

Wattie was trying to swim back towards the bank, holding Scobie's head on his chest, keeping it free of the water. Scobie's head was lolling from side to side, eyes glassy, it didn't look like he even knew what was going on.

Wattie just looked exhausted, face contorted with the strain of trying to hold Scobie's head above the water while fighting the current. He was shouting something but McCoy couldn't make it out above the rush of the water.

'What?' shouted McCoy 'What?' He grabbed at Thomson. 'What is it? What's he saying?'

Thomson turned to him, his face gone white. 'He's saying he can't hold on any longer.'

McCoy let out a moan. 'For fuck sake! Can't we do something?'

Thomson stood there, suit soaking, looking at the water, useless radio in his hand. 'I don't know what to do, Harry,' he said quietly. 'I don't know what to do. I let him go, I shouldn't have fucking let him go.'

McCoy ran into the water, cold hitting him, shouting at Wattie to hold on. Wattie was having difficulty keeping his head up; he dipped under the water once but he came back up.

'Just hold on, Wattie!' McCoy shouted. 'Just hold on!'

And then he went under again.

McCoy scanned the river, tried to run towards the bridge and fell into the icy water. He got back up, spluttering, shock of the cold, looking for

Wattie's head to bob back up, for his big stupid face and dirty blond hair to appear out of the water, but it didn't.

He stopped running and just stood in the freezing water, concentrating hard on spotting him. He waited and waited, praying under his breath, but Wattie's head didn't reappear.

A shout from the bridge and McCoy looked up. Big Gordy was pointing down, over towards the far bank. McCoy caught sight of Wattie and Scobie spinning round in the current, half submerged in the muddy water. Scobie drifted free, Wattie's grip must have gone.

'Wattie! Wattie! Get out the water! Leave him!' he shouted.

He thought he saw Wattie nod, and then the water closed over his head.

'Wattie!' he screamed. 'Wattie!'

He could hear a distant siren, saw the fox turn and disappear into the bushes. Stood there and watched as the river swept the two bodies under the bridge, down the river and out of sight.

The uniforms up on the bridge weren't hollering or clapping any more, just staring at the river where Wattie had gone under. McCoy trudged out of the water, got up onto the bank. Thomson was sitting on an upturned tree trunk, head in hands.

'I fucking told him. You heard me, Harry, I fucking told him not to go in.'

McCoy sat down beside him, put his arm round his shoulders. Couldn't believe what had just happened. Ten minutes earlier, the stupid bugger had been handing him a cup of Bovril and now he was gone. By rights McCoy should have been freezing, but he couldn't feel anything. He patted Thomson's back.

'C'mon, Thomson, there was nothing we could do. You tried your best. He was determined to go.'

'I shouldn't have let him, I shouldn't have let him go. I shouldn't . . .'

Thomson wiped at his eyes with the sleeve of his suit. They sat there for a couple of minutes, Thomson telling himself everything he'd done wrong, McCoy telling him he'd done all he could. The radio crackled into life. Murray was here.

McCoy stood up and wandered over to the bank to see if he could see him up on the bridge. His foot hit against something: Wattie's clothes. Even in the rush to get in the water, he'd left them in a neat pile on the bank. There was a watch sitting on the top. He leant over and picked it up. It was nothing special, a Timex with a worn leather strap. There was an engraving on the back: *Congratulations on graduating from the Academy. Love Mum and Dad.*

McCoy put it in his pocket and picked up the bundle of clothes, turned back to Thomson. 'C'mon, pal, we can't do anything here.'

They walked up the bank, back towards the path, the spinning blue light of the ambulance and the fact that Wattie was gone.

Murray was standing on the bridge waiting for

them. 'Came over the radio. Boys on the next bridge say they saw two bodies float past.'

McCoy looked at him. Somehow Murray saying it, knowing it, made it real.

'Maybe he's okay?' McCoy said. 'Just floating, too tired to swim.'

'How long's he been in the water?' asked Murray.

McCoy tried to think.

'About fifteen minutes now,' said Thomson. 'Twenty maybe.'

'That's too long,' said Murray. 'The water's just above freezing.'

'Christ,' said McCoy. 'It's Glasgow! We're in Glasgow. It doesn't make any sense.'

Thomson had walked off to the side, was crying quietly.

'Is that his clothes?' asked Murray.

McCoy nodded. 'And his watch. His mum and dad gave it to him. Inscription on the back.'

Murray took it off him, read the back. 'What a stupid fucking waste of a life.'

McCoy walked over to the side of the bridge, looked down at the water below. Was only starting to sink in now. Heard a radio calling in. Bodies had been spotted at the bridge by the art galleries. He looked over at Murray.

Murray nodded at him. 'Come on.'

McCoy followed him over the bridge.

CHAPTER 16

'Things people'll do to get in the paper.' McCoy held up a copy of the *Evening Times* he'd bought from the paperboy outside the hospital.

HERO COP SAVES DROWNING MAN

Wattie sat up in the bed and grinned. He'd been given a private room when they brought him into the Western. Him being a hero after all, he was getting the star treatment. He looked exhausted, still pale, but he was grinning, not that far from his usual self.

'I look like a right arse in the picture,' he said.

McCoy turned the paper round. 'Hate to break it to you but that's what you always look like.' He sat down on the chair by the bed.

'I heard you waded in after me,' said Wattie.

'I waded in to get close enough to tell you to stop being an arse, and then I tripped. You owe me for a new suit. How d'you feel anyway?'

'No too bad.' He rubbed at a couple of stitches above his eyebrow. 'Big Gordy did this when he

192

pulled me into the boat, banged my bloody head off the side.'

'Looks good, though,' said McCoy.

'Does it?'

'Aye, makes you look like a right hard bastard.'

Wattie grinned. 'That's a result then. I got a jag in my arse for tetanus and had to drink some horrible thing because of the river water, but other than that I feel okay. Finally warming up. They want me to stay here until the morning, get some rest. As long as I feel okay in the morning they said they'd let me out.'

McCoy poured himself a glass of Wattie's Lucozade and lit a cigarette. 'Murray's put you in for a gallantry medal. Thomson recommended it.'

Wattie grinned. 'Did he? My mum and dad will be pleased.'

McCoy shook his head. 'Fuck your mum and dad. Tell one of the wee nurses in here. You're a real-life hero, with that and the hard man stitches? Her knickers'll be off in a flash.'

The uniforms had picked up the two of them about a quarter of a mile down the river, just past the Kelvin Hall. They'd been swept into a wee pool by the Dunaskin Mill. Wattie was fine. Cold and exhausted, but nothing that couldn't be fixed.

'I thought you were bloody dead, you know. We all did,' said McCoy.

'Did you really?'

'Yep.'

Wattie sat himself up in the bed, grimacing a

bit. 'I just did what I was supposed to. Stopped swimming, conserved my energy, floated until I could see a bit of the bank I could get up on but Gordy got me first.'

'Aye well, don't ever go in a bloody river again. Hear me?'

Wattie saluted. 'How's Scobie?'

McCoy sighed. 'Not good, not expected to come round. You did all you could do, more than anyone could expect.'

Wattie looked crestfallen. 'Wasn't really worth it, though, was it?'

'Don't do yourself down. It was worth it, more than worth it. For all Connolly knows, he's sitting up in bed telling us all about it.' McCoy pointed at the paper. 'Soon as he picks that up this afternoon he's going to be shiteing himself, wondering what Scobie managed to tell us, waiting for the knock. We're not going to let him think anything different. We'll tell the press we interviewed him before he died.'

'Think it'll work?' asked Wattie.

'Hope so. If he gets worried he's more likely to make a mistake, more likely to get caught. That's our best hope.'

'Why'd he put him in the water?'

McCoy shrugged. 'Who knows why that psycho does anything? Maybe it means something, maybe he just—'

'Fuck me, McCoy. Are you following me around like a bad bloody smell?'

194

McCoy turned. Mary from the *Record* was standing in the doorway with a brown paper bag of grapes in one hand, bottle of Irn-Bru in the other. She dumped both on the bed, held out her hand for Wattie to shake.

'Mary Webster, chief features writer on the *Daily Record*.' She looked him up and down. 'You must be the hero.'

Wattie shook her hand, looked somewhat bewildered.

'*Record* sent me to do an interview for the front page tomorrow, all cleared with the top brass. They like the idea of a polis acting like a good guy for once.' She sniffed. 'Makes a change from a polis acting like an untrustworthy two-timing piece of shite who never phones back.'

She sat on the bed, peered at Wattie again, turned to McCoy. 'You didn't tell me the new boy was a looker. Gonnae have to get the smudger up here to take a few snaps, scar looks good.'

'Do I get a choice?' asked Wattie.

'Yes,' said McCoy, just as Mary said, 'No.'

'You can say no, Wattie,' said McCoy.

'No, you bloody can't,' said Mary. 'Not unless you want the Chief Superintendent and my editor up your arse, you can't, so why don't you sit there and have a wee think about the exciting story you're going to tell me while this waste of space and I go and have a wee cigarette. You single, Wattie?'

'Er, yes,' said Wattie, blushing.

'Excellent!' said Mary. She let her hand accidentally fall onto his crotch, had a wee feel.

Wattie froze.

'Just like to check the goods before I commit
myself.' She smiled. 'Feels fine to me, more than
fine. I like a big man to roll me about a bit, no
some worn-out sub-alkie with an attitude problem.
Speaking of which, McCoy, shall we?'

They left Wattie looking puzzled and vaguely
scared, and stepped out into the corridor and
lit up.

'Play nice,' said McCoy. 'He's a bit green.'

'When I need your advice I'll ask for it. He
downstairs?'

'Who?' asked McCoy.

She looked at him. 'Give me a fucking break,
McCoy. It's Jake Scobie, isn't it?'

Didn't seem much point lying, news would be
out there soon if it wasn't already. He nodded.

'Same guy as Charlie Jackson?' she asked.

'Looks like it.'

Mary exhaled, shook her head. 'Elaine's a pain
in the arse but you wouldn't wish that on anyone.
Your fiancé and your dad murdered in the same
week. What the fuck did she do to Connolly?'

'Nothing according to her. Pure as the driven
snow.'

Mary snorted. 'About as pure as my Aunt Fanny.'

'Do you have any proof, Miss Webster?'

'Nope,' she said, blowing a cloud of smoke in
McCoy's direction. 'But she sure as hell wasn't all

196

dressed up last night just to have a drink with me in Rogano's. Managed to fuck that up, didn't you?'

McCoy shrugged. 'Maybe I'm just not her type.'

Mary snorted. 'You're no anybody's type, believe me, not unless they're drunk and desperate. So, what are you going to tell me about Jake Scobie that no one else knows so I can bump your pal off the front page and lead with a decent story?'

'Now why would I want to do that to poor Wattie in there?' said McCoy.

'Because if you do I'll keep an eye on the delightful Elaine and her phone calls and wee trips into town.'

'What trips are they?' he asked.

Mary didn't say anything, examined her nails, took a drag of her cigarette, looked at her watch.

'Okay, I'll bite. Jake had "cunt" carved into his stomach,' said McCoy.

She looked at him. 'I can't use that, as you well know. Family newspaper. Try again.'

'Connolly's not been named yet. I'll give you a picture, name him as chief suspect—'

'Like it—'

'*If* you let Wattie have his front page tomorrow. Hold it a day while I clear it with Murray.'

She looked at him, narrowed her eyes. 'You wouldn't be trying to fuck me about, would you, McCoy?'

'Thought I'd already done that,' he said.

She rolled her eyes, dropped her cigarette on the lino floor and stamped it out. 'Need the photo and the clearance by six p.m. tomorrow or so help me God, Harry, I'll—'

'You'll get it. Promise.'

She nodded, walked back into Wattie's room. 'Right, Wattie, you ready for me?'

Scobie was alive but only just. He'd knife wounds in his torso – one dangerously close to his heart – he'd lost a lot of blood, had hypothermia, been banged up badly in the fast-moving river. Apart from his broken arm, he'd a broken pelvis, a broken leg and numerous cuts and bruises. Hard to tell if they had been caused by him being battered off the rocks in the river or whether they had happened before he even went in. Unsurprisingly, the prognosis wasn't good. He was unconscious and not expected either to come round or survive.

McCoy had gone to see him before he came to see Wattie. He was lying in a bed in a quiet room two floors down, shallow breaths coming out in wheezes. His face was bruised, side of his head shaved, big line of stitches running down it. Two cotton pads on his eyes. The carved CUNT had been stitched up, black threads contrasting with his pale white skin. McCoy almost felt sorry for the poor bugger. Almost.

An elderly minister was sitting by him, holding his hand, Bible open on his lap, reciting under his breath. McCoy ignored him and sat down on the chair on the other side of the bed.

'Are you a relative?' the minister asked. He was looking over at McCoy expectantly.

McCoy shook his head. 'No.'

The door opened and a young doctor came in, looking like they usually do, like the captain of the rugby team with a side shed and a bad smell under his nose. McCoy held out his identity card and the doctor managed to look slightly less superior.

McCoy nodded to the door and they stepped outside, leaving the minister to it. They stood in the corridor, waited for a group of nurses to pass.

'Anything you can tell me?' McCoy asked.

He shook his head, spoke in an Edinburgh accent. 'I don't think he'll last much more than a few hours.'

'Any chance of him coming round?'

'I wouldn't think so.'

McCoy went to walk away.

'One thing, though,' said the doctor. 'Results of his blood tests came in early. Apart from everything else, he's full of Methaqualone.'

'Which is?' said McCoy.

'More commonly known as Mandrax,' he said.

CHAPTER 17

If you were sick and needed cheering up, the hospital canteen wasn't the place to go. Striplights in yellowing ceiling tiles, beige walls, old burgundy lino and various burnt offerings curling up under heat lamps. McCoy and Murray were sitting by the window, half-empty cups of tea in front of them, half-eaten pineapple cake in front of Murray.

Murray'd wanted to see Wattie so McCoy had stuck around until he turned up. Doctor'd told them he'd be out by the morning, no permanent damage done. Now the two of them were silent, glum, looking over at the far side of the room and the only other occupied table.

It was too far to hear anything but it wasn't hard to work out what was happening. The doctor approached the table looking serious, told them something. Elaine Scobie burst into tears and Lomax put his arm around her.

'Must have died,' said McCoy.

'Looks like it. Can't say I'm too sorry to hear it,' said Murray, sipping at his tea.

Elaine's sobs were becoming louder, or if McCoy

was being unkind, more theatrical. The woman behind the counter put down her cloth, crossed herself.

'We should go over there,' said Murray. 'Offer our condolences.'

'You should go over there,' said McCoy. 'I doubt she'll be happy to see me. She asked me last night to put a tail on her dad. She was worried about him being hurt.'

'Oh aye, and what did you say?' asked Murray.

'I told her where to go.'

'Quite right.'

Lomax had produced a hanky from his coat pocket and Elaine was wiping her eyes with it.

Murray stood up, drained his mug. 'Nothing ventured.'

McCoy sat back in his chair, watched the bulk of Murray weave between the Formica tables. He stood in front of Elaine and Lomax, started talking. Elaine looked at him with contempt and Lomax looked at him with something like pity. Elaine stood up, finger prodding Murray's chest, face full of fury. McCoy was glad he couldn't hear what she was saying; didn't need to, he could guess well enough. Murray stood there stoic, took it all while Lomax tried to quieten her down. She was having none of it, still prodding, still shouting.

And then she saw McCoy. Her eyes narrowed and she started walking towards him. Lomax grabbed at her but she got past him.

He stood up as she approached. 'I'm very sorry to hear about—'

Apology cut off by a slap across his face.

He stood there, face stinging.

'You may as well have killed him yourself. I told you, I fucking told you, and all you did was laugh at me.'

'I didn't laugh at—'

Another slap. McCoy took the decision to just ride it out, no point arguing.

'You told me I was stupid, that he wasn't in any danger. Have you seen him? Have you seen what that animal did to him? Have you?'

He nodded.

'And you still stand there telling me how sorry you are? You did this to him!'

She was spitting the words out now, tears and snot running from her nose. She drew her sleeve across it. 'I hope you have somewhere else to go, McCoy, because you're not going to be a detective much longer. Not after this, not after Lomax is done with you. Shame on you. Shame on you!'

And then she spat in his face.

He went to wipe it off and she did it again, eyes daring him to make her do it again. He stood there with her spit sliding down his cheek, watched her walk out the door, Lomax hurrying after her.

He sat down.

Murray appeared, handed him a serviette. 'Charming,' he said.

McCoy wiped at his face. 'She's kind of got a point.'

'No, she bloody hasn't,' said Murray. 'Jake Scobie reaped what he fucking sowed. I hope he died in agony. Things that animal has done to people he fucking deserved everything he got. And Madam has had her fun. I'm getting a bit tired of her routine now. We'll get her in tomorrow. That girl knows much more than she's letting on, and if Lomax says no we'll arrest her as an accessory, make sure the press knows all about it.'

McCoy looked up at him. 'You know something, Murray?'

Murray shook his head.

'I'm glad we're on the same fucking side.'

CHAPTER 18

'Mandrax.'

'What?' said Cooper, still peering down at the map on his knee.

'You sell it?' asked McCoy.

'Naw, hard to get a hold of and no that popular any more. No worth the bother. Why?'

'Where'd I get some?'

'Oh aye,' said Cooper, looking up. 'Fancy a big night, do you? You and that wee bird? She looked the type, mind you. Bit of a raver, I'd say.'

McCoy sighed, put the windscreen wipers back on. Snow had started falling again, thick flakes whirling in the light of the headlamps of the big Austin. 'Not for me. Where would Connolly get a hold of it? Scobie was full of it, and so was Charlie Jackson as it turns out. He must have given it to them before he . . . you know.'

'What? Carved them up?' Cooper pointed through the windscreen. 'Turn right at the next crossing.'

'Aye, you know what Mandrax is like, knocks you skelly. Would make them easier to control, less likely to resist.' He looked up ahead. 'Right? You sure? Sign says Strathblane is to the left.'

Cooper folded up the map, chucked it into the back seat. 'I don't fucking know. I cannae even drive. How the fuck would I know how to read a map?'

He leant forward, switched the radio on, twiddled the knob, looking for the football. Eventually found it. Heard the score. Swore. Switched it back off again.

'How many cars have you got?' asked McCoy.

'Besides this one?'

McCoy nodded.

'Two.'

'What? Three cars, and you can't even bloody drive?'

'Don't need to,' said Cooper. 'There's always some arse to drive me about.' He grinned, glanced at McCoy.

They were deep in the countryside now, hedges at the sides of the road, fields beyond white with snow, stretching off into the distance. Cooper looked out the window as they passed a sign for Helensburgh.

'Were we no in a place round here?' he asked.

'St Andrew's Home,' said McCoy, pointed left. 'It's about twenty miles that way, I think.'

The car was silent, just the noise of the wind-screen wipers. Cooper lit up. 'My front teeth got knocked out in that shithole. Was that the place with that cunt, Brother Benedict?'

McCoy nodded. 'I think Joe was in there too.'

'Was he? I cannae remember. Too many places

like that, too many cunts like Uncle Kenny and Brother Benedict. All started to blur together after a while. How much longer till we get there?'

'Ten minutes or so,' said McCoy. 'As long as this bloody snow doesn't get any worse.'

Strathblane was a pretty wee village, red sandstone houses, church on the left. Even prettier now with the snow making it look like a Christmas card. They drove up the high street, almost back out the other side. McCoy turned off, parked the car beside the back of a scout hall.

'You got the address?' asked Cooper.

'First right after Blainfield House. Not far, we should walk. Don't want anyone remembering the car.'

Cooper nodded. Reached round and picked up the Umbro sports bag sitting on the back seat, opened it and handed McCoy a balaclava and a thick woollen sock with two billiard balls in it. 'Put them in your pocket until we get to the house.'

Cooper did the same with his own set, put a length of clothes line in his pocket too. Turned to McCoy. 'Ready?'

McCoy nodded.

'Good. Let's go and get the cunt then.'

The village was silent, streets deserted under the falling snow. They caught a glimpse of an occasional TV through a window, football on. Looked like England's slaughter of Scotland was still going on. They walked in silence, both of them thinking about what they were about to do. McCoy had the feeling he was about to cross a line he shouldn't be crossing. Maybe he should have left it to Cooper – he wouldn't have minded doing it alone – but he'd let him do his dirty work too many times. He needed to be in on this one.

They walked past Blainfield House. The road was bordered by the long wall of an estate on one side, fields on the other. They turned right and walked up through a field towards the house, avoiding the driveway in case any safety lights came on. The house was a large stone villa, sloped roof running off to the side, smoke from a chimney snaking up into the cold air.

'Done well for himself has old Uncle Kenny,' said Cooper.

A TV was on in the front room, the glow visible through the thin curtains. Lights on in the hall, dining room and one of the upstairs bedrooms too.

'Listen to me,' said Cooper, suddenly serious, businesslike. 'We don't talk at all. If we have to, don't use our names. You get the wife tied up in the other room and I'll deal with Uncle Kenny until you come back. Right?'

McCoy nodded, tried not to think about how he was going to tie up some crying woman.

Cooper held up his sock with the balls in it. 'Try not to hit his head too much, these billiard balls can crack your fucking skull easy. Go for the joints. The knees, elbows, hit as hard as you can, it'll hurt like fuck. If you kick him, kick him in the balls and stomach. I'm going to break his fat greasy fingers one by bloody one. Okay?'

McCoy nodded again. Was starting to feel a bit sick. Reality of what they were doing kicking in. They put their gloves and their balaclavas on and headed down the hill towards the house. They were halfway down when McCoy stopped, held up his hand.

'What's that?' he asked, sure he could hear something.

'What?' said Cooper.

Lights suddenly illuminated the driveway and a car appeared round the corner.

'Fuck!' said McCoy, dragging Cooper to the ground.

As the car approached the house a middle-aged woman opened the door, peered out, then shouted back into the hall, 'Kenneth!'

The car pulled up, and they watched as the passenger door opened and a girl in her mid twenties got out. She'd a fur hat on, multicoloured scarf, long coat.

'Hello, Mum!'

The older woman embraced her, looked amazed. 'Caroline? What are you doing here?'

The shape of a man appeared in the doorway and McCoy's stomach did a flip. He was dressed in slacks, patterned jumper.

'Caroline?' he asked.

'It's us, Dad! Jamie got a few days off so we thought we'd surprise you.'

'Fuck,' said Cooper under his breath. 'Fuck.'

'Let me see if His Majesty is awake,' said Caroline, opening the back door as a man in a car coat and suit got out the driver's seat and embraced Uncle Kenny's wife.

Uncle Kenny padded round the car in his slippers in time to take the sleeping boy off Caroline as she lifted him out the back seat. He kissed the toddler on the top of his head, got his arm under his bum, laid his neck into his shoulder.

'Better get him in quick, Dad,' said Caroline. 'He's only got his jammies on.'

They watched as the car was unloaded, the lights went on all over the house and the snow started to fall again.

'No point waiting here,' said Cooper, pulling his balaclava off. 'Let's go.'

They walked back into town, found a pub that was open. Dirty look from the landlord as they ordered two whiskies. Not locals. Glasgow accents too pronounced. They sat down by the fire, tried to get some heat into their bones. McCoy could feel the weight of the billiard balls in his pocket.

'Did you know he had a daughter?' asked Cooper.

McCoy nodded. 'It's in the file. She lives in Yorkshire, didn't think it would matter.'

'Trust us to pick the bloody night she comes home for a surprise visit.' Cooper shook his head. 'Fuck it, just have to try again another night. We know where he lives, fucker's not going anywhere.'

'Did you see the way he picked up that wee boy?' asked McCoy.

Cooper nodded.

'That's the way he picked me up,' said McCoy. 'The night I had to fight Tommy Dunn. I was exhausted, I thought that was it, it was all over. I thought he was carrying me upstairs to put me to bed.'

'No point in going over it,' said Cooper. 'What's done's done. He's going to pay.'

'Let's do it fast,' said McCoy. He looked at Cooper. 'Before he has a chance with that wee boy.'

Cooper nodded. Threw over his whisky. 'I'll get you another one.'

There was a note pinned to Susan's door when he got back.

IN VICTORIA BAR WITH CLAIRE. COME JOIN!! XX

Just what he didn't need. He sighed, took the note off the door and put it in his pocket.

The Victoria was in Dumbarton Road, just across from Partick Station, nearer his flat than hers. He walked past the library, was tempted to just turn right, go up the hill, go home. Suddenly, all he really wanted to do was go to bed, put the covers over his head and sleep. To stop thinking about Uncle Kenny, St Andrew's, all of it. But he didn't. He kept walking, trying to avoid the slush piling up on the pavement, trying to put a smile on his face.

'Harry!'

He waved, walked over to the table in the corner where Susan and Claire were sitting. She kissed him as he sat down, the two of them already a few drinks in.

'You remember Claire, don't you?' she asked.

He nodded. Unfortunately he did. A total pain-in-the-arse friend of Susan's from the university. Another graduate student, another person who liked to refer to people like him as pigs.

She smiled at him, almost managing to hide the contempt on her face. 'Well, if it isn't our friendly local policeman.'

'Got you a whisky in,' said Susan, pushing it across the table at him. 'Where have you been?'

'Nowhere. The usual. Trying to catch up with paperwork at the shop.'

'Did you ask him?' she asked expectantly.

'Shit! I forgot.'

'Aw, Harry! You promised.'

'I'll ask him tomorrow,' he said. 'Honest.'

Susan turned to Claire. 'One of Harry's friends came to the flat the other day looking for him. Turns out he's a bit of a bad guy. Involved in the vice trade. I've asked Harry if he can set up a meeting between us, for my thesis.'

'And he forgot,' said Claire.

'Yep,' said McCoy, standing up. 'Just another of my many faults. Another?'

He ordered an extra pint at the bar and stood there drinking it, trying to make it last as long as possible. Didn't feel up to Susan and Claire; wasn't really their fault, just didn't feel up to talking to anyone. He was wound so tight he knew Claire would say something that would set him off, they'd have a fight and he'd spend the next day apologising to Susan.

He tried to take his mind off Uncle Kenny and think about what he was paid to think about. Connolly. If he'd killed Elaine's boyfriend, got rid of the reason that was stopping them being together and killed Jake for turfing him out into the wilderness, then maybe that was that. The end of it.

He could see the reflection of Susan and Claire in the mirror above the gantry. Laughing, enjoying themselves. What he should be doing.

Maybe Connolly'd done what he needed to do. Mission over. Somehow he didn't think so. Connolly had burned too many bridges to settle back into normal life. Something big was going to have to happen to finish this, and he had the horrible feeling that whatever that was it was going to involve Elaine.

'Penny for them?'

He turned and Susan was standing beside him. 'What's up? Could tell something was wrong the minute you came in.'

'Nothing,' he said.

She sighed. 'The West of Scotland Man speaks. Nothing's ever wrong, at least nothing you can't drink your way out of.'

He smiled despite himself. 'Where's Claire?'

'Toilets. Not your favourite, is she?'

'Do you blame me? She called me a pig last time I saw her. Seems I'm single-handedly responsible for most of the world's ills. "A capitalist lackey enforcing a corrupt system", no less.'

She kissed him. 'Well, that's true but you're my capitalist lackey. That's what matters.'

She picked up the drinks. 'Go home, Harry. I'll be back soon. There's a quarter of Red Leb in the cigar box. Sean came round this afternoon. I'll drink this, get rid of Claire, be back as soon as I can. Go on.'

He nodded, kissed her and left the pub.

He lay there as she got ready in the bathroom, could hear her brushing her teeth. He was sleepy, pleasantly stoned. He'd been asleep on the couch when Susan had got back, half-smoked joint between his fingers, run-off track of side two of *Sticky Fingers* going round and round. Last thing he remembered was singing along to 'Midnight Mile'.

Uncle Kenny and Strathblane seemed a long way away now. Susan was going to appear in a minute, sit at the edge of the bed, put her glass of water down, set the alarm for uni the next day, just like she always did. He listened to her singing softy as she went to the kitchen to get her glass of water. Shut his eyes for a minute . . .

I dry-swallow another black bomber. Don't want to eat. Need the speed to curb my appetite, keep me awake. I'm sure I am retaining bad energy, that the food I'm eating is collecting round my body, rotting, trying to poison me. I haven't been able to keep track properly since St Enoch's Hotel.

Elaine is in for the night, asleep. No bath tonight, straight to bed. No puff of black hair for me to look at. Pity. So here I am doing what I need to do. Plan. Things are going to change soon and I need to be ready for that. Be precise in deed and thought.

The cars in Dumbarton Road seem very loud as they pass. I think my senses are becoming more acute. Sometimes too acute. The noise is starting to hurt. Headache starting. The taste in my mouth is too strong, can't get rid of it no matter what I do. I can feel the cotton of its shirt on my back, the tiny fibres, the feel of the leather shoes on my feet.

Not long now.

I can see the shadows of people who aren't there. Smell them.

Soon I will be able to see in the dark.

Things are working out.

15TH FEBRUARY 1973

CHAPTER 19

Billy on the desk was stuck on some phone-call, looked fed up, page of scribbles on the pad in front of him. McCoy waved, hurried past before he could signal him to wait. The office was quiet, only one there so far was Thomson. He was sitting at his desk, cup of tea and a Grattan's catalogue spread out in front of him, chewing on the end of a ballpoint pen.

'What you got that for?' asked McCoy, putting a steaming paper bag with a bacon roll in it down on his desk.

Thomson looked up. 'Need a new coat. No bloody money, so need to buy it on the never-never.' He tapped the catalogue with the pen. 'Diane in Records gave me this, said she'd order it for me.'

'Did she now? Very cosy. Lending you her catalogue? She'll be moving in next,' said McCoy, sipping his take-out tea. Rotten.

'So, do you actually want something, Detective McCoy, or are you just here to be a pain in my arsehole?'

'Mandrax,' said McCoy. 'Where would I get it?'

Thomson sat back and grinned. 'Easy. Just need to go and see the Wizard.'

'What?' asked McCoy, opening the bag and trying to avoid grease getting everywhere.

'The Wizard. Lives in Carntyne.'

'As opposed to Oz?'

'Did you get me a roll?'

They both turned and Wattie was standing there. Large as life and twice as ugly.

'Nope,' said McCoy, biting into his.

'All right, Johnny Weissmuller? How's the head?' asked Thomson.

'All right. Couple of stitches and a few aspirin and I was fine,' said Wattie.

Thomson shook his head. 'Thought you were bloody dead for a while. Stupid bugger that you are.'

'I didn't think,' said McCoy, 'I hoped and prayed. I could have got a new partner, someone half decent for a change.' He finished his roll, threw the paper in the bin. 'But looks like I'm stuck with you. You can make up for it, though. Away and get a pool car and meet me out front.'

'Where we going?' asked Wattie.

'To follow the yellow brick road,' said McCoy.

Wattie was driving, singing along to Elton John on the radio, admiring his stitches in the rear-view mirror. McCoy happy to sit in a half-doze, heater blowing hot air as they drove along Duke Street. Weather was still grim. Wet and freezing, slush piled up on the pavements, horrible black-grey colour. He could probably do with a new coat as well, the one he'd on was more cigarette burns than anything else. Maybe he'd have a wee look at that catalogue too.

His doze didn't last that long.

'What is Mandrax anyway?'

'Eh?' said McCoy.

'Mandrax, what is it?'

'Jesus, sometimes I forget you're from Greenock.' He yawned, got his cigarettes out his pocket. 'Mandies. Used to be really popular. Tranquillisers. Knock you loopy, especially if you drink with them. No idea what planet you're on.'

'And that's how Connolly got hold of Jackson and Jake Scobie?'

Horn peeped behind him, lights had changed. Wattie held up his hand and moved off.

'Think so. They both had a lot of it in their bloodstream.' McCoy lit up, waved the match out, rolled the window down a crack, chucked it out. 'Can't see Scobie or Charlie Jackson taking them for kicks.'

'So how did he get them to take them?' asked Wattie.

'Fuck knows. Held a knife to them? Maybe gave them a drink with them already in.'

They turned into Conniston Street then into Dalmahoy Street. Stopped at number 19.

'C'mon, Dorothy,' said McCoy, getting out the car. 'The Wizard awaits.'

Wattie just shook his head. No idea what McCoy was on about half the time.

219

The Wizard answered the door looking half asleep. He was a small guy, long hair, beard down his chest, long fingernails painted black, T-shirt with a map of Middle-earth on it, skinny legs emerging from a pair of baggy black underpants.

'Can you come back later, boys?' he said. 'Just got up, need to sort things out before I set up shop.'

'No,' said McCoy and barged past him into the flat.

A door off the hall opened and a sleepy-eyed girl, looked about sixteen, appeared. She'd a Keep on Truckin' T-shirt on and nothing else.

'Best go back to bed, hen,' said McCoy.

'Are you the fuzz?' she asked, sounding quite excited at the prospect.

'Give us a break,' said Wattie. 'This is Carntyne, no bloody California. Now beat it!'

She closed the door behind her, looking disappointed they weren't going to arrest her.

The living room was dim, smelt of incense and dope. Black walls, curtains pulled over, candles burning everywhere. McCoy pulled the curtains open, let in the flat light of a February morning.

The Wizard looked visibly pained. 'Come on, man,' he said, blinking at the light. 'Stay mellow.'

'Mellow, my arse,' said McCoy and held out his ID card.

'Shite,' said the Wizard, suddenly sounding more like a Carntyne dealer than a spaced-out hippie. He sat down on the couch.

Wattie dug in his pocket, brought out a picture of Connolly, knelt down in front of him and held it out for the Wizard to look at. 'He been here?'

The Wizard looked at it. Pretended not to know who it was.

McCoy sighed. 'I'm only going to ask you this once. Was he here or not?'

The Wizard shook his head. 'Look, man, I don't know who he is. You can't just come in here and—'

McCoy nodded to Wattie. Wattie moved his heavy shoe onto the Wizard's bare foot.

'Christ, man! I don't—'

Protest wasn't worth it. Neither of them was interested. McCoy nodded again and Wattie shifted his weight.

The Wizard groaned, face screwed up. Wattie pressed down harder and he screamed. McCoy was pretty certain he heard a crack.

Wattie gave him one more stamp for luck and stepped away. The Wizard dropped to the floor, moaning and crying.

McCoy crouched down beside him. 'You think that was sore, Mr Wizard? If you don't tell me what I want to know I'll let Wattie here get creative. Unlike me he loves the sight of blood. Kinky that way.'

The Wizard sat up on the dirty carpet holding his foot, one of the toes pointing in a funny direction. McCoy held out his hand to help him up and he flinched. Stood up by himself, hobbled back to the couch.

'The cat was here a week ago. Bought twenty, came back the other night, bought another twenty.'

'He a regular customer?' asked McCoy, noticing to his horror that the Wizard's long toenails were painted black too.

The Wizard nodded. 'Every couple of weeks.'

'Where is he?'

The Wizard shrugged. 'No idea, man. I'm not the kind of business that takes names and addresses.' Wattie moved towards him and he flinched again. 'I don't know! Honest!'

'He say anything?' asked McCoy.

He shook his head. 'A load of shite. If you ask me the cat was loaded on speed. Telling me how things were going to be different for him soon. Better. Said he was going to be with his lady soon. He's been watching her and—'

'Watching her?' asked McCoy.

'Seemed very pleased with himself. Told me how beautiful she was. Said she had to know he was watching her, she was acting so sexy, riling him up.'

'Lovely,' said Wattie.

'He's a strange cat,' said the Wizard. 'Got to be an Aquarius.'

McCoy rolled his eyes. 'He comes back, you phone me at Central. Detective McCoy. Phone me while he's still here. Keep him here. Got it?'

The Wizard nodded.

'Good,' said McCoy. 'And I'll take twenty to go.'

They walked back to the car, McCoy putting the wee plastic bag with the pills in his coat.

'You're becoming a right bastard, Wattie. I think you broke his foot.'

'Learnt it from the master, didn't I? What did you get them for?' asked Wattie. 'They Mandies?'

'What d'you think?' asked McCoy.

'You're going to drug someone?' he suggested.

McCoy laughed. 'Aye. Me. Haven't had any Mandies for years.'

CHAPTER 20

Elaine Scobie had a flat in Princes Terrace. After some pressure from Murray, Lomax had reluctantly given them the address. As the crow flies it wasn't that far from McCoy's flat in Gardner Street but it was miles away in terms of cost and status. Princes Terrace was a prime piece of Hyndland after all. Quiet roads and huge red sandstone flats, well-maintained communal gardens and old money.

McCoy and Wattie were waiting outside number 5 when the patrol car with Murray in the back drew up. He got out, smoothed down his car coat and what was left of his hair, and walked over.

'This better be worth my bloody while,' he growled.

'Nice to see you too, sir,' said McCoy. He pointed up at the windows of Elaine's flat. 'Connolly's drug dealer, the Wizard—'

'The what? What kind of name is that? Jesus Christ.' Murray shook his head. 'Bloody drug dealers should be locked up, not giving you bloody—'

'Told us Connolly told him he was "watching

his lady",' said McCoy, trying to stop the rant before Murray got started. 'The only places Elaine's regularly at are her shop and here. Doubt he would want to hang about Union Street, too easy to notice staring in the window, so I think he's watching her here in her flat. Told the Wiz – the dealer – she was acting all sexy for him.'

'What?' said Murray.

'Think he probably means he could see her when she was getting changed for bed or something like that. Chances are he's deluded enough to think she's taking her clothes off just to give him a show.'

McCoy turned round, looked out over the big gardens in front of Elaine's flat. 'Unless he's living up a tree he couldn't see in the front windows. Has to be looking in the back, which means—'

Wattie held up an *A to Z*. 'He must be watching the back of the flat from somewhere in Crown Gardens.'

McCoy nodded. 'So all we need to do is check all the flats in Crown Gardens that overlook number 5 and hopefully we'll find him.'

Murray looked up at the windows of Elaine's flat. 'Christ, let's hope it's that easy.'

They walked round the back of the flats into Crown Gardens and had a look around. Was quiet. Not many cars in the streets, just a man walking a wee Scottie dog and a fish van discreetly peeping his horn to let everyone know he had arrived.

'I wouldn't mind living round here,' said Wattie.

'Aye, and I wouldn't mind a night with Sandie

Shaw but that's not gonnae happen either,' said McCoy.

He pointed up at number 19. 'Got to be the best bet. Directly behind Elaine's flat, no trees in the way.'

Murray nodded. 'Let's try it.'

There were three bells, McCoy pushed the bottom one. SNEDDON. A woman's voice answered. He told her it was the police and she buzzed them in.

She met them in the hall, her front door half open revealing a riot of plants and antimacassared furniture, small black cat mewing and wrapping itself round her legs. She was a tiny woman, wearing some sort of kimono thing, halo of wispy red hair and make-up that looked like she'd applied it with a trowel. She asked for each of their identity cards, examined them thoroughly. Identified Murray as the boss and addressed herself to him.

'My name is Veronica Sneddon. How can I help?' she asked, staring at Murray's hat long enough for him to get the message.

He took it off. Smiled. 'Just making some enquiries, Miss Sneddon,' he said.

'It's Mrs,' she said. 'I'm a widow of thirty-one years. El Alamein.'

Murray nodded. 'Sorry to hear that. We were wondering if you've noticed anything unusual lately, any comings and goings?'

'Quite the opposite,' she said.

'Sorry?' asked Murray.

'There's me in here, Mrs Campbell on the first

floor and Mr Mitchell on the second. Mrs Campbell is in Australia, visiting her daughter I believe. As for Mr Mitchell, goodness knows.'

'What do you mean?' asked McCoy.

'I've had to take in his milk and his papers, must have gone away on holiday and forgotten to cancel them. Very annoying and a complete waste if you ask me—'

Wattie was already talking into his radio, calling for backup.

CHAPTER 21

Turned out Mr Mitchell hadn't gone away on holiday. He was at home. Dead. Lying in his bath, Gaffa tape round his mouth, ankles and wrists.

McCoy looked down at him. He looked about thirty-five. Shirt, tie, suit trousers, grey socks. Just like any other guy who worked in an office. His hair was brown, just over his collar. Eyes were blue, staring up at the ceiling. He felt Murray behind him.

'His office say he hasn't been in for three days. Thought he had the flu. Tried calling a few times but they didn't get an answer. By the look of it he lived alone. He's the only name on the letters on the hall floor.'

He moved round McCoy and peered into the bath.

'No messages written in his skin, no torture, none of the usual cuts and bruises before the main event. Are we even sure it was him?' asked Murray.

McCoy nodded. 'It's him all right.' He pointed. 'Windows look right into Elaine's flat.' He sat down on the edge of the bath. 'Don't think this guy was of any real importance to Connolly. That's why there's none of the usual stuff. Wasn't personal. Probably didn't even know him. He just happened to be unlucky enough to own the flat that looked into Elaine's bedroom.'

'So he ended up murdered in his own bloody bathroom,' said Murray.

McCoy nodded. 'Looks like it.'

'Poor bugger,' said Murray. 'Poor unlucky bugger.'

Half an hour later, they were sitting at Alan Mitchell's dining-room table, trying to stay out the way of the SOC boys and the ambulance men and Andy the photographer. Wattie, as instructed by Murray, was 'taking charge of the fucking scene for bloody once'.

Mitchell's flat was bright, big windows looking over the snowy gardens, white painted walls. Big picture of Buster Keaton above the fireplace, big one of Geronimo on the opposite wall. The furniture looked like it had come straight out a magazine, modern and stylish. Smoked-glass coffee table with a pile of some old magazine called *Town* on it, long low purple sofa covered in a tigerskin throw and a colour TV in a cabinet. No evidence of anyone else staying there, hardly any evidence of Mitchell himself.

'Quite a place,' said McCoy.

Murray looked round, didn't look impressed. 'If you like that sort of thing.'

Gilroy appeared, sat down at the table. Even with her boiler suit on, she still had an air of ladylike poise. She unhooked her face mask from her ears and peeled off her rubber gloves.

'Sitting Bull?' she asked, nodding at the fireplace.

'Geronimo,' said McCoy. 'Says it at the bottom.'

'Ah,' she said. 'I should know better. Just started a fascinating book, *Bury My Heart at Wounded Knee*, the story of the American West told from the perspective of—'

'Alan Mitchell?' asked Murray pointedly.

'Sorry . . . Back to the matter in hand. I think Mr Mitchell was unfortunate enough to inhale his own vomit. He threw up, and with all that duct tape on his mouth it didn't really have anywhere else to go but into his lungs.'

'Shouldn't he have just swallowed it back over?' asked McCoy.

'In theory, yes,' she said. 'His gag reflex must have been diminished by something.'

'Mandrax?' said McCoy.

She nodded. 'Could be, that or some other opiate-type drug would do it. Sort of thing that seems to happen to musicians quite a lot . . . Jimi Hendrix, for example . . .'

Suddenly noticed Murray was staring at her.

'Sorry again, Mr Murray. Mea culpa. Seem to be easily distracted today for some reason. Yes, Mandrax seems very likely. Given it was present in the bloodstream of Mr Jackson and Mr Scobie, it seems more than likely that we'll find it in the unfortunate Mr Mitchell too.'

She looked at McCoy. 'Do you think this Connolly is going to kill someone else?'

McCoy nodded. 'Don't think he's finished yet.'

'Have you talked to a psychiatrist?' she asked. 'Might help.'

Murray snorted. 'He's no that bad. He's getting better at the blood stuff for a start.'

Gilroy smiled. 'About Connolly, I meant.'

'Ah! Sorry,' said Murray.

'Matter of fact, we have,' said McCoy. 'His old cellmate was a shrink, funnily enough. Said Connolly was the closest he'd ever seen to a pure psychopath.'

'George Abrahams, was it?' asked Gilroy.

'How do you know that?' asked Murray.

'Not many psychiatrists get sent to prison. I remember the case. What did he say?'

'Said he thought Connolly was going to keep on killing or he was going to kill himself,' said McCoy.

'Let's hope it's the latter.' She looked at her watch. 'I've a ten-year-old killed in a farm accident coming in. Sorry I couldn't be more help.'

'Anything else we need to know?' asked Murray.

'One other thing. There seems to be some dried substance around his mouth and nose. Looks like it could be semen.'

'Jesus,' said Murray.

'Semen?' asked McCoy. 'You think Connolly . . .' He stumbled.

'Ejaculated into his mouth?' asked Gilroy. 'Could be, I'll know better in a couple of hours.'

231

'I didn't think Connolly was that way inclined,' said Murray. 'Thought it was Elaine he was after?'

'Also seem to be traces of it in the sink,' said Gilroy. 'If you were to ask me I would suggest that it's not really to do with the sex of the victim in this instance. More a case of any port in a storm as it were. Riled up by the sight of Elaine, well . . . who knows?'

She stood up. 'I'm overstepping my role here so I will retire gracefully.' She looked at McCoy. 'Were I a detective I'd have a look at Hervey Cleckley's list of psychopathy symptoms from 1941. Still stands up after all these years.'

She walked away, stopped, turned back to them. 'By the way, the itinerant who killed himself in the church? Did anything come of it?'

McCoy shook his head. 'Just another depressed alkie.'

She nodded, walked off, pulling the boiler suit from her shoulders as she went.

'Doesn't surprise me she never married,' said Murray. 'Too bloody clever for her own good.'

McCoy grinned. 'I always thought you had a wee soft spot for Madam Gilroy.'

Murray looked at him. 'Shut your trap, Detective McCoy. Not everything is about sex, as you would do well to learn.'

McCoy held up his hands in surrender. 'I never said anything about sex. That was you.'

'Very bloody smart, McCoy. She's an intelligent, well-bred woman . . . she—'

'Sir?'

They turned and Wattie was standing there. 'Come and have a look at this.'

Alan Mitchell's flair for interior decoration didn't seem to have extended to the box room. It had a single bed, a wardrobe, a bookshelf full of art books and a wee armchair. The bed had been slept in, gave off a vinegary smell of old sweat. There was a half-empty bottle of whisky on the bedside table, balled-up fish-and-chip paper beside it, full ashtray. Cashmere coat lying over the armchair.

McCoy looked around. Had a feeling it would be somewhere. He opened the wardrobe, recoiled. 'All his piss and shit is in here.'

Wattie screwed his face up.

'Like the hotel room?' asked Murray.

McCoy nodded. 'Weight's all marked, just the same.'

Murray turned to Wattie. 'Away and get Andy, get him to take some photos.'

Wattie scurried off.

Murray looked defeated. 'How were we ever supposed to find him here?'

'We did.'

'Aye, too bloody late. For all we know he's just chapped someone else's door, tied them up in the bath and made himself at home. Sitting pretty now, watching the racing on the telly. How the fuck do we find him now?'

'Same way we found him here,' said McCoy. 'Doing what you always told us. Following things up, checking things. Police work. And a lucky break.'

'It's always a lucky break,' said Murray. 'I'll call Lomax, tell him what's happened. See if it makes any difference to her coming in. You need Wattie tonight?'

'Don't think so,' said McCoy. 'Why?'

'Boxing's on tonight. St Andrew's Club in the Albany. He's been pestering me for weeks to go. Thought he could do with a wee reward for that river stunt. And it might do him some good to meet some of the other high heid yins.'

'Big do, is it? asked McCoy. 'Why'd you no ask me?'

'Boxing? Blood splattering everywhere? You'd be boaking your load and fainting in five minutes.'

McCoy grinned. 'True.'

'Besides, a night with all the top brass is probably your idea of hell.' He put his hat on, headed for the door. 'I'll let you know what Lomax says.'

McCoy watched him walk out the door. Looked at his watch. Two p.m. More than enough time to find Cooper before tonight.

McCoy sat at his desk chewing the end of a yellow pencil he'd found in his drawer. Time to do what Murray always told him to do when he was stuck. First principles. He wrote

Staying where?

Connolly had to be somewhere. Wrote

Check opposite the Golden Dawn?

He shouted across the room, 'Thomson?'

Thomson looked up, still seemed to be looking at the coats in the catalogue. 'What?'

'Are there any flats in Union Street? Opposite the Lite Bite, Golden Dawn, around there?'

He sat back. 'Don't think so, think it's all offices. If there are, British Rail'll probably be the landlord.'

'Can you do me a favour? Do a check?'

He snorted. 'What's up with Wattie?'

'I cannae find the bugger—'

'Someone mention my name?'

The office turned, and the shouts and the wolf whistles started. Wattie was standing there in a dinner suit, shiny patent shoes, dark blue velvet bow tie. Blond hair wetted down in a neat side shed.

He bowed. Held his hands up. 'What can I tell you? Some of us have just got it.'

'The clap you mean!' shouted Thomson.

More laughter.

Murray emerged from his office, piles of papers in his hand, pipe going. He looked Wattie up and down. Exploded. 'What the fuck are you doing, Watson? We're not going for another three hours! We get changed at the bloody hotel!'

Wattie stood there, going red.

'Get that stupid bloody suit off now and do some bloody work!' He put the papers down on Thomson's desk, walked back into his office and slammed the door behind him.

235

'I feel like a bit of an arse,' said Wattie.

'Penance. Help Thomson with British Rail.' McCoy stood up, put his coat on.

'Where you off to?' asked Wattie, unclipping his bow tie.

'Out,' said McCoy.

Headache is back
can hardly see out my left eye

i don't know how much more of this I can take

Hello Pogba
Hello the Legionnaire
Help an old comrade

please

The light is burning me

help

CHAPTER 22

McCoy was looking at the papers laid out on the big round John Menzies kiosks when someone tapped him on the shoulder. He turned and Stevie Cooper was standing there.

'Did you no see me waving at you?'

'Nope.'

No wonder he hadn't, he could hardly bloody recognise him. He couldn't remember the last time he'd seen him without his red Harrington jacket and jeans, even the blond quiff was gone. His hair looked darker, fact that it had been plastered down with Brylcreem no doubt helping. Umbro duffel bag over his shoulder.

McCoy stepped back and looked at him properly. 'I didn't even know you had a suit.'

'I've plenty,' said Cooper. 'Never wear them.'

'Hate to say it but you look quite good in it, sort of grown-up.'

'Fuck off!' said Cooper. 'I look like every other bugger, which is the main idea.'

He stepped out the way as the tannoy announced the five fifteen to Greenock and the crowd surged towards the platform.

'You fit?' he asked.

McCoy nodded. 'As I'll ever be.'

They turned and made their way through the crowded station, down past the clacking departure boards, out by the taxis and onto Hope Street. The rain was back on, a light drizzle blurring the streetlights.

McCoy stopped for a second, lit up. 'How the fuck are we going to do this without being caught? Place is gonnae be full of coppers, most of who I probably know.'

'No, it's not,' said Cooper. 'It's full of families staying there and businessmen and people who've come to see the fight. No fucker's going to notice us.' He looked at McCoy. 'You sure you want to do this? If you're worried, I can do it myself, keep you out of it.'

'No fucking way,' said McCoy, sounding more emphatic than he felt. 'I'm in.'

The foyer of the Albany was a large double-height room, pale carpet stretching as far as the eye could see. Sets of armchairs and wee tables dotted round, potted plants against the light blue walls. There were people bustling around the front desk, checking in. Could see a couple of guys erecting the boxing ring through the half-open door to the ballroom. McCoy kept his head down, made for the house phone, while Cooper stared at a copy of *Atlantic Crossing* framed on the wall, picture of Rod Stewart with his arm round the hotel manager beneath it.

McCoy picked up the phone and a woman answered.

'The Albany Hotel. Moira speaking. How can I help you?'

'Could you put me through to Mr Burgess? I think he's in room . . . God, I just spoke to him, my mind's like a sieve.'

'Three-three-four?'

'That's it. Thanks.'

'Putting you through now.'

A click and then the noise of a phone ringing. He let it ring twenty or so times in case he was in the shower. No reply. McCoy put the phone back in its cradle. Swore under his breath.

'What do we do now?' asked McCoy, joining Cooper under the picture.

'We could check the bar, but what if someone sees you?' said Cooper.

'Murray said he's a Holy Roller. He'll no be in the bar. Fuck . . .' He stood there for a second trying to think. Realised he could smell something. Chlorine.

'Smell that? Now where would you be right now if you were good old Uncle Kenny?'

Cooper sniffed, smiled. Looked round, saw a sign for the swimming pool. 'This way.'

Down a corridor, through some doors, and there it was. They stood at the big window overlooking the pool, didn't take long to see him. He was sitting on the edge of the pool, podgy body in tight blue swimming trunks. He looked a lot older, black hair greyish now. His burly frame had gone slack, run to fat. But it was him all right.

McCoy could suddenly remember the way he smelled, sweat barely covered by talcum powder. He went to get his fags, realised his hand was shaking, put it in his pocket before Cooper could see.

Wasn't hard to see why he was there. Two women in robes were sitting on the loungers at the side of the pool chatting. Three wee boys in their trunks splashing and laughing in the shallow end in front of them as Uncle Kenny looked on.

McCoy backed away from the glass. Managed to take his eyes off Uncle Kenny, looked at Cooper. He had that look on his face that meant danger: eyes far away, mouth set. Right hand tightened into a fist.

'Stevie?' Nothing. He tried again. 'Stevie? You okay?'

Cooper turned away from the window. 'Let's go,' he said. 'We'll wait for him in the room.'

They took the stairs to the third floor, less chance of seeing someone they knew than the lift. McCoy had a sick feeling in his stomach, wasn't sure if it was from seeing Uncle Kenny after all these years or because of what he was about to do. Cooper wasn't talking, just looked angry. McCoy'd seen what he could do when he was in a mood like that before, wouldn't want to be Uncle Kenny for all the money in the world.

The bedroom lock didn't put up much resistance. Was easy enough to open with the set of wee picks Cooper had in his bag. A quick jiggle in the keyhole and they were in. The room was large, big window with a white net curtain over it, two double beds, one with an open holdall sitting on it. White shirt and dress uniform hanging on the handle of the wardrobe, Alistair MacLean paperback open on the bedside table. Mothercare catalogue. Took McCoy a moment to realise why that was there.

Cooper held his bag open and McCoy took out one of the balaclavas and put it on. Why they were there abruptly became real. McCoy had no doubts about what they were going to do, Joe Brady and his own memories made sure of that, but he felt odd, like he was suddenly on the wrong side.

He sat down on the bed, could see himself and Cooper in the mirror. Looked kind of scary and kind of stupid with their balaclavas on in all this chintzy niceness. The point, really. Cooper reached into the bag again. Pulled out a wool sock with two billiard balls in it, handed it to McCoy.

They waited. Didn't take long. Sound of someone whistling 'Little Baby Bunting', then the noise of a key in the lock and Uncle Kenny opened the door. Stopped. Looked at McCoy on the bed, trying to work out what was happening, and in that couple of seconds Cooper grabbed him round the neck, pulled him into the room and wrestled him to the floor.

'What are you—'

Was all he got out before McCoy stuffed a facecloth he'd got from the bathroom into Uncle Kenny's mouth. Cooper swung the sock above his head and brought it down into his face. Uncle Kenny's nose burst in a cloud of blood. He looked surprised, like he still didn't know what was going on, then the pain hit and his face screwed up as he tried to scream through the balled-up facecloth.

McCoy wasn't sure he was going to be able to hit him, seemed too clinical, until he saw the signet ring on his finger. Remembered it on Uncle Kenny's hand as he reached round the back of his head, pushed it down. 'On you go, son, don't be scared.'

And then he was up off the bed and kicking at Uncle Kenny's body. And then he was punching and then he was swinging the billiard balls in the sock and Cooper was shouting at him to stop and he kept swinging the sock and kicking and hitting and hitting and hitting . . .

He could feel Cooper trying to pull him away, hear him screaming at him. He shrugged him off, brought the sock and the heavy balls down on Uncle Kenny's left hand, heard the snap of fingers. Raised it above his head to bring it down again and Cooper pulled him harder, spun him round. Said one word: 'Enough.'

McCoy looked down at Uncle Kenny, at the mess he was, at the blood and the broken fingers and his elbow joint the size of a grapefruit. Didn't really know how it happened, how long it had taken. All he could really remember was seeing the signet ring and then it was black.

Cooper pulled him up. Let himself be led towards the door. Took one look back. Wave of nausea at the pool of bright red sticky blood surrounding Uncle Kenny. His towelling robe was open, soft white belly black and blue, trunks stained with blood. Cooper pushed him into the bathroom, made him wash the blood off his hands, took the balaclava off his head. Looked him in the eye.

'What the fuck? You almost killed him!' he hissed.

'Sorry,' said McCoy, but he wasn't. Was anything but. Watched the bloody water flow down the drain in the sink. Uncle Kenny's blood. Thought of Joe and Stevie and all the other wee boys who had been lined up in that fucking basement. Thought of himself.

Cooper looked him over, smoothed his hair down, wiped a spray of blood off his neck like a mum getting her wee boy ready to go out.

'Don't walk fast. Don't draw attention to us. Just two guys who've had a drink heading home. Okay?'

McCoy nodded.

Cooper pulled the door open and they walked down the corridor towards the lift. Just two guys heading home.

They ended up in the Victoria in Partick. The two of them sat there drinking pints, not saying much.

Too many memories, too much to think about. Cooper had taken his jacket and tie off, unfastened the top buttons of his shirt. Still looked uncomfortable. McCoy watched him light up, noticed he had dried blood under his nails.

He swallowed back the whisky Cooper had ordered him, wondered what his life would have been like if they'd never met. If Cooper'd never helped him survive when he was a boy. Maybe he'd be as lost as Joe Brady, living on the streets, trying to drink everything away until you couldn't any longer.

Cooper picked up his pint, drained it. Noticed McCoy was staring at him. 'What's up with you?'

McCoy shook his head. 'Nothing.'

'Wanker,' said Cooper, standing up. 'I'll get us another pint.'

He couldn't remember much about beating Uncle Kenny. Remembered him coming in the room, remembered Cooper getting him down on the floor, remembered seeing that fucking signet ring again, and then nothing until Cooper pulled him off, got him into the bathroom and he saw his face in the mirror. White. Saw all the blood on his hands, the spray of it on his cheek.

'Here.' Cooper put another couple of pints on the table, sat down. 'Listen to me. We got in and out. Did it. No one saw us. The cunt deserved it. End of story. Don't you sit there getting all fucking bent out of shape about it. You hear me?'

McCoy nodded.

'Now get that pint down you.'

McCoy took a sip of his pint. Did what Stevie told him. Same as always.

He left Cooper in the pub waiting for Jumbo to turn up. Told him he was going to go and get something to eat, a fish supper. Cooper told him to pull himself together and just forget today. What was done was done. McCoy nodded, said he would.

He didn't go to the chippie. Didn't want anything to eat. He went to the Haddows at the bottom of his street and bought six cans and a half-bottle of whisky. Got home, took them out the bag and lined them up on the kitchen table. Got the Mandies he'd bought from the Wizard, shook three out the bottle and lined them up on the kitchen table too.

The panic was starting to rise again, the fear. What the fuck had he done? Thought he was going be sick, could see the blood on the carpet, Uncle Kenny's broken fingers, the smell of chlorine coming off him, the bruises on his belly, the look on his face when Stevie grabbed him.

He swallowed the pills with the first can. Drank another. And another. All he wanted was to black out for a while, to not be here, to not be thinking about Uncle Kenny or the basement or the fucking signet ring. All he wanted was oblivion.

He opened the bottle of whisky, drank. Sat back on the couch. Could feel the Mandies kicking in, could feel the warmth spreading through his body, could feel the past receding like waves on a beach. He'd missed this, those druggy weekends with Angela. Feeling of letting go, letting the drugs take over. Swallowed another Mandie with the whisky.

Goodbye, Uncle Kenny. Goodbye, St Andrew's. Goodbye to all the fucking homes he'd been left in. His eyes were closing. He could feel the whisky bottle fall out of his hand, onto the floor. Goodbye to the smell of sweat and talcum. Goodbye to . . .

16TH FEBRUARY 1973

CHAPTER 23

He could hear knocking. Opened his eyes, realised there was someone at the door. He looked at the clock, took a while to focus. Eight a.m. Head felt like it was underwater. Waited for the knocking to stop, turned over, fell back down into sleep. A sleep with no dreams.

More knocking. He looked at the clock. Ten past eleven. He groaned. Could hear Wattie at the door, shouting his name. He sat up, waited for the room to steady itself. He managed to get out of bed, realised he still had his suit on, and headed for the front door.

His vision was slightly off, seemed to be a double edge round things, everything just a little out of whack. Couldn't stand straight, kept swaying, wasn't helping him make it along the hall. Put his hand on the wall to try and steady himself. Wished Wattie would stop banging. Managed to get the door open. Heard Wattie say, 'What the fuck happened to you?'

And blacked out.

★　★　★

He could hear Wattie on the phone, must be talking to Murray. He was telling him that he had terrible food poisoning, that he wasn't well at all. He seemed to be back in his bed, wasn't sure how. Felt different. Realised he didn't have his suit on any more, just his skivvies. Bedroom curtains were drawn back, a dim light seeping in, illuminating a bucket by the bed half full of watery sick. There was a pint glass of water on the bedside table. He drank it down in one, fell back asleep.

Two hours later he was in the car, Wattie driving. He'd had a bath, two big mugs of black coffee and a lecture from Wattie, who looked more scared than anything else, and was holding some toast. Sat there trying to eat it, cotton wool in his mouth, while Wattie told him he'd flushed the rest of the Mandrax down the toilet and that he was a fucking disgrace.

He leant against the car window, still feeling like shit. At least his vision seemed back to normal, no double edges. Just a headache that would fell a horse. He closed his eyes, pressed his forehead against the cold window and tried to concentrate on what Wattie was saying.

'He's fucking well done it again,' said Wattie.

'Who?' he asked. Not really sure what he was talking about.

'Fuck sake!' said Wattie. 'Who'd you think? Connolly!'

'Ah,' said McCoy, trying to find his cigarettes in his coat.

'And Murray is going nut job without you there.'

Wattie stopped at a set of lights on Dumbarton Road. Two women with big sprung prams crossed in front of them, fur coats and Rainmates tied under their chins. Wattie rubbed at the screen with what looked like a red football sock with a big hole in it.

'So if he asks, you had a curry last night, got food poisoning, been throwing up ever since. Right?'

McCoy nodded.

Wattie pushed the clutch in and they accelerated away.

'He'll believe you, you look fucking rough enough.' He turned to him. 'What happened anyway?'

McCoy shook his head. Lit up. Drew the smoke into his lungs, felt his stomach rolling. 'Just one of those nights.'

'You better watch yourself, McCoy.'

'Yes, Dad,' he said, sat up in his seat. Fag seemed to be making him feel better. 'So where is she?'

'Who?' asked Wattie.

'Elaine Scobie. You said Connolly had done it again.'

Wattie shook his head. 'You must have been more out of it than I thought this morning. I told you all this already! It's no Elaine Scobie. It's Chief Constable Burgess.'

'What?' asked McCoy. Couldn't have heard what he thought he had.

'The chief constable from Dunbartonshire! Kenneth Burgess. Got done last night.'

'You picked the wrong fucking day to get sick,' said Murray. 'Teach you to eat all that Indian shite. Sick of telling you. You all right now?'

McCoy nodded, couldn't believe he was back in the foyer of the Albany. Felt like he'd fallen through a hole in the floor since Wattie'd told him. Had to stop the car on Bothwell Street to be sick.

Mind spinning, wondering how the fuck Connolly had got to Uncle Kenny. Wondered how the fuck he was going to survive this investigation without getting caught. A chief constable killed, the big boys would be on high alert, no stone unturned. He was fucked. Really, really fucked.

'Come on,' said Murray. 'We've wasted enough time.'

Murray walked towards the lifts, McCoy followed him. Wasn't sure if it was the after-effects of the Mandies but he felt like he was watching himself, that he wasn't really there. He got into the lift and Wattie asked Murray what floor it was. McCoy was about to say 'the third' before he caught himself.

The lift started climbing. He felt too hot, could feel Murray staring at him, not believing the food-poisoning story. He wanted to say something, to try and act normal, but he was too scared he would slur his words.

'You okay?'

He turned and Murray was looking at him, pointing at his forehead. McCoy put his hand up; the sweat was pouring off him. He got a hanky out his pocket, tried to wipe it off. The lift pinged and the door opened. Long corridor in front of them, same carpet that was in the rooms, same carpet that had been wet with Uncle Kenny's blood. Wave of dizziness and nausea.

He stepped out the lift and followed Murray down the corridor towards the group of people standing outside room 334.

The usual crew. Thomson, Andy the photographer, Gilroy, couple of uniforms. Nods and hellos and the crowd moved aside to let them through. If McCoy knew one thing he knew he couldn't go back into that room. He pulled Murray's arm.

'Sir, if I go in that room I'm going be sick or faint, probably both. I'm still not well. I'll just be in the way.'

Murray looked at him, shook his head. Opened the bedroom door.

McCoy waited, listened to the voices beyond the door. Tried to work out what the fuck was going on. Connolly and Uncle Kenny? What was that about? Few minutes later, and Cooper and him could have passed Connolly in the corridor. And what did Connolly think when he opened the door and Uncle Kenny was lying there, half dead already?

Murray reappeared; even he looked shocked. 'Lucky for you you're sick, McCoy. Has to be the worst yet.'

'What's he done?' McCoy asked.

'More like what he hasn't. Seems to have spent his time battering him with some sort of hammer or something. Then he really went to town.' Murray scratched at his bristles. Looked pained. 'Carved BEAST into his stomach. Fucking used flashbulbs lying on the floor again—'

'Christ.'

'Poked both his eyes out as well, left them lying on the carpet.'

Suddenly all McCoy could hear was a loud buzzing. The walls were starting to wobble and blur. Tried to say 'Murray', tried to hold onto the doorframe, missed it. Went down. Saw Murray looking down at him and then nothing.

Wasn't quite sure how he'd got there but when he opened his eyes he was sitting in an armchair in the hotel foyer. Two wee girls were staring at him, eyes wide. Scarpered when he tried to sit up. He sat for a minute watching the comings and goings, breathing slowly, trying to feel normal. Head hurt. He reached up, could feel a big bump on the back of it, must have happened when he fell. The lift door opened and Wattie stepped out, headed for him.

'How's you?' he asked.

'Better. A bit.'

'You went down like a ton of bricks. Andy took a picture of you lying on the floor, says he's going to put it up on the noticeboard.'

'Is he now? Always was a wee prick. Where's Murray?'

'Still up there, talking to Gilroy. Sent me down to see if you're okay.'

'I will be. Soon as you get me a cup of tea.'

Wattie rolled his eyes, walked off towards the bar.

McCoy was beginning to feel human again, like he had a massive hangover but the fuzziness was gone. Could think straight now. Knew what he had to do.

Wattie came back with two teas, handed him one and sat down beside him. 'You gonnae tell me what really happened last night?'

'Nope.'

'Didn't think so.' He slurped his tea to a look of disapproval from a woman in a hat and her elderly mother walking past on the way to the dining room.

'How'd they find him?' asked McCoy.

'Didn't turn up for the boxing last night. Murray thought he'd decided not to come, staying at home, so nobody bothered until housekeeping found him this morning.'

'Lucky them.'

'Tell you what I don't get? What's Chief Constable Burgess got to do with Connolly or the Scobies? Doesn't make any sense. Why would Connolly want to kill him?'

Wattie was on a roll now, musing away. McCoy let him ramble. All he was doing was waiting for Murray to come downstairs.

'Maybe he's decided to just kill polis. Any polis. Gone right off the edge? Or maybe Burgess arrested him once and this is his way of getting revenge? What d'you think?'

McCoy nodded. 'Maybe.'

'Or maybe Burgess was a dirty copper? In cahoots with Scobie and something went wrong, decided to take revenge?'

McCoy nodded again. Was about to tell Wattie to shut up, wasn't sure how many more of his stories he could take, when the lift pinged and Murray and Gilroy stepped out. Wattie stood up, waved them over.

Gilroy looked down at him. 'Mr McCoy, I believe you have some sort of food poisoning?' McCoy nodded. 'Can be very nasty, you know. You need to be careful, keep yourself hydrated and restore your equilibrium. Flat Coca-Cola always does the trick, I find. Try that. Then maybe some dry toast in the morning.'

McCoy nodded. 'Thanks, I will.'

'Good.' She turned to Murray. 'And I'll see you this evening at the autopsy. They taking the body out by the service lift?'

Murray nodded.

'Advisable. Well, gents, I will bid you adieu. And remember, Mr McCoy, flat Coca-Cola!'

They watched her go, walking towards the big front doors, black bag in one hand, umbrella in the other.

'I need to talk to you,' said McCoy.

'Oh aye,' said Murray. 'Do you now?'

'Alone.'

They both looked at Wattie. He shook his head. 'I'll go back up and see how they're getting on.'

McCoy stood up. 'Let's go to the bar. I'm not sure I can do this without a drink.'

They sat at a table at the back, away from what looked like the aftermath of a particularly drunken wedding. Murray had bought two double whiskies without asking, sensed something was up. Put them down on the glass table and sat down. The bar was at the end of reception, an enclosed space lined with strange black-and-white paintings of glens and mountains.

'Well?' asked Murray. 'Why the cloak and dagger?'

'I know why Connolly killed Burgess,' said McCoy.

Murray raised his eyebrows.

'If we do a bit of digging I think we'll find out that Connolly was in a care home or a residential school near Helensburgh when he was young.'

'And?' said Murray.

McCoy took a drink of his whisky, carried on. 'A couple of days ago a bloke called Joe Brady killed himself, hung himself—'

'In the chapel in Firhill.'

McCoy nodded. 'Gilroy gave me his stuff after the autopsy. He had a photo in his wallet cut out from the paper. Burgess at some charity function a few weeks ago. He'd written the number of a Bible verse above his head. "*In God*

I have put my trust; I will not fear what flesh can do unto me."'

'What are you saying to me, McCoy?' Murray looked angry. 'That Burgess beat him? Gave him a doing?'

McCoy shook his head 'No. I'm saying he fucked him.'

'What? Bollocks! He was married, went to the church, he was a bloody elder! I knew him for twenty years. There's no bloody way—'

'Sorry. I'm getting ahead of myself. He wasn't a homosexual,' McCoy said quietly. 'I'm talking years ago. When Joe was ten or so. Little boys. Burgess liked wee boys.'

Murray stared at him. 'What?'

'You heard me.'

Murray sat back in his chair. 'Burgess? Are you sure?'

McCoy nodded. 'I'm sure all right.'

'Christ. If word gets out about this and it's not true you'll ruin his reputation. He's got a wife and kids . . .'

'And that means he has to be a good guy? That's not how it works, Murray, you know that.'

Murray rubbed at the stubble on his chin. 'Man like that? It's hard to believe.'

'Yeah, well, men like Burgess are good at hiding their tracks. Need to be. That's how they get away with it for so long. Brady had a shite life, been in a care home. When he was there he was raped by Burgess. He saw his picture in the paper. The man was on the down spiral already, must have sent him over the edge. Chances are if Connolly was in a care home or an orphanage, he ran into Burgess as well.'

'He was a beast,' said Murray.

McCoy nodded. 'That's why it was carved into his chest.'

'So how come you know all this?' Murray asked. He was looking at McCoy with something like fear in his eyes.

For a second McCoy thought about it, thought about really telling him why he knew. He looked past Murray at the remains of the wedding, some wee boy in a kilt being given a packet of crisps and a Coca-Cola by his half-cut dad in a creased dinner suit. Mum and her pals in the corner with gin and tonics and bottles of Babycham. Normal life. He took a breath.

'Brady's priest told me. He went to confession the day before he killed himself.'

'And let me guess, this priest will deny telling you if we ask him?'

McCoy nodded. 'He has to, sanctity of the confession box and all that.'

'So why did he tell you, Harry?'

McCoy shook his head. Could feel the beginnings of tears in his eyes, knew if he spoke they would come.

Murray sat forward, big hands resting on the knees of his tweed suit. Rubbed at his bristles, settled himself, looked McCoy straight in the face.

'Is there anything you want to tell me, son? You know you can tell me anything, no matter what it is. Sometimes it's better to get these things out in the open.'

McCoy shook his head, could feel a tear running down his cheek, could see that his hand holding the whisky glass was trembling.

'If there ever is, Harry, you can tell me. Okay?'

McCoy nodded, sniffed, wiped his nose with the back of his sleeve.

Murray stood up, picked up his hat, put his hand on McCoy's shoulder and squeezed it. 'Go home, son, eh? Get yourself some rest. Don't tell this to anyone else. Find out what you can tomorrow. Tell no one else, okay? I mean it.'

McCoy watched as Murray walked past the wedding party and out the door of the lounge. And then he started to cry.

Perhaps I have not measured accurately enough. Perhaps my body really is filling up with dead matter after all. I am tired. Tired of blood on my clothes and skin. Tired of trying to wash it off. Tired of waiting and planning and thinking. I want to sleep. To taste something other than shite in my mouth.

I have to conserve what energy I have left. The end is beginning.

Where do I go now?

No more hotels and boarding houses.

I just need quiet.

Room to think, to sleep, to understand what is happening to me.

The past is overwhelming me. Even what I have done has not given me peace.

Things are failing, soon they will go wrong. My head hurts all the time.

I don't have much time left.

The end is beginning. My road is almost run.

17TH FEBRUARY 1973

CHAPTER 24

He was up and out the flat at half four, had managed to sleep for a couple of hours, more than he thought he would. But the sleep he'd had hadn't helped much. Nightmares. Images of Connolly going round in his head, images of Uncle Kenny. Stuff he didn't want to think about. Woke up in a sweat, sheets soaking beneath him. Needed to do something, get moving. Couldn't be alone with his thoughts any more.

If he was quick he could catch Cooper before he went to bed. Friday nights were for going out, that was his rule, didn't often break it. The dark streets outside the flat were covered in a thick frost, white and sparkling in the streetlights. His shoes crunched as he walked up the hill towards Hyndland Road.

No matter what club or lock-in they'd been at, for Cooper and his pals the party didn't stop there, always ended up back at someone's flat. Flying on speed, fuck knows what else, no way were they going to bed yet.

Chances were they would be back at Billy Weir's. Billy wasn't married, liked a party as much as

Cooper did, but he did have a doting mother. Came round twice a week and tidied the place up for him, did the dishes and his washing so the flat wasn't quite the bachelor dump a guy like Billy usually lived in.

Billy lived just off Great Western Road on the borderline of the student flats surrounding the university and the family flats of the normal families who worked in Maryhill and St George's Cross. By the time McCoy noticed where he was, just walking over Kelvinbridge, he was almost there. Had been lost in thought. Wondering what Connolly was going do next. If he was finished with the Scobies and starting to even old scores God knows where it would lead. How many more people had done him wrong? Funnily enough, it looked like Elaine had been right after all. Connolly wasn't interested in hurting her, just the people around her.

He got to Billy's close in Dunearn Street, started climbing the stairs. Up past the graffitied walls and plastic bags full of rubbish dumped outside the doors. Billy was on the top floor, as was every bugger McCoy ever went to visit. He got to the landing, leant on the handrail, stood for a minute, listened. Might be too late, he couldn't hear anything, no music or laughing. Fuck it, he'd come this far, he was going to get Cooper up if he had to.

He knocked the door, stood back in surprise as it was opened immediately. An anxious-looking

Billy, suit and tie still on, was standing there. Was only when he stepped into the light of the hall that McCoy noticed he had blood down the front of his suit and all over his pale blue shirt.

'McCoy? What you doing here? Thought you were Dr Purdie.'

'What's going on, Billy?'

Billy held the door open. 'Come in, he's in the bathroom.'

McCoy walked through the flat. There were a couple of dressed-up girls in the living room he didn't recognise, sitting on the couch under the big Jack Daniel's mirror. Short skirts and long hair, platform sandals. Coffee table in front of them covered in empty glasses and ashtrays, smell of dope in the air. Record was playing quietly, sounded like James Taylor, someone like that. He nodded at them and followed Billy down the corridor.

Jumbo was standing guard by the bathroom door. Jeans, jumper and white sandshoes covered in dark blood. He looked scared, face white, chewing at his nails. 'Mr McCoy.'

'Fuck's going on, Jumbo? Where's Stevie?'

Jumbo nodded to the bathroom. 'I'm not sure you're allowed to—'

McCoy stepped past him and pushed the door open. Cooper was lying in the empty bath, naked but for a pair of bloodstained underpants. McCoy looked at him, looked away quickly, stared at the row of aftershaves on the shelf under the mirror.

'Don't you fucking well pass out,' said Cooper. 'I've had enough shite to deal with tonight.'

McCoy nodded, took a breath, looked back at him. Cooper's blond hair was wet and sticky with blood, jagged slash from his eyebrow disappearing into his scalp. He'd another wound on his shoulder, a gaping six-inch slash seeping blood, and a huge gash going through the thick hair on his stomach. The blood was everywhere: on him, in the bath, on the towels on the floor, the nylon shower curtain. Everywhere.

McCoy tried to breathe slowly, count his breaths. In, out, in, out.

Cooper watched him for a minute or so, shook his head. 'Better?'

McCoy nodded.

'Thank fuck for that,' said Cooper. He nodded down at the bath. 'Billy shoved me in here. Didn't want blood all over his flat.' He grinned and McCoy realised he was drunk or high on something or, knowing Cooper, probably both. 'Cheeky bastard. Said his maw would go spare if she had to clear it up.'

McCoy put the lid of the toilet down, sat on it.

'Purdie's coming. Supposed to be on his way,' said Cooper.

'Why d'you not go to the Royal?' asked McCoy, trying to find his fags in his coat. Found them, lit two, handed one to Cooper.

He took it, inhaled deeply. 'Joking, aren't you? Polis would be all over me like a shot.' He nodded up at the bathroom shelf. 'Pass us that, will you?'

McCoy looked up. Between the old razors and a bottle of Matey there was a bottle of Whyte & Mackay's. He got it off the shelf, took a drink himself before he passed the bottle to Cooper.

'So what happened?' he asked. 'Who'd you annoy this time?'

Cooper took a long swig. When he lifted his arm up to drink McCoy could see the long pink rope of scar disappearing down his back. Sword'll do that to you.

'I didnae annoy anyone. Just went for a nice night out.'

'And?'

'And the king is dead, that's what's happened. No Scobie now. Take someone like that out the equation and all his boys start jostling for position. What better way to set your stall out than by carving me up? Wee warning to keep out of it. No takeovers. Keep it in the family. Stupid bunch of cunts.'

'Where were you?' asked McCoy.

'Started off in the Muscular Arms, then the dancing at Clouds, then some lock-in at a pub in Byres Road. One got me when I came out.'

'How'd he know you were there?' asked McCoy.

He shrugged. 'Someone in one of they places will have telt them, quick phone call. Twenty quid earned.' He grimaced, raised the bottle to his lips. 'What are you doing here anyway?'

'Uncle Kenny's dead.'

'What?' Cooper lowered the bottle.

'He's dead,' said McCoy.

Cooper shook his head. 'No way. I got you off him in time. You were like a fucking animal, mind you. Never seen—'

'It wasn't me that did it.'

Cooper looked at him.

'It was Connolly. Took him apart, made a right mess of the bastard.'

'Connolly? Scobie's Connolly? What the fuck has it got to do with him?' asked Cooper.

'Must have seen the same picture you and Joe Brady did. Chances are he was in a home too. Got Wattie trying to find out.'

Cooper lay back in the bath. 'Fucker should have turned up earlier, saved us the trouble.' He lifted the bottle. 'To Connolly, at least the mad cunt did something useful this time.'

A knock on the door and Jumbo poked his head in. 'Mr Cooper, the doctor's here.'

He stood to the side and Purdie was standing there, leather bag in hand. He was forty-odd, thin, reddish hair. Took the cigarette out his mouth.

'Gents, how are we? Sorry, not familiar with this area, took me a while to find it.'

McCoy nodded at Cooper. 'I'm fine, it's him you're here to see.'

Purdie took in the blood and the slashes and sighed. 'Been in the wars again, Mr Cooper?'

'Something like that.'

Purdie moved in, took his coat off, handed it to Jumbo, and knelt down on the fluffy bathmat.

He rolled up his shirtsleeves, revealing burgundy-striped pyjamas underneath, and started examining Cooper's cuts, sucking the air through his teeth every so often as he did.

'How much you in for now?' asked McCoy.

Purdie was rummaging in his bag. 'Two and a half grand.'

McCoy whistled. 'You like the horses that much?'

'Seems so,' said Purdie. 'Unfortunately they don't seem to like me.' He poked about in his bag, emerged syringe in hand.

Cooper's face fell. 'What's that? I hate fucking jags.'

'Local anaesthetic. Up to you, Mr Cooper. I would, however, strongly advise it. Going to be grim otherwise. Plus, I don't need you squirming and moaning while I'm trying to stitch you up.'

Cooper looked at him. 'Three hundred off the debt.'

Purdie just stood there saying nothing, syringe in hand. Waited.

'Fuck sake, five hundred. Now get on with it.'

Purdie grinned, moved in, injected Cooper's shoulder. Cooper was stoic; didn't flinch but made sure he didn't look either as Purdie injected his side, hands gripping tighter onto the sides of the bath as the needle went further in.

'Now, I should be honest, this one might hurt,' Purdie said as he eased the needle into Cooper's scalp.

McCoy looked away, not before he caught the horrified grimace on Cooper's face.

Purdie took the needle out. 'All done. Now we wait five minutes.'

'Thank fuck,' grumbled Cooper. 'You got anything else in that bag?'

Purdie sat on the edge of the bath, had a rummage about. Held up a red capsule. 'Take this.' He handed it over and Cooper swallowed it over with a slug of whisky. He turned to McCoy. 'You want one?'

'Why not? he said, putting it in his pocket. 'Keep it for a rainy day.' He stood up. 'I'll leave you to it for a while.'

He stepped out the bathroom, almost walked straight into Jumbo. The boy's face was full of fear.

'He's all right, Jumbo. You know what he's like. Take more than a few slashes to do him in.'

Jumbo nodded, looked relieved. 'Okay, Mr McCoy.'

McCoy looked at his watch, wasn't even six o'clock yet. He yawned. 'Come on, Jumbo, you can make me a cup of coffee. Might wake me up.'

They stood in the kitchen waiting for the kettle to boil. Was cold, just old lino on the floor, no heater, windows dripping with condensation. No sign of Billy or the girls, although the creaks and the giggles from the bedroom next door were a fair indicator of where they were. Jumbo carefully spooned some Mellow Bird's into a couple of mugs, added hot water and milk, handed it over. They sat down at the table.

McCoy brushed the toast crumbs aside and put his mug down. 'How's the reading getting on?'

Jumbo brightened. 'Good. Do you want to hear?'

McCoy nodded – why not? – and Jumbo got a folded copy of *Commando* out his back pocket, spread the wee comic out on the kitchen table and started to read. He was slow, a bit painful to listen to, but he was definitely getting better.

'"I reckon it's time the Jerries had a warning. You know what to do, mate . . ."'

'Sounding good, Jumbo.'

He let him read on, mind drifted from the battlefields of Dunkirk. He had to connect Connolly with Uncle Kenny and quick. If he could prove Connolly had a reason for doing what he'd done and with the physical evidence – the BEAST and the rest of it – the investigation would be over before it began.

No reason to think anyone else had anything to do with what happened that night, least of all him or Cooper. And even if Connolly started to blabber when he was caught, say Uncle Kenny was already badly beaten when he got there, hopefully no one was going to believe him. Or care.

'"British sab . . . sab . . . sabo?"'

McCoy held out his hand and Jumbo passed him the comic. He looked at it. 'Saboteurs. Don't worry, Jumbo, that's a hard one.'

Jumbo nodded, was about to start again when Purdie poked his head round the door.

'Chaps? That's me done.'

They followed him back to the bathroom. Cooper was now lying in a warm bubble bath, beatific smile on his face.

'Matey,' said Purdie. 'Saw it on the shelf. My kids love it. I've stitched him best I could. Hopefully the one on his forehead won't scar too much. I've also put a bottle of Dettol in the bathwater. Let him lie there for twenty minutes or so, let it do its disinfecting duty. Then get him out the bath and get him into bed. That Seconal is strong stuff, don't want him slipping under the waves.'

McCoy nodded. 'Jumbo, make Dr Purdie a cup of tea before he goes.'

'Much obliged,' said Purdie. 'Call me Fraser. Doesn't seem like the kind of occasion that calls for formality. Until the next time.'

They left and McCoy sat back down on the toilet lid. 'Better?' he asked.

'Aye' Cooper said. He'd his arms stretched out along the sides of the bath, head above the water. McCoy could see the black stitches running up his side and shoulder, ones on his forehead were much finer, thinner, less likely to leave a scar, he supposed.

Cooper ducked his head under the water then sat up, pushed his wet hair back. 'Tell you something, McCoy, whatever that pill was, it was fucking good. Should have had one.'

'Can't. Have to get to work.'

Cooper shook his head, as if he was trying to clear it, looked at McCoy through half-closed eyes.

'Those clowns that did this? Scobie's half-arsed boys? They have no fucking idea what's about to happen.'

'That right?' asked McCoy, reaching for the whisky bottle.

Cooper nodded. 'Them, Naismith, Collins in the Southside, no fucking idea.'

McCoy decided to humour him, took a swig, wiped his mouth. 'So what's gonnae happen then?'

Cooper smiled lazily, tapped the side of his nose. 'All in good time, Harry, all in good time. But things are gonnae change, change big time. Believe me.'

'Got a favour to ask you,' said McCoy.

'That right?' said Cooper sleepily. 'All I ever do is your fucking favours. What is it this time?'

'Susan wants to interview you. For her uni work. That okay?'

Cooper's eyes were closing. He laid his head on the side of the bath. 'Fine by me. As I said, tasty wee bird that you've . . .'

McCoy shouted on Jumbo and he appeared round the bathroom door.

'Better get your boss out the bath before he drowns himself,' said McCoy.

CHAPTER 25

'Harry! It's half past bloody six!' said Susan. 'Get in here before I bloody freeze.'

McCoy held up a bag of rolls and a packet of bacon.

'What are you doing here at this time anyway?' she asked, closing the door behind him and pulling her dressing gown tighter round her.

'Was passing. Thought I'd make you breakfast. Rolls in twenty minutes!'

'Great. I don't even like bacon.'

'Bollocks! Everyone likes bacon rolls,' said McCoy.

Susan walked into the bathroom shaking her head and McCoy headed for the kitchen.

Twenty minutes later they were sitting in Susan's kitchen with bacon rolls and mugs of tea in front of them. Place was finally warming up, all three bars of the electric fire on along with two of the gas rings. The windows were steamed up, smell of fried bacon, felt cosy. With all the clothes hanging from the pulley above them, it felt like they were in some kind of tent.

'Wattie was up here looking for you yesterday

morning,' said Susan, cutting her roll in half. 'Couldn't get an answer at your door.'

'Was he?' said McCoy through a mouthful of roll. 'I had food poisoning, been puking all night, then I fell asleep. Was exhausted.'

She smiled. 'And here was me thinking you were out living it up with your fancy woman.'

'Well, that too. By the way, you still want to talk to Stevie Cooper?'

She nodded, put down her mug. 'Did you ask him?'

'Yep. How about this afternoon? He's in a flat in Dunearn Street. Wee bit under the weather so he'll be glad to see you. Nothing else to do.'

'What's up with him?'

'Cold, I think, got the sniffles. You want that?' He pointed at the half roll on her plate.

'You have it.' She pushed her plate towards him. He picked it up and shoved the whole thing into his mouth.

'You could have given me more warning, Harry.' She stood up. 'I better get my notes together.'

'What? Now?' he managed through his chewing. 'I thought we might go back to bed for a wee hour.'

'Did you now?' she asked. 'Need to call your fancy woman then. I've got an interview to prepare for.'

'But I made your breakfast!' he said.

She looked at him. 'You think you can buy me for a cup of tea and a roll?'

'I'll wash up afterwards as well.'

'Need the bin taken down.'

'Christ,' said McCoy. 'You're a heartless woman, Susan. Deal.'

She smiled. 'Now that's what I call a decent offer.' She looked at her watch, looked at him. 'Better be quick, though.'

He stood up, grinned. 'Always am.'

Eight a.m. and the shop was already running at full speed. The death of a senior policeman had consequences, big ones. Suddenly the race to find Connolly had gone up a few gears. Extra staff from Eastern being called in. Budget for any and all overtime authorised. No stone to be unturned. McCoy sat down at his desk and looked round. Thomson was calling in anyone on leave, ticking off a long list. Murray was in his office with the door closed, been in there for an hour already apparently. Meeting with big brass.

McCoy started tidying up the papers on his desk, couldn't find any notes from Wattie about the children's homes records he'd asked him to look for. Looked through again, wasn't concentrating on what he was doing, too busy trying to sit on the rising panic that had been bubbling up since he'd got there. Told himself they were looking for Connolly, not him and Cooper. Found himself watching Murray and the two suits in his office through the dimpled glass. Had a flash of himself in court charged with manslaughter. Was about to go out and buy more fags, anything to get out of there, to try and calm down, when Wattie appeared.

He walked in carrying a white paper bag, a cardboard cup of tea, hair still wet. If the fact that he was whistling didn't give it away, the fact that he was still wearing his good suit definitely did.

He sat down at his desk, pointedly not looking over at McCoy.

McCoy leaned back in his chair. 'Mr Watson, nice of you to join us. Out last night were you?'

Wattie nodded, opened his bag and pulled out a square sausage roll.

'Nice time, did you?' asked McCoy innocently.

Wattie nodded, bit into his roll, brown sauce dripping onto his notes. He cursed, wiped it off with a paper serviette.

'Fuck off, McCoy,' he said.

'Knew it!' said McCoy. 'Someone got their hole last night.'

Wattie kept eating his roll, refusing to look at him.

'Who's the unlucky lady?' he asked. 'Anyone I know?'

Kept eating.

'Let me think. Had to be a first date for you to try and impress her with that flash suit.'

Wattie stuck two fingers up at him.

'So must be someone you've just met.' And then it dawned. 'No!'

Wattie nodded.

'Mary from the *Record*? Fuck me. You're a better man than I!'

'Yeah, that's what she said too.' Wattie rolled up the empty bag, dropped it in the bin. 'Now, do you want to know about Connolly or not? Come on.'

McCoy stood up, followed Wattie down the back corridor into the old part of the station. It was mostly unused, a room still full of horse tackle. Seemed Wattie had been busy after all. He'd commandeered one of the old meeting rooms, walls still covered in photos of police football teams and *Have You Seen This Man?* Bible John posters. The big wooden table in the middle was completely covered in huge lists of children's homes, care homes, approved schools. Phone and scribbled-on bits of paper beside them.

Wattie sat down on one of the chairs. 'Spent last night doing this while you were at home with your food-poisoning-my-arse. Fucking nightmare.' He pointed at the lists. 'Some of these places are run by the council, some by the church, some by charities, Barnardo's, that sort of thing. Trying to find anyone who knows anything is a bloody nightmare. But,' he did a drum roll on the table with two pens, 'I did.'

He flicked through his notes. 'St Martin's Approved School, Bishopbriggs. Our man Connolly was sent there in 1956 with two of his pals for trying to rob a tobacconist in Ashgill Road.'

'What age was he?' asked McCoy.

Wattie looked at his notes. 'Hang on . . .' Looked up. 'Ten. Now, are you going to tell me what this is all about?'

282

'You know Diane in Records, don't you?' asked McCoy, ignoring him.

Wattie sighed, nodded. 'Aye, she comes from Greenock, same as me. As a matter of fact her brother was in the same football team as—'

'Go and see her. Find out where Kenneth Burgess was stationed in 1956. Then meet me outside in twenty minutes. We need to get out of here before Murray puts us on the funeral recce.'

Wattie sat there.

'What you waiting for?' Struck him. 'Fuck sake! Thank you, Watson, for your endeavours with the care homes and thank you for going to see Diane, and no, I still don't want to know about her brother's bloody football team. Happy?'

'No problem.' Wattie stood up. 'And remember, Detective McCoy, manners cost nothing.'

The only pool car McCoy could get was a clapped-out Viva, crack in the windscreen and a heater that didn't work properly. Still, at least the engine sounded fine. He was getting into it when a police van pulled up by the garages and six uniforms from Eastern got out. Jake Scobie was being buried tomorrow morning. A whole lot of villains expected to attend and maybe Connolly as well. Murray wanted every aspect of the route covered and that meant a recce that afternoon. No way was he sticking around for that. Having to go to the funeral was bad enough, without having to go over the route of the cars this afternoon as well.

He drove round the block, pulled up outside the front of the station. Wattie was standing there blowing his hands. He got in, tried to turn the heater up, realised it made no difference.

'Better not be muddy where we're going, I'm not getting this suit ruined.'

'So where'd you get to last night then, you and the lovely Mary?' said McCoy, pulling out into the traffic.

'Not that it's any business of yours, went to the Berni Inn for something to eat then back to hers.' He rubbed at the condensation on his window. 'She's quite a lassie, that Mary. Not backwards in coming forwards.'

'That's one way of putting it. Diane?'

'Ah,' Wattie dug in his pocket, got out a folded bit of paper. 'Seems that in 1956 our man was stationed in Lennoxtown. Seconded there for six months covering someone's leave.'

'What's that? Twenty minutes or so from Bishopbriggs? Not very far.'

'So what exactly are we going to this approved school for?' asked Wattie.

'Evidence. Need someone who remembers him coming to the school,' said McCoy.

'From 1956? You'll be lucky.'

They were past Springburn now, heading out towards the hills. They were covered in snow, sun shining on them, looked like a biscuit thin.

'Why would Burgess come to the school?' asked Wattie. 'I don't get it.'

McCoy sighed. Last thing he wanted was to go through it, tell Wattie how he knew Uncle Kenny liked to visit places like St Martin's. Besides, he'd told Murray he'd keep it quiet.

'Seems Burgess went to schools to give career talks to the boys. Theory is he might have met Connolly there, maybe he did something that pissed Connolly off and he never forgot it.'

'What?' Wattie looked at him. 'Who came up with that load of shite?'

'Me,' said McCoy. 'Shite it might be, but has to be better than walking the fucking funeral route in this weather.'

'That's true,' said Wattie. 'Can't believe Murray fell for it, though.'

Bishopbriggs was just past Auchinairn, at the northern edge of Glasgow, almost in the country. An old high street surrounded by acres of new houses, every one the same as the others. Every good citizen's dream home. Three bedrooms and wee garden. Bishopbriggs was where the working-class people who had done well moved to as soon as they had enough money to leave the council houses of Milton and Springburn. Taxi drivers, electricians, painters and decorators, those kinds of people.

When St Martin's was built it was probably in the middle of farmland, nice view of the Campsie Hills behind; now it was slowly being encircled by the new houses. They turned off and drove up the long and bumpy drive. McCoy hadn't been in

St Martin's but it looked exactly like all the other homes he had been in. Grand Victorian building surrounded by cheaply built extensions covered in white pebbledash and ringed by playing fields. Last thing he wanted to do was visit a place like this but he didn't have a choice. He had to make the connection between Uncle Kenny and Connolly, shut the investigation down as soon as he could.

'So what's the plan?' asked Wattie.

'Fuck knows,' said McCoy as he parked the Viva in front of the entrance. 'Play it by ear.'

Wattie rang the bell. McCoy lit up while they waited. Noise of locks being undone, call of 'Hang on!' and eventually the door opened to reveal the last thing McCoy expected. An attractive young woman, red hair piled on her head, jeans and a peace symbol T-shirt.

'Sorry, bloody door's a nightmare. How can I help?' she said.

They held up their police identity cards.

'So you found the wee bugger?' she asked.

'What?' asked Wattie. 'Found who?'

She looked puzzled. 'Are you not here with Barry Armstrong?'

'Nope,' said Wattie.

'Ah. To be honest I thought it was a bit early to have found him. Normally manages about three days on the run before he gets caught.' She smiled. 'I'm Alice. Come away in.'

They followed her through into the main hall. Was much like it would be in any other school:

notice boards, kids' paintings on the wall, smell of floor polish. Only difference was the set of keys around Alice's waist jingling as she walked. She led them past a group of sullen-looking boys in jeans, blue jumpers and white sandshoes being marched towards the stairs, and into a cluttered office, sat down behind the desk. Wattie and McCoy sat down opposite her.

'I'll say it again,' she said, sipping from a big mug with a picture of Tweedledee and Tweedledum on it. 'How can I help you?'

'Bit of a strange one. We're hoping to speak to someone who was here in the mid fifties,' said McCoy.

'God! Now you're asking, not sure there is anyone. Not me, plainly. Let me think.' She put her mug down, drummed her fingers on the desk. 'Mr McBride left two years ago. He'd been here since the Middle Ages, I think.'

'He live local?' asked McCoy.

'Did. Passed away at Christmas, I'm afraid. Can I ask what it's in regard to?'

'Murder investigation,' said McCoy.

'Golly!' she said. 'Does it have to be a teacher?'

McCoy shook his head.

'In that case you might be in luck. Mr Spence, the caretaker. I'm sure he's been here a long time, not quite sure he goes that far back, but he's probably your best bet.'

'Where'll we find him?' asked Wattie.

'Behind the sports pavilion. He's got a wee hut

thing, think he lives in the bloody place. Weather like this, he'll definitely be in there with the fire on not doing his job.'

The playing fields were rock hard with the cold, slippy with frost. Didn't stop them being used. Teams of boys were playing football, or more accurately using the game as an opportunity to knock lumps out each other. Referee's whistle blowing every five minutes followed by cries and protests.

'They must be bloody freezing,' said Wattie as they walked past the pitches. 'Shorts in this weather.'

'Character-building, or at least that's what they used to say. There it is.' McCoy pointed over at a green wooden hut, smoke coming out a chimney in the corner. 'What did she say his name was again?'

'Spence,' said Wattie.

Spence turned out to be a small wiry man with thick black hair. Looked like a Beatle wig sat on top of his wrinkled face. Effect wasn't pleasant. He let them into the hut, sat them down on an old park bench and sat himself back down on a battered armchair by the fire. The hut was tiny, full of junk from the school. Broken benches, big clock with one hand missing, pile of gym mats, broken tennis rackets. Smelt of smoke and some sort of fertiliser.

'What was it you were wanting?' asked Spence, poking at the fire.

'How long is it you've been here, Mr Spence?' asked Wattie.

'Me? Christ, now you're asking.' Thought, counted on his hands. 'Thirty-three years. Since I got demobbed.'

'So you were here mid fifties, aye?' asked McCoy.

'I told you, didn't I?' He shook his head at their obvious stupidity. 'Thirty-three bloody years.'

'Fair point,' said McCoy. 'You ever remember a policeman, Kenny Burgess, coming to the school?'

The poker gave it away. Stopped dead for a few seconds, no more rearranging the coals.

Spence shook his head, started poking again. 'No. What would a bloody policeman be coming to a school for? And even if he did I cannae remember that far back. Who bloody can?'

McCoy sat back on the bench. 'Wattie, do me a favour. I left my jotter in the car. Go back and get it, will you?'

Wattie looked at him like he was mad. 'You're joking, aren't you?'

'Just go and get it,' said McCoy.

Wattie stood up looking murderous, stomped out the hut.

McCoy waited until Wattie was definitely gone, Spence sitting there poking the fire, muttering to himself. Took out his cigarettes and lit one up.

'Thirty-three years,' he said. 'That's pretty good going. You must have led a charmed life to get away with it that long. Charmed life and a bit of protection from a certain boy in blue. Nice wee arrangement, right enough. Neat. You're here with all these young boys and he's out there making sure any complaints they make come to nothing.'

Spence looked at him. 'I don't know what you're talking about.'

'That right? Well, let me make it crystal clear for you, you fucking cunt. Either you pimped out the boys to Burgess so he could fuck them, or here's my more likely scenario, you weren't just a pimp. Sampled the goods before you handed them over.'

Spence stood up, sat back down again. Looked at the door.

'Bet you never thought when you got out your bed this morning that this was going to be the day. Must have known it was coming sometime, though. And here it is. Gravy train has just derailed, Spence. Big time.'

Spence looked at him again. McCoy had never seen a trapped rat but now he knew what one looked like.

'Easy way or hard way?' he asked.

Spence swallowed. 'Don't know what you're on about.'

'Always the fucking same,' muttered McCoy.

He stood up and moved towards Spence.

Spence held the poker out at him. 'Get away from me! I mean it!' he shouted.

McCoy kicked it out his hand. Spence cowered back in his chair. McCoy grabbed him, pulled him out of it and onto the floor. Stood on his hand with his left foot, ignored the scream and started kicking at his body with the other. Good few kicks in the balls as well. Within a few minutes Spence had stopped screaming, was down to a low moan every time McCoy's shoe thudded into him.

One last kick and McCoy knelt down by him. Punched him in the mouth hard, then did it again. Sat back against the park bench and got his cigarettes out. Spence lay there sobbing and moaning, wiping the blood from his mouth.

'Here's a wee heads up, Spence,' said McCoy. 'That's fuck all compared to what's going to happen to you every fucking day in Barlinnie. It will be all that and worse. They'll batter you every day, throw boiling water with sugar in it at you. Put shite in your food, piss in your tea. Chances are you'll last a month or so of that until someone finds out where you worked and realises that's where their wee brother or their nephew was. Then they'll kill you as slowly and painfully as they can.'

Spence was wailing now. Reached out, held on to McCoy's foot. 'Please . . . please, I'm sorry . . . I . . .'

McCoy blew out a cloud of cigarette smoke, waved it away. 'Sorry, are you? Well, that's nice, but I couldn't give a fuck. I want you in Barlinnie. I want you to suffer every fucking day.' The wailing was increasing. 'But I'm in a hurry, so there's a deal on the table.'

Spence nodded, face looking hopeful. 'Yes, please, anything.'

'Okay. This is it. Non-repeatable, non-negotiable.

291

You're going to tell me everything I need to know now. Right now. And when we get to the station and you're in your cell I'm going to take the turnkey for a cup of tea before he takes away your belt and your shoelaces. Should give you enough time, eh?'

What he was proposing dawned on Spence. His face crumpled.

'What? Don't tell me you thought you were getting off?' McCoy shook his head. 'That's the only deal. It's up to you, you fucking piece of shite.'

CHAPTER 26

Wattie was talking to Alice in her office when he saw McCoy walking back across the playing fields to the main building. He hurriedly said cheerio, ran out to meet him.

'I've got the jotter,' he said, holding it out. 'Sorry, got a bit waylaid.'

McCoy held out his hand. 'Give us it.'

Wattie handed it over. McCoy tried to take it and get his hands in his pocket before Wattie saw but he didn't manage it.

'Why've you got blood all over your hands?' asked Wattie. He looked up. 'Christ, it's all over your shirt as well.'

McCoy slipped something into the notebook. 'Tripped on the way out the wee hut. Go back and get that wee cunt and get him into the car.'

'What? Now? Did you find anything out?'

McCoy nodded.

'That it? No sharing?'

'Nope. Just get the cunt. And get his fucking biscuit tin.'

McCoy walked back into the building, sat down

293

on a bench in the main hall. Put his head in his hands, tried to breathe. They were all the same, these guys, couldn't help themselves, took pictures. Some they could put into Boots to get developed, some they had to take to Dirty Ally at Paddy's market, or someone like him. He opened the notebook and looked at the one he'd taken from Spence.

A Boots one. Couldn't face going through the other ones he had in the biscuit tin under the floorboards. Uncle Kenny in a pair of shorts standing on a riverbank. Two lads in the water with their underpants on. One of them was Connolly; even at twelve years old you could recognise him. Squinting at the camera, one arm wrapped round Burgess' leg. The photo was going to be enough to convince Murray, he was halfway there already.

If they wanted to look at Spence's other ones, find more evidence about what Uncle Kenny really liked to get up to on these wee camping trips, that was up to them. He'd done his bit. No way he was looking at photos like that, not for all the tea in China.

He went to the bathrooms, washed the blood off his hands. Supposed he could have spent hours interrogating Spence, would probably have broken, an old man after all. But he was too tired, too sick of it all; the denials, the crying, the horrible fucking details. He dried his hands on a stale-smelling roller towel. Took the picture out his wee red jotter and had another look. Maybe it was the fact that Connolly had a shock of dark hair in the picture that did it but McCoy thought he could remember where he'd seen him now, seen him before he started shaving it off.

The car crunched round on the gravel and Wattie stretched over and opened the passenger door. McCoy got in, pulled the door shut. Burgess was in the back – black eye, broken nose, cut over his eye and a look of terror on his face.

'You get the tin?' asked McCoy.

Wattie nodded. 'In the boot.'

'You have a look?'

'Started to. Stopped.'

'Don't blame you,' said McCoy.

'Back to the shop?'

McCoy shook his head. 'Not yet. Woodilee Asylum, about ten minutes up the road. Head towards Lenzie.'

He had to make sure. Glasgow was ringed with them. Woodilee, Dykebar, Leverndale. Asylums. Most of them were full of women, women who for the most part just couldn't cope any more and either broke or just gave up. Poverty, drink, husbands who beat them to fuck, the slow crushing horror of a life always led in fear and terror of what the next day would bring.

His mum had been one of them. He remembered coming to visit her a few times in Woodilee when he was a boy. Once with Dad, once with a woman from the council. She was still his mum, looked like her, smelt like her, but something had happened. Only found out later it was the electric shocks. They had undone her. Whatever was left of her had spooled away, slipped through her fingers in the fog of lithium, Seconal and fuck knows what else. His Auntie Mary was in there too, smiling at everyone, trying to show them her stuffed rabbit when all anyone could do was look at the ruin in her eyes, at what was left of her after the lobotomy.

McCoy wasn't even sure what had been wrong with his Auntie Mary in the first place. He knew she'd had a baby when she was fifteen who got taken away, knew her dad, his Great-uncle Donny, used to thrash her from room to room for 'being a fucking whore'. She ran away when she was twenty and he didn't see her until fifteen years later, sitting on a windowsill in Woodilee, dark circles round her eyes, rabbit in her hand, thumb in her mouth.

'This it?' asked Wattie as they pulled up. Woodilee looked as much like a stately home as anything else. Ornate red sandstone building topped with towers and arches, immaculate grounds.

McCoy nodded.

'You going to tell me what the fuck we're doing at a loony bin?'

'Just want to double-check something,' said McCoy. 'Sure I saw Connolly here years ago, just want to make sure.' He turned to Wattie. 'You all right to stay in the car with this cunt?'

'Long as he doesn't open his mouth.'

McCoy nodded. 'Won't be long.'

He checked at the reception desk. Mrs McCoy was still in Ward 9. And no, he couldn't see her out of visiting hours. He took out his badge, told the torn-faced cow behind the desk it was police business and headed for the corridor leading to the wards.

The ward sister was a large woman with her hair in braids and a red birthmark on her cheek. She smiled when he came in, got up from her desk, told him Mrs McCoy was sleeping but he was welcome to go and have a look if he fancied. Told him she'd told her all about him. Her big handsome son in the polis.

The ward was bright, full of light from the tall windows, walls painted a pale yellow colour. He walked down the line of beds. Some held old women more skin and bone than anything else, eyes bright, wondering what was going on; some just mounds beneath the covers, sleeping their days away.

Sister had told him his mum was in the bed at the end, beside the glass doors. They looked out onto a vast lawn, trees in the distance. He sat down on the chair by the bed, took his mum's hand in his. His hand was huge compared to hers now, his covered in scars and calluses, hers dry and warm, but they still fitted together. He was back holding his mummy's hand. She didn't move, looked out for the count. The drugs, he supposed.

He laid his head on the bed, could smell lilac talc; someone must still be bringing it to her.

'She's a good sleeper.'

He turned and his Auntie Mary was there. Her toy rabbit's fur was almost worn away now but she looked much the same.

'I know your name,' she said. 'You're Mary's boy.'

He nodded. 'Harry.'

She held out her rabbit. He took it, gave it a kiss and gave it back.

'Peter,' she said.

A nurse appeared behind her, guided her back towards the entrance to the ward. He looked back down at his mum. Wasn't really sure what he was doing here. He'd stopped coming a couple of years ago, didn't seem much point any more. Whatever was left of his mum had gone a long time ago. He stood up. Told her goodbye, kissed her hand and left.

He knew it was somewhere around here. Could remember sitting in the waiting room waiting to talk to some bored doctor about his mum's condition. He passed a room with a lot of women sitting at tables making cuddly toys and turned into a long corridor. Sign on the wall: DOCTOR'S OFFICES THIS WAY.

He kept going and then he saw it, green door with a frosted window and WAITING ROOM written on it. He opened it and went in. There was an elderly woman sitting there, coat and hat on, bag on her knees. She looked surprised to see him. He nodded to her and sat down on one of the orange plastic chairs.

'You all right, son?' she asked.

He nodded.

'Waiting to see the doctor?'

He nodded again, trying to put her off. Didn't work.

'Me too. My sister. Nerves. In for her nerves.'

He tried to remember being here before. Connolly had been sitting by the window, suit on, black hair cut into the wood. Looked like any other visitor.

'Been coming for years.'

He'd stood up when a receptionist came in and called his name. 'Mr Connolly? Doctor's ready for you.' Connolly'd walked past him on the way to the door, run his hands over his head as he did, smiled at the receptionist.

And that was it. Nothing else. So he was right. He'd seen Connolly before, didn't get him anywhere, though. Maybe he was just kidding himself coming here, thinking he would remember something important. Maybe he was just looking for an excuse to see his mum, hold her hand. Knew why. He still had the fear deep down inside him, the fear of being found out, the fear of having to tell everyone why he and Cooper had done it. Fear of what would happen to him. Maybe he was just a scared boy looking for his mum to make it all right. He stood up. She couldn't make it all right, not this time. Only way he could do that was to make sure everyone knew why Connolly who killed Burgess.

Time to get on with it.

Wattie had gone home. Spence was in the cells waiting for his duty officer. He'd walked him down there, told the turnkey he was on suicide watch. Turnkey nodded, wrote it on the chalkboard outside his cell. Took his laces, his belt, the blanket, his clothes, put him in a paper suit. Spence watched him dully. Knew what was coming to him, knew he was heading for Barlinnie. McCoy told the turnkey to check him every twenty minutes. No way that cunt was killing himself before he got what was coming to him.

'You lied to me,' said Spence.

'That's right,' said McCoy and shut the heavy iron door.

Now he was sitting at his desk, watching the clock and waiting for Murray to come out his office. Tried to think about where Connolly could be now. They still hadn't found him, not a clue as to where he was, even with all the extra men on the job. Maybe that psychiatrist weirdo was right. Maybe he had killed himself, was lying in some empty flat or shitey hotel room, or even in the woods somewhere. Maybe they were looking for a ghost.

Murray's door opened and he stood there in his shirtsleeves, rolled up over his meaty arms, empty pipe in his hand. He looked exhausted. Waved at McCoy. 'Come on in.'

By the time McCoy got in the office and shut the door Murray was easing himself back into his seat behind the desk. He yawned widely, shook himself. Looked up at the clock. Eight o'clock.

'Twelve bloody hours I've been in here. Fuck it!'

He leant back, opened the drawer of a filing cabinet and took out a bottle of Whyte & Mackay and two glasses. Poured a couple of measures into each, handed one to McCoy.

'All the funeral stuff done?' asked McCoy.

Murray took a swig, scowled, nodded. 'Yep. Tight as a crab's arsehole.'

'You think he'll turn up?'

'Connolly? Never know, he's fucking mad enough to. Even if he doesn't, every other fucking villain in this city will. Big day out. Got Andy and another two photographing everyone, help us to see the runners and riders now Scobie's out the picture. Gonnae get ugly in the next few weeks.'

'Aye, so everyone keeps telling me,' said McCoy. He took another swig of the whisky. 'You speak to Spence?'

Murray nodded. 'Wasnae saying much, wants to wait for his solicitor. Had a look in the fucking biscuit tin, though.' He rifled through his papers until he found the photo of Burgess on the riverbank, peered at it. 'It's definitely him, isn't it?'

McCoy nodded.

Murray rifled around again. 'I told Thomson to go through the tin. See if he can identify anyone.

I couldnae face it.' He held out a photo. 'He found this.'

McCoy's stomach lurched. Was scared of what he was going to be looking at. Of what it might be. Of whom it might be. He took it, looked down. It was Connolly, thick black hair, smile on his face. It looked like he was in some sort of tent. He was naked, Burgess sat beside him in a pair of underpants, arm round his shoulder. He handed it back.

'It's enough to connect them, to give us a motive for the murder. Don't need any testimony from anyone else.'

McCoy poured himself another belt, drank it over. 'That's good.'

Murray looked at him. 'Something I need to tell you.'

'Oh aye, what's that?' asked McCoy, voice sounding wobbly. Fear rising. Him and Cooper arrested. Convicted.

'Nobody's going to know.'

'What?' asked McCoy, not understanding.

'Burgess was an elder of the church. A decorated senior police officer with forty years' service. Wife and two kids, grandkids. Right Worshipful Master of the Chief Super's Lodge. All-round pillar of the community. Chief Super would rather it stayed that way.'

He could feel Murray watching him, looking for a reaction.

'Connolly was a psychopath with a hatred of the

police. Picked Burgess at random and that's why he got killed. No rhyme or reason to it. Just bad luck. You okay with that?'

McCoy nodded. Truth was he didn't care. No connection to him and Cooper was all that mattered. Cooper and him had done what they needed to do. The fucker had been tortured to death. The account was settled.

'Spence?' he asked.

'Be spending the rest of his life in Barlinnie getting battered every week and drinking tea with piss in it,' said Murray.

McCoy stood up. 'All's well that ends well.' He finished the last of his whisky, put the glass down on the desk.

Murray looked at him. 'You sure you're okay about all this, Harry? You know you can speak to me if—'

McCoy held his hands up. 'I'm fine. Honest. Now, why don't you buy me a drink and we'll talk about something rather than the bloody case? You can even talk about bloody rugby.'

Murray smiled, took his coat off the peg, followed him out the door.

After an argument about where they were going to go they ended up in Macintosh's in Cambridge Street. Not too loud for Murray, far enough from the shop that they wouldn't meet any other polis for McCoy.

Murray sat at a table while McCoy went up to the bar. There was a group of young guys in the corner, sports bags at their feet, wet hair, must have come from playing football. Other than them and a few couples, the place was quiet. McCoy ordered two pints and two whiskies and carried them back over to Murray.

He'd got his pipe out and was happily puffing away despite the theatrical coughs of a woman a few tables away. 'Need you to do me a favour,' he said, trying his pint.

McCoy had just swallowed his whisky over in one, frowned. 'What's that then?'

'Like you to talk to David,' said Murray.

'He still staying with you? Him and Colin?'

Murray nodded. 'Haven't got rid of the buggers yet. Were supposed to be with us for six months, coming up for three years now.'

McCoy grinned. 'What's Margaret got to say about that?'

'You know her, she'd keep any of them for ever but they're almost seventeen now.'

'You no getting a bit old for all this fostering malarkey?'

'Far too old. But the council called Margaret the other day. Thirteen-year-old twins. Nowhere else to go. Colin and David need to make way.'

'So what is it I'm supposed to be doing?'

'Colin's all sorted. Starting an apprenticeship next month. David's a bit lost. Just finished school, no idea what he wants to do. Want you to talk to him about joining the polis.'

McCoy shook his head. 'Things don't change much in your house, do they?'

'Nope,' said Murray. 'He's a big lad, sensible. Would suit him. You can tell him how it made a man of you.'

'Did it?' McCoy grinned.

'Don't push it, son.' He held up his glass. 'Another?'

They had a couple more pints. McCoy told Murray he'd talk to the boy. Murray told McCoy all about how the Police Rugby League was getting on and he nodded, not listening to a word. Was getting to half nine when Murray stood up to go, started putting his coat on.

'What you doing?' he asked.

McCoy took his wee red jotter out his pocket, held it up. 'Going to have another pint and a think.'

'I'll see you at the funeral at nine. See if you can come up with something by then.'

McCoy said he would, watched him go. Was only a mouthful left in his pint glass, time for another, but time for a pee first. He swallowed the dregs, headed for the toilets. They smelt like most pub toilets did, of piss and those wee yellow cakes that sat in the trough. He stood up on the ledge, unbuttoned his fly and started peeing. He heard the door open behind him but did as toilet etiquette required and kept staring at the wall in front of him.

He felt a hand on the back of his head for a

second before it rammed his forehead hard against the wall. Held it there, his face squashed into the cold tiles. He tried to move but whoever was holding him was strong, stronger than he was. Could feel the pee running down his leg, felt warm breath in his ear, squirmed, tried to get away.

'You weren't on my list,' the voice said. 'But you are now.'

CHAPTER 27

McCoy could feel Connolly's breath against his check, smell it. Smelt like something rotten, dead. He couldn't move, forehead scraping against a cracked tile on the wall. Felt a punch in his side, another, and Connolly pressed his head harder into the tiles. McCoy tried to kick out backwards, make contact with something, a leg, anything. Was hitting air.

Connolly hissed in his ear. 'Think yourself lucky you only got spat in the face or you'd be getting worse than this.'

Smell of him was revolting. McCoy tried to struggle. Sickeningly he could feel that Connolly had a hard-on, could feel it pressing into his back. Then he was in his ear again.

'You dirty little fucker, you're going to get what's coming.'

McCoy managed to move his head slightly, get his face off the wall. 'Get off, you cunt!'

Connolly laughed, punched him again. 'It's the ones like you I enjoy. Ones that start off like big men and end up peeing their drawers and crying for their mammy. And believe me, McCoy, you're going to cry.'

Another punch and McCoy tried to cry out. His whole side felt like it was on fire. He could hear the jukebox outside in the pub, someone laughing. All seemed very far away. Tile was cutting into his skin, could feel blood running into his eye. Knew he was in trouble, visions of Charlie Jackson on the roof.

Then the noise of the door opening behind him and a surprised-sounding voice. 'What the fuck's going on here?'

Felt a sharp pain down his side and the hand grabbed his neck, pulled it back and smashed his face off the wall again. He fell down, half in, half out the trough, turned in time to catch a glimpse of the back of a bald head and a razor being lifted then brought down on the face of the old man standing at the toilet door.

The man's face opened, a sheet of blood appearing.

Connolly turned back to him, grinned, drew his finger across his neck. 'I'll see you later, McCoy. I'm nowhere near finished with you yet.' Stepped over the old man and the growing puddle of blood and disappeared out the door.

McCoy tried to stand up, didn't feel good, put his hand on the tiled floor to try and steady himself and it slid in the warm blood covering the floor. The old man was on the ground, hands up at his face. The door closed and McCoy was left lying there in his own piss and blood. He scrambled to his feet and wobbled into the wall, looked down. Blood soaking through his shirt.

The door half opened. A woman's voice. 'Willie? You okay in there?'

'Help us,' said McCoy. 'Help.'

Susan was sitting at the kitchen table when he got in, notepads and books spread all over it. He leant over and kissed the back of her neck. Put the four cans of Export down on the table.

'Someone smells like they've been to the pub already,' she said and looked up.

'Jesus, Harry! What happened?'

He had stitches in his eyebrow, a burst lip and a pyjama top from A&E on under his coat. He sat down on the couch, winced in pain. 'I'm okay, honest.'

But he wasn't, not by a long shot. Tried to look better than he felt. Smiled.

Susan was beside him, staring at his face. 'Okay? Then why are you sitting funny? Why have you got bloody pyjamas on? Harry? Harry?'

He held his hand up. 'Don't make me laugh. It hurts.'

He eased his coat off. 'Gonnae help me get these pyjamas off?'

She moved in, unbuttoned them and gingerly eased the top over his arms. 'Oh, Harry.' She looked like she was about to cry.

'It looks worse than it is. Honest,' he said, lying.

He'd a bandage wrapped round his torso, specks of blood showing through it already. Twelve stitches underneath them. A razor slash across his ribs. Would have been a heck of a lot worse if he hadn't been wearing a jumper under his jacket. They weren't sure what the 'punches' he'd felt were but they weren't punches, more like hits from a cosh, something heavy. Two cracked ribs and black and blue bruises around his body.

Susan peered at the bandage. 'What happened?'

He was too sore and too tired to explain it tonight. 'Got hit by a car coming out of Macintosh's. My fault. Wasn't looking where I was going. Was just a bump. I'll be fine in the morning.'

'Christ, Harry, you're a bloody idiot. You had me worried.' She stood up. 'All that and you went to the off sales on the way home?'

He tried a smile. 'Knew we'd finished the Red Leb. Needed some kind of anaesthetic.'

She shook her head. 'Bed. Now.'

He was about to protest then realised how tired he was. Bed suddenly didn't seem like such a bad idea.

Took a bit of manoeuvring and a lot of moans and groans to get him in there. Eventually he was in and propped up on the pillows. Susan re-appeared with two aspirins, some sleeping pill she'd found and a couple of cans of the beer.

'Here,' she said. 'These might help you sleep.' Got in beside him.

He tried not to groan as she snuggled in to his

side. He opened the can, covered the top with his mouth as it foamed up and took a drink, swallowed over the pills. 'You go and see Cooper?'

'Oh yes, had quite the afternoon.'

'How come? He tell you stuff?'

'Told me stuff and had a smile on his face when he did it.' She looked up him. 'Do you know what he does?'

He nodded.

'And you're still friendly with him?'

McCoy sighed. Had a feeling this was going to happen.

'I've known him for twenty years. He's like a brother—'

'A brother who ruins women's lives.'

McCoy reached for his fags on the bedside table. 'You asked me to speak to someone in the vice game. All info for the dissertation. What did you think he was going to be like?'

'I didn't think he would be so unrepentant. So fucking proud of himself.'

'You're a good-looking girl, he's just showing off.'

He lit up, could feel the sleeping pill and the beer starting to work. Didn't let on they'd already dosed him at the hospital.

'You're not taking this seriously,' she said. 'He's a monster.'

He shrugged. This wasn't an argument he wanted to have. Especially not tonight.

'You don't even care, do you?' she asked.

He tried to sound even, take the sting out of things. 'I thought I was doing you a favour. Among other things, Cooper is a pimp, no better or no worse than the rest of them. Unless the entire vice trade disappears tomorrow there will always be people like him—'

'Men like him.'

'Men like him who'll run prostitutes. I can't stop that.'

'Or even try. All boys together, aren't you?'

He'd tried, but now he was getting angry. 'Fuck sake, Susan, give me a break. I'm not the bloody enemy here.'

'You sure about that?'

There was silence for a minute. He lay back on the pillows. 'Look, I'm going to go to sleep. I'm tired, and I'm in pain. I think if we keep going we'll both say things we don't really mean. But if you really think I'm the enemy then you're wrong.'

He woke up a couple of hours later. Side was too sore to really sleep. Rain battering against the window. He turned over in the bed, trying to find a more comfortable position, and Susan was looking at him.

'You're awake,' he said.

She nodded.

'You okay?'

'You're not the enemy, Harry. I'm sorry.'

She cuddled into him and laid her head on his chest. He closed his eyes. Pretended to go back to sleep.

My judgement is going fast.
like my sight
like my control
i can hear voice voices
voices that hate me
the voice of my mum and the voice of my dad inside
my head my head that hurts all the time now

i should have waited. time is not mine to control

done him outside.

in the street
in an alley
alone
i am sick and fat with dead material

idontwantoliv e this lif

timeis runnn nnnning out.
one day eft.

justenoughtime

18TH FEBRUARY 1973

CHAPTER 28

McCoy recognised him by the cut of his expensive coat. Tall figure standing outside the Terminus Cafe looking a bit lost. Didn't suppose Lambhill was his normal habitat on a Saturday morning. Or any other morning come to that. He crossed the road, side hurting like fuck, and headed towards him.

'Didn't think you'd be here,' said McCoy as he approached.

'No. Wasn't sure whether to come.' Lomax peered at his face. 'Been in the wars, Mr McCoy?'

McCoy rubbed at his stitches. 'Something like that.'

'You heard, I suppose?' asked Lomax.

McCoy nodded. 'Heard this morning. Elaine gave you the big E.'

Lomax looked pained. 'Not quite the way I'd put it but accurate enough. "Services no longer required."' He looked like he still couldn't believe it had happened. 'Still, I did work for her father for almost twenty years. Felt like I should show my face.'

McCoy pointed. 'Mourners are going in across the road.'

They watched as the funeral cars made their slow way down the hill. A long line of shiny black Daimler and Jaguar limousines stopping the traffic on Balmore Road. The crowd outside St Agnes' Chapel had been getting bigger since McCoy had arrived a couple of hours earlier. People come to pay their respects to the great man, curious passers-by, the press, and of course the police.

Lomax wiped snowflakes off the shoulders of his coat. 'So they are. I should get in soon. You joining us?'

'Think I'll just spectate from over here,' said McCoy.

Elaine Scobie hadn't been shy about putting her hand in her pocket. Three mourners in top hats led the cortège, heads bowed. Glass-sided carriage pulled by six black horses following behind. Horses snorting and stamping, breathing big clouds in the cold air, black feather plumes stuck in their bridles.

Scobie's coffin was almost obscured by all the flowers covering it. Huge mound of white lilies and roses. A sign with DADDY spelled out in floral letters ran the length of the glass panel. If McCoy was a betting man there'd be a wreath in there with a note saying 'From the Twins' on it as well.

Lomax said goodbye and hurried across the road to the chapel entrance and disappeared into the crowd of black coats and black umbrellas held up against the falling snow. McCoy scanned the crowd. Didn't know what he was expecting.

Connolly to be standing there, black armband on and an 'Arrest Me' sign around his neck? He chucked his empty paper cup of rotten tea into the wire bin at the bus stop and walked up towards where Murray had positioned himself outside Lambhill Police Station.

'Nice of him to get buried here,' McCoy said, pointing at the chapel directly across the road. 'Very convenient.'

'What's this I hear about last night?' Murray asked.

'Wattie tell you?' asked McCoy.

Murray nodded. 'The bare bones. You sure it was Connolly?'

'Think so. Only got a glimpse, but who else with a bald head is going to attack me in the toilet of Macintosh's? Besides, he said I was lucky she only spat in my face.'

'How come he knew that?' Murray asked.

'Well, he wasn't in the hospital canteen as far as I could see. Only really leaves one option.'

'Elaine told him.'

McCoy shrugged. 'Looks like it.'

'Christ, she's a piece of bloody work. You're lucky you got away without any more damage.'

'That's the thing,' said McCoy. 'Whole thing was a rush, all a bit of a mess. Jumping me in the toilets of the pub? Not the greatest idea. Not like him. Everything else he's done has been precise, organised. Last night just feels like he wasn't thinking properly.'

'Maybe. Let's hope so. How's the old boy?'

'Fine apart from the scar he's going to have. Wife nearly had a heart attack.'

'Not bloody surprised.' Murray was craning his head, trying to see up to the roof, sheepskin jacket straining. 'Is that wee prick Andy up on there?'

McCoy looked up at the two-storey police station behind him. Couldn't see much of anything. 'Should be. Wattie told him enough times.'

'Wattie!' shouted Murray.

Wattie appeared from the station doorway as if by magic. Looked about ten times better than McCoy did in his suit and black Crombie, even had a black armband on. 'Sir?'

'That clown up there, is he?' asked Murray.

'Yep. Just left him. Tripod, bags of film, big long lens. Whole kit and caboodle. All right, McCoy?'

'Knows what he's doing?' asked Murray.

Wattie recited, '"Mourners, crowd, anyone lurking about. Cover them all. Get clear face shots." He's been told fifty times.'

'He better be ready,' said McCoy. 'Show's about to begin.'

The lead Daimler had drawn up at the chapel entrance. The priest opened the door and Elaine Scobie stepped out. Every inch the chief mourner in a long fitted black coat, hat with veil piled on top of it. Shiny black high heels adding a touch of sombre sexiness. The crowd parted to let her through; men took their hats off, ladies looked down respectfully.

She stopped at the entrance, looked back at the crowd for a minute, flashbulbs going off, lowered the veil over her immaculately made-up face and stepped into the chapel. You had to hand it to her, she knew how to make an entrance as well as an exit.

They watched the limousines slowly empty. Relatives, associates, gangland faces.

'See your girlfriend's here,' said McCoy as Mary stepped out the second limo. She looked almost normal for once: black fur coat and hat, make-up just this side of panto slightly undermining her serious demeanour.

'Very funny,' said Wattie. 'By the way, you better stay out her way, said you owed her some exclusive.'

'Fuck! I forgot about that.'

The crowd of photographers rushed towards a car, flashbulbs going, as Frankie Vaughan stepped out, all teeth and hair and skinny black suit. The real villains were keeping well out the way, didn't need their faces in the paper. They were gathered at the back, Crombies and trilbies to a man, faces down. All except one.

After twenty years of jeans it was the second time he'd seen Stevie Cooper in a suit in a couple of days. Looked like a new one as well. Dark blue, black tie, snow-white shirt. He was standing tall, making sure everyone knew he was here, Billy Weir by his side. A few slashes weren't going to stop him. Here to let all the contenders to Scobie's throne know that he was still very much in the game.

'You really think Connolly will show his face?' asked McCoy. 'He'd have to be mad.'

Murray shrugged. 'Fuck knows. Worth a try. Got men up and down the road to the cemetery, couple in the chapel. Have to try and get a few into Mallon's afterwards.'

'That where the big do is then? Mallon's? No exactly Ferrari's, is it?'

'Scobie grew up round here, maybe that's why. Old times' sake.'

'I'm going to walk up to the cemetery, have a look around while they're all in there,' said McCoy.

'Suit yourself,' said Murray. 'You get a whiff of Connolly, you call it in. Clear?'

McCoy nodded. 'Don't worry.' He held up the walkie-talkie he'd been given and had no idea how to work and started walking.

Lambhill Cemetery was only ten minutes up the hill. Stood right on the edge of the city, fields and then the Campsie Hills beyond. Wind was bitter, coming in from the north, driving the snow, chilling McCoy right through. He walked through the big stone archway at the entrance, nodded at some uniform he half recognised who pointed off to the left.

Didn't have to walk far before he saw the black hole of the grave in the field of white, diggers in donkey jackets and woolly scarves standing by the tarpaulin-covered earth that was about to be returned from whence it came. He wandered amongst the graves, finally found a big mausoleum thing that he could shelter behind. He leant against the eulogy to Samuel Sneddon 1856–1912, lit up a cigarette and tried to ignore the throbbing in his side.

He looked around, just rows of graves, few wind-blasted trees. Knowing Connolly, if he was here there would be no way McCoy would see him. Murray seemed to be pinning a lot on this, with polis all the way up the hill, Andy and his pictures. Pressure must be getting to him. Papers would be full of it again tomorrow, funeral kicking it all up again. A fat seagull landed on a nearby grave, squawked at him. He looked around again. Nowhere here for Connolly to be. Well, at least not as far as he could see.

The gravediggers heard the engines first, looked up. The line of limos and cars was inching its way up the hill towards the graveyard. McCoy flicked the last of his cigarette away and started walking down towards the gate, thought he'd leave them to it and have a look round Mallon's while they buried him. Maybe a whisky or two to try and get the warmth back into his bones.

He stood back from the road and took off his hat as the first limo approached. Elaine was sitting on his side, looking out the window. She took her sunglasses off as the car drew near. Before he knew it he'd bowed his head and crossed himself. Autopilot. When he looked back up she was looking back at him. Could have sworn she had a half-smile on her lips. Did she know what had happened to him last night? Did she ask him to do it?

The rest of the cars followed. He couldn't help smiling when Mary threw him a vicky as her car passed, mouthed 'You're fucking dead, McCoy'.

Dignified as always.

Mallon's was just along from the chapel. A strange-looking building. It had a round tower at the front covered in white pebbledash, looked a bit like a wee lighthouse. Behind it was a red-brick building that held the bar, lounge and function suite. It did well out of weddings, funerals and the normal evening trade. Was always packed on a Friday and Saturday night, people getting up to sing or tell some jokes.

He pulled the big front door open and walked in. Was immediately hit by a wave of heat and the smell of sausage rolls and egg sandwiches. Buffet was being laid out by two young girls in waitress uniforms. Sandwiches, pies and slices of cake all being arranged on big trestle tables sitting adjacent to the bar.

'Christ, no seen you in here for a while,' said the bartender as McCoy walked up to the bar. 'You have an argument with a brick wall?'

'Closer than you'll ever know, Bobsy, closer than you'll ever know. You all right?' asked McCoy.

'As I'll ever be. You want a pint?' he asked, moving towards the pumps.

'Not today,' said McCoy, peeling off his soaking coat and scarf and hanging them on the back of a chair. 'I'm fucking freezing and I'm dying for a pish. Double Bell's and where is it again?'

Bobsy pointed over to a door in the corner and moved over to the optics. 'You're paying for this, you know!' he shouted after him.

'Aye, in your dreams,' said McCoy, smiling as he pushed the toilet door open. He stopped, smile frozen on his face. 'Christ,' he said under his breath. 'Fucking hell . . .'

The three of them stood there – Murray, McCoy and Thomson – just looking, trying to take it all in.

The gents' toilets looked like the inside of an abattoir. The floor was slick with blood, was even in the urinal trough. Was everywhere. The long mirror across the row of sinks had been smashed, half of it on the floor, half still clinging to the wall in long shards. A black spray-painted message was written along what was left of it.

PROMISES MADE. IT'S TIME.

McCoy took a hanky out his pocket, held it over his mouth; smell of the blood making him feel sick. 'Bastard must have been in and out quick. Staff cleaned it twenty minutes ago.'

Wattie opened the swing door of the gents', walked in, started coughing.

'Fuck sake, you weren't joking, were you?' he said, spitting on the floor. 'Can even taste it in my mouth.'

'You held them at the cemetery?' asked Murray.

'Aye. No happy about it, though. Three poor uniforms lined up under the arch blocking the way are getting pelters. Family want to know what's going on. Think we're just noising them up for the sake of it.'

'Gonnae have to move it, sir,' said McCoy. 'They can't have the reception here. That mad bastard could be somewhere in here waiting for them. It's too dangerous.'

Murray was tapping the pipe against his teeth. 'What the fuck am I supposed to tell them?'

'Gas leak? Pipes frozen?' suggested McCoy.

Wattie coughed again, held up his hand. 'Sorry, right in my bloody throat. I spoke to The Inn up the road. They'll take them, got a function suite about the size of this one. Just move all the sandwiches and stuff up there. Pub's a pub.'

'Fine,' said Murray. 'Tell them it's a burst pipe and move it there. Better get going.'

Wattie nodded, made for the door and something resembling fresh air.

'You think he's in here somewhere?' asked McCoy.

Murray shrugged. 'Soon find out. Got half the polis that were out there crawling over this building.' Looked disheartened. 'If you ask me he's gone.' He nodded at the mess. 'He's made his point.'

'Which is?' asked McCoy.

'Christ knows. A warning? Whatever he's done, whatever he's doing, it's coming to an end.'

'You reckon Elaine's got something to do with the murders after all? Promised him something in return for getting rid of her fiancé and her dad?'

'I didn't, but now I'm no so sure. Is she really that manipulative? That cold-blooded?'

'Would you be asking those questions if she was a man? You'd just assume she'd done it to take over.'

'You're probably right. Maybe we've all been taken in by her womanly charms, not seen what she really is.'

'Mary at the *Record*'s convinced she's got someone on the go. A boyfriend.'

'Connolly?' asked Murray.

McCoy shrugged. 'Could be. Would make sense. Maybe she's trying to welsh on the bargain now and he's not having it.' He nodded at the spray-painted message. 'Would explain that if she was having—'

They turned as the door swung wide open again, banged against the tiled wall.

'I was told you were in here. What on earth do you think you're playing—'

Archie Lomax stopped, mouth open, staring at the blood and the message on the wall. He stepped back, colour draining from his face.

'How did he get in here?' asked Murray, looking at Thomson.

'Don't know, sir, doors are supposed to be—'

Didn't get a chance to finish.

'Well, get out there and make bloody sure they are!'

Thomson made himself scarce, pushed past the stunned Lomax on the way out.

'What is this?' asked Lomax. 'What in God's name's going on?'

'Connolly,' said McCoy.

'Anything you want to tell us, Mr Lomax?' asked Murray.

'Me? About what?' he spluttered.

'About your ex-client?'

'Elaine? What would she have to do with this?'

'A lot, maybe. You absolutely sure she has had nothing to do with what's going on? Boyfriend out the way, father out the way. Even you out the way. She's a very rich young woman all of a sudden. A rich young woman who has an empire to run.'

Lomax leant back against the tiled wall, held his hand up and was tidily sick on the floor. 'Sorry,' he murmured, wiping his mouth with a mono-grammed handkerchief. 'Smell really is quite appalling.' He dropped the handkerchief into a bin by the sinks. Evacuation completed, he was back in full lawyer mode.

'What you're trying to imply is nonsense. There's no way Elaine would conspire with that lunatic to kill her father and fiancé. The whole idea is absurd.'

'Is it?' asked Murray. 'You sure? She got rid of you without a blink. You sure she's the nice wee girl you think she is?'

Lomax looked at them. He was thinking about it, maybe starting to doubt. Moment went.

'Nonsense,' he said. 'An ill-advised business decision to fire me hardly makes her a conspirator to murder. The other chap said something about moving to The Inn? Is that what I tell everyone?'

McCoy nodded and Lomax went to go.

'Mr Lomax,' said Murray. Lomax turned back. 'If you're right, and I hope you are, do one thing for me. For fuck sake get her to come into protective custody. Whatever her relationship with Connolly is, I think it's broken down. He's out of control. Way past the point of no return. I can't protect her unless she comes in. You know that and I know that. Help us out here.'

Lomax nodded, stepped over the puddle of his own sick and left.

'Twenty-eight polis I've got on overtime. Half of Central up here as well as the Lambhill boys and it's all been a waste of fucking time, hasn't it?'

'Come on, Murray. What else could you do?' asked McCoy.

'I could catch the cunt, that's what I could do. Do the job I'm supposed to.' He buttoned up his coat. 'C'mon, I need some fresh air.'

They stood outside on the pavement. Snow was going off. McCoy could still taste the blood at the back of his throat. He spat into the snow and lit up a cigarette. Murray was standing over by the side watching the last of the snow whirl round the lampposts on Balmore Road. McCoy handed him a whisky he'd got from Bobsy behind the bar. He took it, took a sip.

'I think they're gonnae take me off this tomorrow,' he said. 'Get some new blood in from Lothian. He's killed three people already, including a cop, probably got more in his sights. It can't go on.'

'What's the point of that?' asked McCoy. 'You know Glasgow better than anyone, you know him better than anyone—'

'Aye, but I can't fucking find him, can I? One man. One deranged lunatic on the loose in Glasgow, and with all the time and resources in the world I can't get him.'

'You will. We will.'

Murray half smiled. 'You sure about that?'

'Sure as sure. C'mon, let's see how the purvey's going.'

The Inn was a low modern building with a big orange plastic sign above the door in groovy modern type. Trouble was the sign was the only thing that was remotely groovy or modern about the place. It was a drinkers' pub, not really for socialising, just for seeking a lonely oblivion. Probably the last place Elaine Scobie imagined seeing off her dad. Murray and McCoy had a drink in the bar, keeping an eye on the comings and goings in and out of the function suite, ignoring the dirty looks thrown at them. Was getting on, crowd was starting to thin out. Just the diehards left.

McCoy was just about to go to the bar again when Billy Weir emerged, looking for the toilets. He saw McCoy and nodded over to the other end of the bar.

McCoy waited until Murray wandered off to the toilets and went over. 'You still here, Billy?'

Billy nodded, didn't look too happy about it. 'No my idea, I can tell you. It's Cooper that wants to stay.'

'Stevie? Why's he so keen on being here?'

'Think he just wants everyone to know he's still in the game. Been glowering over at Scobie's goons the whole time. I keep trying to get him to go home. The amount he's drinking, this could end up nasty.' Suddenly struck him. 'Why don't you go and have a word?'

'Me?'

'Aye, go on, Mr McCoy. You're good with him when he gets like this.'

McCoy looked back at the toilets. 'Need to be quick.'

The function suite was a long room with a stage at one end. Grimy red carpet, chairs and tables arranged in two lines, remnants of some Christmas tinsel hanging from the ceiling. What was left of the guests was scattered round the different tables, men with shirtsleeves rolled up, pints in their hands. Women were down to black dresses, fags and wee sherry glasses. Some sort of moany Irish ballad playing over the tannoy.

Cooper was standing with his back to the bar,

pint in hand. His tie was undone, suit jacket gone, reddish watery stain on his shirt where the blood was seeping through his stitches. He looked drunk, the mean kind of drunk that always spelt trouble. Billy was right; his eyes were firmly fixed on the corner table where Scobie's lieutenants had settled themselves. McCoy wasn't looking forward to trying to get him out of there, not one bit. Still, he had to give it a try. Anything would be better than a free-for-all with a room full of tooled-up hard men.

McCoy was heading for him when Mary suddenly appeared in front of him, blocking his way. She prodded him in the chest. 'You, you lying bastard, are in deep trouble. Confirmation, my arse.'

'Mary, lovely to see you. Looking for Wattie, are you?'

'Very funny, McCoy. At least I've discovered one polis who isn't a total arsehole.'

'That right? Don't speak too soon. Hasn't told you he's married, has he?'

She stopped. 'Whit?'

McCoy grinned. 'Come on, where's your sense of humour, Mary?'

'It's where my boot's going to be in a minute, right up your arse. You, arsehole, are going to tell me exactly what you know about a certain senior policeman's death to make up for fucking me about. Right?'

Murray had reappeared. 'Miss Webster.'

Mary smiled at him, all angelic. 'Evening,

Inspector Murray.' Turned back to McCoy, prodded him again. 'DO NOT MOVE. I'm not finished with you yet. I'm going to the bogs to see if her ladyship's all right. She's been in there so long I think she's fallen down the bloody plughole.'

McCoy nodded, saluted. Mary muttered 'prick' under her breath and headed for the toilets.

'Interesting young woman, that,' said Murray.

'That's one word for her,' said McCoy. 'You want another pint?'

Murray nodded. 'Why not?'

McCoy hadn't even reached the bar when he heard his name being shouted. He turned; it seemed to be coming from behind the toilet door. He walked over, pushed it open.

Mary was standing there, looking distraught.

'What? What is it?'

'She's no here,' she said. 'She's gone.'

CHAPTER 29

Murray was looking up at the ceiling of the ladies' toilets. Two of the big white plasterboard tiles were gone, leaving a hole a couple of feet across.

'Fuck sake!' he shouted. Kicked in the bathroom door; it swung back, clattered against the wall. 'We're standing next bloody door! Twenty feet away and he's got in here and taken her!'

'Sir, we couldn't—'

'Couldn't what? Organise a fucking piss-up in a brewery? Jesus Christ!' He turned to McCoy. 'I tell you what, if I wasn't off the case before, I sure as hell am now. And do you know what? I don't bloody blame them. What a fucking fiasco.'

'There's a search going on outside—'

'What, after the barn door's bloody shut?'

McCoy was going to say something else, thought better of it, decided to just let the storm blow itself out.

'How the fuck am I supposed to explain this away?'

McCoy didn't say anything. What was the point? Murray was right. It was a fucking fiasco.

'So he was up there all the time?' Murray asked.

'That's the theory,' said McCoy. 'Sat up there until she came in alone, dropped down, somehow managed to get a hold of her, and took her back up into the loft, out the skylight and away. She can't weigh more than seven stone or so, she's tiny.'

'What is he? The bloody Scarlet Pimpernel?'

McCoy looked up again. 'Nope. But he's a mad enough bastard to do it, wait up there for hours.'

Murray shook his head. 'So that's what all that blood was for up at Mallon's? To get her down here while we searched up there.'

McCoy nodded. 'Looks like it, and we fell for it hook, line and sinker. Oldest trick in the book.'

'How'd he get back up?' asked Murray.

McCoy pointed over at the row of sinks. 'Just stand on there, then pull yourself up. Not that difficult.'

'Not that easy with a struggling woman, though,' said Murray.

'Maybe she wasn't struggling much,' said McCoy. 'Not enough time for his usual Mandrax trick though. Must have had a knife, a gun maybe.'

'Poor cow,' said Murray.

'Or maybe she waited until everyone else had gone back into the hall and tapped on the ceiling, let him know she was here.'

'You really think they're in this together?'

'Makes sense.'

Murray looked up at the hole in the ceiling again.

'Why wouldn't she just meet up with him later?' he asked. 'Why go to all this trouble?'

'She's not stupid, Elaine. Even if she is involved, there's no way she'd want anyone to know it. Wants people to think she's the helpless victim in all this. She's got Connolly wrapped around her finger, nothing he wouldn't agree to, not with—'

The toilet doors burst open. They turned to see Stevie Cooper standing there. He was swaying, tie undone, face flushed, but he looked serious, deadly serious.

'I need to talk to you,' he said, pointing at McCoy. 'Now.'

Murray looked furious. 'This is a bloody crime scene, Cooper! Get the fuck out my sight before I take you in for obstruction. You hear me?'

Cooper didn't even flinch, just kept his eyes on McCoy. 'Now,' he repeated.

Murray went to go for him and McCoy put his hand out, held him back.

'I'll be two minutes, sir. Easiest way.'

He pushed Cooper out the door, left before Murray could say anything. Cooper marched across the dancefloor, out the back doors and into the car park. Stood there waiting for McCoy to catch up.

'You trying to get me fired?' hissed McCoy. 'Want to tell me what the fuck is going on?'

'He's got her,' he said.

'Aye, think we'd gathered that,' said McCoy. 'What's the big deal?'

336

'You need to find her before he kills her,' he said. 'You need to find her.'

McCoy looked at him. Hadn't seen fear in Cooper's eyes very often but he was seeing it now. And then it struck him. How wrong he'd been.

'It's you, isn't it?' he said.

Cooper looked at him, realised he'd given himself away.

'You're the one she's been having wee chats on the phone with, the one she's been getting dressed up—'

'Just fucking find her, McCoy!'

'So when did all this start? Before or after her fiancé got his cock stuck in his mouth?'

Cooper moved so quickly McCoy didn't have a chance to react. Next thing he knew he was lying on his back in the snow, Cooper's knees on his shoulders, his hands at his neck. Cooper bent his face down into McCoy's, spat the words out. 'Just fucking find her. Right?'

McCoy could smell the beer and cigarettes on his breath. See the panic in his eyes. 'Get off me,' he said.

Cooper eased his grip, stood up and walked away.

McCoy lay there watching him go, watched him walk out the car park and into a waiting car, Billy at the wheel. Lay there wondering why he could have been so stupid not to have guessed before. Lay there thinking back. How Cooper'd known about her dad having cancer, how he'd known Connolly was obsessed with her. Everybody knows, he'd said.

Maybe they did and maybe it was just him and he'd missed it. Just back from his three weeks, head all up his arse, thinking it was all about him.

Changes were coming, Cooper had said. Big changes. He wasn't joking. Stevie Cooper and Elaine Scobie were going to take over the Northside. All she had to do was survive long enough to do it.

CHAPTER 30

The shop was chaos. Too many people crammed into too small a space. Extra desks along the walls, new phone extensions. McCoy couldn't think with all the noise and the orders being shouted. Extra lads from Eastern weren't helping his mood either. All of them acting like the cavalry come to save the day. He needed some peace, some space to try and work out what was going on. He took his coat from the back of the chair, told Wattie he was going out to buy some fags and left.

He hated the Eskimo but it was the nearest pub so he headed there. Still couldn't get his head round Cooper and Elaine. Wondered if it was just a business arrangement, whether they were really seeing each other. Whatever it was, it made sense for both of them. Two of them together were a force to be reckoned with. Her dad's money and clout and his young Springburn lads were enough to challenge anyone. No wonder her dad's boys had tried to warn him off. Must have rumbled what was happening and tried to stop it before it was too late.

He pushed the door of the Eskimo open and walked into the warm and smoky fug. He got a pint, sat down at a wee table and got his fags and his red jotter out. Cursed when he realised he'd forgotten his pen.

Where would Connolly take Elaine? If he'd found out about her and Cooper she would be in real trouble, no matter how much she believed Connolly wouldn't hurt her. Connolly wasn't going to be happy if he'd killed one boyfriend for her and she'd gone and got another one, one that wasn't him. He would need somewhere quiet, somewhere he wasn't going to be disturbed. Maybe that was the idea, maybe he was just going to keep her like some kind of pet. Store her away where no one else could get her but him. Whatever he was going to do, it didn't look good for Elaine.

He took a draught of his pint, opened the jotter, flicked through. All that was in there was a list of names and times and dates, no great inspiration there. The pamphlet from Dr Abrahams fell out onto the beaten copper table, corner into the puddle from his pint. He picked it up, wiped it on his coat, stuck it back in the jotter with the picture of Uncle Kenny from the paper that had been in Brady's wallet.

The pub door opened. He felt a blast of cold air and looked up. Mary was coming towards him, still dressed in her funeral best.

'Wattie said you might be in here,' she said,

sitting down. She looked around. 'Should have known it would be a dump.'

McCoy could hardly disagree. The only other people in there were three old men who were making their pints last the night and a middle-aged woman who seemed to be having an in-depth conversation with herself.

'Look, Mary,' he said. 'If this is about exclusives or what happened to Burgess can we do it another time?'

'It's not, luckily for you. It's about Elaine.'

He got her a gin and tonic and himself another pint, sat back down at the table.

'Did you always know who it was?' he asked.

She took a sip, shook her head. 'Not at first. Then I saw him dropping her off one night. Knew I recognised him from somewhere. Looked up the photo files at the paper and there he was. One Steven Patrick Cooper, rising star of Glasgow's bad boys.'

'When did it start?' asked McCoy.

'Not sure. Think it was before Charlie got himself killed. No real reason to think that, just the way she talks sometimes. Makes me think not everything in the garden was rosy with her and him before he died.' She looked at him. 'You know him, don't you? This Stevie Cooper?'

McCoy nodded.

'What's he like then?' she asked.

'Cooper? I'm the wrong man to ask. I've known him since he was a wee boy.'

'Hang on, doesn't that make you exactly the right person to ask?'

He shook his head. 'I see a different side of him to most people. He's brighter than people think but he's dangerous as well. Doesn't take no for an answer. Ambitious.'

'Sounds like the ideal man to help her run the business.' She smiled. 'And more.'

'You think they're together?'

She shrugged. 'It's hard to tell with a woman like Elaine. She's so wrapped up in what she looks like, how sexy she is, the whole image thing, I don't think she can separate business and pleasure that easily. Two sides of the same coin for her. Both about getting what she wants.'

She hesitated for minute, said it. 'Do you think she's dead?'

McCoy couldn't think what to say. 'Maybe. You know what Connolly's like.'

'Aye, and I know what he did to the other ones.' She looked down at the table, shifted her glass. 'Christ, she was a right pain in the hole, but you wouldn't wish that fate on anyone.'

The middle-aged woman finished her conversation with herself and headed for the door. Stopped by their table to tell them that the Daughters of Isis walked amongst them. Mary said she'd look out for them. The woman seemed satisfied, left with a smile on her face.

'You think she goaded Connolly into killing them?' asked McCoy.

342

Mary thought for a minute. 'I don't know. I really don't know. She seemed pretty broken up about her dad but . . .' She shrugged. 'Hard to say anything definite about Elaine. She's a cold one.'

'Cold enough to get Connolly to do her dirty work then not keep her side of the bargain?'

'I don't know. Yes. Maybe.'

'She say anything useful about Connolly at all? Any idea where he is?'

'That's what I've been trying to think. She didn't talk about him much. Said he used to be different, reckons he came off his medication.'

'What medication?' asked McCoy.

'Don't know, she didn't say. Stuff to make him less loony, I suppose. She thinks it's when he stopped taking it that he got obsessed with her.'

'We checked all this after Charlie Jackson. He's not registered with any doctor.'

'Isn't he? That's weird. Where'd he get it then?'

McCoy sat back in his chair. Opened his jotter to write down 'Double-check doctors' and it fell out again.

Mary bent over, picked it up, looked at the front. 'Where did you get this shite?'

McCoy took the pamphlet from her, swallowed back the rest of his pint, kissed her on the head and made for the door.

'McCoy!' she shouted after him. 'Where the fuck are you going?'

I know how to do it before the light burst in and
together together the ties thatbind
    e   l   aine.

19TH FEBRUARY 1973

CHAPTER 31

'You never saw Connolly after you left Barlinnie?' asked Murray.

They were in the interview room. Too small, too hot, stink of stale cigarette smoke and unwashed clothes. They'd sent a couple of uniforms to pick him up before he went out on his daily walk with his sign. Didn't want to come in, didn't see why he should. He may have been disbarred and a borderline nutcase but he was still a psychiatrist, a learned professional, not used to being treated with disrespect.

Abrahams shook his head, looked like he was enduring the most tiresome morning of his life. 'I already told your colleague all this. I'm not entirely sure why I've been dragged in here this morning to go over it all again.'

'Never prescribed him any medication?' asked McCoy.

Abrahams sighed. 'How could I? As you are so keen on reminding me, I'm no longer a practising doctor. Even you must realise that means I'm not able to prescribe anything any more.'

'Come on, Abrahams,' said McCoy, sitting

347

forward. 'I'm sure you've still got some prescription pads lying about, samples from drug companies, stuff you stockpiled when you knew you were going to get struck off.'

Abrahams gave a weak smile. 'For a policeman you really do have a very vivid imagination.' He sat back in his chair, looked round the interview room with a mixture of distaste and curiosity, looked at his watch. 'Is there anything else?'

'Any idea where Connolly is now?' asked McCoy.

'No.'

'He's kidnapped a young woman.'

Abrahams looked alert all of a sudden, practised boredom gone. 'Ah well, that is unfortunate, very unfortunate.'

'What do you mean?' asked Murray. 'Of course it's bloody unfortunate!'

Abrahams took his wee round glasses off, started to polish them with his jumper, suddenly looked older, vulnerable. 'It's not good because it probably means that he's entering his final stage.'

He put his glasses back on. Looked at the two of them. 'Even psychopaths have a sense of self-preservation. They want to keep doing what they're doing. If he has taken this girl the chances are he's not much concerned with his fate any more, or indeed the fate of the girl.'

'You mean he's going to kill her?' asked McCoy.

'When was she taken?' asked Abrahams.

McCoy looked at Murray.

He shrugged, didn't seem any point in keeping it secret. 'Yesterday afternoon.'

Abrahams sighed. 'In that case I imagine he already has.'

They let him go. Didn't have any reason to hold him, or to think he wasn't telling the truth. McCoy knew they were clutching at straws, didn't know what else to do. Murray was going to Pitt Street to give them a progress report, didn't look very happy about it. He wasn't surprised. What was he supposed to tell them? No progress whatsoever since the last time he spoke to them and by the way, Elaine Scobie is missing?

He walked back into the office, sat back down at his desk, felt useless. Even with all the extra staff, the phonelines, the door-to-door, the alerts on the TV and the radio, he had a pretty good idea of what was going to happen next. Soon, probably tomorrow, someone would call 999, say they'd found a body. They would rush there, sirens going, lights flashing, and they would find out what they already knew, that the body was Elaine.

Elaine, as dead as she would have been if they'd spent the time since her disappearance sitting on their arses playing dominos. Whatever they were doing to try and find Connolly, it wasn't working. Maybe Murray would get pulled after all. Maybe that's what they really wanted him at Pitt Street for. He hated to say it, but maybe that's what the

349

case needed. Someone new to look at things, to make new connections.

He looked up and Wattie was standing in front of him.

'What are you doing staring into space like some loony?' he asked.

'Thinking,' said McCoy.

'Aye right. Catching flies, my mum used to call it. Any luck with the Abrahams interview? Stupid old bastard left a pile of his pamphlets on the duty desk.'

McCoy shook his head. 'Waste of time. Which is what I'm doing sitting here.' He stood up. 'Get a pool car, eh? If I sit here any longer doing nothing I'm going to go mental.'

'A car? Why? Where are we going?'

'Springburn. Time for you to meet the big boys.'

Wattie shook his head, walked off to get the car.

He wasn't at Memel Street, was only the young lassie there. She told them he'd gone somewhere with Billy but she didn't know where. Offered them a cup of tea, line of speed. McCoy was tempted but the disapproving look on Wattie's face was enough to put him off. They walked back out the close, headed for the car.

'Where now?' asked Wattie.

'Let's try Billy Chan's.'

Wattie stopped. 'The China Sea? You're kidding? All the way back into town?'

'You got something better to do, Sergeant Watson?'

'No.'

'Well, shut the fuck up then.'

They walked on. The scrubby lawns and broken-down fences in front of the tenements were covered in a thin layer of snow. McCoy stepped over a bent pram wheel.

'You think the fact she's a girl'll make any difference? He's killed three guys, tortured them, even cut bloody words into them. You think he would do that to a woman?'

'Not sure,' said McCoy.

Wattie got the car key out his pocket. 'Maybe she is alive. Maybe he just wanted to talk to her, try and convince her that he's the man for her. Might not hurt her at all.'

McCoy blew into his hands. 'That, Wattie, is not the most stupid thing you've ever said. And if it's true, at least it gives us more time to find her before he changes his mind and decides to carve her up. Either way we need to find the bugger, and while we're clutching at straws we may as well clutch at them all, hence the search for Stevie Cooper.'

'Was he going out with her? That the sketch?' asked Wattie, unlocking the Viva.

'Not quite sure. Might have been more of a business arrangement. Now hurry up and open the bloody door. I'm freezing!'

Wattie did, and they got into the car. Wasn't much warmer than standing on the pavement.

'Either way, Cooper's been talking to her. She might have said something to him about Connolly, something that helps.'

'You've not told Murray, have you?' said Wattie, starting the car.

'Do I look stupid? The name Cooper is like lighting the bloody touch paper. He just rants, doesn't get us anywhere. Let's see if I can find anything out, then I'll worry about Murray.'

They'd just driven out onto Hawthorn Street when McCoy spotted one of Cooper's boys coming out the baker's across the street, carrying a big cardboard box with steam coming off it. Recognised the Rod Stewart feather cut and the leather jacket. Couldn't remember his name. He'd come to pick him up in Cooper's Zephyr once. John? James?'

Told Wattie to pull over beside him. He rolled the window down. 'Get in, they'll get cold. John, isn't it?' he said.

'Jamie,' he said, looking uncertain. 'I'm fine, I can—'

'I wasn't actually asking, son. Now, get in the bloody car.'

Jamie reluctantly got in the back, put the cardboard box down beside him. Smell filled the car.

McCoy leant over the seat. 'Scotch pies?'

Jamie nodded.

'So,' asked McCoy cheerily, 'where we off to?'

The Viking was on the corner of Maryhill Road and Ruchill Street. About ten minutes away via

Bilsland Drive. McCoy had the occasional look at Jamie in the rear-view mirror as they drove there.

He looked worried, chewing on his bottom lip. No doubt trying to work out how Cooper would react to him telling the polis where he was. Not well, probably.

'Any of these pies going spare?' asked Wattie. 'I'm starving.'

Jamie rustled about in the box, handed one over.

Wattie bit into it, swore as hot fat poured out the bottom of it and splashed onto his shirt and tie. 'For fuck sake!'

Jamie handed over one of the papers they were wrapped in and Wattie proceeded to scrub away at his front, spreading the stain everywhere.

'Many's in there?' asked McCoy, catching his eye in the rear-view mirror.

'Twenty,' said Jamie unhappily. 'Well, nineteen now.'

'Cooper must be awful hungry, eh?'

Jamie didn't say anything. Just looked out the window, chewed his lip.

CHAPTER 32

They pulled in to the car park behind the Viking. It was deserted. Was a Sunday, pub was shut. They got out and Jamie stood there looking lost, box in hand.

'On you go, son,' said McCoy.

Jamie nodded, knocked on the back door. It opened and Billy Weir was standing there. Didn't look happy.

'Where the fuck have you been? We're bloody starving. Did you get—'

Looked even less happy when McCoy stepped in front of the doorway.

'All right, Billy? How's things? The boss in?'

Walked past him into the pub before he had a chance to answer.

McCoy had been in the Viking's function room before, someone's retirement do. Had been brightly lit then, balloons, streamers and a table with a big cake on it. Wasn't quite the same this time. Lights were dimmed, stop anyone walking past thinking the place was open. Jukebox in the corner was on, turned down low. Faint rumble of 'Brown Sugar'.

Twenty or so guys were sitting at the tables in

groups of three or four. All early twenties. All looked much the same. Leather coats or denim jackets, pale indoor skin, long hair in middle partings, fags in hand, trying to look hard. Troops. They looked at McCoy and Wattie with studied indifference, giving nothing away, waiting for the boss to let them know what they thought. The atmosphere was tense, ugly, like something bad was about to happen.

Stevie Cooper was standing in the middle of the room. He was dressed in a pair of jeans and a blood-splattered vest, open razor in his hand. He had the look in his eyes that McCoy always dreaded, that faraway look that meant he was out of control. There was a guy tied to a chair in front of him. He was naked, head hanging down onto his chest. Arms and chest a mess of slashes, blood pouring out the cuts and pooling on the floor. His nose was broken, eyes swollen, but McCoy still recognised him. He'd seen him at the funeral, one of Scobie's lieutenants. Been in the shop a few times as well, arrested for aggravated assault. Could even remember his name. George Hughes.

He felt Wattie step in behind him, trying to get out of Cooper's sightline. If McCoy had been sensible he'd have got the two of them out of there as soon as he could, said sorry, maybe another time. But being sensible didn't always work with Cooper, sometimes you had to be as fearless as he was. He hoped to God he had judged it right and this was one of those times.

He moved into the light, felt the heart beating in his chest. Tried to look calm.

'McCoy,' said Cooper evenly.

'Full confession,' said McCoy. 'Wattie here ate one of your pies, but the rest are here.' He took the box off Jamie. 'Want me to give them out before they get cold?'

Cooper smiled. 'Aye, go on then. Make yourself useful for once. Billy! Get the beers!'

Tension was broken. McCoy tried not to look too relieved. Colour came back into Wattie's face. McCoy walked round the tables holding out the box, the troops took the pies, made a few jokes about the polis delivery service and him being a shite waiter. McCoy laughed with them, joined in, didn't care. They were here-today-gone-tomorrow boys, cannon fodder, half of them would be in Barlinnie this time next year.

Billy appeared with a wooden crate of beer bottles, started handing them out too. Cooper grabbed a couple, motioned to McCoy to follow him, disappeared through into the bar.

Wattie grabbed McCoy as he walked past, hissed in his ear, 'What am I supposed to do?'

'Just stay calm, don't do anything stupid. Speak to Billy about the football or the fucking price of tea, just don't ask any questions about what's going on. Okay?'

Wattie nodded, didn't look okay at all. Nothing McCoy could do about it, he'd have to sink or swim. He followed Cooper through the door.

Cooper was sitting in the shadows. Table right at the back of the bar. He pushed the chair opposite him out with his boot and McCoy sat down. Cooper put a beer in front of him. He looked less distant now, seemed to be back to normal.

'You sure can pick your moments,' he said.

'Was that George Hughes?' asked McCoy, taking a slug.

Cooper nodded. Now they were this close, McCoy could see the blood on his chest and up his arms, on his bruised knuckles, in his fingernails as he grasped the bottle. There was even a spray across his neck. Looked like Cooper had been at it a while.

'Tell you what you wanted to know, did he?' McCoy asked.

'Finally.' Cooper took another slug. 'They always do.'

McCoy sighed. 'This what's gonnae happen, is it? You're gonnae make me winkle it out of you bit by bloody bit?'

Cooper smiled. Didn't say anything.

McCoy stood up, started pacing. 'Right. Let's see if we can hurry it up. Scobie's gone, firm's in a mess, no anointed successor, so this is a perfect time to strike – with or without Elaine on board.' He nodded towards the function room. 'You and the boys in there are going to do it tonight while the iron's hot. By the looks of him, Hughes has told you what you needed to know so it's pies, a beer, few lines of speed

357

maybe and you send them off into the night to cause chaos. Right so far?'

'Pretty much.'

'Good. So they smash some pubs up, do over some of his taxis, hammer a few of Scobie's more senior lowlifes. Now his boys know which way the wind is blowing you give them a one-off chance to come join your merry band while you and Billy storm the Citadel, or as it's normally known, the Top of the Town, and take out Waller. The king is dead, long live the king.'

He sat down, took a swig of his beer. 'That the sketch?'

Cooper shook his head, smiled. 'You know something, McCoy? You always were too fucking smart for your own good.'

'What can I say? It's a gift. Now your plans for world domination are out the way, can we talk about what I really came here to talk about?'

'And what would that be?'

'Elaine,' said McCoy. 'You hear anything? From her? Connolly?'

Cooper shook his head, started peeling the paper label off his beer. 'What's to hear? She's dead.'

'You don't know that,' said McCoy.

Cooper looked up at him. 'Yes, I do, and so do you.'

McCoy was about to argue with him, tell him he could just be holding her hostage, that he might have let her go, that they would find them before he did anything, but he didn't. He knew it as well as Cooper. Elaine Scobie was dead.

'I'm sorry,' he said.

Cooper shrugged. 'No great loss.'

McCoy had known Cooper long enough to know when he was lying. Also knew if Cooper wanted him and everyone else to think he didn't care about Elaine then it was best left at that. But he remembered his face at The Inn, the simple plea – 'Find her'. He had cared about her.

'How much do you know about her and Connolly?' he asked.

'Enough.' Cooper sat forwards, face emerging from the shadows. 'So what is this now, a police interview?'

'No. It's me asking you a few questions that might help me find her body quicker and get Connolly put away so you can do whatever you've arranged for him when he gets into Barlinnie. That okay with you?'

'Still sounds like a fucking polis interview to me,' Cooper grumbled.

'Was she in it with him?' McCoy asked. 'Did Connolly and her plan it together?'

Cooper shook his head. 'Not at first, not with Charlie Jackson. That came out the blue. That was all Connolly.'

'But she was in it when it came to her dad?'

Cooper took a swig from his bottle. 'Let's just say she had a wee word in his ear. Helped him understand how happy she'd be if her dad was gone.'

McCoy shook his head. 'Charming. First thing you think about after your boyfriend's been murdered is how to hatch a plan to use the same guy to kill your father.'

Cooper didn't rise to the bait. 'She was smart, knew her dad was fading away, and if she knew that then soon enough everyone else would. And by then it would be too late, too much competition. Had to move fast to make sure she was going to get what was rightly hers.'

'What? By killing him?' asked McCoy.

'That's how these things work, McCoy, you know it as well as I do. You don't get fucking elected, you take it.'

'And what was Connolly going to get out this deal?' he asked, knowing full well.

'She was going to let him fuck her brains out,' said Cooper evenly. 'Or so he thought.'

'Maybe that's what she's doing now,' said McCoy.

'Don't think so. And if she is it's not her choice.' Cooper shouted towards the door, 'Billy!'

Second or two later, Billy's head appeared round the door.

'Get us another two bottles, eh? And my fags are in my jacket.'

Billy nodded. 'Hughes has come round by the way, crying and babbling. What do you want me to do with him?'

Cooper sighed, stood up. 'Hang on.' Walked through to the function suite.

McCoy sat there, straining to hear. Couldn't hear

anything, just the low music from the jukebox. Whoever had put the money in was a Stones fan. 'Jumping Jack Flash' now. Couple of minutes went past and Cooper reappeared, bottle in each hand, fag in the corner of his mouth. Gave a bottle to McCoy and sat down.

'What did you do with Hughes?' McCoy asked.

'Thought you said this wasn't a police interview?' Cooper took the fag packet out his pocket, got a wrap out of it, cut two big lines of speed on the table.

'Where did you come into the equation with Elaine and Connolly?'

'This really is a fucking police interview now,' said Cooper, sniffing one up. He rubbed his nose, winced. Held the rolled-up fiver out to McCoy, who shook his head. Then thought differently.

'Oh, fuck it,' he said, took the note, did the other line.

Cooper rubbed his nose again, sniffed a few times, took another swig of beer. 'Plan was I was going to get rid of Connolly after he'd done the dirty deed, but that didn't really work out. Cunt was madder than she thought. He disappeared, said he was hiding until his mission was complete.'

'His mission?'

'That's what he said. Was always reading these books about Nazi troops and all that kind of shite.'

'Sven Hassel?'

Cooper nodded. 'She was going to tell him to meet her in a hotel and when he turned up I'd be there instead. But after he did Jake Scobie, he didn't appear again. She couldn't get a hold of him, fucking vanished into thin air. First time she saw him must have been when the fucker pulled her up into the roof, and by that time he knew all about me. Game was up.'

'It was him that slashed you, wasn't it? Nothing to do with Scobie's boys.'

He looked genuinely surprised. 'Smart arse, right enough. Fucker came at me like a bat out of hell. Billy battered him with a hammer and he ran for it. Thank fuck.'

'What did he tell you?'

'Nothing.'

'Come on, Cooper. He told you something. That's why you're so sure she's dead, isn't it?'

Cooper had that look on his face again, trying to look like he didn't care. 'He told me they were going to be together for ever.' He smiled sadly. 'Only one way that can happen, eh?'

'You think he's killed himself?'

'Yep.' He stood up. 'Now, if you've finished your fucking interview, Detective McCoy, beat it. I've got stuff to do.'

she's holding my hand.
Her eyes have opened again
she's watching me with love.
I crush another two and put them in the red wine
hold it p to hermouth

she drinks it.

her ey es close again.

I ease her dresss off herbrahertights her knickers

Whatever I

have

done i have done fr

this moment
  it is worth it

CHAPTER 33

'You going to tell Murray?'

'Tell him what?' asked McCoy.

'You kidding me?' Wattie sounded incredulous. 'Hughes sitting there half fucking slashed to death for one. What Cooper and his troops are up to for another!' He stopped the car at the lights at Bilsland Drive. Looked at McCoy.

'Now why would I do that?'

The lights changed and Wattie moved on. McCoy started looking for his cigarettes, was sure he'd left them in his coat pocket. Speed was starting to kick in. He really needed a cigarette. Found them. Looked up and realised Wattie was pulling the car over.

'What you doing?'

Wattie stopped the car, took the keys out the ignition. The Viva spluttered to a halt. 'I need to talk to you,' he said, turning to face McCoy.

'Why?' asked McCoy, lighting up. 'What have you done?'

'Me!' Wattie shouted. 'I've not done anything! It's you! You're not going to tell Murray!'

McCoy sighed. 'Start the car, keep driving until we get to the Round Toll, turn into Possil Road.'

'Why?'

'Two reasons. One because I fucking told you to and two because I want to show you something. That all right with you, is it?'

Wattie turned the key in the ignition, started the car. Couple of minutes later they turned into Possil Road, started up the hill.

McCoy pointed. 'Turn right just after the bridge.'

Wattie peered out the window. 'The Whisky Bond? That where we're going?'

'Yep.'

Wattie pulled up by the big brick building – no lights on, all shut up for the night – and parked the car by the far wall. Turned to McCoy. 'What now?'

McCoy opened the car door. Immediate blast of cold air. 'Follow me.'

Wattie cursed, shouted after him, 'It's freezing out there!' No response. 'McCoy!'

McCoy stood by the wall overlooking the canal, managed to get a fag lit in the wind. Canal was inky black, surface rippling in the wind. Wattie appeared beside him, hands deep in pockets, scarf round his neck.

'Well?' said Wattie. 'We here just so I can freeze my bollocks off?'

'What exactly is it you're wanting me to tell Murray?'

Wattie pushed the hair back from his forehead,

looked frustrated. 'That Cooper slashed fuck out that guy! That they're going to wreak bloody mayhem tonight!'

'Look,' said McCoy, pointing out over the canal towards the city. You could see most of it from up here, lights shining through the rain and the mist. The high flats at Cedar Street, Park Church Tower behind that, new flats being built at Farnell Street, city centre beyond.

'Remember when you and I had that wee chat in Wypers a few weeks ago? When I told you this was the big bad city? Did that no go in?'

'Yes, but—' said Wattie.

'But what? You still think we're here to solve crimes like Dixon of bloody Dock Green?' He pointed at the city laid out in front of them. 'Look at it! It's nearly a million bloody people! Wheels need to keep turning. Life needs to go on.'

'How d'you mean?' asked Wattie, looking puzzled.

'What we're really here to do – me, you, all the bloody Glasgow polis – is minimise damage. That's what I told you this afternoon. Time for you to meet the big boys. Time to start dealing with them. I'm no always gonnae be with you holding your hand.'

Wattie looked dubious.

'What? No believe me?'

'No, it's just him sitting there all covered in blood, slashes everywhere. It was horrible.'

'Fuck him. He's done worse to other people and done it more than once. Scobie's gone.' McCoy gestured back over his shoulder. 'There's a vacuum on the Northside. Sooner and quicker that vacuum gets filled, the better for everyone. Cooper's going do it tonight. By tomorrow he'll be running things. One night of mayhem is better than a month-long fucking full-out war, believe me. I've been through it before.'

McCoy dropped his cigarette in a puddle, watched it fizzle out. 'And now Cooper and Billy Weir know who you are, you managed not to act like a total arse—'

'Thanks a fucking lot.'

'—and so now they'll be okay when they have to deal with you and you've got what you wanted. A direct connection with the new kings of the Northside. More than any other lazy cunt in the shop has. Now, come on, I'm fucking freezing out here and we need to go and tell Murray that Elaine was playing us along all the time. Just like he said she was.'

They drove back, stopped at the lights by Millie's Motors on the way. Rows of Cortinas and Hillman Imps covered in snow in the forecourt. Huge sign with a drawing of a woman with a low-cut black dress, blonde hair and a huge speech bubble with 'See Anything You Fancy??' coming out her mouth.

McCoy smiled to himself. Didn't know if it was the speed or he was just in a good mood, but sometimes he really did love Glasgow.

CHAPTER 34

'She was the one that suggested to him that he kill her father. Cooper said she didn't know about Charlie Jackson but I have my doubts. Either way, she's a nasty piece of work. If by some chance she's still alive we could charge her with accessory to murder at least.'

He waited. Nothing. 'You were right all along.'

Murray sat forward in his chair, put his elbows on his desk, looked McCoy in the eye. 'Are you telling me your pal Stevie Cooper knew what was going on and we didn't?'

'Well, I'm not sure he knew before the actual—'

Murray held his hand up. McCoy shut up.

'Are you telling me he had vital information about a murder case and didn't tell you?'

McCoy sat there. Looked glum. Stupidly thought Murray would be happy that his suspicions were right, that Elaine was up to her neck in it. Red was spreading up Murray's fat neck into his face; he was holding his pencil too tight, knuckles going white.

'And where is Cooper now?' he said quietly.

This was getting worse and worse. Usually when

Murray was angry he would shout and scream and it would all blow over in a couple of hours. Not this time. He was staying calm, deadly calm.

'I don't know,' said McCoy.

'Let me tell you something, Detective McCoy. I'm getting mighty sick of your wee chats with that cunt Cooper. He helped you out in that bloody house in Park Circus so I was going to look the other way for a while – not any more. You're getting far too fucking pleased with yourself. Hanging about with your gangster mates, thinking you're a fucking big man.'

McCoy was going to say something but suddenly didn't know what. Half of him knew Murray was right. Had been showing off to Wattie taking him up to the Viking. Letting him think he was part of the new power in the Northside.

Murray was off again. 'The minute this Connolly business is over, I'm going for Cooper and believe me I will get him. I am going to get the cunt in and I am going to charge him with obstruction and any other fucking thing I can think of.'

He leaned forward, face inches from McCoy's. 'I am going to nail that cunt to the wall. Do you understand me?' McCoy nodded. 'And if I hear one fucking whisper that you tried to warn him I'm going to nail you up next to him. Understood, Detective McCoy?'

McCoy nodded again, wishing this was over.

'Now get the fuck out my sight.'

McCoy walked out Murray's office, sat back

down at his desk. Wasn't quite sure how it had gone so wrong. Was his fault. Too bloody eager to tell Murray without thinking it through. Too eager to show off what he'd found out.

He opened his jotter, looked at the names and dates. Couldn't think about anything else but what Cooper was going to do when he found out Murray was on a personal crusade against him. All because he couldn't keep his trap shut.

'Wakey, wakey!' He looked up and Thomson was standing by his desk. 'There's someone waiting for you at the front desk.'

For one stupid minute his heart raced, thought it might be Cooper. 'Who is it?'

'Didn't give his name, just grabbed me as I was coming through. Told me he needed to speak to you urgently.'

McCoy opened the door to the front office, saw who it was, cursed Thomson. Charlie the Pram was sitting on the bench beneath the 'Don't Be an Amber Gambler' poster. Last thing he fucking needed.

Billy the desk sergeant looked up from the ledger, grinned. 'That's Mr McCoy here for you now, sir.'

Charlie looked relieved, took off his battered trilby. 'Mr McCoy. Thank God you're here.'

McCoy sat down beside him, tried to breathe through his mouth. He wasn't looking good, Charlie. Painfully thin, eyes going everywhere, forehead bleeding and scratched.

'What's up, Charlie?' asked McCoy, realised

what it was as soon as he said it. He didn't have his pram with him.

'They took it, the bastards took it.'

'Christ, Charlie, I'm sorry. When did you last have it?'

His eyes were brimming with tears. 'This morning, hadnae slept all night, lay down by the bins behind Arnott's, forgot to tie it to my leg.' He looked at McCoy, clean lines down his face where the tears had cut through the grime. 'I had everything in there – everything.'

'I know, Charlie, I know. Look, it's bound to turn up. I'll get the boys to keep an eye out for it, see if we can find it, okay?'

He nodded, looked utterly dejected. One last boot in the face he didn't need.

McCoy dug in his pocket, got a fiver out. 'Take this. Get a room in the Great Eastern tonight, get warm. Then tomorrow go down to Paddy's. Should be enough left to get you another pram just in case, eh?'

Charlie took the fiver. McCoy noticed he had something folded up in his other hand. One of the pamphlets that wanker Abrahams had left on the desk.

Charlie saw him looking at it. 'Maybe he's right. Maybe that's what I need, eh? A lobotomy. Says here you'll never feel depressed again, cures it.'

McCoy held out his hand. 'Give us it, Charlie. That's the last thing anybody needs.'

Charlie handed it over. McCoy stood up. Helped

371

Charlie up. 'Come on, get to the Eastern before it fills up, eh?' Charlie nodded. 'Get the new pram tomorrow, come back and see me in a couple of days, see if we've found the old one, okay?'

Charlie put his hat back on, headed for the door. McCoy watched him go. Even with this shit with Cooper he couldn't feel too sorry for himself. Charlie, Joe Brady, things could always be worse. He turned to Billy. He was looking at him shaking his head.

'You're a soft touch, McCoy.'

'Aye well, someone's got to be.' He realised he still had the pamphlet in his hand. Unfolded it. Held it up.

'See the wee speccy cunt that left these here?' Billy nodded. 'He comes in here again, chase the wee fucker.'

He walked back through into the shop. Murray was standing at his desk, file in his hand.

'Sir?'

Murray didn't look happy, handed it to him. 'Got Williams from Eastern to have another look at Kenny Burgess' murder.'

McCoy took it, sat down.

'He's not sure the same person that killed Charlie Jackson and Jake Scobie killed Kenny Burgess.'

'What? How?' McCoy's stomach was flopping over. Thought he'd got away with that one, proved that Connolly did it. No further investigation, no danger for him and Cooper.

'One of the maids at the Albany reports seeing

two men coming out Burgess' room about five o'clock. She was off, had flu, didn't get interviewed until yesterday.'

McCoy was trying to hold it together. Could see his hands shaking on the desk.

'It's probably nothing. You and Wattie check it out. Let me know if you find anything.'

McCoy nodded. 'Will do.'

Murray went back to his office. McCoy sat there trying to breathe slowly, to not panic. All he had to do was make sure he didn't find anything else out, let Murray know it was a false alarm, a dead lead, and everything would be okay.

He opened the report, started reading. All the maid said was that she came out a room a few doors down to get some more furniture polish off her cart and she saw two men come out of Burgess' room. Said they both looked normal, nothing special, wearing suits and ties, one of them had a sports bag. She went back into the room she was cleaning and didn't think any more about it until she got back to work and Williams asked to interview her.

He closed the file. Felt something like relief. He could get rid of that. Wasn't much to get rid of. Wondered if this was what it was like to commit a major crime, worrying about getting found out all the time. To always be looking over your shoulder, holding your breath. Knew one thing, he was never doing anything like Burgess again. Never.

Realised the report was sitting on the desk next to Abrahams' pamphlet. Last thing people like Charlie the Pram needed was reading shite like this, promising a cure to all their ills. Picked it up to put it in the bin. Stopped dead. Just kept looking at the pamphlet.

'I don't fucking believe it,' he said to himself. 'I don't fucking believe it.'

CHAPTER 35

He couldn't find Wattie anywhere, decided not to wait. For all he knew Elaine's life could depend on it. Wasn't keen on driving, especially not in this weather, but he got a car from the pool, set off through the city and headed for the Southside.

Pinetrees, Beverley Road, Newlands, Glasgow, was set back from the road. Like most of the houses in Newlands, it was massive, built so servants could live on the top floors and never be seen. The house was surrounded by large gardens with mature pine trees at the back, big double garage off at the side. Front was a huge lawn, flower beds, monkey puzzle tree in the middle. Despite its grandeur, it looked like it had seen better days. Weeds growing up through the paving stones leading to the door, peeling paint on the iron railings, general air of neglect.

McCoy sat in the car looking at the house, pamphlet in his hand. 'To order more pamphlets, contact Pinetrees, Beverley Road, Newlands, Glasgow' written on the back. He felt a bit daft now, rushing out the shop at full tilt, and for what?

To look at an empty house. He knew Abrahams was hiding something, just didn't know what. Seemed like another address might be it. Wasn't so sure now.

He called in from the car. House was registered to a Mr Cuthbert Abrahams, according to Diane from Greenock, and according to the electoral register he was eighty-three. What if that was all it was? His dad's house where he stored his extra pamphlets?

Fuck it, was worth a look.

The snow on the path up to the house was pristine. He trudged up, feet sinking into the wetness. Closer he got, the more neglected the house looked. One of the panes in the upstairs window was cracked, moss growing up the wall by the front door. Maybe his dad didn't even live here any more, probably off in an old folk's home.

He rang the bell. Didn't hear anything. Hit the door with his fist a good few times. Nothing. He put his hands up to the windowpane to hide the glare from the snow and peered in.

'Shite,' he said under his breath.

Took three good goes for him to kick the door open. Wood was starting to rot which helped but it was still a big bastard of a door, didn't give way easily. Wood cracked and then the Yale lock gave way and the door swung open. He went in, walked through the dusty hallway shouting hello, trying not to breathe in the smell of cat piss, and into the big front room.

Mr Abrahams was a thin man dressed in a variety of stained blankets wrapped around himself, shoes that looked too big for him and a knitted balaclava. A kitten popped its head out from his blankets, sniffed, retreated again. A shackle round his bleeding and scarred ankle was attached to a chain secured to an old-fashioned iron radiator.

'Mr Abrahams?' asked McCoy.

He nodded. 'Are you the Home Guard? I told that bloody girl the blackout blinds in the drawing room were too small.'

McCoy sighed. Not only was this trip a waste of time, now he was going to have to deal with this. There was a covered bucket by the couch, packet of biscuits, a torch.

McCoy smiled endearingly, or at least he hoped he did. 'Mind if I sit down for a bit?'

The old man looked at him. Kitten appeared again. 'You'll have to be quick. I have to get dressed for dinner, car's coming in half an hour.'

'Quick it is then,' he said, sitting down on a dining chair by the window.

The old man seemed to be living in the front room. Bed was in there, old black-and-white TV, wee three-bar electric heater, empty tins of cat food everywhere. He hoped to God they were for the cats and not him.

Mr Abrahams arranged his blankets around himself, looked exhausted. 'I'm cold,' he said. 'Very cold.'

'It's okay, we're going to get someone here to help you.'

He nodded, seemed to understand. 'I don't even know what day it is,' he said, eyes welling up. 'I don't know where everyone's gone.'

'Your son comes to visit?'

He nodded again. 'He brings bread and milk and the food for the cats. I keep asking him where everyone is but he doesn't answer.'

McCoy wondered if he could get Abrahams done for parental neglect, wondered if there even was such a thing. Was going to get him done for something, that was for sure. Decided he may as well double-check things while he was here.

'Do you have a phone, Mr Abrahams?' he asked.

Mr Abrahams looked at him, lost. 'I'm sorry,' he said apologetically. 'I can't remember where it is.'

'Don't worry,' said McCoy. 'I'll find it.'

House was pretty much as he expected. Most of the rooms seemed to be abandoned and unused. Colder in the draughty rooms than it was outside. He pushed the door open to the front bedroom and something scurried under the skirting board, disappeared. Cardboard boxes full of Abrahams' pamphlets were everywhere – on the bed, piled up on the floor.

He wiped some of the condensation off the window and looked out. House faced a wee park covered in snow, didn't look like it was used much. Snow was unmarked. No snowmen or kids playing, not in Newlands.

He pushed a box over, sat down on the bed and lit up. Bit of a wild goose chase all in all, no Abrahams and certainly no Connolly. There was a picture in a silver frame on the bedside table. Mr Abrahams looking neat and smart in his suit, standing in front of a boat. Funny how things turn out. Drive past this place and you would think the people inside were rich, happy, living in one of the biggest houses in Glasgow. Little would you know. A cat put its head round the door, jumped up onto the bed and settled down beside him, purring. He put his hand out to stroke it, realised it was crawling with fleas just in time.

The back bedrooms were the same: empty, damp and freezing, no sign of a phone anywhere. He stood at the window looking out over the back garden. Had to be the size of a couple of tennis courts. He rubbed at the grime on the window and tried to see where it ended. Wherever it was, was lost in a tangle of bushes and overgrown pines.

Finally found a phone under a wee table in the hall. Got it out, blew the dust off it and called into the shop. Told them to send an ambulance and somebody from the Cruelty. He was just about to head downstairs when he noticed something.

The black felt roof of the garage was wet, glistening in the sunshine. No snow. The garages of the other houses were all covered in a thick layer of it. Snow on Abrahams' garage must have melted, which meant the garage was heated. Why would anyone heat their garage and not the house?

He stepped out the back door and walked down to the garage. The two double doors at the front were locked. Padlocks on them thick with rust, looked like they'd been there for years. He tramped round the back, feet crunching in the snowy gravel. There was a back door, a normal-sized one, and it was lying half open.

'Abrahams!' shouted McCoy. 'You in there?'

A figure stepped into the doorway. Bald head. Long metal bar in hand. 'No, but I am,' he said and swung the bar.

McCoy tried to step back but he was a fraction too slow. The bar hit him hard on the temple. There was a burst of pain. As he fell he saw Connolly raising it to swing it again and then everything went black.

He could hear voices – not what they were saying, just the noise of them fading in and out.

He opened his eyes. White light. Bright white light. That's all he could see.

McCoy closed his eyes, opened them again. Realised he was looking at striplights in the ceiling. Realised if he could see the ceiling he was lying down. Realised he couldn't move.

He tried to look down his body. There was a broad leather strap across his chest, another one across his ankles, wrist straps. Felt like there was one over his forehead; could hardly move his head, couldn't move his body at all.

He strained his neck, tried to move his head

sideways. Straps tight, could only shift an inch or two, but it was enough. The inside of the garage was bright. Lamps as well as the striplights in the ceiling. Walls painted white, half tiled. White metal cabinets with glass doors full of bottles and boxes of medicines.

Next to him was something like a metal autopsy table. Thing is, autopsy tables didn't have leather wrist and ankle restraints unbuckled and hanging over the side. Big leather strap that looked like it would hold someone's head in place at the top. Realised that's where he was. Strapped to a table in Abrahams' garage and he remembered who hit him. Connolly. And suddenly he was scared, very scared.

Turned the other way and there was a machine in the corner, a kind of box on wheels with a meter on the front, two wires coming from it ending in two black-handled things with suckers on the end. He knew what it was. An ECT machine. His stomach rolled. He knew what they were for too. They zapped your brain, gave you an electric shock; you have a fit. His stomach rolled again. And then they lobotomised you.

'Well, well.'

He turned. Abrahams was looking down at him. Smiling. 'I thought Mr Connolly had killed you. That blow to the head looked very nasty. Seems not.'

McCoy tried to speak but his tongue was thick in his mouth, couldn't really get any words out.

He turned his head. There were two chairs by the wall. Connolly was sitting in one, Elaine in the other; her head bowed, body slack. He tried to scream but his throat was too dry, too sore. A kind of strangled moan came out and Connolly looked over at him. Smiled.

Connolly stood up, stretched. 'About fucking time,' he said.

He walked over to the table. Leant down, face right into McCoy's. His breath stank of cigarettes and a weird sweet smell, chemical. 'You almost ruined it, you fucking cunt.'

McCoy felt his heart running too fast, like it was exploding in his chest. He'd been scared before but now he knew what real fear was. What terror was. He wanted away, wanted to be anywhere but there. He tried to speak, to plead, but Connolly clamped a hand over his mouth.

'You listen to me. I'm going to finish what I started in that pub. And this time there'll be no old cunt to save you. You understand, McCoy? Going to be just you and me and all the time in the world.'

McCoy started to writhe, tried to pull at the straps. Tried to stop thinking about Charlie Jackson on the roof – the blood, the cutting.

'And you know something?' Connolly said. 'I can't fucking wait.'

He turned to pull a small wheeled metal table towards him. McCoy twisted his head, saw what was on the table. The fear was everywhere now, whole body singing with it.

'Help me,' he managed to get out. 'Don't, please.'

Connolly picked up a scalpel, held it up to the light. He could see Elaine behind him, still sitting in the chair, head down. Tried to call to her.

'Please . . .'

'She can't hear you, McCoy,' said Connolly. 'Nobody can.'

He leant over him with the scalpel and McCoy screamed, twisted his head back and forwards.

'Stay still or it'll be worse,' said Connolly and then he cut the first button off his shirt.

CHAPTER 36

He couldn't remember if it was the third or fourth time he'd come back round. He didn't even care what happened to him any more. He just wanted to black out again and for the pain to go. But it didn't. It was coming over him in waves, the worst pain he'd ever felt.

He could see Connolly bent over him, concentrating as he carved another letter into his chest. He had told him what he was going to write but he'd forgotten. Pain just overcame everything. Couldn't think of anything but wanting it to stop, couldn't remember anything but the pain.

'There,' said Connolly. He looked up, grinned. Sprays of drying blood on his face.

McCoy heard Abrahams behind his head.

'That's enough for now,' he said.

'Fuck off,' said Connolly. 'I haven't even started.'

Abrahams sighed. 'Okay. If you must.'

Connolly put the bloody scalpel back on the metal table. Looked through the other instruments like a kid picking his favourite toy.

All McCoy wanted was for him to hurry up. To hurt him so bad he passed out. To escape back into the darkness. Hide there where Connolly couldn't get to him.

Connolly held up a small bone saw, showed it to McCoy. 'This one, I think,' he said.

He pulled it along McCoy's arm experimentally, teeth pulling and cutting through his flesh. McCoy screamed as the pain hit. Connolly grinned happily, went to draw it through McCoy's arm again and stopped. Looked confused. He swayed a bit, then fell, slumped over McCoy's chest.

Abrahams appeared behind him, syringe in hand. 'He's had his fun,' he said. 'Now it's time for mine.'

McCoy felt the black calling him back, felt the weight of Connolly being lifted off his chest, and drifted away.

He thought he could smell burning, like an electricity transformer overheating or a plug before it blew. He opened his eyes, wave of agony from his body. Turned his head, thought he saw Abrahams undoing the straps holding Connolly's body down on the other table. Blinked, tried to focus. Thought he was going to black out again. Did.

The smell again. The burning. He turned his head. Elaine was strapped to the other table, Abrahams holding the paddles of the ECT machine to the sides of her head. A warning tone and then she shuddered and jerked; the smell of burning got stronger. Her legs were kicking under the straps, body writhing. Abrahams took the paddles away and her body suddenly became still.

Abrahams bent over her, took the leather block out from between her teeth. Caressed her cheek, kissed her.

McCoy turned away.

He told himself he wouldn't turn back, that he'd keep his eyes on the far wall. Waited, could hear Abrahams wandering around, whistling as he picked up things from metal trays. McCoy knew exactly what it was he was picking up. A hammer and a long pointed probe.

He told himself he wouldn't turn, wouldn't look. He didn't. Not even when he heard the hammer hit the probe. Not even when he heard the faint crack of her skull giving way and he started crying. He felt sick when he heard the scraping. Kept his eyes on the wall, tried not to believe he was next. The scraping went on. He willed himself back into the darkness.

'McCoy!'

He came to suddenly. Abrahams was undoing the strap across his chest. Helping him sit up. As he did, the pain across his chest hit him. He tried to breathe, to ride it out, tried not to pass out.

'Breathe,' said Abrahams. 'Try to breathe.' He held a cup of water up to his mouth and McCoy tried to drink it, most of it spilling onto the cuts on his chest.

'Better?' Abrahams asked.

McCoy nodded.

'Good.'

Abrahams cocked his head. Distant sound of a siren. Smiled. 'Perfect timing.'

McCoy raised his head, blinked. He felt woozy, tried to focus.

Kevin Connolly and Elaine Scobie were sitting in the two chairs dressed in hospital gowns. They both had black eyes, bruises on their foreheads, dried blood around their nostrils.

McCoy's head spun, thought he was going to pass out again. Tried to hold on. Blinked a few times, tried to believe what he was seeing. The sirens got louder. The two of them were holding hands.

CHAPTER 37

'Could have been worse, I suppose,' said Wattie. 'Could have said cunt.'

'Watson! For fuck sake!'

'Sorry, sir,' said Wattie.

McCoy was lying on Abrahams' kitchen table getting stitched up by one of the ambulance men who had come to take the old man away. He was a huge guy, fingers like bunches of bananas, but he seemed to be doing a good enough job.

'Should really be getting this done at the hospital,' he said, sticking his needle in.

'I'm not going to the hospital,' said McCoy through gritted teeth.

'Are you sure that's—'

'I said I'm not going, Murray! That's that.'

Murray sat down on the kitchen chair, held his hands up in surrender.

McCoy looked away as the needle went in again. Wasn't quite sure why but he wanted to be here with Murray and Wattie. Wanted normality. Them bickering at each other, the stink of Murray's pipe. He'd thought he was going to die, really believed it. Now all he wanted was to be here with people he knew, not alone in a hospital.

The ambulance man finished. 'There'll be scars but they should fade. A scalpel, was it?'

McCoy nodded.

'Goes in deep but it's a thin cut, shouldn't be too bad. I'm going to say this once more, even though you're no listening to me. If you start getting a headache or light causing you pain go straight to A&E. That's a nasty hit to your head. Need to be careful.'

McCoy nodded again. Watched as he packed up his stuff. He stopped by Murray on the way out, bent down, talked in his ear, but McCoy could still hear him.

'Keep an eye on him, good chance he could go into shock. If he feels dizzy, starts to sweat, throws up, get him into the hospital no matter what he says.'

'Here.' Wattie put a cup of tea down in front of him. 'Found the tea in the back of the cupboard. Probably been there since the First World War but give it a go.'

McCoy sat up, pulled the jumper Wattie had taken off and given him over his head, and tasted the tea. Wasn't bad.

Murray rubbed his stubble. Looked pained. 'So what the fuck do we do with the two of them in there? Never seen anything like it.'

'You sure she's okay in there with him?' asked Wattie.

'Let's just see what the doctor says, eh?' said McCoy.

Murray nodded.

'Phillips turned up pished one too many times so it's some new guy.' He began patting his jacket, looking for his pipe. 'You remember much?'

McCoy shook his head. 'I remember being hit by Connolly and waking up on that fucking table. Remember him cutting me, but after a bit I kept passing out. All gets a bit hazy.'

'Not bloody surprised,' said Murray.

'I remember the smell of burning, Elaine on the table.' Flashes of her fitting, the noise of the hammer coming down, the look on Abrahams' face. 'Think he must have done it to Connolly first.'

'Christ.' Murray winced, hit the bottom of his pipe on the heel of his brogue. 'I think I'd rather be bloody dead.'

The door opened and Dr Purdie came into the kitchen. McCoy recognised him immediately; last time he'd seen him he was patching up Cooper in the bath. By the look of Purdie he recognised him too; both decided to pretend they didn't.

Purdie sat down at the table.

'Well?' said Murray.

'Well,' said Purdie, 'this is certainly one of the strangest cases I've ever seen. Mind you, once I was working in Edinburgh—'

Murray was holding his hand up.

'Sorry,' said Purdie. He settled himself. 'Both of

them appear to have been lobotomised.' He coughed as Murray's pipe smoke drifted towards him. 'It seems to have been done correctly, undoubtedly by someone who has done it before.'

'Abrahams did them at Ninewells,' said McCoy.

Purdie nodded, continued.

'The actual procedure itself is not that physically damaging. Couple of days until the swelling goes down and they'll be right as rain. The problem is its inaccuracy.'

'What do you mean?' asked Murray.

'I was going to say lobotomy is kind of a blunt instrument but that seems a bit tactless. However, it's true. The reason it's fallen out of favour is twofold. Our pharmaceutical solutions to mental health have become hugely more advanced than they used to be and the problem with lobotomies was that you were never quite sure what you were going to get.'

Purdie took out his fags, lit up. 'The original aim of the procedure was to ease the suffering of deeply distressed patients. Help with the horrors of severe depression, schizophrenia, mania and so on. However, its use began to become somewhat indiscriminate, began to be used as a matter of course on almost any patient who was exhibiting even the mildest mental problems.' He took a draw, blew out. 'And after the operation the effects were hugely variable. Some patients were calmer, albeit a bit absent, and some were practically destroyed, reduced to walking corpses, not much higher than a vegetative state. Memory non-existent, loss of bowel function, motor impairments and so on. They were calm all right, but largely because they were virtually destroyed as human beings, no real aspect of their personality left.'

'What about those two?' asked Murray.

Purdie frowned. 'It's probably too early to say, but I fear they're on the more damaged end of the scale. Their motor function is okay, but even in a cursory examination you can see their memory and mental capacity is hugely diminished. Neither of them seem to have a clear idea of who they are or what they are doing here. Blessing is they don't seem very upset about it, quite the opposite in fact. They also seem to have some sort of bond, constantly holding hands. Were they married?'

'Not exactly,' grumbled Murray. 'Knew each other, though. So what happens now?'

'Well, they could become more cognisant over time but I would think it unlikely. Far more likely prognosis is that they will deteriorate further.'

'The man in there, Connolly, is a murderer. A very fucking nasty one at that,' said Murray. 'Almost did for McCoy here as well.'

McCoy held up his jumper.

'Ah,' said Purdie. 'Nasty, very nasty indeed.'

'And we're not going to be able to try him, are we?' asked McCoy.

Purdie shook his head. 'I wouldn't imagine so. Any lawyer would point out that in this state he would be unable to understand even the most basic tenets of a trial.'

'Unfit to plead,' said McCoy.

Murray smashed his fist down on the table. Purdie just about jumped out his skin. 'He's done it, hasn't he! That fucker's got away with it.'

Purdie stood up, looked a bit taken aback. 'If that's it, gents, you'll get my written report in the morning.' Made himself scarce.

Murray hit the table again. Swore again. 'He's got everything he wants. He's got away with murder and that poor bloody girl is hanging on to him like a fucking long-lost lover.'

'That's one way of looking at it,' said McCoy.

Murray looked at him. 'Is there another bloody way?'

'The two of them may as well be dead. Both of them got what was coming to them. Didn't think their big plan would end up like this.'

Murray didn't look convinced.

'Come on, Murray. You think being like the two of them is a victory? That they've got away with something?' said McCoy. 'If you ask me, at least some sort of justice has been done. The most we're going to get, anyway. We should take it.'

They heard the crunch of a van on the gravel drive.

'Other ambulance must be here,' said McCoy.

It was. They followed the two ambulance men into the front room. Connolly and Elaine were sitting on the couch smiling, hand in hand, rugs wrapped around them. The lady from the council who came with the ambulance stood up.

'Okay, you two,' she said. 'Ready for a wee trip?'

Elaine nodded. Connolly didn't seem to even understand that. They stood up, took the woman's hand. Elaine looked at McCoy as she passed him. He caught her eye, felt he was looking into nothing. Couldn't help but remember the last time she'd looked at him, from the back of the limousine at the entrance to the cemetery. The way she'd looked then: beautiful, smart, dangerous. Now she was just an absence, less than a person, less than alive. He wouldn't be her for all the money in the world.

CHAPTER 38

McCoy steeled himself, sat down at the interview-room table, flinching at the pain from his cuts. Looked across at Abrahams.

Abrahams smiled at him pleasantly, as if he'd just walked past him in the park. 'How's the chest?'

'Fuck off,' said McCoy.

The door opened behind him. Abrahams' solicitor no doubt.

'Afternoon, Mr McCoy,' said Lomax, sitting down opposite him.

'You've got to be fucking kidding me,' said McCoy.

Lomax smiled. 'Not at all. My client Mr Abrahams engaged me a few hours ago, as soon as he was brought into custody.' He turned to Abrahams. 'Isn't that so?'

Abrahams was polishing his glasses on his jumper. He put them on, looked at McCoy. 'Indeed it is. Nothing but the best for me. And, as we all know, Mr Lomax is the best.'

The door opened and Murray stepped in.

Looked at Lomax. Looked at McCoy.

395

'What the fuck's this?' he said.

Lomax smiled again, was enjoying himself. 'And good afternoon to you, Mr Murray. As I have just explained to Mr McCoy, I am Mr Abrahams' legal representative.'

'Isn't that a conflict of interest or something?' asked McCoy as Murray sat down beside him, pulled his chair up to the chipped laminate table.

Lomax was pleased to explain. 'The short answer is no. Were my client pleading not guilty it would of course be so, but he is pleading guilty. Any momentary professional relationship I had with Miss Scobie is therefore not a problem.' He sat back in his chair. 'Now, can we get on with it? After all, my time is money.'

Murray took a bunch of files out of his bag, dumped them on the table. One of the bulbs in the cage above them fizzed, flashed. He looked at Lomax. 'If I find out this is some kind of funny buggers to try and get a mistrial I'll—'

Lomax held his hand up. 'Be assured it isn't. Now, please, can we proceed?'

Murray nodded reluctantly. Couldn't have looked more suspicious if he tried.

'Excellent,' said Lomax, sitting forward. 'Now, my client has a statement he wishes to make about what happened at Pinetrees.'

'You mean in his own wee Dr Mengele garage?' asked McCoy.

Lomax sighed. 'In the garage at the property, yes. He is more than content for you to do what you wish with this statement. His only concern is that he gets to explain his side of what happened.'

'That right?' said McCoy. 'Well, let's be honest, it's not like the other two can, is it? Not after what he did to them.'

'Get on with it,' grumbled Murray.

Lomax turned to Abrahams as if he was introducing the next turn at the Palladium. 'Mr Abrahams, over to you.'

Abrahams coughed, arranged the bits of paper he had in front of him. McCoy was starting to get angry, wasn't quite sure how Abrahams seemed to be running this interview.

He started. 'I first met Kevin Connolly when he came to see me at Woodilee Hospital. I soon—'

'You did what?' said McCoy. 'You lying little cunt, you said you'd never seen him until Barlinnie!'

'Mr McCoy!' said Lomax. 'Please let my client finish his statement, that is all he asks.'

McCoy was furious with himself, should have made the connection quicker. Connolly wasn't there visiting when he saw him, he was an outpatient. Should have fucking guessed.

'McCoy, you all right?' asked Murray. 'You sure you want to be in here?'

McCoy nodded, face set.

Abrahams went on. 'I quickly discovered he was in nature psychopathic. A continued danger to himself and others. It soon became apparent to me that he was never going to benefit from any sort of therapeutic cure. Consequently I decided to start him on a course of Seconal and Librium. The hope was to keep his most dangerous behaviour at bay. He attended the hospital intermittently but as far as I was aware was still picking up and taking his prescriptions.'

Another page turn. 'I lost contact with him when I went to Dundee and only met him again after—'

'You got struck off,' said McCoy.

'After the unfortunate incident at Dundee and my arrival at Barlinnie. There I found his state worsened; his mind seemed to have deteriorated quite considerably. Despite his aggressive demeanour, he was a very frightened individual, scared of what was happening to him. He was desperate for any kind of solution.'

'And you were just the one to provide it,' said McCoy.

Abrahams ignored him. 'I helped him with new medication but it became apparent a couple of months ago he had stopped taking it. He believed it was poisoning him and making him store what he called "dead food and water" in his body – something, along with crippling headaches, he found incredibly difficult to deal with.'

New page, looked up at Murray and McCoy. 'When the police failed to apprehend Mr Connolly after the three horrendous murders I saw it as my duty to put an end to his killing spree—'

'You what?' asked McCoy, amazed.

'I was on my way to my father's house to

telephone the police and report what I had done when I was picked up by the uniformed officers—'

'You let him fucking carve me up!' said McCoy. 'Two of you were in it together!'

'—to inform them that Connolly's reign of terror was over. That I had done what the police failed to do, stopped the killings.'

He sat back, smiled. 'Thank you. I would like a copy of that statement to go to all the major newspapers along with a copy of my pamphlet.'

McCoy was holding onto his chair, knew if he let go he would punch the wee fucker. Murray was red-faced. Lomax had the good grace to look embarrassed.

'That, gentlemen, concludes my statement. I did what any good citizen would do with the means I had. Ended the terror, did the job the police couldn't.'

Murray lurched forward but McCoy got his hand out, managed to stop him. 'Lomax,' he hissed, 'did you know about this?'

Lomax shook his head. 'Mr Abrahams wanted to keep the exact wording of his statement a secret until he could address the police. Had I been—'

'The girl,' said McCoy, ignoring him. 'Elaine Scobie. Where does she fit into all this? She hadn't done anything but you were happy to butcher her too.' McCoy turned to Lomax. 'And this cunt watched as Connolly carved me up, even lent him his fucking scalpel to do it.'

'Are you suggesting my client was present in the garage when Connolly attacked you?' asked Lomax.

'He was fucking there all right.'

Lomax looked puzzled, or pretended to look puzzled. 'My client informed me that he arrived at the garage to find Mr Connolly in the process of wounding Mr McCoy. Thinking quickly, he injected Connolly with a tranquilliser to prevent him doing any further damage. In point of fact, Mr McCoy, my client saved your life.'

McCoy couldn't believe what he was hearing. Realised what Abrahams was doing; it would come down to McCoy's word against his. And Connolly's medical report would no doubt show that he had been drugged.

Abrahams sat back in his chair, shook his head. 'It's quite remarkable how incompetent you people really are. You know nothing, do you? Elaine Scobie and Connolly boasted to me about how they had hatched the plan to kill three people, including her fiancé and her father. She was as guilty as he was. She needed to be helped.'

McCoy scrabbled about in the pile of files in front of him. Found it. Held it up. 'This is Dr Purdie's medical report on Elaine Scobie. Her blood tests show she was so full of Mandrax she could barely walk or talk. I saw her like that. She couldn't even fucking sit up straight!' He opened the file, pointed. '"Close to a fatal dose," he said. And yet you're telling me that even in this state she willingly came with Connolly, the man who had just kidnapped her, to your fucking house of horrors?'

'I don't—'

'And she sat down and had a chat with you over a nice cup of tea about her motivations for helping to kill three people. I don't fucking think so.'

He threw the file at Abrahams. It bounced off his chest and fell to the floor, papers spilling everywhere.

Lomax tried to take charge again. 'Mr McCoy, that consists of an assault. My client is—'

'A lying fuck. Elaine didn't have a fucking clue where she was. Only reason she didn't try and run, to get away from you and Connolly, was because she was so drugged up she couldn't even move. You thought it was your lucky fucking day, didn't you? A wee bonus. Another young girl you could butcher, just like you did in Dundee.'

Abrahams was unfazed. 'She described to me in great detail the pleasure she took in Connolly's actions. She found his descriptions of what he had done sexually arousing. As his lover she was complicit, egging him on to further obscene acts.' Abrahams smiled. 'Just like Myra Hindley and Ian Brady. Heard of them, have you?'

That was enough. McCoy did it before he could help himself. Punched Abrahams full in the face as hard as he could. He felt his nose break under his fist and Abrahams fell backwards off his chair.

McCoy was round the table and standing over him before he could get up. He could hear Lomax

401

and Murray shouting at him and he didn't care. He was shouting too, right into Abrahams' terrified face.

'Listen, you twisted cunt. When Cooper finds out what you've done you're going to wish you'd killed yourself when you had the chance.'

He could feel Murray pulling at him, yelling at him to stop, heard Lomax ringing the emergency buzzer, shouting on the turnkey.

Abrahams tried to sit up, to put his smashed glasses on. 'My actions were those of a concerned citizen, I did what—'

McCoy kicked him in the face.

CHAPTER 39

Murray finally stopped shouting into his face and sat back down behind the desk. Looked like he'd worn himself out calling McCoy every name under the sun. Short version of the bollocking was simple. His fate as a polis depended on whether Lomax made a formal complaint. And why wouldn't he? McCoy had just kicked fuck out of his client right in front of him. And if he did, McCoy was out.

'Nothing to bloody say for yourself?' asked Murray.

McCoy shook his head. Wasn't much he could say.

'Should fucking think not. I've a good mind to suspend you anyway. If half the shop wasn't off with bloody flu I would. Hear me?'

McCoy nodded. Kept his eyes on Murray's rugby pictures on the wall behind him, tried to stay calm.

'You ever, ever do anything like that again you're out, McCoy – Lomax complaint or no Lomax complaint. Straight out the fucking door.' He looked vexed suddenly. 'I know you'd been through hell, probably shouldn't have let you in that interview room, but still . . . What bloody possessed you?'

'He did. Sitting there lying through his fucking teeth.'

Murray snorted. 'Ninety-nine per cent of people in that interview room lie through their bloody teeth! Why was he so different?'

'Because he really thinks he'll get away with it,' said McCoy.

'Aye well, I don't, and I'll make sure the wee cunt—'

A knock on the door.

It opened and Lomax was standing there. 'Gents, mind if I come in?'

McCoy's heart sank.

Murray waved him in and he sat down beside McCoy.

'I suppose you can guess why I'm here?' said Lomax.

Murray nodded. McCoy waited for the hammer to fall.

'I've known Elaine Scobie since she was a baby,' he said. 'And I've just read the doctor's report.' He turned to McCoy. 'I now have to continue as that piece of scum's lawyer just so he can't ask me to testify about what happened in there. If I could I would walk away right now, but I have no wish to see your career ended by someone like Abrahams. What you did was not advisable but it was understandable. I took him on to show what

404

a big man I was and that's my mistake, something I'll have to live with.'

He stood up, held his hand out to McCoy. 'Until the next time, Mr McCoy.'

McCoy shook it, amazed. Lomax nodded at Murray and left.

Murray sat back in his chair. 'I wasn't expecting that.'

'Me neither,' said McCoy, relief flooding his body.

'You're fucking lucky,' said Murray. 'Won't happen twice. Now fuck off.'

McCoy stood up, headed for the door.

'Hang on,' said Murray. 'I forgot.'

McCoy sat back down.

'Burgess. The Albany. Definitely something funny going on there.'

'Aye?' asked McCoy, fear rising.

'Gilroy now. Her report's in. He had Mandrax in his throat. Was pushed down there post-mortem.'

'Eh?'

'Exactly. Why would you give someone Mandrax when they were already dead? Doesn't make any sense.'

'Maybe Connolly just wanted to do what he always did?'

Soon as he said it McCoy knew how stupid it sounded.

Murray looked at him.

'Sorry.'

'Whatever it is, something's not quite right.

I might hand it to Eastern right enough, get them to look at it as a separate case. Can't do any harm.'

'No,' said McCoy. He felt as if he was going to be sick. New investigation. No way they weren't going to find out about him and Cooper beating him up first.

'When are you going to decide?'

'When I decide. That okay with you?' asked Murray, sounding annoyed.

'Gonnae be hard with Connolly the way he is, isn't it?'

Murray sat back. 'Not if he didn't do it, it isn't. Crammond from Eastern's good. He'll get to the bottom of it.'

McCoy nodded. Just when he thought things couldn't get any worse. Crammond. He was a fucking terrier, good detective. Everyone expected him to be a chief inspector in a few years. If Murray got him on the case he was fucked, truly fucked.

Murray pointed at him. 'And by the way, I meant what I said. I'm going to get Cooper whatever it takes and if I ever hear you use him to threaten anyone again, even a cunt like Abrahams, I'll batter fuck out you myself.'

McCoy nodded. Didn't disbelieve him.

CHAPTER 40

McCoy sat down at his desk. Looked at the clock. Half past seven. Chest hurt like fuck. Kept thinking about being on that table, not able to move, Connolly with the scalpel. No wonder he felt like a drink. Usually, after a case like this, with someone like Connolly in custody, there would be a big piss-up. Murray putting thirty quid behind the bar at the Eskimo, everyone ending up merry with the drink and flushed with the success of getting the bastard.

Not this time. Nobody really had the heart for it. Least of all him. Connolly was downstairs in the cells but it wasn't really him that was there. Was like he'd escaped his body somehow, had the last laugh. Pulled a fast one on them. No trial, no prison sentence, just a lifetime spent staring at a wall in somewhere like Woodilee, vacant smile on his face.

Elaine Scobie was gone. Whisked away by some auntie, was at her house in Lenzie, it seemed. Auntie wasn't stupid. Elaine was a very wealthy young woman, her father's death had seen to that. Whoever was in charge of her welfare would get their hands on it soon enough.

Wattie appeared beside him. 'You okay?'

McCoy nodded. Wasn't. Was still thinking about bloody Crammond.

'Heard Murray had a right go at you.'

'I deserved it.'

'How's the stitches?'

'Sore. I'll live.'

'The forensic boys are dismantling his wee torture chamber now, seeing if they can find any trace of him doing it to anybody else.'

'Don't think he did,' said McCoy. 'Wee bastard was so proud of himself he'd have told us.'

'Probably right.' Wattie pulled the chair from his desk over, sat opposite McCoy. Looked round to make sure no one was listening. 'It's started,' he said.

'What?'

'The Viking. Stevie Cooper. Heard it on the radio. Waller and Tommy Simons are in an ambulance on the way to the Royal. Waller's not expected to make it.'

'Christ,' said McCoy.

With all that had happened today he'd forgotten about Cooper's plans.

'That's not all. The Silver Bells is on fire, so're two houses in Bishopbriggs and there's about twenty troops in A&E waiting to get stitched up.' He sat back. 'Looks like your pal's the new boss of the Northside.'

'Does Murray know?'

'Will do in about ten minutes. Thomson's just

checking everything before he goes in to tell him. Wouldn't want to be Thomson for all the bloody tea in China. He'll go fucking mental.'

McCoy stood up.

'Where you off to?' asked Wattie, looking surprised.

'Need to go and see Cooper. And need to get the fuck out of here before Thomson breaks the news.'

Wattie grinned. 'You off to congratulate him?'

'No. To give him the news. Let him know his girlfriend's a fucking vegetable. You stay here. No matter what anybody says, you and I were never in the Viking, right?'

Wattie nodded.

'I mean it, Wattie. Not a fucking word or both of us are fucking toast.' Chances were he was toast already but he didn't need Wattie knowing about that.

Wattie held his hands up. 'Okay. Okay. Christ . . . calm down.' He thought a minute. 'What do you think he'll do?'

McCoy shrugged. 'Abrahams will be dead within the week. Can tell you that for a fact.'

'Fuck.'

Thomson was getting up from his desk, couple of pages of foolscap in his hand, heading for Murray's closed door. McCoy picked up his coat from the back of his chair and hurried towards the door as Thomson started knocking.

CHAPTER 41

Memel Street seemed to be the best bet. He got a cab outside the station. When he told the driver where he was going the man said he'd take him to the corner but there was no way he was driving down there. McCoy just said okay. Couldn't be bothered arguing.

He sat in the back, watching the city go by, feeling sorry for himself. Tried to scratch under the bandage on his arm. Seemed like it was all piling up, wasn't sure he was going to make it through the next couple of weeks. If Murray gave Crammond the go-ahead to look at Uncle Kenny's murder he and Cooper were fucked. No way Crammond wouldn't find out what really happened.

Even if he got away with that, Murray was so intent on bringing Cooper down he was going to get caught in the crossfire. Way his record was he'd never survive a disciplinary meeting. He'd be out on his arse, charged with something, if he was lucky, and if he wasn't he was heading for Barlinnie.

The taxi dropped him on Hawthorn Street and he started walking up Memel. Chances were Cooper already knew what had happened to

Elaine. Always seemed to know what was going on before most of the police did. Still, he owed it to him to tell him the story, even if he wasn't much looking forward to it.

He was about halfway up the road when he started to hear the music and the shouts and the laughing. Seemed the victory party was in full swing already. Just what he felt like. A bunch of kids were hanging out outside the close. Looked for the wee girl with the cardigan but couldn't see her. He pushed past them and climbed the stairs.

Couple of guys were standing guard halfway up, recognised him from the Viking, let him through. One of them had a thick cotton patch attached to his cheek with tape, blood seeping out from under it.

'That looks sore,' said McCoy.

The boy shrugged. Boom-boom of the music from the party louder now. He took a gulp from his bottle of Whisky Mac, held it out for McCoy. He took a slug, was grateful for it, grimaced as the cheap whisky burned his throat. Handed it back. 'Anyone else get hurt?'

'Few of the boys. Tam Mullen's in the Royal. One of the cunts had a hatchet.'

'Nasty.'

The boy grinned. 'Should have seen the state of them, but.'

McCoy trudged up the stairs. 'The Jean Genie' finished. 'Virginia Plain' started. The door of the flat was ajar. McCoy pushed it open and the music was deafening. The flat was boiling hot, mobbed; most of the crew he'd seen at the Viking plus loads of young dressed-up and made-up girls. The air was thick with dope smoke and the smell of incense and perfume. A girl dressed in her bra and knickers was hammering at the bathroom door.

'Billy!' she shouted. 'Billy! Let me in!'

The bathroom door opened and McCoy caught a glimpse of Billy Weir, naked but for his Paisley patterned underpants, holding an album cover covered in white lines up to a girl's face. The other girl jumped in, slammed the door shut behind her.

He elbowed his way through the crowded hall, took a few drags of a joint that was offered to him, made it to the kitchen. Table was covered in cans and bottles. Someone was unwrapping a big news-paper parcel full of steaming fish suppers. Jumbo was sitting on a chair at the back looking about as unhappy as McCoy had ever seen him, long-haired girl sitting on his lap, arms round his neck.

'Where is he, Jumbo?' shouted McCoy above the noise.

'He's in the Central Hotel,' said Jumbo. 'I know where it is. I'll take you.'

He stood up so quickly the girl fell off his lap onto the floor. She looked disgusted, started brushing herself off.

They walked out the close and back along the muddy gardens. Even though it had started to rain again, a cold drizzle turning the light round the lampposts a hazy orange, the fresh air felt good. Jumbo seemed to have been decked out by someone. No plimsolls and woolly jumper any more. He'd smart black slip-ons, shirt with repeat patterns of Charlie Chaplin on it, leather jacket. Looked like every other member of Cooper's troops.

'I know where the Central is, Jumbo,' said McCoy. 'It's the biggest bloody hotel in Glasgow.'

'Thought I'd make sure,' he said.

'You no want to stay for the lassies?' asked McCoy. 'You want to go back?'

Jumbo shook his head, face going red. 'I'll show you where Mr Cooper is.'

'Suit yourself. So how'd the big battle go?'

'It was horrible,' said Jumbo.

McCoy stopped, realised Jumbo was close to tears. Even with his flash clothes, he still looked like he always looked, like a lost boy in a hulking man's body.

'Why? What happened?' asked McCoy.

'I went with Mr Cooper to the pub.'

'The Silver Bells?'

He nodded. 'Mr Cooper stabbed the two men before they knew what was happening to them. He stabbed them and stabbed them, they were crying and screaming, and one of them fell on the floor and he stamped on his face, did it three times. Then he—'

He stopped, wiped at his eyes. 'The other one had a big knife—'

413

'A machete?'

Jumbo nodded. 'He went for Mr Cooper with it but he managed to get it off him and he hit him across the face with it.'

'Jumbo, you don't—'

'And half his face was hanging off and the blood was all over Mr Cooper and he was shouting he was going to fucking kill him and Billy was trying to pull him away and I thought he was going to kill Billy he looked so angry.'

McCoy put his arm round him. Could feel the sobs shaking his body. 'You sure you're cut out for all this, son?'

He managed to get it out through the sobs. 'I don't have anywhere else to go.'

McCoy patted his back, told him he was going to be okay, that he was just upset, he'd be fine tomorrow. Almost believed it. Felt like it was half his fault. In trying to save Jumbo he'd managed to sell him into a terrible kind of life, a life his body was right for but his mind wasn't. Horrible thing was he was right. He really didn't have anywhere else to go.

A taxi emerged from the mist and rain. McCoy hailed it and they got it in. Told the driver to take them to the Central Hotel. Lit up a fag. Tried to convince himself things could be worse. He could be Jumbo. Failed.

The taxi stopped at the rank under the canopy outside Central Station and they got out. Rain was

414

really coming down now, line for the taxis stretched all the way back to the hotel. The Central was a huge railway hotel – ornate building, all towers and carved stone. Unlike the St Enoch, this one was booming. Everybody had stayed there, from Laurel and Hardy to Judy Garland. Even Led Zeppelin. Until they got banned that was.

'He's in the penthouse suite,' said Jumbo, looking up.

'Okay,' said McCoy. 'How come you're no with him? Thought you two were joined at the hip?'

'He said he wanted to be by himself tonight,' said Jumbo.

'What you going to do now? Go back to the party?'

Jumbo shook his head, looked a bit embarrassed. '*The Jungle Book*'s on at the Odeon. I saw it when I was a wee boy.'

'It's a good film.'

Jumbo nodded. 'Tell Mr Cooper I'll be downstairs in the hotel from seven in the morning if he needs me.'

McCoy nodded, watched Jumbo lumber up the street towards the cinema. Wondered how long he was going to survive this new life.

CHAPTER 42

The best-looking girl McCoy had ever seen answered the door of the suite. She was as tall as him, long blonde hair, figure barely hidden in what looked like one of Cooper's short-sleeved shirts.

'I'm looking for Stevie,' he said, trying not to stare.

She smiled. 'Sure.' American accent. 'He's in the big bedroom.'

Big bedroom implied there was more than one. Suite must be even bigger than it looked from the door.

'Through the seating area, can't miss him.' She opened the door wide and turned, shouted, 'Steven! You got a visitor!'

Steven? He hadn't heard Stevie called that since they were at school. He smiled at her, feeling slightly awkward, and walked into the big seating area, stood for a minute, took it in. Two couches facing each other, glass coffee table with a big arrangement of flowers on it in the middle. Long windows overlooked Hope Street and the lights of the city beyond.

His shoes sank into the carpet as he walked towards a pair of double doors on the back wall, passed a silver tray on the sideboard loaded with gleaming crystal tumblers and shiny bottles of spirits. Memel Street and Billy's party couldn't have been further away.

Cooper was sitting up in a huge double bed, bare-chested, hair all over the place. Was propped up on what looked like four or five crisp white pillows, big grin on his face.

'So I guess all this means your plan worked out?' said McCoy.

Cooper laughed. 'Ellie!' he shouted. The girl appeared in the doorway. 'Do us a favour, hen, get us a couple of beers?'

She nodded, walked away, bum looking like it was chewing toffees.

'Where the fuck did she come from?' asked McCoy, watching her backside disappear.

Cooper grinned. 'Akron. Wherever the fuck that is. She's a model. Here to do some fashion show thing for Fraser's. Met her in there when I was buying another suit.'

'You don't even wear suits,' said McCoy.

'Might start now. Now that I'm living the high life.'

'Fair point,' said McCoy. 'She's certainly made herself at home, I'll say that for her.'

Cooper patted the side of the bed. 'Come and sit down.'

'Nope,' said McCoy, pulling the chair out from

the dressing table. 'Not falling for that one. Don't need my head rapped, thank you.'

'Would I do that?' said Cooper, patting the bed again.

McCoy sighed. Cooper was in one of his good moods. Was liable to keep this going until he did what he asked. May as well get it over with.

He sat on the side of the bed. Cooper smiled, did nothing. Then grabbed him in a bear hug, got his head under his shoulder, arm across his neck.

'Surrender!' he shouted.

'I surrender,' said McCoy, trying to breathe through the stranglehold.

Cooper squeezed harder, rapped the top of his head with his knuckles. 'Didn't hear ye!'

'I surrender!' he gasped.

Cooper laughed, let him go, pushed him away, and McCoy tumbled off the bed and ended up on the floor. Sat up.

'You know something, Stevie? The fact you still find that funny after twenty bloody years is really fucking sad.'

'What's fucking sad is you fall for it every time,' said Cooper.

McCoy was about to explain but didn't. Sat on the chair, tried to smooth himself down. 'You okay then? Survive the war intact?'

Cooper twisted round, long fresh cut intersecting the scar that was already on his back. Pulled the covers back to show McCoy a deep gouge on his calf that seemed to have been bandaged with duct tape. Then he held up his left hand. Tip of his middle finger was missing.

'Like Dave Allen,' he said, grinned.

'Yep, except you're not funny. That's not too bad, could have been a lot worse. Heard you put some people in the hospital.'

Cooper shrugged. Nothing was going to spoil his good mood. 'Nature of the game. Fuck them. They'd have done the same to me.'

'Boys.'

They turned and Ellie was standing there with four bottles of beer on a tray. She put it down on the end of the bed, winked at Cooper and left again.

'Is she actually real?' asked McCoy. 'Looks like Miss World, appears with trays of beer and she seems to actually like you.'

Cooper grinned again. Was like a cat that had got the cream, all of the cream. 'You ever slept with an American bird?'

McCoy shook his head, took a swig from his beer bottle.

'Whole different ball game—'

'If you'll pardon the expression.' McCoy held out his bottle. 'Cheers!'

They clinked bottles, drank.

'So what happens now?' asked McCoy.

'This is what happens now,' Cooper said, waving his arm about. 'Places like this. Northside's mine now. Billy Chan's back from Hong Kong. Sorted out his connection. All systems go. No more fucking Memel Street and all the shite that goes with it. That's Billy's now. I've done my fucking time at the coalface. Time to kick back and enjoy life for a change. Gonnae stay here for a while, starting to get used to it.'

'She staying too?'

'Yep.'

McCoy didn't want to say anything to sour the mood. He was enjoying himself as much as Cooper. Had never seen him this happy before, this contented, but it wasn't what he'd come for and he had a right to know.

'Elaine,' he said. 'You heard?'

Cooper nodded. 'I told you she was going to end up dead.'

'She's not dead, Stevie. She's been lobotomised, but she's alive.'

'You call that alive?'

'Suppose not.'

Cooper shrugged. 'She was dead the minute Connolly got a hold of her.' He took a swig of his beer; for a second his real feelings showed on his face and then they were gone. Smile came back.

'That wee prick Abrahams goes to Barlinnie tomorrow, I hear,' said McCoy.

Cooper nodded. Both of them knowing why McCoy was telling him. Both of them knowing he would be dead by the end of the week.

Ellie appeared at the door holding a wooden cigar box. She sat down on the bed. 'You sure about this, honey?'

'Try anything once, that's my motto.'

She smiled, opened the box. There was a Zippo lighter in it, a spoon, a length of rubber tubing, a folded wrap and a syringe.

McCoy looked at Cooper. 'What are you doing, Stevie? You don't need to start on that.'

Ellie raised her eyebrows.

'Stevie, for fuck sake!'

Cooper stared at him. Although he was in as good a mood as McCoy had ever seen him, he still didn't like being told what to do. 'Ellie, can you go and have a bath or something—'

'You mean give you boys some time?' She stood up. 'Sure. I'll go powder my nose.' She left, cigar box tucked under her arm.

Cooper waited for her to leave, turned to McCoy. 'Do you think I'm fucking stupid? It's a one-off. See what it is I'm selling.'

'You know what you're selling. Smack. Smack that gets you addicted just like Janey, gobbling off old men for a ten-bob note to buy more then ending up dead in a fucking deserted tenement. What more do you need to know? You want to sell it, then that's your business, but for fuck sake don't be stupid enough to start doing it.'

'You saying I'm stupid?'

McCoy realised he'd better go easy. 'No, Stevie. I'm not saying you're stupid, I'm saying you're about to do a stupid thing. There's a difference.'

'That right?' said Cooper, voice becoming colder.

'And how would you know? It's not like you've ever done anything stupid, is it?'

McCoy looked at him. 'What's that supposed to mean?'

Cooper shook his head, started on the other bottle.

'Come on, Cooper. What are you saying?' asked McCoy, starting to get annoyed.

'Nothing,' said Cooper. 'Nothing you need to know anyway. Just me getting you out of trouble like I always have. Making sure Harry McCoy goes on his merry way thinking the world's his fucking oyster. You want me to stop doing it, just ask.'

McCoy stood up, angry now. 'I don't have a fucking clue what you're on about, Cooper. And if you think we're still back in school and you're going to protect me from some hard man or Uncle fucking Kenny—'

'I did.'

'I know you did, but that was a long time ago—'

'Not that long,' he said quietly. 'About four days ago to be exact.'

McCoy sat back down on the chair, confused. 'What?'

Cooper leant over, opened the drawer of the night table, took out a wrap of speed, cut two lines on the back of the room service menu, rolled up a note and snorted one. Held the menu out to McCoy. A test.

McCoy took it, snorted the line, rubbed at his nostrils, took a swig of his beer.

'Connolly didn't kill Uncle Kenny,' said Cooper. 'You did.'

Cooper had got out of bed, put some jeans on. McCoy was sitting on one of the couches, noise of the traffic on Hope Street a dim background rumble. Cooper poured a good measure of whisky into two crystal tumblers, set one down in front of McCoy, sat down on the couch opposite him, scratched at the thick hair on his chest.

'What are you saying to me?' McCoy felt like he was watching himself, the two of them. Couldn't understand what Cooper was telling him.

'Connolly killed him, it was Connolly,' he said.

Cooper shook his head. 'You just thought he did.'

McCoy took a gulp of the whisky, burn in his throat as he swallowed. 'I don't understand.' He was looking at Cooper, at his familiar face, at the couch and the whisky tumbler and the curtains. Everything was normal except nothing was now, not any more.

'You don't remember much about what happened, do you?' said Cooper.

McCoy shook his head. 'I remember I started to hit him and then . . . I don't know, something happened . . . wasn't even me any more. All I wanted to do was hit him and hit him and then I remember you shouting, grabbing me, pulling me off him.'

'I've never seen you like that,' said Cooper.

'Never really seen anyone like that.' He smiled. 'Except me, probably. Was like you'd gone, wasn't you any more, didn't care about anything but hurting Uncle Kenny.'

'And I did,' said McCoy. 'Didn't I?'

Cooper nodded. 'You did. You really did.'

Ellie walked in, towel wrapped round her body, another round her hair. 'Don't mind me,' she said. Picked up her handbag from the sideboard, disappeared back into the bedroom.

Cooper got the bottle from the sideboard, poured some more into their tumblers. Sat back down. 'By the time I got you off him it was too late. Damage was done.'

'What damage?'

'He was going to die. No question.'

'He was going to what?' McCoy thought he was going to be sick, faint, do something; was like when he saw blood. He tried to calm himself, started his breathing, took a slug of the whisky.

'I know what men look like just before they die,' said Cooper. 'Seen it happen a few times. He was still breathing but it was wrong, sounded wrong. Oxygen wasn't getting into him. I think you'd smashed his windpipe or something. You stamped on his neck a good few times.'

'What? I did what?' McCoy put the glass down. Room was fuzzy, Cooper suddenly seemed very far away. He sat back, tried to let it pass.

'You okay?' asked Cooper.

McCoy nodded, but he wasn't. He really wasn't.

'I had to get you out of there before he died, before you realised what you'd done. If you found out we'd both have been fucked. You wouldn't have been able to handle it.'

McCoy knew he was right.

'So I left you in the pub, went back. And I was right. He was dead. Senior police officer dead in a hotel room, they were going to chuck everything at it. No way we were going to get away with it.'

He picked the big onyx lighter up off the table, lit two fags, handed one to McCoy. He took it with trembling hands. Couldn't believe what Cooper was telling him. Didn't want to believe it.

'The only way they weren't gonnae dig too deep was if they thought they already knew who had done it.'

'Connolly,' said McCoy.

'Connolly. So I made it look like he'd done it.'

McCoy was starting to understand. 'Elaine?'

Cooper nodded. 'She'd told me what had happened to Charlie Jackson and her dad, all the details that weren't in the paper—'

'The writing carved on the body.'

Cooper nodded. 'And then you did the rest.'

'Found out Connolly was connected with Uncle Kenny.'

'And now, thanks to Abrahams, Connolly's in no position to say anything different.'

'How did you know what Abrahams was going to do?'

'I didn't. I'm no bloody psychic. I was just hoping

425

that if Connolly said he didn't do it no one would believe him.' He took another swig from the tumbler, smiled. 'Long as nothing else happens we're home free.'

'Why didn't you tell me? Tell me what had happened?'

Cooper looked at him. 'You're joking, aren't you? I know what you're like, McCoy. I shouldn't have even told you now.'

'Why?'

He sighed. 'Because you'll do what you always do. Worry about it, torture yourself, think about it until it drives you half mental. I hurt people for a living, you don't. You try and help them, all those fucking jakies that think you're God's gift. All the wife-beaters and the nonces and the evil bastards you put away. You try and work out what's right and what's wrong with the world, try to do the right thing. Me? I just do what has to be done. Keep moving forwards.'

McCoy stood up, felt shaky and nauseous, sat back down. Didn't know what he was doing. Thought he might scream or start crying or just sit there and never move again.

Cooper looked at him. 'See? You're doing it now, aren't you? Trying to work out how you could have killed someone, trying to work out how you're going to deal with it.'

He smashed the tumbler down on the glass table, a long crack appeared on it.

McCoy jumped.

Cooper leaned across the table at him. 'Well, don't. Uncle Kenny was an utter fucking cunt of a man. Ruined hundreds of boys' lives just so he could get his fucking kicks. He deserves to be dead. I'm glad you killed him, I'm glad he fucking suffered, I'm glad he knew he was going die alone on the fucking floor of a hotel room. I only wish it had taken longer and you'd hurt him more. So don't you fucking well start regretting what's happened. For once in your fucking life just let it go. It's done. Got me?'

McCoy nodded.

'Fucking remember what I've just said whenever you start to think about it. Don't let that cunt get into your head. Don't let him win.'

McCoy nodded again.

'Good.'

Cooper stood up, walked through to the bedroom.

McCoy sat there. Had no idea what he was going to do. If Crammond got the case he was going to be charged with murder. He'd get fifteen years at least. Fifteen years in Barlinnie. A cop in prison. Everyone knew what that was like.

No point telling Cooper what might happen. Less he knew, the better. Far as he was concerned it was all fixed. The future was rosy. And then he thought again. Realised Crammond would find out the two of them were there. No way were they going to believe someone like Cooper was an innocent party. They would get him for murder too. Especially the way Murray felt about him.

He stood up. Went into the bathroom. Washed his face in the basin. Looked at himself in the mirror. He was white. His hands were shaking. He was fucked and Cooper was fucked. All for fucking Uncle Kenny. Where was the justice in that?

He walked back through, sat down on the couch.

Cooper reappeared. 'C'mon through.'

'I've got to go, Stevie—' but he was talking to nobody.

He got up, went through to the bedroom.

Ellie was sitting on the bed, open cigar box in front of her. 'Care to join us?'

McCoy looked at the cigar box, sat down on the bed. Ellie smiled, undid his cuff button, rolled up his sleeve, tied the rubber tubing tight round his bicep. Watched his arm, veins swelling up.

Cooper had a tube round his arm as well. Was watching Ellie as she tipped a little of the brown powder into the spoon, added some water and lit the lighter under it. The liquid started to bubble, thicken.

'Not long now, boys,' she said, smiling. 'Not long until everything just floats away.'

And at that moment that was exactly what McCoy wanted, wanted more than anything – the pain to go away. The pain in his body, the pain of what had happened to him, for everything to go away. No more thoughts of Connolly standing over him with a scalpel in his hand. All he wanted was for him and Cooper to be stoned, free. No Crammond. No Murray. No Barlinnie. No murder.

He stood up, pulled the tube off his arm.

'What?' Cooper was looking at him.

'Be careful, Stevie. Please. I've got to go.'

He walked out the room, could hear Cooper calling after him.

'McCoy! Fuck's up with you!'

CHAPTER 43

The taxi headed up Crow Road. McCoy looked at his watch. Half nine. Would still be out walking the dog. He didn't really know what he was doing, what he was going to say. Just knew he had to do something and this was all he could think of.

He got the driver to drop him off at the corner of Borden Road. He stood for a while smoking, watching the corner. Rain had turned into snow falling down in clumps, dissolving on the wet pavement. He heard Bruno before he saw him. A deep bark and the Labrador was running towards him, tail wagging. He was older now, fatter, but he was still as friendly. Jumping up, trying to lick his face.

'I see you, Bruno, I see you!' he said, pushing him down.

A whistle, and the dog ran back along the road. Wasn't long before Murray appeared. Pipe in one hand, rolled-up dog lead in the other. He stopped for a second and McCoy stepped under the streetlight so he could see it was him.

Murray bent down, got Bruno on the lead.

Walked towards him. 'Don't think you're here to see Bruno, are you?'

McCoy shook his head.

'Thought not,' said Murray. 'What's up?'

'I need to talk to you,' said McCoy.

'Oh aye,' said Murray. 'Better come in then.'

Ten minutes later they were sitting at the kitchen table, Bruno already half asleep in his basket in the corner. Colin and David had grunted hello, gone upstairs to watch the football.

'Where's Margaret?' asked McCoy, looking round.

Murray put a bottle of Bell's and two glasses down on the table. 'Away at her sister's. She'll no be happy she missed you. You don't visit enough.'

'I know,' he said. Least of his sins.

Murray sat down, poured the drinks. He'd his at-home gear on. Old cords, a Tattersall shirt and the same green cardigan he'd had for donkey's. Stubble was through on his chin, reddish-grey. McCoy looked at him. Didn't know where to start, how to start.

'All the way here unannounced on a night like this. Can't be good news,' said Murray.

'It's not,' said McCoy. 'I need to ask you a favour, the biggest favour I've ever asked anyone in my life.'

Murray bristled. 'If you're here to ask me to lay off bloody Stevie Cooper you can forget it.'

McCoy shook his head. 'It's not that.'

Murray looked at him, blinked. 'Okay.'

'Don't let Crammond look at the Kenneth Burgess murder,' said McCoy.

Murray's glass stopped halfway to his lips. 'What?'

'I don't want you to let Crammond look at the case.'

'And why's that?'

'Because he'll find out I killed him.'

There was silence for a second or two. Ticking of the clock on the wall, Bruno snoring.

'You did what?' said Murray quietly.

McCoy just hoped he could get through it without crying. Took a breath, started. 'I killed Burgess. I went to the hotel and I beat him to death, and then I made it look like Connolly had done it.'

Murray was just looking at him, like he was someone he didn't even know. 'What are you talking about? Why would you do that?'

'You remember when you came and got me?' McCoy asked. 'At Lochgelly School?'

Murray nodded, still looked completely bewildered.

'You remember what I was like?'

'They said you hadn't spoken for a few weeks, couldn't get you to eat anything. They wanted to put you away, in Woodilee.'

'But you wouldn't let them,' said McCoy.

'Margaret was having none of it. Said you were coming here. Mind you, we were half up the bloody wall with you. Nobody knew what was up with you. Doctor said it was hysteria, that it would . . .' Murray stopped. Had suddenly realised what McCoy was telling him. 'Kenny Burgess?'

McCoy nodded, poured himself another shot of whisky, hand shaking. 'I'd been transferred to Lochgelly School. Stevie was a year older. After a few months he was transferred, so it was just me.' He swallowed hard. 'Kenny Burgess, Uncle Kenny, had been paying me visits for weeks.'

'Harry, I . . .'

McCoy held his hand up. He couldn't stop. Knew he wouldn't be able to start again.

'The headmaster told him I was there. He'd seen me at St Andrew's. Tried it there but it didn't happen. Stevie stuck to me like a fucking limpet. He was big by then, had already knifed one of the brothers. They were scared of him. But at Lochgelly he wasn't there any more.' McCoy looked at Murray, smiled. 'Just me on my lonesome.'

Murray was looking at him with a mixture of pity and fear in his eyes.

'Wasn't just me Uncle Kenny liked to visit. Been doing it for years and years. Must have been hundreds of boys, I think—'

'Harry, why didn't you tell anyone?'

And that was when he started to cry. No sobs, no wailing, could just feel the tears running down his cheeks.

'I did. I told Father Mulholland. Told me I was wicked and making it up. Came to visit the next night. "Once the seal is broken," he said to me, "the vessel has no worth."'

Murray was just staring at him, looked close to tears himself.

433

McCoy sniffed, wiped his nose with his sleeve, carried on.

'He retired, picture in the paper. Stevie was in the hospital when he saw it, just like Joe Brady did.'

Murray nodded.

'Stevie and I decided to give him a kicking, revenge. Wasn't going to change anything but it was something, however small. Wanted to do it for us and all the other boys.'

Murray stood up, went over to the sink, ran the tap. Turned away. McCoy knew he was crying, didn't want him to see.

'Why didn't you tell us? Me? Margaret?'

'Because when I came here it was the first place I'd ever felt safe. I knew nothing bad would happen to me here. I didn't want to go over it all again. Not even with you or Margaret. I knew you would believe me and that was enough.'

Murray was still looking out the window, out over the snowy garden. 'What happened? In the Albany?'

'I don't really know,' said McCoy. 'I was hitting him but when I saw his signet ring, smelt him, I lost control. I hit him too hard. Stevie pulled me off him but I knew the damage was done, he was going to die.'

'Christ, Harry.'

'So I went back later without Stevie, made it look like Connolly had done it. I knew what to do. Then I started looking for the connection between Connolly and Uncle Kenny. Knew if Connolly had been in care my chances were good.'

Murray turned, sat back down at the table. 'And now you want me to stop Crammond?'

McCoy nodded.

'Christ, Harry, how did you get into this mess?'

McCoy tried to smile. 'I have no idea. But I can't get out, not without you.'

Murray put his head in his hands. 'Oh, Harry, Harry, what have you done?'

McCoy looked at him. For the first time he was scared. Scared Murray wasn't going to help him. Maybe he'd misjudged the whole thing.

Murray looked up, tears in his eyes. 'You killed a man, Harry. You're a polis. No matter what happened you can't do that, you just can't.'

McCoy nodded, panic coursing through his body.

'No matter how much he deserved it. We can't do things like that. That's what separates us from them. You understand that, don't you?'

McCoy nodded again.

'Understand what it means? What has to happen?'

McCoy was crying properly now, wiping at his nose with his sleeve. 'I'm sorry.'

Murray pushed the bottle of whisky across the table at him. 'The boys are staying up in the attic now,' he said. 'Your old room's there, bed's made up.'

He stood up. Put his hand on McCoy's shoulder. 'Nothing we can do tonight. Try and get some sleep.'

He whistled and Bruno got up immediately, followed him upstairs.

McCoy watched them go. Picked up the bottle.

The garden was quiet, snow muffling everything. He walked across the square of snow that was the lawn and sat down on the bench beside the tree. Remembered sitting here when he first got to Murray's. Throwing the ball for Bruno for hours on end. Was all he wanted to do then, throw the ball for Bruno, not think about anything.

He got his fags out, lit up. Took a swig from the whisky. The light in the bathroom upstairs went on for a couple of minutes, went off again. Snow kept falling. He didn't feel cold, was just happy to be on this bench again, in Murray's garden. The one place in his life he'd felt safe.

Maybe this was where he should stay. He felt around in his pockets. The Seconal Dr Purdie had given him, four Mandies left over from the Wizard's stash. Maybe that and the whisky and the cold would be enough.

He sat there for a while.

He woke up, could hear Murray shouting at the boys to get going or they'd be late. Bruno barking. Doors slamming.

He didn't think he would but he'd slept. Must have been the old bed that had done it. His room was still the same. Wallpaper with Olympic rings and different sports on it. Wardrobe with a crack in the door. Desk with books piled on it. Picture of a racing car above his bed.

Had spent a few hours in the cold but decided not to let Uncle Kenny win. He wouldn't be another Joe Brady. He wasn't giving them that satisfaction. No matter what the top brass had said, there was no way Uncle Kenny was going to his grave a family man and a respected elder of the church. Not if he had anything to do with it. If he was going down he was taking Uncle Kenny and as many of his pals he could remember down with him. Fuck the lot of them.

Could hear Murray on the stairs, still recognised his tread after all these years. He sat up. The door opened and Bruno jumped up on the bed, started licking his face. Murray appeared, cup of tea in hand, put it on the bedside table. Didn't look like he'd slept much.

'Tell me honestly,' he said. 'Did we let you down, me and Margaret?'

McCoy shook his head. 'No. You were the only ones that didn't.'

'You sure?'

McCoy nodded. 'Never been surer of anything in my life.'

Murray stood up. 'Well, best not start now, eh?' He whistled on Bruno, walked towards the door. 'Last night didn't happen. Crammond isn't going to happen. Now get out your bloody bed. You're late for work.'

helpme